MATT BROLLY

Following his law degree where he developed an interest in criminal law, Matt Brolly completed his Masters in Creative Writing at Glasgow University.

He is the bestselling author of the DCI Lambert crime novels, Dead Eyed, Dead Lucky, Dead Embers, and Dead Time as well as the acclaimed near future crime novel, Zero, and the US thriller, The Controller.

In 2020 the first of a new crime series set in the West Country of the UK will be released by Thomas and Mercer (Amazon Publishing)Matt also writes children's books as M.J. Brolly. His first children's book, The Sleeping Bug, was released by Oblong Books in December 2018.

Matt lives in London with his wife and their two young children. You can find out more about Matt at his website www.-mattbrolly.co.uk or by following him on twitter: @MattBrollyUK

ALSO BY MATT BROLLY

The DCI Lambert series:

Dead Water - prequel novella

Dead Eyed

Dead Lucky

Dead Embers

Dead Time

DI Blackwell Series:

The Crossing

Other novels:

Zero

The Controller

For children (As M.J.Brolly)

The Sleeping Bug

First published in the United Kingdom in 2019 by Oblong Books

Copyright © 2019 by Matt Brolly

A CIP catalogue record for this book is available from the British Library.

978-0-9957747-3-5 – Paperback

978-0-9957747-4-2 – E-book

978-0-9957747-8-0 – Hardback

THE CONTROLLER

MATT BROLLY

OBLONG
BOOKS

For Beth and Warren Eardley

1

The knocking came in the middle of night. It took a few minutes for the sound to register - the incessant rhythmic thud of fists on wood the sound of a train rattling along the tracks. Opening his eyes, Samuel Lynch suffered the same teasing sensation he experienced every morning of being somewhere else, of being someone else; and then he saw the mess from last night and reality returned in a wave of nausea. He dragged the back of his hand across his eyes and sat up in bed. The sound of the banging was replaced by a similar noise in his head, accompanied by short, staccato stabs of pain. On the dressing table, five empty beer bottles fought for space amongst piles of unfiled paperwork - he never drank more than five, but still suffered the raging headaches every morning.

'Mr Lynch?' The banging on the door continued. Lynch couldn't remember the last time he'd had visitors and no one, not even his ex-wife, knew his address. Something about that should have made him sad, but he was too piqued by curiosity. His rent, bills included, was paid in cash and he was methodical about entering and leaving the building. No one should know his location.

He jumped from the bed and tiptoed to the closet, avoiding the mounds of paper on the threadbare carpet. He pulled on his robe and from the inside shelf took out his Glock 22. He unclipped the magazine, checked it, and clipped it back in place.

The banging resumed. The same four beats, the rhythm identical as if somehow he was being mocked, matched the exact tempo of his growing migraine. 'Sir, this is Special Agent Lennox from the FBI. I need to talk to you.'

Gun in hand, Lynch moved to his desk. His laptop was buried under sheets of paper. Throwing them to the floor, he switched on the machine hoping the webcam outside his front door was still active. Clearing a pile of dirty laundry off the chair he sat down, glancing at the giant maps hanging on the wall above his desk.

Bang, bang, bang-bang. Bang, bang, bang-bang.

'For Christ's sake, Lynch, open this goddamn door.'

Lynch checked his gun again as he entered the password for the laptop. He was surprised to see the webcam still worked, surprised further to see what it revealed. Three men stood outside his apartment door. Two wore SWAT vests, covered in Kevlar panels. The third was suited, and was about to hit the door again when he noticed the light on the webcam. He looked up and waved at the lens. 'Mr Lynch, please open up.'

Lynch picked up the laptop and scurried to the side of the room, so he was no longer in line with the front door. 'I want to see credentials. All three of you, up to the camera.'

The suit sighed, and pulled out his card and held it to the

lens. 'Don't move,' shouted Lynch, studying the ID of Special Agent, Bill Lennox.

'Next.'

Agent, William Benson. Agent Ralph Barnes. If they were fakes, they were good fakes.

'Now will you open the door?' asked Lennox.

Lynch placed the gun in his robe pocket and unbolted the door, poised for surprise movements.

'Samuel Lynch. I'm Special Agent Bill Lennox. May I come in?' The man was in his forties. Medium build, slightly bigger around the gut than was healthy.

Lynch opened the door. 'Your buddies coming in as well?'

'If you don't mind.'

Lynch held the door open for the two SWAT guys. Both men were grotesquely over-sized. At six-two, Lynch was well above average size. He trained daily and had a strong build, but was dwarfed by the two muscle-bound men.

Lynch shut the door as the men acclimatized themselves. Lennox glanced at the maps on Lynch's wall, the SWAT guys at the mess.

'You carrying?' asked Lennox.

'You?'

Lennox nodded. 'Quite a piece of work,' he said, pointing to the larger map.

The map was Lynch's creation. Five meters wide, it displayed the entire network of railroad lines in the USA. Next to it was a two-meter map of Texas' active and disused railroad lines. Each map was dotted with hundreds of colored pins.

'What do you want?'

'Can we sit, or are we going to do this standing up?'

'What do you think?'

'Fair enough. Have you heard of a man who goes by the name of Gregor Razinski?' The two SWAT guys had stopped looking at the mess and were staring at him.

'No.'

'He seems to know you.'

'Well, good for him, Lennox, is it? But I have no idea who he is, so unless you can tell me what this is about please kindly fuck off.'

Lennox smirked, and Lynch came close to wiping the expression from his face, three armed agents or not. 'Mr Razinski is currently involved in a situation in Asherton County. He's taken a family of four hostage in their home. He has killed the father of the family, and has killed one police officer.'

Lynch felt last night's pizza, and the last of the five beers rise up in his throat.

'He refuses to speak to anybody but you,' continued Lennox.

Lynch didn't know the name. He had almost faultless recall ability and, although he'd encountered hundreds if not thousands of people in past operations, he was sure he didn't know Razinski. 'Never heard of him. I have no connection to that area,' he said.

'We know. We have a team in place. They're ready to go in but we thought it prudent to speak to you first. To see if you could shed some light.'

'Who does he have hostage?'

'He has killed a man by the name of Edward Gunn. He's detained Gunn's wife, Eleanor, and their two young children.'

Lynch shook his head. 'Motive?'

'Not clear. We can't trace Razinski. We're yet to secure any photo ID.'

'When did he mention my name?'

Lennox was clearly holding something back. 'Two shots were heard from the house, prior to Razinski attempting to leave. Five minutes earlier one of the Gunn children had made a call to the police explaining that a man had broken into the house and taken the rest of the family hostage. Two cops on foot patrol nearby came to the scene and caught Razinski leaving. They opened fire. Razinski retreated to the house, managing to take one of the cops down as he retreated.'

Lynch nodded. 'And?'

'Back up arrived, and they eventually made contact. Razinski confessed to killing Mr Gunn and informed the Sherriff's team he had the rest of the family with him.'

'This is a great story, Lennox, but when are we going to get to the bit about me?'

Lennox glanced at the two SWAT guys.

'Just fucking spill it, Lennox.'

'It seems Mr Razinski was under a miscomprehension. He demanded to speak to Special Agent Samuel Lynch.'

Lynch nodded, now understanding the covert glances between the three men.

'San Antonio FBI field office team were called in. Obviously, they checked your file. As there was no sign of Razinski on the databases we couldn't link him to you anyway. Our team talked to him, tried to push him for more. And eventually he gave us something.'

Lennox exchanged glances with the two SWAT guys once more. Seven years ago, Lynch had headed up the San Antonio field office SWAT team. Now the very same type of men he'd once led were treating him like a victim. In his mind's eye, he pictured himself taking the Glock from the inside pocket of his robe. He was sure, even now, he could get three shots off before they reacted. He had the element of surprise, and they were making the mistake of underestimating him.

Lennox scratched his chin, the sound of his nails dragging through his rough stubble audible in the room, and glanced again at the maps above Lynch's desk.

Catching him in the movement, and wondering what that might mean, Lynch experienced a surge of adrenaline.

Lennox sighed before speaking. 'Look, there's no easy way to say this, Mr Lynch. Razinski said he wanted to speak to you as he had some information which might be of interest.'

Lynch nodded, trying to control his increasing pulse rate.

'It's about your son. Razinski claims he's still alive.'

2

'We've found him.'

Special Agent Sandra Rose took the phone from her colleague. 'Lennox? Speak.'

'We have him.'

'What does he know?'

'In my professional opinion, nothing whatsoever. He was asleep when we called. Says he's never heard of Razinski.'

'But he's agreed to assist?'

Lennox paused. 'Reluctantly, yes.'

Rose handed the phone back to her colleague.

An officer from the Dimmit County office, Captain Iain Haig, sitting next to her in the unmarked van looked at her for information. 'We're going in?' he asked.

'I'll speak to him one more time, then my team will enter the house. I'll need your men to stay back.'

Haig curled his lip. 'You want to tell them that?'

Haig's file was impressive. A former marine, he headed up the criminal investigation division in the small county. Rose was confident he could have handled the situation. But

Razinski had mentioned a former FBI operative, and Haig had been good enough to call it in. Now she was here, it was her responsibility.

'Listen, Iain, I understand it's an awkward situation but we both want the same outcome. Your guys are baying for blood. Let me go in and get this guy. Get some justice for your officer.'

Haig had no option, it was her operation now. The Captain shook his head, suggesting she was making a mistake, and left the van.

'Get me Razinski,' said Rose.

It was her fourth hour at the scene. Most of it had been spent in the back of the van, with five other operatives. What little oxygen left in the confined space smelled of cheap cologne, sweat, and nicotine. For a moment, she envied the retreating Haig and the fresh air he was enjoying.

One of the techs, a quiet, almost monosyllabic man by the name of Charles McCarthy, handed her a pair of earphones. Rose's heart rate spiked as she heard the ringing tone.

She'd spoken to Razinski twice since arriving. During their brief conversations, she'd been unable to detect any sense of fear. He'd remained calm and considered, despite having just murdered a policeman and being surrounded by practically the entire County police force and two field teams from the FBI. He'd admitted to killing Edward Gunn, and told her that he had Gunn's wife and their two young children, one boy, one girl, as hostage.

The ringing stopped. McCarthy's eyes drooped like a lost schoolboy, confused and alone. It took her a second to remember he was looking to her for support, that she was in charge.

'Yes?' Razinski drew out the word with an almost comical intonation.

'Mr Razinski, this is Special Agent Sandra Rose, again.'

'That is disappointing.'

Rose's neck flushed. 'I have some good news for you. We have located Special Agent Samuel Lynch.' She'd decided now was not the time to tell Razinski that Lynch no longer worked for the FBI, though she suspected he already knew.

'Congratulations.'

'He's agreed to meet with you.'

'I look forward to his appearance.'

'I'm afraid it's not as simple as that, Mr Razinski.' Rose hated pandering. If Haig had his way, the house would have been stormed hours ago. 'It will take Lynch four to five hours to get here, and I'm afraid we can't wait that long.'

'That's too bad, Agent Rose. Do remember I have very little to lose. I gutted that little piggy friend of yours, and Mr Gunn here is, how should we say, beside himself at the moment. I don't imagine I'll be experiencing a sense of freedom anytime soon.'

The insinuation was clear. 'Let's not be rash, Mr Razinski. Let us come in, get the family, and I'll personally take you to see Agent Lynch when he arrives.'

Razinski went silent. 'I'm sorry, Miss Rose. It is Miss, I presume, but no.'

The faint sound of Razinski's breathing faded. 'Listen, Razinski, we're reaching critical point here. I found Lynch for you, I upheld my side of the bargain, now uphold yours. I have an entire department here who would gladly come for you en masse. Would risk a random bullet for the opportunity to get at you. This is your last chance. Let my team come in and take you to safety, and I'll give you my word you'll be unharmed.'

The line went silent. McCarthy nodded, confirming Razinski was still on the call. She couldn't speak again until Razinski spoke.

'Okay, Agent Rose, I'll take you at your word,' he said, an eternity later. 'I'm getting a bit bored cooped up here anyway.'

Rose pointed to Agent Glen Phelan, who headed up the SWAT team. Phelan rushed from the van and began barking orders at his team. 'Mr Razinski, my team will be entering the house now. For your safety, lie down on the ground. Link your hands together above your head. Can you do that for me?'

'For you, Rose, dear, anything.'

'If you move from that position, my team will terminate you.'

'Understood,' said Razinski, laughter in his voice.

Phelan returned to the van, joined by Haig. 'Ready,' said Phelan.

Rose gave Haig an earpiece so he could hear the rescue operation. 'Iain, we're not going to have any trouble from your guys?'

'Get that fucker away from here immediately, and there'll be no trouble.'

Rose nodded and Phelan left the van.

The mission was one of the simpler ones Rose had overseen. Phelan sent in four of the SWAT team. They smashed down the Gunn's front door on the first attempt and secured the lower floor with no resistance. Moving upstairs, Rose heard a brief commotion as the team found Razinski. Thirty seconds later she heard, 'subject and area secure.' A short period of silence followed as Phelan entered the area.

'Jesus fucking Christ,' he muttered into his headset. 'Ma'am, we're going to need you up here.'

Rose couldn't equate the quiet, drawn out voice on the other end with Phelan. She'd always admired the man's strength, especially under duress. His last sentence didn't sound like him. Like Rose, Phelan had seen unimaginable things in his time as a field agent. What had he seen to affect him so?

Pandemonium struck as she left the van. Cuffed, and secured by two of the SWAT team, Razinski was being led into a waiting van when one of Haig's team attacked. An obese figure in a check shirt, one of Haig's deputies, surprised Rose with a burst of speed which resulted in his fist connecting square with Razinski's jaw. The agents let the blow go. Razinski had murdered the man's colleague, and a free punch was the least they could offer. Then, as Razinski began laughing, they were forced to intervene.

Check Shirt's face reddened, deepening into a dangerous looking shade of purple as he lunged for Razinski again. Two of his colleagues had reached the scene and were trying to tear Razinski from the SWAT team.

Rose withdrew her firearm. 'What the hell is going on?' she shouted.

The police officers stopped their attack. Check Shirt glared at her as if she was somehow to blame. 'You know what he did,' he said.

'Let us handle it now. He'll get what's coming to him.' Rose softened her voice but left an edge to it so the officers were under no illusion about who was in charge. Captain Haig left the van. One look and his team dispersed.

Razinski smirked as the officers retreated.

Rose didn't speak as Razinski was cuffed and bundled

into the back of the secure van, accompanied by one of her team. She turned to see the ashen face of Phelan staring at her from the front door of the house. She walked over, and nodded to him to check he was ok. 'Seal this entrance,' she instructed one of Haig's deputies. 'No one is to enter until they have my clearance.'

'Prepare yourself,' warned Phelan, accompanying her into the house.

She sensed it immediately. She'd visited hundreds of crime scenes in her time, and it was always the same. Stillness seeped through the house, a sense that something had changed irrevocably. Her stomach muscles clenched, a tight feeling spreading across her chest.

'The master bedroom,' said Phelan.

She tried to ignore the photographs adorning the walls next to the staircase. She caught glimpses of stylized photos, individual portraits of each family member, and one larger picture of the family together. Her eyes betrayed her and she lingered on the picture of the young daughter, smiling at the camera as if nothing could ever hurt her.

The smell guided her to the bedroom. One of the SWAT team guarded the door. He stood aside, failing to look her in the eye. Rose held her breath and entered the crime scene.

She'd already known by Phelan's reaction that the whole family had been slaughtered but she wasn't prepared for what she saw.

She took in the whole scene in one glance. The mother and children were tied to chairs in a line. Each was gagged, a tear across their necks. They faced a fourth chair where the decapitated body of their father sat, his head stuck between his legs like a sick Halloween doll.

Rose didn't need ERTU, the Bureau's evidence response

team, to check the bodies. She knew the family had witnessed the decapitation before being killed. 'Ok, get ERTU in,' she told the guard.

She followed Phelan downstairs trying not to rush. The fresh air hit her like a slap. She took a couple of seconds to compose herself and continued working.

'All of them?' asked Haig, resigned to the fact.

Rose nodded. 'I think he killed them before he tried to leave last time.' She'd requested that Razinski allow the mother to speak to them but he'd refused. Rose couldn't suppress a shudder as she thought about the family being forced to witness the decapitation of the father. What it must have done to them, how long they must have sat in terror with that image ingrained in their visions, waiting for their fate.

ERTU had arrived and were being briefed by Phelan. 'I want to be present for all questioning with Razinski,' demanded Haig. He had a towering presence, and Rose sensed the man's natural authority. He'd been nothing but reasonable considering the events and she understood how his team would follow him unwaveringly.

'You can accompany me to the offices. I'll do as much as I can.'

One of the SWAT team, Trevor Khatri, joined them. 'Excuse me, Ma'am, we've discovered something you might want to see.'

Haig accompanied her to the van. Khatri opened the back doors. Razinski sat on the right hand side. His arms and legs were chained to a steel bar running the length of the van. A second SWAT member sat opposite him. 'Lean forward,' ordered Khatri.

Razinski smirked but didn't move. Khatri looked at Rose

and she nodded. Khatri placed his forearm on the back of
Razinski's neck and shoved him forward. Razinski didn't
fight, his smirk a constant on his face.

Khatri pulled the man's shirt up revealing a crude
marking on Razinski's back. It was half tattoo, half scar tissue.
The image looked like a ladder or a train track. Two parallel
vertical lines had been carved on Razinski's back from his
neck to his waist. Rose counted the horizontal lines joining
the two lines. The lines were welt-like, colored blue. Rose
numbered them as eighteen.

'What am I looking at?' asked Haig.

'A myth,' said Rose.

3

Lynch was used to false starts, and empty leads. It had plagued his time as an agent, and had only become worse since. He'd never completely given up hope that his son was alive, would never do so until the day he died or the day he saw his son again. But he could treat it only as that. Hope. Nothing Lennox told him changed the fact that it was the loosest of leads. The hostage taker, Razinski, had mentioned both his name and his son's. He'd told the agent in charge that Daniel Lynch was alive.

Hope.

Lennox left him alone to call the agents at the scene. The two SWAT agents looked away. Once his breathing returned to something close to normal, Lynch retrieved his laptop. Uploading a piece of software, he entered Razinski's details. The search results were empty.

'Razinski surrendered. They have him in custody,' said Lennox, hanging up his phone.

Lynch shut the laptop. 'The family?'

Lennox shook his head.

'I'll get changed.'

After showering, Lynch retrieved a packed suitcase from the bottom of his wardrobe. He removed the three forged passports, five stacks of dollars, and two handguns, and placed them in his safe. He stared at his phone, trying his best not to think about his son.

Daniel had gone missing six years ago, aged seven. Lynch left the FBI a few months later.

He picked up the phone and called his ex-wife, Sally. 'Hello, stranger,' she said.

'Hi.' He couldn't face small talk at the moment. 'Listen, I'm going away for a few days.'

'Okay, thanks for the update.' She sounded bemused, but her tone remained soft.

'What?' said Lynch.

'Well, I haven't seen you for four months, Sam. I'm a bit surprised you're updating me about your movements.'

Lynch gripped the receiver. Everything he wanted to tell her became lost in the rage rising within him.

'What is it, Sam?'

He couldn't tell her about Daniel. It was almost definitely a hoax, the Razinski character having read up on the case and using him as a bargaining chip. Not that Sally would have listened anyway. She hadn't exactly given up on Daniel but had come, in her own words, to an acceptance.

'It's nothing,' said Lynch, realizing he'd been holding his breath. 'I might be out of contact for a time, that's all.'

'Sam, you can come see me at any time. You know that, don't you?'

'I know,' said Lynch, hanging up.

Lynch opened up a second laptop from the sideboard in his bedroom and downloaded some documents onto a flash drive. He hesitated, staring at a chest of drawers in the far corner of the room. He didn't know how long he'd be away, when he'd next return to his apartment. His hands shook as opened the top drawer and pulled out a woolen garment.

It was little more than a rag now, a piece of lifeless material. Daniel had been wearing it the day before he'd disappeared, an innocent seven year old unaware of how his life was about to be changed forever. In the last six years not a day went by where Lynch hadn't gazed at the pullover. He placed the material to his face, inhaling the fabric, before placing it in a holdall.

Lennox and his team were waiting downstairs. They'd made themselves comfortable, sitting around the kitchen table as if waiting for a meal. Lennox held a touch screen tablet in front of him and was studying the screen with intense purpose.

'Angry birds?' said Lynch.

'Completed that years ago. Come have a look. Some images of this Razinski guy you might find interesting.'

Lennox handed him the tablet, his eyes wide in anticipation. 'Any luck tracing who he actually is?' asked Lynch, trying not to respond to what he saw on the screen.

Lynch squeezed the image on the tablet and scrutinized the image. It was a Railroad tattoo. Carved by machete onto the man's back, colored by blue tattoo ink. Two long parallel lines stretched the length of Razinski's back interspersed with a number of horizontal lines joining the two lines together.

'There are eighteen sleepers if you're interested,' said Lennox, pointing to the thin horizontal lines.

Lynch glanced at the FBI agent. In the past six years, he'd tracked down three other people with similar tattoos. The sleepers, the ties connecting the tracks, were meant, as far as

Lynch had been able to ascertain, to symbolize a kill. Of the three men with the matching tattoos Lynch uncovered, one had seven sleepers, one seventeen, and the other twenty-one. All proved to be false starts - copycats of a rumor, an urban legend. Under severe duress, the three men confessed the tattoos were elaborate fakes, created by the same tattoo artist.

In turn, Lynch tracked down the tattoo artist, an elderly man by the name of Cooper. Cooper explained to Lynch how he'd created the effect on the three men; the techniques he'd used to desecrate their bodies with his barbaric practice. Also under duress, Cooper denied any link to the Railroad. That it was a joke, a request by the three men he'd obliged for money. Lynch informed the tattoo artist that he would no longer be involved in such obligations, and helped him to agree by shattering both his hands.

Lynch was used to false starts, but the image on the screen was different to those three tattoos. The ragged lines of the Railroad tracks and sleepers were visceral. Each sleeper uneven, the resulting welts different sizes. It looked disjointed, as if the work was completed over a number of years. As if someone had taken the occasional knife to the man's back.

'You think it's the real thing?' asked Lennox.

'Depends what the real thing is, I guess,' said Lynch.

Lynch scrolled through the images on the tablet until he came to Razinski's face.

'Recognize him?' asked Lennox.

Lynch shook his head, not taking his eyes off the image of Razinski. The man had a slim, gaunt face. His cheeks were well defined, his blue eyes bulging from their sockets. The man's hands were cuffed but he smiled for the camera as if on a photo-shoot. 'I've never seen him before,' said Lynch, unable to hide the disappointment in his voice.

'Well, he's receiving some serious attention. They're moving him to a secure unit. He still insists on speaking to you.'

'What are we waiting for, then?' said Lynch.

'It's very secure, if you get my drift,' said Lennox, producing a blindfold from his back pocket.

They waited until he was in the back of the van to blindfold him. The windows were blanked out. 'Is this necessary? I can't see a thing, anyway.'

'Procedure,' said Lennox.

'Ah, yes, I'd forgotten about procedure. Any beer for the journey?'

'I wish.'

Lynch spent the first ten minutes tracing the route the van took in his head. Unfortunately the driver was wise to the technique. He drove in concurrent circles and soon managed to disorientate him enough that Lynch gave in. The secure unit could have been anywhere. They could drive for hours, only for the unit to be a mile from his house.

He tried to sleep but had only been awake a few hours. He pictured Razinski, his gaunt smiling face, and thought about why he had asked for him. Even if what he said was true, that his son was alive, there was nothing for Razinski to gain by speaking to him.

Three hours later, the van stopped. 'Wait here,' said Lennox, pulling open the side door.

Lynch held his breath and listened. The lack of traffic noise suggested they were somewhere remote. The fresh air was a welcome relief from the cloying air-conditioned interior of the van. He heard muffled words between Lennox and another man, someone different from his two SWAT companions. Lennox raised his voice and returned to the van.

'I'm afraid I must bid you adieu,' said Lennox. 'Somehow we don't have clearance to go any further.'

'Must be serious. Shall I keep the headgear on?'

'Just awhile longer.' Lennox took his hand and shook it. 'Best of luck going forward,' he said.

'Thanks.'

Lennox slid the door shut and the van sped off. Ten minutes later, Lynch experienced a change of pressure and a dimming of light. They were underground. Lynch pulled off the blindfold as the van continued downwards. The blacked out windows prevented any view of the outside. 'Much further?' he asked the replacement driver.

'Nope.'

The van entered a spiral continuing for another five minutes before pulling to a stop.

4

The replacement driver pulled up and opened the door of the van. 'Please wait here, sir,' he said, leaving Lynch alone in the relative darkness. Lynch had been in similar places before. The FBI black sites were not supposed to exist but he knew of at least five locations nationwide. It took the highest security level and such a clearance came at a price. It was one of the reasons he was still monitored by his former employers, and explained how they'd located him so quickly.

He couldn't tell if he'd been here before, having no idea where he was currently located. The black site shared a uniformity of design. They were effectively underground prisons, with one way in and one way out. The CIA used such places for suspected terrorists and other threats to security. The FBI used them for interrogation purposes, reserving them for persons of particular risk to the public.

His presence there suggested they were taking the Razinski character seriously. Unofficially, Lynch was the ultimate expert on the organization called the Railroad; mainly because the FBI had denied all knowledge of their existence.

Shortly after Daniel's disappearance, Lynch's research into the group was disbanded. An outside agent, Lawrence Balfour, was recruited to lead Lynch's department so Lynch resigned to conduct his own investigation.

The replacement driver returned. 'With me please, sir,' he said, moving towards a small tunnel entrance lit by a line of faded neon lights.

A hint of ammonia hit him as he followed the silhouetted figure down the narrowing corridor. The driver walked with military precision, and Lynch found himself matching the man's stride until eventually he stopped at the entrance to a second section of the black site, a cavernous area lit by powerful beams of light. At the center of the space was a glass dome. At the center of the dome, his arms and legs cuffed, sat the man Lynch presumed was Gregor Razinski.

A pair of officials walked towards him, the suited figures dwarfed by the backdrop of the glass prison. 'Mr Lynch,' said one of the pair, a bespectacled man in his early fifties.

'Special Agent Balfour,' said Lynch, recognizing the man who'd replaced him in his role at the FBI. Since Lynch's departure, Balfour had been promoted. He was now an ASAC, Assistant Agent in Charge, at the San Antonio field office.

Balfour smiled at Lynch and offered his hand. 'Thank you for agreeing to assist us. It can't have been easy for you.'

'Nor for you,' said Lynch, alluding to the fact that they were acknowledging the possible existence of the Railroad. He shook hands with the man, holding eye contact.

'This is Special Agent Sandra Rose,' said Balfour, glancing at the woman to his left while maintaining his practiced smile.

'Samuel Lynch.'

Rose nodded. She had a slim, athletic build, a couple of inches shorter than Lynch. Her red hair was tied in a bunch. Her face was unreadable. No smile but no sign of hostility. 'I headed up the operation resulting in Razinski's capture,' she said.

'Where he mentioned my name?'

'Yes.'

'What can you tell me?' said Lynch.

Rose replayed the scene at the Gunn household: the death of the local deputy, the supposed hostage situation resulting in the massacre of the entire Gunn family.

Lynch pictured the scene, detaching himself from its brutal reality by viewing it in the abstract, as if it were a training exercise rather than the brutal slaying it was. 'Were the family already dead when Razinski mentioned my name?'

Rose hesitated, displaying a hint of emotion for the first time. 'The initial examinations would suggest they were.' She sighed. 'He enjoyed the game, toying with us. Obviously, we had no reason to believe he'd already executed everyone so we bided our time.'

Lynch caught a sense of defensiveness in Rose's words which had been picked up by Balfour who shifted balance from left to right foot. 'Why do you think he mentioned me?' said Lynch.

'I was hoping you could provide that information,' said Rose, regaining her initial composure.

'I don't know him,' said Lynch, not elaborating further.

'He knew about you and your son,' said Balfour, still smiling.

'That's public record,' said Lynch, picturing the newspaper headlines ingrained in his mind. FBI Agent's Child Goes Missing. Daniel's face smiling out from the front page.

Balfour nodded, exchanging looks with Special Agent Rose. Lynch knew they were thinking about his reaction to his son's disappearance. His obsession with the organization dubbed the Railroad, and their leader, a figure known only as the Controller. How that obsession had soon rolled out of control, until Lynch had mapped out a century of crimes and attributed them to this mysterious and, as far as the FBI were concerned, fictitious group. How Lynch's work began to suffer until his superiors had no option to let him go and replace him with the man standing in front of him.

'He was adamant that he wanted to speak to you. As you know, he claimed to have details of your son's location,' said Rose.

Lynch's heart fluttered at the mention of his son. He wouldn't let hope dictate to him now. He considered the prisoner in the glass dome, only meters from him, as an imposter and would treat him as such until proven otherwise. 'Did you consider he was just playing with you. That he was using his supposed knowledge to negotiate his escape from the site with his life?'

Rose's demeanor didn't change in reaction to what was effectively an accusation. 'As I said, we had no way to know if the family were alive or not. At the time it was the only logical negotiation technique.'

'You've interrogated him?' asked Lynch.

Balfour pinched his nose, frowning. 'We've begun the process. He claims his name is Gregor Razinski and he is a member of this so-called organization.'

'The Railroad,' said Lynch, goading Balfour.

'Yes. He's refused to elaborate much further either about

his involvement with the group, or about the group itself.' Balfour hesitated. 'Listen, Lynch, I understand your past involvement with this organization and I know what Razinski is promising you, but as far as the FBI are concerned the Railroad do not exist.'

'I got that message a long time ago, Balfour.'

Balfour didn't respond.

The appearance of Razinski and his tattoos were far from proof of the Railroad's existence, but what would they need for the group to be recognized? 'What's your take, Rose?'

'I don't know enough about the Railroad to offer an opinion at the moment. All I know is that Razinski slaughtered that family without remorse. He is highly intelligent and manipulative. He obviously didn't expect to be caught and it's possible he'd created this scenario of you and the Railroad as a backup, should he ever get into such a situation. That said, we've taken a closer look at the Railroad tattoos on his back and, as far as we can ascertain, the tracks go back over a number of years. There is significant scar tissue on his back. Our best guess is that the last three tracks were carved onto his body less than a year ago. The first track as long as ten to fifteen years.'

Lynch thought about the word *carved*. His research suggested that only a fellow Railroad member could carve a track onto a body. The process involved the use of a machete. It was crude and dangerous. 'It's one hell of a backup plan.'

'There is possibly a simpler explanation,' said Balfour.

Lynch studied Balfour, his coiffured hair and lightly tanned face, the whiteness of his teeth and false smile, and wondered how much action the man had ever seen. 'Let me guess, you think that Razinski is the Railroad?'

'It would make more sense,' said Balfour, smile still intact.

'Than what?'

'Than some rogue organization which abducts people on or near train tracks never to be seen again.' Balfour paused and Lynch noticed a hint of steel in his eyes. 'We have to consider that Razinski has created this myth of the Railroad over the years, and that...'

'And that he knows about my son because he is the one who took him?'

For the first time since meeting him, Balfour looked uneasy. 'It has to be considered,' he said.

They walked towards the glass dome where Razinski was being held. The glass was one way and Razinski couldn't see them. He sat with perfect stillness, staring into space. 'What do we know about the Gunn family?' asked Lynch, peering through the glass into the domed prison.

'We're yet to uncover a link between the Gunn family and Razinski. Edward Gunn was an architect, high-level stuff. Eleanor Gunn a housewife,' said Rose, moving next to him. 'That said, we've been unable to trace Razinski on any system. He had no identification on him and doesn't appear on any of our databases. It's highly probable he's using an alias.'

Lynch continued studying the man in the prison. Razinski's calmness was serene, trance-like. He would know he was under surveillance and yet sat if he was alone in his room, lost in thought. Lynch understood what was likely to happen next and it filled him with dread. He thought about Daniel. His last known whereabouts was at a public pathway next to a mainline train track. Lynch could picture the area in perfect clarity as if he'd just left the place. The tinged brown of the playing fields, the rusted metal on the swings, and the rip in the corrugated iron of the perimeter fence separating the

Railroad track from the playing area. Since Daniel's disappearance, two other children had gone missing in a three-mile radius of the spot. Prior to his disappearance, seventeen children had gone missing in a five-mile radius of the spot, each disappearance less than a mile from a sightline of a railroad track. Balfour and Rose would want to discuss Daniel's disappearance, and Lynch wasn't sure he had the energy to go through with it. Only the sight of Razinski, and the possibility he knew about Daniel's fate kept him in place.

'Let's get a drink,' said Rose, as if reading his thoughts.

She led him through to a makeshift canteen, where drinks and food were spread out buffet-style on a long table. Lynch poured himself a cup of oily coffee and piled his plate high with thick-cut sandwiches, his appetite returning after his long journey.

The three of them sat, Razinski still visible through a glass partition. Lynch was aware of the sound of his eating in the stillness of the room. Balfour and Rose sipped at their drinks, waiting.

'What do you want to know?' said Lynch, gulping his coffee.

'You understand our position,' said Rose, delaying.

Lynch held his hand up, his palm facing the woman. 'You don't need to treat me with kid gloves. I understand the drill, and your suspicions. Just get on with it.'

'Have you ever met the man through there, the man we know as Razinski?'

Lynch understood they had to ask the questions, had to repeat themselves, and was happy to answer. 'I've never met him, never came across him in my research.'

Rose glanced at Balfour. 'Your research, what can you tell us about that?'

Lynch smiled. Balfour knew of his research, would have examined what files he hadn't managed to smuggle out of his headquarters at the time. 'No one cared about my research before,' he said, staring at Balfour. Now was not the time for pettiness but he wanted to make his point.

'Wouldn't now be a perfect opportunity to put that record straight?' said Rose, interjecting as if sensing the tension between the two men.

Lynch took himself back to that time six years ago and the rudimentary connections he'd made, and how those connections had grown over the years. In retrospect, he understood he'd become too close to the case and that he should have taken more time off work following Daniel's disappearance. He finished his coffee, and leant back in his chair.

With the sight of Razinski in his periphery vision, he looked at Balfour and Rose. He was in no mood to speak. 'I uncovered patterns, at first state level, then nationwide. The stats are there for everyone to see. I'm sure you've read my reports. A significant amount of children, and adults, had gone missing near railroad tracks nationwide. A big enough discrepancy to suggest we take notice.' He sounded defensive, petty even, but the lack of support he'd received from the Bureau still nagged at him.

'You were given time to work on this,' said Balfour, more statement than question.

'To begin with,' said Lynch, unable to hide the sneer on his face. 'It became apparent the project was too big for one small team.'

'They took you off it?' asked Rose, a hint of softness in her eyes.

'I was told to put it on the back burner.'

'But you didn't,' said Balfour.

'I'm not here to argue. How could I? Those families wanted answers. Can you comprehend what that's like? The loss of a child is horrendous but the not knowing, the thoughts that come with that lack of clarity, you can only imagine. I wasn't about to let those people down.'

Balfour and Rose didn't reply for a time, appreciating Lynch was speaking from personal experience. It was Balfour who broke the silence first. 'You were close to an arrest when you were...'

'Fired?' said Lynch, not hiding his sneer.

'You weren't fired. You left after I arrived.'

'Oh yes, I forgot. I had uncovered a possible location for a man known as the Controller, the head of the Railroad. I went to meet my informant, only to find that he'd been executed.'

'Manner?' said Rose.

'Professional. Gunshot to the chest, double tap to the forehead. When my superiors found out I was still working on the case they put me on leave, wanted me to get over the disappearance of my son. Get over it,' he repeated, his scorn centered on Balfour. 'Six months later I was out. And Mr Balfour here was in.'

Special Agent Rose brushed her hand across her nose as she studied him, ignoring his dig at Balfour. 'The agents who picked you up at your house found some maps,' she said.

'Yes.'

'You've continued your work?'

'I think that's a poorly kept secret.'

'And how's that panned out for you, Mr Lynch?' said Balfour.

Lynch pursed his lips together and expelled air. He'd made his mind up years ago about Balfour and the verdict was not positive. 'I know people are still going missing. I've reported as such - as you well know.'

The three of them sat for a time in silence. Lynch understood he was being assessed. They were deciding if he was in the right mind to interview Razinski. That was why he'd kept as calm as he was able during the discussion, had contained his emotions when he wanted to lash out.

Rose had yet to question him about the actual day when he'd been instructed to take extended leave from the organization. The accusations he'd made about a cover up within the department, accusations leveled in part at the man next to him. It was this that effectively forced him to leave. He'd seen it in the eyes of his colleagues, the mixture of pity and disgust that he'd lost it. That the disappearance of his son had pushed away at his sanity until he'd finally snapped.

Tired of the silence, Lynch spoke. 'You got me all the way here,' he said. 'You may as well let me speak to Razinski.'

Balfour stared at him. Lynch matched the assessing glare and saw a weakness within Balfour. 'Okay, Lynch,' said Balfour. 'You'll go in there with Special Agent Rose. The first sign of anything untoward and you'll be straight back out. Understood?'

Lynch glanced at Rose who maintained her neutrality. 'Crystal,' he said.

5

They were about to depart the seating area and head for the dome when an operative interrupted them. 'Sir, may I have a word,' said the suited man to Balfour.

'Wait there,' said Balfour, getting to his feet and walking the operative to the other side of the room.

'How long have you known Balfour?' asked Lynch, once he was out of earshot.

Rose didn't immediately answer. She held his gaze, and once more Lynch felt he was being analyzed. He put himself in her position. For all she knew, he was a crazy who'd lost it following his son's disappearance. But however unlikely she might consider Lynch's theories, she wouldn't be able to argue with the fact that Razinski had requested to speak to him. 'Never met him until today,' said Rose. 'Seems nice,' she added, with a hint of a smile.

'Were you aware of any of this beforehand?'

'What, the Railroad? I've heard of the legend, that's why I recognized the tattoo on Razinski's back.' Rose shifted in her seat, and glanced over at Balfour who was deep in conversation with the operative. 'If you don't mind me asking, how has your research been going for the last six years?'

It was an innocent enough question, and she'd asked it without any judgment so Lynch answered. 'The short answer is nowhere,' he said with a small laugh.

'The long answer?'

'No time for that. Let's just say that every time I get close to a breakthrough something happens.'

'Such as?'

'People generally go missing,' said Lynch.

Rose nodded. He couldn't tell if she was humoring him. More likely, she was using their friendly chat as a mode of interrogation. 'Did your investigations have anything to do with the Gunn family?'

Lynch noticed a narrowing of her eyes as she spoke the surname of the butchered family and wondered how horrific the crime scene had been. 'You're heading down the wrong road, Special Agent Rose, if you think I have anything to do with whatever happened to that family.'

'I wasn't suggesting that.'

Lynch paused, composed himself. 'Not directly, no. I would be interested in reading their files. From what I've been told, it sounds like an opportunistic home invasion gone wrong. It doesn't sound as if Razinski had any particular motive for targeting the family.'

Rose went to speak only to stop as Balfour returned. The ASAC was flustered. He pulled at the lapels of his jacket, shifting from foot to foot. 'Okay you two, let's get this thing up and running,' he said, not offering an explanation. 'I'll be watching on the screens.'

Lynch followed Rose to the glass prison where a desk and two chairs had been laid out. Armed guards surrounded the entrance to the dome, and one of the gigantic men followed them into the glass area as if the prisoner had some Houdini-like escape ability.

Gregor Razinski didn't respond as the side door of the glass dome opened. Rose pressed a button on a side panel, and the chair holding the captive in place made a slow turn so that Razinski faced them. Razinski was firmly secured. His hands and legs were locked into the metallic contraption, and a steel band curled around his neck making it difficult for him to move his head. The chair stopped moving so that Razinski sat facing them. Razinski blinked before making eye contact with them in turn before finally settling on Lynch.

Razinski smirked and Lynch saw the look of a man perfectly at ease with himself. His eyes were devoid of humanity and Lynch understood at that moment there would be no great revelation from him. Razinski was beyond empathy. He would have no regrets about what he'd done to the Gunn family, and would offer no assistance unless it benefited him.

'Special Agent Lynch,' said Razinski. His voice was coarse, guttural, as if his throat was bone dry. 'Or should I say Mr Lynch?'

'You have me at a disadvantage,' said Lynch.

Razinski attempted to laugh, the sound emanating from his mouth more of a yelp. 'But I know all about you, Lynch.' He tilted his head, as far as able considering his restraints. 'And your little boy. Though he's not so little anymore.'

The world in front of Lynch faded out of focus. White noise filled his ears at the mention of his son, and for one horrendous second he thought he would pass out. He blinked, mirroring Razinski's earlier movement, and reality rushed back at him. He composed himself, hoping he hadn't given away too much in his reaction. He sensed Rose in his peripheral vision willing him to continue. 'Shall we stop playing games now, Mr Razinski. You obviously know I'm no longer with the FBI. Why did you request my presence here?'

Razinski narrowed his eyes, feigning sympathy. 'Poor Lynch. We've been watching you all this time you know. Your tedious attempts at tracking us down.'

'So you admit you're part of a wider organization,' said Rose, interjecting as Lynch tensed up.

Razinski didn't look away from Lynch. 'We could have snuffed you out at any moment,' he said, widening his eyes. 'But where would be the fun in that?'

Lynch matched the man's glare. He'd often wondered why he'd never been a target for the Railroad and maybe this was the answer. 'Last chance, Razinski. They already think you're wasting their time. Tell me what you want, tell me why you killed the Gunn family, or I'm out of here.'

A coldness descended over the captive man. It spread outwards from his eyes. His facial muscles tensed, the tendons on his neck sticking out like wires. 'The Gunn family,' he said, taking a deep breath. 'A regrettable folly. An opportunistic error on my part. I apologise for the crudeness but then I was forced into reacting.' For the first time, Razinski raised his voice, turning his attention to Rose.

'How long had you been planning your siege on the Gunn family?' said Rose.

'I'm not here to talk to you, Madam,' said Razinski, breathing in again and turning his attention back to Lynch. 'Mr Lynch, it is under regrettable circumstances that we meet but possibly it is fortunate for you.'

'Stop wasting time, Razinski.'

'Okay, okay, you have me. I'm metaphorically holding my

hands up. I have the information you need. I can give you the Railroad. The Controller. You have only a vague idea of what you've stumbled on. I can give you the world, Lynch. So many unsolved crimes, so many crimes you didn't even know existed. And more than that, Mr Lynch, I can give you the one thing you really want. I can tell you where your son is.'

Lynch controlled his breathing, refusing to give Razinski the satisfaction of seeing him flustered again. Despite which, he couldn't help but think of his boy. He always pictured Daniel the same way, as he was the last day he saw him. The close cut crop of his hair, the green t-shirt with the legend 1967 stitched across the front, his wide eyes and wider smile as he threw the football around the back yard. The following day, Lynch had left to speak to an informant. By the time he'd returned on Monday afternoon, Daniel was gone.

'Speak then,' said Lynch.

Razinski frowned as if Lynch was acting simple. 'Oh come on, Lynch, what do you take me for. Give and take and all that.'

'What do you want?' said Lynch, losing patience with the man.

'I want what is rightfully mine,' said Razinski, a darkness to his voice.

Lynch sighed.

'Full immunity. Authorized and signed by the District Attorney, and verified by legal counsel of my choosing.'

Heat spread across Lynch's face. He'd feared such a ludicrous ultimatum but now he was here, with this man suggesting he had information on his son's whereabouts, it was tough to handle.

He turned to Rose who tapped her pen on the desk. 'This is a non-starter,' she said, not bothering to humor the man.

'Take it or leave it.'

Rose didn't sound fazed by Razinski's resolve. 'Razinski, you're obviously psychotic but you're not completely without intelligence. We both know what you did at the Gunn residence. You beheaded a man, made his family watch, and then murdered them in cold blood without a hint of remorse. You murdered a police officer.'

Razinski grinned, as if savoring the memory. 'And?'

Lynch fought his rising heartbeat. He was meters away from Razinski, could get to him within seconds. He could do extensive damage in that time and doubted anyone would be in a huge rush to stop him. All that held him back was the possibility that Razinski was telling the truth and had answers for him.

Special Agent Sandra Rose picked up her pen and placed it in the front pocket of her jacket. 'If you can't be serious about this, Razinski, then our time here is up. We'll return you to the system and you can see how you fend there.'

'I wouldn't,' said Razinski.

'Wouldn't what?'

'I wouldn't fend. I would be dead within forty-eight hours.' He sighed, and shook his head as far it could move within his restraints. 'I don't think you quite understand the information I'm willing to share with you.'

'Why did you request me?' said Lynch.

'Isn't that obvious, Mr Lynch? You're the only one who believes in our existence.'

Lynch shrugged. 'That's not going to make a difference. Not after what you've done.'

'Bullshit,' said Razinski, for the first time displaying emotion. 'I know for a fact that you've got people in protection who've done worse than this.'

'Jesus, you do live in a fantasy world,' said Rose.

'You've got worse people than me working for you. If you don't realize that, Agent Rose, then you're either naïve or don't have the clearance.'

It was Rose's turn to laugh but Lynch sensed her growing unease and feared she would end the interview before Razinski had the chance to offer them anything. 'Why don't you help yourself by giving us something,' he said.

'What, like where poor little Daniel Lynch is? It's the last thing I'm going to share with you, but I will. I give you my word on that.'

Lynch didn't respond. His heart rate was past a hundred now as shots of adrenaline raged through his bloodstream.

'It's okay, Mr Lynch, I understand. You're impotent. Not even worth one of those pointless badges the lady next to you possesses. You lost your son and think it was your fault. Let me tell you something, Mr Lynch. It was.'

Lynch pushed himself up from his seat, only for Rose to grasp his wrist and ease him back down.

The movement was manna to Razinski. 'See,' he said, with unhidden joy. 'We took him because of you, Lynch. I think you know that. We took him because you were close to finding us and we wanted to, and please do pardon the pun here, derail you.'

'That's enough,' said Rose, getting to her feet. She waited for Lynch who remained in his seat staring at Razinski, considering what damage he could inflict on the monster before him.

'I can give you everything,' said Razinski. 'So many are still alive. So, so many. I can tell you where they are. I can give you the Controller,' he shouted, as Lynch finally got to his feet and followed Rose out of the glass prison.

6

Lynch returned to the makeshift canteen where Balfour was waiting.

'Well, that was a bust,' said Balfour.

Lynch reminded himself he no longer worked for the FBI and debated internally if it was worth knocking the man out. 'What the fuck is going on here?' he said.

'I think that's obvious,' said Balfour, rattled by Lynch's insubordination.

'I agree. I think you've got something on the Railroad, otherwise you wouldn't be humoring this fuckwit.'

Balfour squirmed, his face shaping itself into something both uncomfortable and smug-looking.

'You fuckers. You got rid of me but you followed up my work. That's why you knew where to find me. Do you know about this?' said Lynch, turning to Rose.

Rose shook her head, her scorn reserved for Balfour.

'Did you really expect to be notified, Lynch? May I remind you that you're no longer a member of the FBI. That you left in disgrace.'

Heat rose in Lynch at the word disgrace. Balfour had finally revealed his true self and it wasn't pleasant. Lynch ignored the jibe, the same way Balfour was ignoring the fact that Lynch had lost his son due to his work. 'Even from a professional viewpoint you should have consulted me. Maybe we wouldn't be in this position if you had.'

Balfour's cold eyes bored into Lynch, reminding him of the lack of empathy he'd seen in Razinski. He was convinced now the FBI had been monitoring his actions ever since his departure.

'Where do we go from here?' said Rose, trying to dispel the tension between the two men.

'What do you suggest, Agent?' said Balfour, not taking his eyes off Lynch as if expecting an attack.

'We could negotiate on his demands,' said Rose.

Balfour snarled. 'Full immunity? Even we couldn't pull that off.'

'She said negotiate,' said Lynch, tired of the man's attitude. In his time with the Bureau, he'd seen stranger things. It would never be acknowledged officially, but deals were made with criminals, even ones as extreme as Razinski. If it wasn't a possibility then Razinski wouldn't still be sitting there in his glass prison. He would have been taken somewhere even more secure than his current surroundings.

Balfour placed his fingers on his mouth, the second nervous habit Lynch had spotted since being reunited with the man. 'We may have a possible negotiation tactic,' said Balfour. He sounded reluctant, as if it pained him to share the words.

Rose glanced at Lynch, her frustration made clear. Neither of them spoke, waiting for Balfour to speak.

'As you were interviewing Razinski, a call came in from

one of our field teams. We've managed to trace Razinski's family. What's left of them anyway.'

'What's left of them?' said Rose.

'Apparently Razinski has an estranged wife. Or did. She was discovered outside her residence in Victoria, two hours ago. She was not long dead.'

'Cause of death?' said Lynch.

'Exsanguination. Both wrists were slashed.'

'And she was discovered in the street?'

Balfour pulled open the iPad on the desk and turned towards Lynch and Rose. A series of images played before them. A woman in her late forties, early fifties, spread-eagled in a quiet back street. Her body positioned horizontally across the road, her legs and arms pulled to her side so she made a straight line. Blood pooled around her creating a maroon lake. It was apparent whoever had placed her in the road wanted her discovered.

'That's not the worst of it,' said Balfour, taking the iPad back. 'Six other members of Razinski's family have been found.'

'Six?' said Rose, incredulous.

'Razinski's mother, was found outside her care home in Lufkin. His uncles, Bill and Joss Turner from his mother's side, and Blyth Razinski from his father's side. And then there's his sister, and her husband,' said Balfour, clicking the iPad and handing it back to Lynch.

Lynch held the iPad at arm's distance as if the images on the screen could be contained. He squinted his eyes, trying to make sense of the pixelated shapes. The corpses of Razinski's sister and her husband lay side by side. Like Razinski's estranged wife, their arms and legs had been pulled in to create two horizontal lines. They were placed two feet apart, in Lynch's opinion the opening rungs of a Railroad line. Lynch gulped and, fighting the rising nausea, peered closer at the photo. Next to him, he sensed Rose's apprehension.

'Scroll through,' said Balfour.

Lynch swiped image after image, panoramic view to close up, until he was left in no doubt as to what he was seeing. Like Edward Gunn, Razinski's sister and her husband had both been decapitated though the assailants hadn't stopped there. They had switched heads on the corpses, so Razinski's sister's body had the head of her husband and vice versa.

'It couldn't be a clearer message,' said Lynch. 'They obviously know we have Razinski in custody.'

'But why kill all his family?' asked Rose. 'What do they gain?'

It was the wrong question. 'Who haven't they killed?' said Lynch

Balfour nodded. 'We have been unable to trace Razinski's father, Wayne, and his eight-year old daughter, Ellie. Ellie lives with her grandfather in a small rural area called Hardwick near Waco, ninety minutes out of Dallas. We have a sighting of them four hours ago in a grocery store, but from what we can ascertain they never returned home.

Lynch glanced at the images of Razinski's daughter, struggling to comprehend how the monster in the transparent prison behind them could have a child. He assumed Ellie had been an accident, unwanted by mother and father, and had therefore been abandoned to the care of her grandparent. Did she know the man her father was? Did Razinski's father understand what he'd created? 'Have we received any word from them?' he asked.

'Them?' said Balfour.

'We can stop with the pretense now, Balfour. The Railroad, or whatever we want to call them. The killings are a warning, the kidnapping a motivation for Razinski not to talk.'

'Does Razinski know?' said Rose.

'Not yet,' said Balfour.

Rose lent forward on her desk. 'So what do we do? Go back and tell Razinski what has happened. Then what? Hope he gives us the lowdown on this supposed organization? If anything, this puts us in a worse negotiating position.'

'Not necessarily. We can tell Razinski we will find his father and daughter if he cooperates,' said Balfour.

'That's if he even cares,' said Rose.

Lynch nodded. 'They've obviously targeted the father and daughter. If Razinski does have any allegiance or empathy, I imagine it is focused on one of them. I guess we have nothing to lose by discussing it with him.'

Lynch stood, an old instinct taking over. 'Let's go,' he said.

Rose didn't wait for confirmation with Balfour. Lynch heard her get from her seat as he walked towards the door. He glanced sideways at Balfour who remained sitting but didn't try to interfere.

RAZINSKI CHUCKLED as the hydraulic doors of the prison sighed open. 'Back so soon,' he said.

Lynch followed Rose to the safety line where she told Razinski the news about his family, holding back the details of his father and daughter. Lynch scrutinized the prisoner's face for a reaction but saw nothing beyond a slight elevation of the eyebrows.

'You wish me to comment?' said Razinski, as if the brutal murder of six family members was a mundane issue.

'They're trying to warn you off,' said Lynch.

Razinski's eyes widened in mock appreciation. 'Wow, what a deduction. Of course they're trying to warn me off. Bit of an overkill, as usual. At least it proves one thing though.'

'What's that?' said Rose.

'That I have something to offer you. So what do you have to offer me, Agent Rose?'

'Full immunity is off the table, Razinski, but I think you knew that. Some arrangement could be made for home custody though in a secure area.'

Razinski stared blankly ahead. After some time, Lynch realized the man was in thought. 'I want legal representation and official documentation before I speak.'

Rose nodded and turned towards Lynch as if looking for confirmation.

'Tell him,' said Lynch, keeping his gaze on Razinski for a reaction.

It wasn't much, a mere narrowing of the eyes, but as Rose told Razinski about his father and daughter the man, for the first time, looked concerned about his predicament.

The three of them sat in silence for a period, eventually broken by Razinski. 'Why would you tell me that? You know they are effectively buying my silence.'

Razinski sounded vulnerable and Lynch was quick to exploit this momentary weakness. 'We can help you, Razinski. We're the only people who can. Tell us what you know now and I promise we'll do everything in our power to find your missing relatives.'

Razinski thrust his chin forward, his skin catching on the metallic restraints. 'You forget, Mr Lynch, you're no longer a member of this esteemed organization.' Spittle flew from his mouth as he spoke, his face coloring in anger.

'Mr Lynch is representing the Bureau in this, Mr Razinski,' said Rose. 'I can confirm we will put all our resources into finding your family.'

Razinski relaxed, his head dropping onto his restraints as if someone had drained the power from him, before tensing again. Lynch noticed the veins on the man's forearms pop into view as he clenched his fists, his face blossoming into color as the rage spread throughout him. 'You fucking morons. You think you can do anything?' he said, his voice rising until he was screaming at them, his face so contorted that he was unrecognizable. 'They are gone, gone for ever. It isn't a bargaining tool. It is a sign of power. It's not meant for me, it's meant for the rest of them. It's meant for you.'

As quick as the anger arose, it vanished. The color drained from him as his body relaxed once more. 'Thank you for your concern but my original demand remains and there will be no further discussion until I have a document to sign and an attorney to witness it.'

LYNCH CONSIDERED the enormity of Razinski's statement as he followed Rose out of the prison area. If what he'd said was true, the Railroad were prepared to commit multiple and graphic executions simply to serve a point.

Balfour was waiting for them in the secure area where he'd monitored their second interrogation of Razinski. Lynch counted the armed guards surrounding the prison, and positioned in various points across the hangar. The underground compound should be one of the securest places on earth. The extended guard presence smacked of overkill.

'That went well,' said Balfour, as the hydraulic doors clicked shut securing the three of them in the enclosed area.

'Tell me what you know,' said Lynch.

As he spoke a second door, a hidden element directly behind Balfour, slid open and two Agents dressed in SWAT gear entered the room.

'Thank you for your help, Mr Lynch, but we can take it from here.'

Lynch glanced at Rose, dismayed but not surprised by this latest development. He was no longer one of the team and had served his purpose by talking to Razinski. What happened next was beyond his level, which at present was non-existent.

Rose grimaced. 'Sir, I think it would be wise to keep Mr Lynch here for the time being. He has a connection with Razinski and whatever group he is part of. I think his disappearance would affect the possibility of co-operation.'

'Thank you for your suggestion, Agent Rose, but Razinski will cooperate with us, one way or another,' said Balfour.

Lynch poised himself as the SWAT officers moved towards him. Although there was little he could do, he wanted to leave with some dignity. Rose glanced at him, as if questioning him over Balfour's last statement.

What had he meant? That he was prepared to go beyond what was legal to get answers from Razinski? If that was the case, Rose would probably soon have to make a decision as to whether she was prepared to go along with such a procedure.

The first of the SWAT guys held out his arm. 'Please come with us, sir,' he said.

Lynch nodded to Rose. 'A pleasure,' he said, as the sound of an explosion ripped through the compound area.

The five agents in the secure area froze. The SWAT members looked at Balfour for instructions and Lynch took a step away from them.

Balfour barked questions into his walkie-talkie but received only static in reply.

'They've come for Razinski,' said Lynch, as the first set of gunshots rang out in the hangar.

Balfour hesitated, the lack of decisiveness highlighting the potential coward in the man.

'We need to get him out of there,' said Lynch. 'Razinski is our only link to the Railroad.'

Balfour glanced around the room as if an answer could be found in the reinforced concrete walls, bulletproof glass, and steel doors separating them from the rest of the hangar.

'He's right, sir,' said Rose, who'd withdrawn her firearm.

In the compound, a team of FBI operatives had moved to surround Razinski's prison. The explosion and gunfire sounded as if it came from some distance away but the thick walls of their room dampened the noise.

As if in answer, one of the guards surrounding Razinski's prison took a hit in the chest. He was wearing his Kevlar vest but the impact knocked him off his feet. As he fell, three canisters were thrown into the area, each releasing smoke on impact.

'Tear gas,' said Lynch.

The attack was enough for the two SWAT operatives to jump into action. 'There are masks through here,' said one of the men, pointing to the hidden door. Before Balfour could object, they disappeared through the opening.

'I need a gun,' said Lynch, as outside the room guards returned fire on an unseen enemy. As he spoke one of the guards took a bullet to the head, the impact ripping half of the unfortunate man's head clear away.

'Balfour,' shouted Lynch.

Balfour was rooted to the spot, watching events unfold with a mounting horror. 'We're staying here,' he said.

Lynch glanced at Rose for support. 'Protocol,' she said, sounding unconvinced of her words.

'Do you have a spare weapon?' asked Lynch.

Rose shook her head, as a second guard took a bullet to the head and the scene outside their window clouded over as the tear gas spread.

'Where does that door lead?' said Lynch, pointing to the opening where the SWAT team had exited.

'Leads back into the hangar,' said Balfour.

'And there are masks? What are we waiting for?'

For the first time since the initial attack, Balfour turned to look at him. 'They won't be able to penetrate this area.'

Lynch stepped towards Balfour, amazed by the man's relaxed manner considering his men were under attack. 'Really? Then can you tell me how the hell they penetrated this hangar in the first place? Isn't this supposed to be high security? Even Special Agent Lennox wasn't allowed access.'

Balfour nodded and turned his back on him. It was enough to confirm Lynch's suspicions. As Balfour turned away to face the smoke-filled exterior, he made his move. He had the element of surprise on his side, but Balfour was quicker than he'd expected. As Lynch reached for him, grabbing him by the throat, Balfour launched a counter attack. Both men were locked together, Lynch raining blows into Balfour's kidneys as Balfour tried to fight back.

'What the hell are you doing, Lynch?' screamed Rose.

In the blur of the encounter, Lynch made out the form of Special Agent Rose standing in perfect gun-firing pose. Legs shoulder-width apart, gun held out in front with two hands.

'He's one of them, Rose,' said Lynch, managing to slip his left leg behind Balfour and bringing him to the ground.

Balfour crashed onto the ground, the back of his head slamming against the concrete and bouncing back up to face Lynch's elbow which was careering towards him. The crunch of bone echoed around the hollow interior as Lynch reached for Balfour's gun.

'Drop it,' said Rose.

He could feel her behind him, imagined the gun pointed between his shoulder blades. He had little option. Rose was extremely well-trained and with a gun in his hand she wouldn't listen to his pleas of negotiation. 'I'm going to drop it,' he said.

'Nothing sudden,' said Rose.

Lynch nodded and bent his knees, allowing the gun to drop. He kicked it away as Balfour gurgled and moaned next to him. 'You must see it was him who let them in,' he said, turning to face Rose.

'We have absolutely no proof of that. For all I know it could be you.'

'Think straight, Rose. Why would I stage this?'

'Razinski requested you. What better way to stage an escape? You're the only civilian here.'

Rose's gun was pointed at his chest but Lynch could see her resolve fading. 'They took my child, Rose. I wouldn't help them even if I could. I have no idea where we are. I was blindfolded when they took me from my house and we drove for hours. We could be anywhere.'

Rose didn't respond. She kept her gun aloft.

'We need to make a decision, Rose. They're going to kill Razinski.'

Beyond the divide, still clouded with smoke, the muted sound of gunshots continued. Rose and Lynch stood staring at one another, stuck in an impasse until finally Rose lowered her gun.

Balfour was unconscious and didn't stir as Lynch put him into the recovery position. 'He's going to be fine. Safest place for him. May I?' he said, pointing at Balfour's gun.

Rose lowered her gaze. 'So help me God,' she said.

Lynch picked up the gun, his gaze fixed on Rose. He saw the hesitation in her eyes but she kept her gun lowered. 'What do you know of the layout?' he asked.

'About the same as you. This is the first time I've been here as well. Did you see any of the shooters?'

'No, impossible to tell.'

'You been through that door?' said Lynch, picking up his rucksack

'No, but it doesn't seem to be code protected.'

They moved in formation, Lynch kicking open the door as Rose secured the area beyond. The door led to a second room where the tear gas had yet to penetrate. 'Here,' said Rose, pointing to a store cupboard which the SWAT members had left open. She reached in and handed him a SWAT gas mask. Lynch had his eyes fixed on the row of rifles and machine guns. He took a Koch MP5 machine gun and one for Rose. Rose didn't question him, taking the offered gun and pulling the strap across her shoulder before opening the steel door.

Rose pointed, her breathing heavy in the mask's inbuilt headset. They edged their way into the main hangar area. The gas was clearing but their vision was still limited. Rose stumbled and Lynch raised his gun in anticipation. 'Jesus,' said Rose, gazing down at the murdered colleague she'd stumbled over. They crouched down, scanning the area for the gunmen but the whole area was still.

Lynch's mind tended to switch into a different gear in these situations. It was a type of coping mechanism. He stopped considering danger, hesitation his enemy. Only on reflection did he marvel at the risks he was prepared to take. 'How many guards did we have on duty,' whispered Lynch.

'At least twenty, if not more.'

'This strike you as weird?'

'Maybe the explosion accounted for more than we imagined.'

They edged forward, the gas dispersing enough so they could see inside Razinski's prison. 'Shit, they got to him,' said Lynch.

Razinski was still in his elevated position strapped to the metallic chair. His head lolled to one side, held in place by the metal strap curled around his neck. Lynch made out the red patch blossoming across his chest.

'Where the hell are they?' said Rose.

Bodies surrounded the glass dome. They secured the area and edged forward. Lynch stopped by one of the fallen agents, one of Razinski's guards he'd nodded to earlier. The man had no pulse but Lynch couldn't find any gunshot wound. 'Keep your mask on,' he said to Rose.

'No wounds here,' said Rose, bending down next to another of the guards. 'I think we need to get out of here. God only knows what's in this gas.'

Lynch didn't want to contemplate what was in the tear gas. Although they hadn't breathed it in, their skin was exposed and it was possible they'd been infected. I need to see if Razinski is alive,' said Lynch, moving towards the prison, trying his best to avoid the corpses lining his path.

'We need to go,' repeated Rose, who held the MP5 in front of her moving it in a continued circle surveying the area for danger.

'They've gone,' said Lynch, reaching the entry to Razinski's prison where the second guard lay on the ground, jamming the entrance open. Lynch touched the man's neck, dismayed by the coldness of his skin, the stillness where he should have felt the throb of his pulse. He held Balfour's gun in front of him as he edged towards Razinski.

The man reeked. Up close, Lynch could see the bullet hole in Razinski's shoulder. The entry point suggested the bullet had entered from above. Lynch glanced upwards from Razinski's vantage point towards a stanchion area. It was possible that the gunman had positioned himself there, had waited for the guard to open the bulletproof divide before squeezing a shot towards Razinski.

'Let's go,' came Rose's voice in his ears.

Lynch cursed and was about to leave when Razinski's eyes flicked open.

8

'He's breathing,' said Lynch, shaking himself into the present. The dome was free of the tear gas but he kept his mask on.

Rose followed him into the prison, her gun still held in front of her. They were sitting ducks unless the assailants had either fled or been killed in the fight. Rose moved towards Razinski and examined the bullet wounds. 'One shoulder hit, two to the stomach,' she said into the mask's inbuilt microphone, the words crackling with static.

Without hesitation, Lynch smacked Razinski open-palmed across his cheek. 'Razinski,' he shouted.

Razinski's eyes blinked opened only for them to close once more.

'No time for that, Razinski,' said Lynch, smacking the man again.

The second impact shook the man awake, a smile creeping across his lips as he became accustomed to this situation. 'I told you,' he said, his voice a dry rasp.

'We can help you,' said Lynch.

Razinski glanced down to his wounds. 'Face it, Lynch, you've got nothing to offer.'

'We need to get out of here,' said Rose.

'They have your father and daughter,' said Lynch, containing his mounting desperation. It felt ludicrous negotiating with a man such as Razinski. He was a pure psychopath. It was inconceivable that he had an ounce of compassion, even for close family members, but impending death could do the strangest things to a person. 'Tell me where to look and I'll find them. Who is the Controller?'

'As if you'd do that for me.' Razinski coughed, a well of blood spewing from his mouth.

'I wouldn't do it for you, I'd do it for me.'

'And your son?'

Lynch's body tensed. 'And my son, yes.'

Razinski struggled for breath but was determined enough to utter his dying words. 'Some things are best left alone, Lynch. You wouldn't recognize your son now. The boy you know is gone.'

Rose heard the words, and inched towards Lynch as if in support. It was too late. Lynch wanted to stay professional but Razinski's words spoke to him, painting pictures in his mind he wasn't ready to contemplate. He went to punch Razinski in the face, only to change course at the last second instead landing a blow to the bullet wound on Razinski's shoulder. Razinski smiled so Lynch held his hand on the wound and began to squeeze.

A brief period of silence ensued, followed by a howl of pain which reverberated around the glass prison. Lynch was thankful Rose didn't try to intervene. She kept her eyes on the vacant hangar as he kept his fingers pressed into Razinski's yielding flesh.

'Okay,' screamed Razinski.

Lynch released his grip. 'That was your only chance. I meant what I said, I will do everything I can to find your daughter and father. Tell me where to go.'

Razinski fell in and out of consciousness. As he began to slip away, Lynch pressed his fingers further into the wound. 'Not yet, Razinski,' he said.

Death was a great leveler. With the binds holding him in place, and the blood oozing from his wounds, it was almost possible to have sympathy for the dying man. Lynch reminded himself of Razinski's crimes. 'Tell me,' he repeated, trying not to plead.

'We need to go,' said Rose.

'Lean closer,' said Razinski, like a character from a dark fairy tale.

Lynch lent in, disgusted by the smells drifting towards him, the sourness of the man's breath, the pungent body odor, and the distinctive smell of the blood leaking from his body. Lynch waited for the comeback, the final biting comment from a dying man, but Razinski surprised him. Spittle tinged with blood frothed from his mouth as he spoke. 'Mallard,' he said.

Lynch nodded, hiding his shock. Still holding his breath as he listened to Razinski's dying breaths. He glanced over to Rose unsure if she'd heard the name, her focus on the vacant bunker site, her knees bent ready to flee. 'You're sure?'

'Yes. Finish it,' said Razinski.

Lynch glared down at the man, pulling his gun from its holster and pointing it to his head. Razinski closed his eyes, the outline of the smile forming on his lips as he waited for oblivion but Lynch kept the gun raised and followed Rose out of the glass prison. As they made their way across the body-laden ground of the hangar, the sound of Razinski's cries and curses reverberated around the compound.

They stopped at the entrance to the secure room. At their feet lay the bodies of the two SWAT members they'd encountered during their meeting with Balfour.

'We can't leave Balfour here,' said Rose.

Lynch cleared his mind. In principle he agreed with her but taking Balfour with them was a risk. He didn't know for sure if Balfour was involved but the safer option was to leave the man behind. 'He'll be fine here. I don't think we should risk it.'

Rose gazed at him, an alien visage with her gas mask protruding from her face. 'I'd lose my job,' she said, making her way through the barrier.

Lynch nodded. He followed her into the room but Balfour was no longer there.

9

Lynch held his gun aloft as Rose secured the area where they'd left Balfour. 'We need to get out of here,' said Lynch.

They moved deeper into the hangar, Rose taking the lead. 'Through here,' she said, her labored breath clear in Lynch's ear-piece. They moved downwards into the heart of the building, Lynch hoping Rose knew what she was doing.

'There's a car pool down here,' she said, as if reading his thoughts.

Lynch remembered the journey he'd made underground once Lennox and his colleagues had been relieved of their duties and wondered how deep underground they were.

Two steel doors blocked their path to the car pool area, the body of a fallen SWAT agent wedging the door open. Rose bent down and checked the pulse of her colleague, mouthing the word, 'no,' into her mouthpiece.

Lynch stepped over the body of the agent, careful not to touch the corpse out of an ingrained form of respect. He noticed as he jumped clear that the agent's semi-automatic rifle was still tight against his chest suggesting he hadn't had time to defend himself. Gun raised, he watched Rose make the same journey. He wondered if she blamed him for their predicament, and for her fallen colleagues. Her life had certainly taken a turn for the worst since he'd been introduced into her life. It was impossible to tell, her headgear masking all but the subtlest signs of body language.

He followed her to the blacked-out van that had driven him into the compound. 'Shit,' said Rose, as she opened the driver's door to discover the sight of another agent slumped against the steering wheel, a gaping wound where the side of his head should have been. 'Help me move him, Lynch.'

Together they hauled the heavyset figure from his resting place. 'Sorry buddy,' said Lynch, as the corpse fell to the ground.

The keys were still in the ignition. 'Get in,' said Rose, wiping blood and other matter from the driver's chair and dashboard. 'Keep your mask on,' she added, as she started the engine, taking the words from Lynch's mouth.

The engine roared into life and Rose began the long ascent to the top of the building. Lynch kept his window wound down, his gun at the ready for any surprises.

'Fuck,' said Rose.

The way forward was blocked by another set of doors, these ones not wedged open.

Rose switched off the engine and they left the car both still wearing their headgear, their guns pointed in front of them as extensions of their bodies. Lynch wanted to take off his mask, its tight confines combined with the cloying remnants of the smoke bomb adding to his sense of claustrophobia.

'Through here,' said Rose, guiding him to a side door.

'Careful,' said Lynch, realizing as he spoke how redundant his words were. Rose had proved to be nothing but professional and it was churlish to expect any different now.

If his comment bothered her, she hid it well. She kicked open the door, ducking to the left as Lynch held his gun aloft and cleared the room.

The room was desolate, the agents on duty having most likely joined the battle beneath. At the other end of the room, a second set of doors was open and Lynch caught a glimpse of something he feared he would never see again.

Daylight.

Rose signaled for them to move to the side and they edged their way to the opening. Lynch was sure whoever was responsible had long since departed but was happy with the cautious approach. They followed the same routine as before, Rose securing the outside area as Lynch made his way out into the fresh air.

In the commotion, Lynch had lost track of time. From the light he estimated it was mid to late afternoon. They scanned the outside area, Rose taking a particular interest in the rooftops. It was five minutes before they lowered their weapons.

'I think we should keep these on until we're clear of the space,' said Rose, knocking the exterior of her mask.

'I agree. Let's get the hell out of Jacksonville, Agent Rose.'

Rose stared at him, her face unreadable behind the gas mask. 'Whatever you say, Lynch. Let's try over there.' She pointed to a lot of six identical vans, each blacked out like the one currently trapped within the hangar.

They tried each of the vans, but none held a set of keys. Rose got into the driver's seat of the last van. 'FBI training 101,' she said, bending down and opening the casing protecting the ignition.

The heat of Lynch's breath circulated around his mask as he waited for Rose to start the van. His heart drummed at a steady pace as he surveyed the small parking lot area, a jet of adrenaline rushing his system as the engine finally roared into life.

Lynch kept his window wound down as Rose maneuvered the car through a checkpoint which had been blown open. 'Where are we?' said Lynch, as Rose drove the van through a desert-like area. The land was level, the ground beneath them a coarse yellow-brown. Above them, a perfect blue sky beat down. From the position of the sun, Lynch estimated it was between two and three in the afternoon.

'I could tell you but I'd have to kill you,' said Rose, a lightness to her voice as she recounted the hackneyed joke.

Lynch made an educated guess. 'West of San Antonio?'

'A couple of hours out west,' said Rose, her masked expression not giving away any sense she was impressed by his deduction.

'I think it's safe now,' said Lynch, pulling off his gas mask. The relief was staggering. He hung his face out of the window, allowing the air to rush his face.

Rose followed suit, sighing loudly as she inhaled the fresh air. A thick red line outlined her face where the mask had dug into her skin.

'I forgot what you looked like,' said Lynch.

Rose pressed some buttons on the dashboard to no avail. 'Signal is still jammed.'

'Strange there are no response units. You would have thought word would have got out by now,' said Lynch.

'This is a highly secure area, Lynch. I'd never heard of it before. Just look at our location. With communication cut, it's not surprising no other units have arrived.'

Lynch rocked in his chair. He lowered his gun, the tension easing from his shoulders. It highlighted how intensive the last hour had been. He glanced at Rose whose focus was straight ahead on the endless road before them. As they continued in silence, Lynch remembered what Razinski had said to him.

Mallard.

Mallard was the name of a family legacy. The current heir, Wilberforce Mallard the 6th, was an enigmatic billionaire. Lynch had come across him in his investigation into the Railroad. The original Wilberforce Mallard had been one of many to invest in the Railroad system laid on American soil in the 1830's. The Mallard family fortune had been built from those beginnings. Lynch's knowledge and investigation went no further than that and he had no way of determining if Razinski had just given him a name he wanted so he would end his life. He wanted to discuss the matter with Rose, but at that present moment felt unable to trust anyone; even the agent who'd helped him escape.

'Land ahoy,' said Rose.

Lynch blinked and focused on the perimeter they were approaching. The steel chain link fence was covered in barbed wire. At its heart was a gantry post. The reinforced gate separating the compound from the wider world was blown open. Lynch lifted his gun as Rose slowed the van to a stop.

A now familiar sight greeted them as they disembarked. The bodies of three agents lined the exterior of the gantry, each with a single bullet wound to the forehead. 'Take cover,' said Lynch, fearing the sniper who'd executed the agents could still be at large.

They waited within the reinforced gantry building, each

hunched on the ground, the bodies of the agents meters away. Lynch tore his gaze from one of the men whose face was inches from his, eyes wide open, a red tinged yellow substance dripping from his mouth.

They waited in the stifling atmosphere of the shelter for five minutes. Lynch's clothes soaked with sweat, his body on edge waiting for action.

'What do you think?' said Rose.

'I think they're long gone. We're sitting ducks. If they were still out there we would have been attacked.'

Rose nodded and they both got to their feet. Rose tested the guards' walkie-talkies. 'Still no reception,' she said.

'The sooner we're out of here, the better,' said Lynch, heading towards the van. He glanced back on the desolate land they'd retreated from, the compound somewhere beyond the horizon. He was about to enter the van when a sound assaulted his ears.

A spilt second later, a rising plume of smoke became visible as the full extent of the explosion became apparent.

10

It was an hour before they reached the beginnings of civilization, Rose's phone receiving signal as they drove through a second check point leading onto the dirt track of a back road. They stared at the mobile device Rose had stuck to the dashboard as message after message filtered onto the screen.

'You going to answer that?' said Lynch, as another batch of messages pinged onto the screen.

Rose pulled the van over. With the engine still running, she took the phone from its handle and studied the information. 'They're all from head office, complaining of radio silence from the compound. They are generalized, nothing specific for me.'

The red circle had disappeared from Rose's face replaced by a sprinkling of freckles around her nose and cheeks Lynch hadn't noticed before. 'They would have latched onto my signal by now,' she said.

They sat in silence considering what that meant. 'Who can you trust?' said Lynch.

'Good question.'

'They may see you as a suspect unless they hear from you.'

'It had crossed my mind.' Rose furrowed her brow, a set of white lines cutting into the pale flesh of her forehead. 'I think they'd be more concerned by your presence.'

'That had crossed my mind too,' said Lynch.

Rose gripped the steering wheel. Lynch watched the steely determination in the Agent's eyes as she came to a decision. 'I know a safe place, two hours from here. We can regroup, make a decision. In the meantime...' Rose snapped off the back of the phone and withdrew the battery and Sim Card, and handed the remains to Lynch. 'Let's get something to eat.'

Thirty minutes later they were on the I-37 heading south of San Antonio. The landscape a never-ending roll of green-brown fields dissected by the concrete of the interstate.

'Here we go,' said Lynch, spotting a sign for a truck stop two miles in the distance. As Rose rounded a corner, she pointed to the outline of a Railroad track running parallel to the road. Lynch closed his eyes and pictured the spot. Using techniques he'd acquired over his years in the FBI, he'd created a mind map of the Railroad lines covering the wall of his office. He moved around the mind map and pinpointed their exact location. He saw the pins on the map as if he was back in his apartment. Four red pins, five greens pins. One yellow. Four girls, five boys, one adult female. He moved further into the labyrinth he'd created and located the files of each of those missing people who had disappeared along this stretch of Railroad.

'Wake up,' said Rose, jolting him from his memory.

Lynch bolted upright, his eyes wide and alert. He felt the heat of Rose's glare on him. 'Must have dropped off,' he said.

'Dispose of that, will you?' said Rose, pointing at the remains of her phone.

Lynch jumped from the van and moved around the various trucks until he found an open window. He glanced around, depositing the Sim card through the window, satisfied as the card fell into a heap of garbage on the passenger side of the truck. He deposited the battery and casing into two separate trashcans and joined Rose in the restaurant area.

The agent had taken a seat in the far corner near a second exit. She noticed him as soon as he entered the room, her head dropping an inch in acknowledgement. They ordered burgers and cups of black coffee, each devouring their meals within minutes, Lynch only now appreciating how hungry he'd been. He savored the juices of the meat, and various sauces, and drank heavily of the lukewarm coffee as if it was nectar.

'You need to come clean with me, Lynch,' said Rose, once they'd finished.

Lynch wiped a napkin across his mouth, nodding to the waitress offering him a refill. His last few years in the organization had taught him not to trust anyone, but he had no option now. Rose could never have masterminded their escape from the compound. There had been too many variables, situations when either of them could have easily lost their lives. Furthermore, he could see no logical reason why she would have helped him escape if she was part of the team responsible for the break-in and destruction of the compound in the first place.

He held Rose's gaze, taken by the sprinkling of freckles spreading across her face. 'You know everything there is to know.'

'Everything?'

'Until this morning, I was out of the game. Yes, I've been working on my own research ever since I left but from what Balfour admitted that was common knowledge.'

Rose recoiled at the mention of Balfour's name. If, as they suspected, he was part of the team sent in to execute Razinski, it was possible he was alive and had escaped when Lynch had been listening to Razinski's dying words.

'You have to report Balfour, before he tries to turn the tables on you,' said Lynch.

Rose's eyes widened but she didn't respond. 'What did Razinski say to you?'

The name Razinski had given him played in his mind but he didn't speak it. 'Much the same as before. Grotesque threats and comments about my son.'

Rose lent back in her seat, her face relaxing. 'I can only imagine what you went through when he talked like that about your son,' she said. 'I'm sorry you had to endure that.'

'Thank you.'

'How old was he when he went missing?'

Lynch sucked in a breath, his nostrils filling with the smell of days old grease and fried onions. The scene at the house filled his mind's eye, as vividly as the sight of Special Agent Rose sitting opposite him. Sally beating her fists at his chest, something missing from her eyes which would never return. The jumbled words of his colleagues as they updated him, consoled him, made soon-to-be broken promises about finding Daniel alive. 'Seven,' he said, unable to hide the croak in his voice.

'What was he like?'

Lynch smiled. The question seemed genuine, but he couldn't shake the feeling that Rose was still working, using standard techniques to get information from him. He didn't care. He rarely spoke about Daniel. It was always too painful to talk to Sally, and there was no one else in his life. 'He was a good kid. It's easy to see him through rose tinted spectacles, but he was a good kid. Polite, intelligent, he was a beautiful little boy. He was still young enough to have that sense of innocence about him. He loved baseball,' said Lynch, as an afterthought, his voice losing his composure.

Rose lent towards him and surprised him by placing her hand over his. For a second, he wanted to drag it away, the naked intimacy of the situation too much for him to deal with. Rose held it in place and smiled at him, her pale skin erupting into a cascade of freckles. 'Let's get out of here,' she said, breaking eye contact as she looked at one of the various television screens on the walls of the truck stop.

Lynch withdrew his hand, noticing his heightened pulse rate as he glanced up to the screen showing an overhead picture of a building devoured by flames, below which read the headline, 'Fire at local government building.'

They kept their heads down as they made their way through the restaurant area of the truck stop, even though the information on the television was limited to overhead views of the fire.

The sun was still high outside but the temperature had dropped. Rose drove the van to the filling station and filled the tank as Lynch purchased provisions including two six packs of beer from a local brewery. Rose joined him in the small shop area and handed him some cash. 'Better not use cards,' she said, her voice hushed. 'Get two of those burner phones as well.'

Lynch avoided eye contact with the clerk as he paid. He

wasn't sure at the present time what concerned him most - the FBI finding him, or the Railroad.

'Tell me about your research,' said Rose, as they joined the traffic on the interstate.

Lynch took in a deep breath, accepting he wouldn't be able to avoid the discussion forever. It made it easier that Balfour was absent. 'It started with a missing person's case I was involved in three years before Daniel disappeared. It started off routine. A missing teenage girl, thirteen years old. She lived in a trailer park in Brazos County. Alcoholic parents, and from what we could gather an abusive father. We were only called in as she was the fifth child to go missing in that area in a year. The trailer park was adjacent to a railroad line though I didn't give that a second thought. The line was only used for industrial transit, three to four trains passing through a night.'

'That's a lot of missing children. How specific was the area?'

'All from that trailer park. It was a sprawling place, some permanent structures spread over a number of acres, a community of ten thousand or so.'

'Still, five missing children in a year.'

Lynch closed his eyes and accessed the photos of the five children from his memory place. 'Not one word from any of them, to this day. Vanished without a trace.'

Lynch let the information settle in as Rose ploughed through the thickening traffic. She would know as well as he did what the disappearances meant.

Razinski's taunts about his son played through his mind. The suggestion that he wouldn't want to see Daniel now stung most, though it offered the briefest glimmer of hope.

The first sign he'd had that Daniel was still alive since the day he'd gone missing.

'What gave you the link to the Railroad?' said Rose, bringing the van to a stop in the stationary traffic.

'Like most of these things, pure coincidence,' said Lynch. 'There were far too many residents to interview, and too little manpower. We concentrated on the family, as you would expect, and interviewed the families of the other missing children. The way they lived their lives.'

Lynch shook his head. 'You couldn't have blamed any of those children for running away and I wish that's what had occurred. Alcohol and drugs, suspected sexual abuse in at least three of the cases, it was tragic but I couldn't imagine any of them having the wherewithal to pull off such a set of disappearances. Anyway, I was leaving the trailer of the father of an eight year old who'd disappeared. It was night, and the walk back to my car ran adjacent to the railroad line. As I was approaching the car, a man stopped me. He was the girl's grandfather and I had interviewed him earlier that week. He must have been in his eighties but he had a hardness to his eyes of a much younger man. "It was them," he said, pointing to the railroad lines. He'd been drinking so I didn't push him, simply asked for clarification. That was when he said it. "The Railroad." I didn't pay much attention until the following day when his body was found hung from a tree outside his trailer.'

'Jesus,' said Rose, a look of genuine shock on her face.

'Indeed. I was the last person to see him alive which didn't help the investigation and when I included the Railroad in my report my career was changed irrevocably. And soon my life.'

'They take you off the case for that?'

'No, but resources dried up as soon as I started my research on the Railroad. I may as well have been starting an x-files investigation. As far as everyone was concerned, the Railroad were a myth and investigating them was career suicide.'

'But you continued?'

'Covertly. I read of the few arrests over the years. The tattoo you saw on Razinski I discovered on other suspects. I studied the contradictory conspiracy theories and agreed that it all sounded like so much hokum. And then I began investigating the railroad disappearances.'

The traffic had started moving again, Rose taking her time weaving through the vehicles not wanting to draw attention to them. 'And?'

'The statistics were an anomaly. The amount of missing children in the country was staggering enough to comprehend, so I had to narrow it down state to state, county to county. Even then, the numbers were incredible. But the amount of children disappearing on or within a small radius of a railroad line was so statistically disproportionate that I had to investigate further. I made the evidence fool proof. Obviously, millions of people live near railroad tracks so, working first on my own district, I eliminated all but the most obvious cases. Incidents where children had last been seen playing on or within a small radius of a track, those children who lived within a hundred yard radius of a railroad line. Still the numbers beggared belief. I started looking closer at the Railroad myth. I stripped away the bullshit and investigated the possibility that there were a group of people abducting, for whatever reason, children close to railroad lines.'

Rose pulled off the highway onto a back road of a small town. 'And what did you find?'

'A number of dead ends, false leads, and then when I finally got close they took Daniel.' Lynch closed his eyes, and inhaled deeply through his nose.

'How were you close?'

'I found one of them,' said Lynch, eyes still closed. 'That was why I was away. I uncovered an informant who'd given me a name.' Lynch thought about Razinski's dying words, Mallard, and wondered if that was another false trail. 'I was on the way back when they took Daniel. The following day the informant was discovered with his neck slit, and the lead had disappeared. Or so I was told.'

'And still they wouldn't believe you?'

Lynch opened his eyes. 'I thought they chose not to, but after today I'm not so sure.'

They drove for another thirty minutes in silence. Lynch felt as if Rose wanted to ask him something, and eventually she did. 'Did Razinski say anything to you?'

He wanted to tell her but wasn't ready. 'He asked me to kill him,' he said.

'That's all?'

'That's all.'

Lynch felt guilty for not revealing the truth but he had to analyze the information Razinski had given him. He needed to go over his research on Mallard and consider where that left him.

Rose didn't push him further and he decided to change the subject. 'So two first names?' he asked. 'Ever cause confusion?'

'Sure does. Half the people in my field office think my first name is Rose.'

'What do you prefer?'

'Well, I can't stand the name Sandra.'

'Sandy?'

'Grease put paid to that. My high school staged a version and I didn't hear the end of it for some time. People tend not to call me that now.'

Lynch held his hands up. 'Understood.'

Rose smiled. Ten minutes later she pulled off the interstate, a secondary road leading to a dirt track surrounded on both sides by overgrown trees and bushes. She parked up and retrieved a key from under a rock. The safe house was little more than a trailer, reminiscent of those Lynch encountered during his initial investigation into the Railroad.

'It's not much, but it will do for tonight,' said Rose, opening the door of the building.

The place was minimalist, clean and tidy. Lynch had set up a similar place during his time in the Bureau, a spot where he wouldn't be reached, where he could prepare for an unexpected departure. He didn't enquire, but was sure Rose would have a bug out bag somewhere in the vicinity with false identification and enough cash to help her survive undetected for a number of weeks.

'I'll charge these,' she said, opening the phones they'd purchased from the gas stop.

'Who are you going to call?'

'Yet to be decided. There's a shower through there, towels in the cupboard. I'll see if I can find you a change of clothes.'

'Thanks. I'm not sure I'd fit into anything you'd have though.'

Rose grinned. 'I'm prepared for most eventualities.'

The bathroom was little more than a box room, big enough for a shower, toilet, sink and a small cupboard where

Lynch found some towels. He sat on the toilet, exhaustion hitting overcoming him. He must have been awake for over twenty-four hours but felt too twitchy to sleep. He stripped and ran the shower. It took a while to heat up but soon a haze of steam blurred his vision. The hot jets soothed his aching joints. He tried to plan his next move but struggled to focus. He imagined his apartment was, or soon would be, under surveillance and as he had no transport of his own he had no way of getting back anytime soon.

He was about to leave the shower when there was a knock on the bathroom door. 'You ok in there?' said Rose.

'Yeah, fine,' said Lynch.

A small period of silence followed, punctuated by the sound of Lynch's heart hammering in his chest, and then the door creaked open. Rose walked in, dressed only in a towel. She looked unsure of herself. 'I thought you might like some company,' she said.

Lynch hesitated. After everything they'd been through, he could think of nothing he wanted more at that moment but still he remained silent.

'Don't keep a girl waiting,' said Rose.

'No, sorry,' said Lynch, flailing like a nervous schoolboy as he opened the shower door.

Rose stared at him, the steam flushing her face. Hesitantly, she removed her towel and moved towards him.

11

Lynch jerked awake for at least the third time that night. Next to him, Special Agent Sandra Rose slept with a peacefulness he envied. Although there had been other women since Sally, Lynch couldn't remember staying the night with any one of them. They had been regrettable one-night stands, driven by the occasional animal need or dose of uncontrollable loneliness. He would usually sneak out during the middle of the night, a miscreant leaving the scene of the crime. But no such option was open to him now, and he had no desire to leave. He simply wanted to sleep and it was the one thing evading him.

Every time he shut his eyes his mind played tricks on him. He was back at the compound interviewing Razinski; he was on a flight returning home after being informed of Daniel's disappearance; he was pushing his fingers into Razinski's wounds demanding an answer; he was on his hands and knees trawling for clues on the railroad line where Daniel had disappeared; he was in the shower, a raven-haired woman dropping her towel and moving hesitantly towards him.

At some point he must have dropped off. He awoke with a judder, the room still dark, drool falling from his lips onto the rough stubble of his chin. Inaction was crippling him. He had a point of reference and needed to utilize it. He crept from his bed and changed into the set of clothes Rose had provided him. He located his rucksack and, checking Daniel's sweater was still within, filled it with his dirty clothes and some of the provisions from last night, including all the beer and one of the burner phones. Cursing himself, he took some cash from Rose's bag and the van keys.

He tried to ignore the guilt as he sneaked from the trailer. Rose would have a contingency plan. A second vehicle would be nearby, and she would have to call in at some point that day whatever her reservations about the Bureau at that moment. He adjusted the seat of the van, checking everything was ready before starting the engine. He feared Rose would appear and try to stop him, but he managed to start the engine without any trouble and minutes later was on the highway heading for a location close to his home.

It was early morning, the sky still dark and the roads empty. Although still guilty at abandoning Rose, Lynch was buoyed by possibility. The lead from Razinski was the closest he'd come to the Railroad since his investigation began. It would be difficult to get near Mallard. The man was a recluse and his wealth would make it difficult to get near to him, but he had something to work with now. He needed to access his files, and the Internet, to find out more. The assault at the compound was proof enough to him of the organization's existence and that, coupled with the revenge tactics used, proved that Razinski had been an integral member of the organization. The explosion at the secret FBI compound also brought into play other significant issues, none more so than the Bureau's complicity in the success of the Railroad. For now, it was an issue for Special Agent Rose and her colleagues. Lynch took no satisfaction in being proven right. His only goal was infiltrating the organization, finding his son, and destroying the Railroad from within.

He couldn't go home. He pictured Special Agent Lennox and his accomplices waiting outside his apartment. He'd registered the steeliness in the agent's eyes and knew he would be less inclined to go soft with him following recent events.

Fortunately, Lynch had his own safe house albeit a less salubrious one than Rose's. Three hours later he pulled off the interstate into Mable, a small area outside Houston. He came here once every six months to check the location. Considering how easily the FBI had located his apartment, it was possible they would also know this location. He made three circuits of the small town, analyzing the vehicles and the few pedestrian walking the streets, searching for anything out of the ordinary.

As satisfied as he could be, he drove the van to a parking lot on the outskirts of town. He slowed his pace as he approached the lot's entrance, checking the interior of a parked sedan, before punching an eight-digit code into the control panel by the lot's gates. The gates clicked open, and he eased the van through the opening his eyes alive to potential danger. Parking outside a white brick building, he made a cautious approach to the entrance punching in a second eight-digit code to gain access.

Lynch's safe house was a storage container on the first floor of the building. A lone security guard would have seen him gain entrance and was probably watching him walking down the corridor to his lock up. Lynch walked around the corner where the cameras stopped rolling. He'd chosen the place for this very reason. Although he would never be able to stay there for longer than twenty-fours, it was important to have the option of being undisturbed. He punched in a final eight-digit code and the door to his container opened revealing a box room, eight by eight feet, empty apart from a cast iron safe built into the reinforced wall and a bed settee Lynch had purchased should he need to rest.

From the safe, Lynch retrieved everything: two handguns with matching holsters, and a box of ammunition. A manila envelope with a set of false identification, two credit cards, a burner phone and enough cash to sustain him for a few months. He pulled out a rucksack and changed into a new set of clothes, including a new pair of running shoes. He placed the holsters over a white t-shirt and placed the loaded guns inside before pulling on a jacket. Taking a deep breath, he stepped out into the corridor and secured the room.

He took the back route away from the storage container, completing a full lap of the first floor before reaching the exit. Before opening the door, he peered through the darkened glass of the building into the parking lot in time to see two men taking more than a passing interest in his van.

The glass was one way so he was able to view them unde-tected. They were poorly dressed in loose jeans and hockey tops. The taller of the two was heavyset, his paunch drooping over the waistband of his faded denim. His companion was barely five-foot, the shape of a firearm bulging from his waist-band. Unless they were playing the part to perfection, they had to be amateurs. Still, Lynch didn't want to take any chances.

He opened the door of the building and made his way past the men. Careful not to make eye contact, he noticed their quizzical looks in his peripheral vision. As he moved past the larger man he made his move, thrusting his elbow into the man's midriff and following the impact with two sharp jabs to his throat. The smaller man stood frozen as his companion dropped to the ground his hands clamped to his mouth in a silent scream. By the time the smaller man decided to act, Lynch had his gun pointed at him.

Lynch could see the man was thinking about reaching for his gun. 'If you have any idea who I am then you know you would be dead before you even made contact with that toy weapon,' he said.

If there was any fight in the man, it all but disappeared. Lynch stepped forward and kicked the fallen man in the groin. 'This is what's going to happen. On the count of three you are you going to retrieve the gun from your pants. You are going to turn it so the handle is facing me and then very gently you are going to place it on the ground. If at any point, even if by accident, the muzzle is pointing anywhere vaguely in my direction you will be dead. Do you understand?'

The man nodded, his eyes not leaving Lynch's.

'No, not good enough. You need to speak to me. Do you understand my instructions?'

'Yes,' said the man. His voice was calm enough, suggesting to Lynch that he was less likely to engage in heroics. He kicked the fallen man for a second time, lest he decide to get involved, and counted to three.

The smaller man reached into his pants, never the best place to keep a weapon in Lynch's opinion, and withdrew the gun. Lynch was poised in perfect balance as the man did as requested. 'Kick the gun over and get on your knees,' said Lynch.

Lynch had chosen the lock up area for its privacy. It was off-grid but he needed to get the two men out of sight as quick as possible. 'Put your hands behind your back,' he said, unclipping the ammo from the man's gun. 'And lie on your front.'

The man did as instructed and Lynch repeated the order to his fallen comrade. Satisfied both men wouldn't move, he opened the back of the van and recovered two sets of flexi cuffs never once taking the aim of his gun away from the potential assailants.

He cuffed the smaller man first, concluding he was the leader of the pair and most likely to flee. The man struggled but it was easy enough. The larger man barely moved as Lynch repeated the maneuver. He was still out of breath and in considerable pain. Lynch hauled both men to their feet and instructed them to get into the back of the van. As they tottered on the edge he pushed them forward, both men landing on the metallic flooring of the van with a satisfying thud. Lynch jumped in after them, shutting the van doors behind him.

'Jesus, man,' said the smaller of the two, as Lynch rammed his elbow into his back and pulled up his shirt. 'What do you want from us?'

Lynch ignored him, searching for clues on the man's skin. Not finding any tattoos, he repeated the move on the man's silent friend. The pair were clearly civilians, and for a second Lynch wondered if he'd made a mistake. 'Who sent you?'

'No one sent us, man,' said the small one.

Lynch located a pressure point on the man's shoulder and kept his grip firm as the man began to scream. 'You have no idea what you've walked into,' said Lynch. 'I will give you one more chance to answer the question. You will not get another opportunity. Do you understand?'

The man murmured and Lynch found the pressure point again. 'Do you understand?' he repeated, once the man's screams subsided.

'Yes,' said the man, through erratic breaths.

'Who sent you?'

'It was some guy in a bar, man. He offered us a thousand bucks to put the scares on you. Five hundred up front, five hundred afterwards.'

'Some guy?' said Lynch, turning the smaller guy onto his back so he could see him face to face.

The man tried not to look at him. He'd stepped out of his league and wanted to return back to a more comfortable place. 'Yeah, some guy. Big guy, biker look. He had the cash on him, told us you would be here.'

'He knew that for sure?'

'Seemed to.'

'Did he tell you what I was driving?'

'He wasn't sure. Said it might be a black van. That's why we were checking it out.'

Lynch breathed through his nose, the smell from the men having filled the interior of the van. 'What were you supposed to do when you found me?'

The man closed his eyes, and shook his head.

'Tell me,' said Lynch, hovering over the man close enough to scare, far enough back not to risk being head-butted.

'We were supposed to give you a beat down,' said the man, his voice laced with defeat.

'How's that working out for you?'

Lynch got the name of the bar from the man before jumping into the front of the van.

'Where you taking us?'

'You don't want to know,' said Lynch, laying his gun on the passenger side.

He drove for thirty minutes to a secluded woodland area he'd used in the past for shooting practice. The big man had yet to speak up, but the smaller man protested his innocence every few minutes. Lynch concluded that whoever had sent the two jokers in the back had known about the lock up but not that Lynch would be there. He imagined a similar greeting was waiting for him at his apartment. If it was the Railroad, why had they gone to the trouble of sending two civilians? With what Lynch knew of them, they had the resources to have sent a couple of hardened professionals. Maybe even a sniper to end Lynch's interest once and for all.

If the last couple of days had taught him anything, it was that he wasn't as off grid as he'd imagined. He would have to revise his security procedures if he ever got the chance. The thought made him think about Sally, and he promised himself he would contact her as soon as he'd seen off the two men in the back.

'Out,' he said, having driven the van down a back lane into the woodland.

As he pulled the larger man out of the van, he noticed he was crying. 'You're kidding me,' he said, pulling the smaller man out to join his partner.

'Come on, man,' said the smaller man. 'We didn't mean no harm.'

'No harm? I thought you were going to give me a "beat-down",' said Lynch, mimicking the man's voice. 'Through there,' he said, pushing the men into the trees.

They walked for twenty minutes, Lynch guiding them in a spiraling direction so they would be unsure of their whereabouts. He stopped at a clearing where he'd nailed a target for his firing practice to a birch tree. 'On your knees,' he said lowering his voice.

The big guy collapsed to the ground bubbling away like a child as the smaller guy sunk to his knees with a weary resignation. Lynch pulled some thin rope from his jacket and tied the men's wrists before removing the handcuffs. 'Don't want these being used in evidence,' he said. With the men on their knees, propped up against the tree, he lent down on the smaller man's calves digging his knee into the relaxed flesh. 'I like your boots,' he said, tearing at the laces with a hunting knife. He repeated the process on the man's partner who cried at every turn, until he had two sets of boots.

'I'm going to give you a last piece of advice,' said Lynch. 'You have wandered into something you can not imagine. Whoever told you to scare me knew something like this would happen. He played with your lives, and that is the sort of thing he does. I would not return to that bar ever again. I would leave this area as soon as you are able. Though you're going to have to do so on bare feet. And if I ever come face to face again, I will be the last thing you ever see.'

He pushed both men against the tree, and smiled as they tumbled into the overgrowth.

BACK IN THE VAN, he called Sally from the burner phone as he searched the interstate. Someone was playing a game with him as Razinski had suggested, and he feared his ex-wife was in danger.

'Hello,' came a gruff voice from the other end of the line.

Lynch took a deep breath. 'Rob, it's Samuel Lynch. May I speak to Sally?'

'Oh, Samuel, hi, of course. I'll just get her.' Rob had been seeing Sally for the last couple of years. Lynch had only met him on one occasion and was ashamed to admit he'd played the hard man act. He'd obviously intimidated Rob and regretted his behavior, even though he'd never admit as such to Sally.

If anything, his relationship with his ex-wife had strengthened since she'd started dating Rob. Initially, Lynch had thought it was because they had something else to fight over but now he realized it suited them both that she had someone else in her life. Rob had helped her cope with the loss of Daniel, and although Lynch wasn't prepared to accept his son was gone for ever he was pleased that Sally had managed to come to terms with the loss.

'Twice in a week, I'm honored,' said Sally.

Lynch held the cell phone to his ear. It was good to hear her voice. For an absurd moment, he wanted to tell his ex-wife about his night with Sandra Rose. He had no idea where the notion came from and he dismissed it with the same immediacy as it appeared. 'You won't feel honored when you hear what I have to say.'

Sally didn't respond. He sensed her gripping the phone, thought he heard a sharp intake of breath. 'I'm not sure I want to hear this,' she said, finally.

'No, but you're going to have to trust me.'

Sally's voice raised an octave. 'No, Sam, I do not want to hear that from you.'

'Sally, you know I wouldn't contact you if it wasn't important.'

'What have you done, Samuel?' Her voice had changed

from a high-pitched protestation, to a deeper tone of accusation. Lynch understood. She would forever blame him for Daniel's disappearance, however much she denied it.

'I need you and Rob to go away with immediate effect. Take a vacation, anything, but stay away from family and friends and get out of the house.'

'What the hell are you talking about, Sam?'

'You need to trust me,' he said, realizing too late that the repetition of trust was a mistake.

'Trust you? Trust you, Sam? Now, why the hell would I do that?' In the background, Lynch heard Rob questioning her.

'You're in danger. I'm sorry but that's how it is. If you stay where you are, you risk your own life and Rob's.' Lynch didn't want to be so hard on her but it was the only way he knew to make her see sense.

'Is this to do with Daniel?' said Sally, a new sound to her voice. Lynch couldn't tell if it was contempt or pity.

'In a way. Listen, Sally, this is serious. Two men came for me yesterday. They found me, do you understand?' Even Sally didn't know where he lived. 'If they found me, they will find you. Pack now, and get the hell out of there. Don't take your cell phones. Take down this number and call me on it when you've purchased some burners.'

Sally was incredulous. 'Some fucking burners? We're not in an episode of the Wire. I've got work today for heaven's sake.'

'Please, Sally.'

Lynch heard a muffled conversation between Sally and Rob and hoped her new man would help her see sense. 'You win, Sam. You always fucking win. We're leaving now. I want this over though or I'm going to the police.'

It was an idle threat as Lynch knew deep down that part

of her did trust him in these matters. 'Whatever you do, Sally, do not mention this to anyone. Especially the police. That is how they will find you.'

'Fine.'

Lynch sighed. 'Thank you, Sally,' he said. 'Sorry,' he added, hanging up before she could respond.

12

Rose heard Lynch depart. She'd kept her eyes shut, in the end deciding she had no right to stop him leaving.

The seduction had been her choice. He'd been a reluctant participant at first, which she'd found charming, and there had been a tenderness to him she hadn't expected. Afterwards, they lay together in a companionable silence until they'd both drifted off to sleep despite the incidents of the previous day. She should have made him stay, should probably have held him under arrest but she'd chosen to let him go hoping that at some point he would trust her and let her in on whatever he had planned.

She ran the shower and filled the coffee machine as she waited for the heat to reach the streams of water. Exhaustion crept over her. It had been the first real sleep, save for a couple of stolen minutes, she'd managed since the Gregor Razinski incident, and she felt the full force of that exertion in every inch of her body. She took the coffee into the shower and washed the previous night off her skin.

Time was precious and she regretted taking the luxury of

sleeping for so long. She needed to make contact with her superiors but first needed to work out who could be trusted. The incidents at the compound were still fresh in her mind, yet the scene she'd left at the Gunn house was most prominent in her memory. It wasn't the gore so much - she'd encountered her fair share of dead bodies in her years at the Bureau - as the layout of the bodies; the coldness of the way Razinski made the children watch their father die before killing them. During training one of her tutors, a serial killer profiler, had stated he'd rarely encountered true evil in his years of investigating. His suggestion was purely clinical and he'd been at pains to point out that he wasn't defending the actions of the killers. The vast majority of serial killers were past victims of extreme abuse in their childhood years. It was no excuse but went some way to explaining their behavior. However, Rose felt sure she'd encountered something different at the Gunn house and her further interactions with Razinski only confirmed her suspicions that she'd come face to face with pure evil.

The attack at the compound had been militaristic in its precision. The dead agents were the FBI's elite and whoever was responsible had breezed through them without trouble. She agreed with Lynch that there had to be an insider, and the fact that Balfour had escaped pointed to him as a chief suspect.

THE QUESTION now was did they know that she'd escaped with Lynch? It was possible Balfour was at large spreading lies about what went down at the compound. And then there was the conundrum of the Railroad. Lynch made a compelling argument for the existence of the group, and despite what she'd read about his obsessiveness following his son's disappearance it was something she could no longer dismiss.

She changed and ate as much as she could force down for breakfast, not knowing when she would next eat. She packed up her EVAC bag and was about to lock up when she heard a noise from outside.

Rose fell to the floor, reaching for her gun. They'd been very careful on the journey here and she would be staggered if anyone had followed her. She played through the idea of tracking devices on the van and concluded that was the most logical explanation.

She lay on the floor, feeling the controlled rhythm of her heart reverberating against the wooden boards when there was a knock at the door. Rose held the gun in front of her, remembering to take shallow breaths. It was possible Lynch had returned but she needed to hear a voice before responding to anything.

A second knock on the door, five long beats followed by two short taps, a familiar weight behind the sound. 'Sandra, you in there?'

Rose held her breath, a wave of relief coming over her. Aside from family members, only one person ever called her by her first name. The voice came from her partner, Special Agent Dylan Stillman. Dylan had been on annual leave during her time at the Gunn house. She checked the date on her watch. He'd been due back today.

'Sandra, open up it's me.'

Rose kept low. Dylan was the only person who knew about her safe house. He was the closest she came to fully trusting someone in the Bureau but that didn't mean he'd come alone. But alone or not, she had to answer the door. She lifted herself up to her knees and glanced through a gap in the binds but all she could see was the drooping branches of an acacia tree.

'You alone?' said Rose.

'Sandra, thank God. Jesus Christ, what have you got yourself into?' It was a relief hearing Dylan's baritone, the hint of humor in nearly everything he said.

'Are you alone?' she repeated, creeping to the door.

'I'm alone, Agent Rose, but there is a team stationed about five miles away. I'm afraid your safe house has served its purpose.'

'Bastard,' she said, opening the door.

Special Agent Dylan Stillman looked momentarily alarmed as he noticed the gun in Rose's hand. He was about the same height as Lynch but bulkier. His most prominent feature was his chin. It was elongated, wide and granite-hard. 'I'm afraid I didn't bring you anything,' he said.

Rose smiled. 'I guess you better come in.'

'You've done the place up,' said Stillman, moving through the interior of the trailer, a huge grin on his face.

'Shut up, Dylan,' said Rose, unable to hide her smile. She was surprised at the visceral feeling she felt at seeing him again and wondered if the few days had taken a heavier toll than she'd imagined.

'Coffee?'

Stillman took a look at the coffee machine and grimaced. 'I'm fine. Care to tell me what the hell is going on before I call it in?'

Rose sat and ran her hands through her hair. She always wore it tied back at work and she searched for a band before telling Stillman what had happened. She explained everything: from the multiple murders at the Gunn house, through to the siege at the compound, and Balfour's disappearance, omitting only the fact that Lynch had stayed the night with her. She explained that they'd gone separate ways after escaping the compound.

Stillman whistled. 'Jeeesus, I sure pick the wrong time to go on vacation.'

Rose stood, and began packing. 'I'm going to need you to hide this,' she said, handing Stillman her EVAC pack.

'The weapons all accounted for?'

'Yep.'

'Okay, I'm going to call this in now.'

Rose placed her hand on Stillman's forearm. 'What's the general feeling, Dylan?'

'No one thinks you've gone rogue, if that's what you're thinking.'

'Balfour? Lynch?'

Stillman nodded. 'Balfour is not accounted for. The sensible money is that Lynch is behind this.'

Rose sighed, regretting letting Lynch go and lying to her partner. 'I'll tell you now that I don't think he had anything to do with this. He was with me the whole time at the compound and helped me escape. There was no way he could have led anyone to that place.'

Stillman shrugged. 'Let's get going.'

Rose turned everything off, and locked up. As she stepped off the concrete porch towards the van, two vehicles roared up the dirt track towards her. She turned to Stillman whose face softened. 'Sorry, Sandra,' he said as a team of SWAT officers left their vans. 'We had to make sure you were safe.'

13

Diesel and exhaust fumes mingled with the smell of wild flowers. Sandra Rose stood rooted, staring at Stillman with accusation.

'It's just procedure, Sandra. What was I supposed to do? You were seen on CCTV at a garage off the I-37. They would find have found this place sooner or later. Tell them what you told me and you'll be fine.'

Rose shook her head. 'Fuck you, Dylan.'

Stillman ran his hand across his over-large jawline, up his face, and through his hair. 'Jesus,' he said, moving away as two suited men walked towards her.

'Special Agent Sandra Rose, come with us please,' said the first of the men, a short stocky figure with a prominent patch of hairless scalp on the back of his head. The man was wearing shades and looked like the archetypal FBI agent portrayed in film and television.

'You are?' said Rose, not moving from her spot.

'Special Agent McBride, and my colleague Special Agent O'Callaghan.'

'The Irish contingent,' said Rose.

'We haven't heard that one before. Now, if you don't mind.'

'Where am I going?'

McBride sighed. 'Headquarters in San Antonio. Now, please get in.'

Rose positioned her hands in the air as he went to grab her. 'I wouldn't,' she warned, walking towards the car. She positioned herself in the back seat and was surprised when McBride and O'Callaghan sat in the front.

She caught a glimpse of Dylan as they moved down the dirt track. He lifted his hands in the air in mock surrender, his face lined with guilt. He wouldn't have been able to see her response through the darkened windows of the car and she was pleased he would be carrying the guilt around with him. Not that she could blame him. He'd claimed he'd been making sure she was safe, and though she doubted that was the full reason he'd guided the Bureau to her safe house she imagined his heart was in the right place.

She played memory games as they made the journey in silence. She realized they hadn't patted her down and she still carried her Bureau firearm, as well as the burn phone she'd purchased with Lynch. She recounted his number in her head until it was fixed. She wondered where he was now, and what Razinski's last words had been to him.

Three hours later they pulled into the underground carpark at the FBI headquarters in San Antonio. Rose noticed a higher security presence than was usual. McBride's car was checked for explosives and she was patted down by one of the security personnel. 'Apologies, Ma'am, new protocols,' said the guard, relieving her of her firearm.

Rose nodded, wondering how effective such protocols

would be should there be another attack. Rose worked out of the Laredo field office, but had worked at headquarters in the past so was used to the winding corridors McBride and O'Callaghan led her down. She was less familiar with the secure elevator that opened into a deserted bullpen where lines of desks and chairs collected dust. McBride nodded to her and she stepped out of the elevator as the door shut on the two operatives.

Rose walked across the vacant office checking the walls and ceilings for security cameras. To her left, a door slid open and a woman's head popped through. 'Special Agent Rose through here,' said the woman, disappearing within.

Rose moved towards the door, feeling incomplete without a firearm. The woman was waiting for her behind the opening. 'Sandra Rose, I'm Assistant Agent in Charge, Janice Roberts. This is Senior Agent in Charge, Dwayne,' she said, pointing to a man sitting behind a large oak paneled desk.

Rose knew both agents and their titles.

The SAC, Miller, smiled. 'We've met before,' he said, getting to his feet. 'Under more salubrious circumstances. Special Agent Rose, please take a seat.'

Rose did as asked, Roberts closing the door of the office. She glanced around the room which aside from the gigantic desk was devoid of features. It was only the three of them.

Miller picked up a file from the desk, studying it through his steel rimmed glasses. 'You've been doing well, Rose,' he said, glancing at the document. 'Quite a little career you had going for yourself.'

'Had, sir?'

Miller broke into a smile. 'Semantics, Rose. Apologies. However.'

'However,' repeated Janice Roberts, taking a seat next to

her. 'We would be very interested to know what the hell happened at the compound. You see, we've recovered forty-one personnel from the compound. Forty-one members of this organization. Your organization, Special Agent Rose.'

'Plus the body of the one prisoner,' added Miller, smiling as he savored the role of good cop.

'Yes, and the body of Gregor Razinski,' said Roberts.

'In fact, the only bodies we didn't find were yours, thankfully, and those of Samuel Lynch and Special Agent Balfour.' The smile disappeared from Miller's face. 'Now would you like to tell me what in the goddamned hell went down, Rose?'

Rose glanced at each of her superior officers in turn, wondering if they wanted the truth or a scapegoat. The pair of them were career officers. Like Balfour, she imagined it had been a long time since either of them had experienced the day-to-day activities of a field agent. Yet, she wasn't hardened enough to doubt their concern over the tragic losses at the compound. Nor could she blame them for questioning her with such directness, despite the implied accusations. She explained everything from the Gunn house onwards, repeating the story she'd told Dylan back at the safe house. Her only omissions were the fight between Lynch and Balfour, and Lynch accompanying her to the safe house.

'Where did you get the gas masks?' asked Roberts, brushing a loose strand of grey hair from her wrinkled face.

'Two of Balfour's guards explained where they were stored.'

'What happened to them?'

'They both wore masks but were shot,' said Rose.

Miller searched through the second file on his desk, and nodded to Roberts.

'At any point did you suspect Lynch?'

Rose shook her head. 'I keep playing everything back but I can't see it. It was his idea to leave the office and to speak to Razinski. He helped me escape. If he was part of the breakout then surely it would have been easier to have eliminated me.'

'Did he have that opportunity?' asked Roberts.

'I gave him a firearm.'

Roberts' eyes widened but she didn't comment.

'He could have shot me at anytime. I had my back to him when he was speaking to Razinski,' said Rose.

Miller rubbed his chin. 'What do you know about the work Lynch was engaged in before leaving the Bureau?'

'Nothing until the last couple of days. I'd heard of the Railroad before.'

'You commented on the scar tattoos on Razinski's back?' asked the SAC.

'Yes. The tracks are an open urban legend within the Bureau. I'd never paid it much heed before.'

'And now?' said Miller.

'Someone came for Razinski. Whoever they were, they were highly effective. Lynch clammed up when I spoke to him. I know about his son of course. During our interrogation, Razinski kept stating that Lynch's son was still alive. Naturally, Lynch didn't respond too well to that suggestion.'

Miller exchanged a look with Roberts. Rose wondered if Lynch knew either of the pair, if they'd been responsible in any way for his departure from the Bureau.

'How do you think security was breached at the compound?' asked Roberts.

Rose considered how best to respond. She pictured the fallen guards at various checkpoints, the expediency and unexpectedness of the attack, and could come to only one conclusion. 'It's difficult to see beyond a leak from within.'

Roberts stared at her stony-faced. 'All communication is monitored from within that compound, Rose.'

Rose shrugged. 'I imagine if they are organized enough to stage such an attack, that communication would not be much of an issue for them.'

'Did you see anything suspicious. Anyone we should be looking closer at?'

Rose thought back to Balfour and kept silent.

Miller hesitated as if he knew what she was thinking. He surprised her by changing tact. 'Where is Samuel Lynch now?'

'I don't know,' said Rose, pleased she didn't have to lie. 'We split up.'

'Split up?' said Roberts.

Rose repeated the lie that they parted ways after exiting the compound.

'Why haven't you contacted us?' asked Roberts.

'I needed some time to think. After what had happened at the compound, my initial thought was that we must have a leak within the Bureau. I didn't want to risk communication. Thankfully, my hand was forced.'

'Lynch mention where he was going?'

Rose recalled him speaking to Razinski before they left the compound. Lynch insisted that the man hadn't divulged any information but she wasn't convinced. 'He didn't say. As I mentioned, Razinski had taunted him that his son was alive. If I was to hazard a guess, I would imagine he is following up on that. Have you located him?'

Miller shook his head. 'What happened to Balfour?'

A picture of Lynch tussling with Balfour flashed in Rose's mind. She considered the best way to answer. For all she knew, Balfour had returned and explained exactly what had happened. 'The last I saw of him was in the compound safety room.'

'Did you check on him before leaving?'

'We checked on Razinski before fleeing. We went back to the room where we'd last seen Balfour but no one was there.'

Miller was about to question her further when a figure appeared in the doorway of the office. Rose hadn't heard the man approach, and tried to hide her surprise at seeing the stocky figure of McBride filling the gap of the doorframe.

'There's been a development,' said the agent.

Roberts glanced at Miller who nodded. 'Go on, McBride,' she said.

'We've found two more bodies. We believe they belong to Gregor Razinski's Father and daughter.'

14

Adrenaline still pumped through Lynch as he pulled onto the interstate. Talking to Sally was a tricky proposition at the best of times. Their conversations always followed a pattern. They guided one another from the painful reality of their lives. If they mentioned Daniel they did so with love, with fond remembrance. Now he'd broken the unwritten rule. In the matter of a few seconds, he'd destroyed the years of rebuilding he'd gone through with his ex-wife. They were back to the start. He'd forced Sally back into a game she'd never wanted to be part of, and with that came the anguish of reliving everything which had come before.

He zigzagged through the traffic, receiving a number of horn blasts as he showed total disregard for everyone else on the road. He pushed his foot harder on the accelerator, a force within guiding him onwards. He considered how easy it would be to keep going, to press his foot as far down as it could go, to close his eyes and let the car lead him to oblivion.

The elongated sound of a trucker's horn tore him from his reverie. Lynch slowed down, cursing himself for his melan-

choly and selfishness. This wasn't about him. This was about
Daniel and Sally. He was to blame and had no right to take
the coward's way out.

He eased into the inside lane and considered his next
move. He wanted to speak to Sandra Rose but couldn't take
the risk. Her field office was compromised and Rose would be
under surveillance. He needed to follow up the lead given to
him during Razinski's dying words. He had meager research
on Mallard but at least he had something to work towards
and for the time being it would be best to do it alone.

He pulled over at a diner and ordered lunch. He was only
an hour from Hardwick where Razinski's father and daughter
had last been seen. He'd given his word to Razinski that he
would help his father and daughter but that wasn't why he
was heading to the trailer park. If he was to find Mallard, or
whoever potentially held Daniel, then this was the natural
next step. Though he would have to watch from a distance.
Rose would have returned to her field office by now and the
FBI would have begun scanning the area.

Taking a seat at the edge of the counter, he ordered a
burger and fries and drank greedily from a mug of black
coffee. He examined the diner's patrons suspicious of
everyone from the young family huddled in one corner of the
room, to the elderly gentleman four chairs down from him.
Experience told him danger could come from anywhere.

The burger was limp and bland, smothered in ripe
mayonnaise and salty relish. He drank a second coffee to
wash away the taste, the burner phone placed on the counter.
Only Sandra Rose had the number - if she'd placed it to
memory as he had hers. He stared at it a bit longer, willing
her to call, before settling his bill and returning to the van.

The burger growled in his stomach as he pulled the van

back onto the highway and set off for Hardwick. Images from the compound played through his mind as he meandered through the interstate traffic and onto the back roads. Lynch had never experienced death on such a grand scale and in remembrance the scenes had a dream-like quality. In part, this was because he'd experienced them through the fog of a gas mask. Trapped with the sound of his own breathing, he'd moved through the smoke-filled arena like a character in a first-person shoot-out game. He'd stepped over the corpses of his former colleagues with a worrying dispassion. He'd convinced himself this was due to his professionalism, the need to survive, as well as reaction to the sheer absurdity of what had happened but this resolution faded each time he remembered.

A jeep, polished red with oversized wheels, overtook him, blaring its horn. It was only then Lynch noticed how slow he was travelling. He was close now. Hardwick was a ten-acre site on the outskirts of Waco. The small town had a population of circa ten thousand according to the battered signpost welcoming Lynch to its city limits.

Hardwick was a non-descript American small town. Lynch pulled over into an Esso garage to check his map, in time to see a cascade of black vehicles each with tinted windows, roll by the main road.

Lynch shut his eyes and took in deep breaths. He hadn't seen the personnel within but the convoy was clearly FBI and it would be too much of a coincidence if they were headed anywhere but Hardwick. Why now? They would already have a presence there from yesterday. Something must have happened?

He purchased some water from the gas station pondering his next move. They'd want to question him, minimum, so turning up at the scene uninvited wasn't the smartest move. He didn't want to waste time being interrogated. His sole focus now was on finding Daniel and he couldn't let anything get in his way. Back at the car, he drank from the cold bottle as he studied the map. He needed to access the scene without being noticed and his finger trailed the most promising location.

Twenty minutes later he stood on high ground gazing down at the unfolding scene below. Two canvas tents had been erected on the harsh asphalt ground. Yards from the tents ran two sets of train tracks. From his vantage point, the rusted metal of the tracks suggested they were disused. Weeds poked through the stone covering between each sleeper, some reaching over a meter high. Lynch scanned the area searching for a sign of an active train, his eyes following the tracks until they disappeared to the south behind a set of hills and to the east towards the horizon.

The tents suggested that bodies had been discovered and with such a large FBI presence, Lynch presumed this meant the Railroad had reached Razinski's father and daughter.

Had it all been a ploy? Razinski had led him to this place but Lynch felt he was being played. Why had they gone to the trouble of taking Razinski's father and his daughter, only to dispose of them a day later? Lynch watched the ERTU agents work the scene. In a matter of days, the Railroad had gone from obscure legend to staging the mass slaughter at the compound; and now this. If nothing else, it was a statement. Razinski had been seen as a threat and had been eliminated in the most extreme way. Who now would dare to cross them?

Lynch retrieved a pair of military-grade binoculars from his rucksack and zoomed in on the railroad lines. The significance couldn't have been any clearer. Turning back to the agents, he spotted a lone figure standing motionless in the hive of activity surrounding her. She was staring out at his location. He zoomed in closer onto the figure, until he was able to see the smudged outline of the freckles decorating her pale face.

Sandra Rose gazed back at him as if they were only meters apart, as if she knew she was being watched. She blinked, her nostrils opening as she took a breath. Lynch reached for the burner phone in his pocket as Rose drew the back of her hand across her cheek and turned away.

15

Rose agreed to work on the case with one caveat, that her partner Dylan Stillman wasn't allowed any part in the process. Following his deception at her safe house, she wasn't sure she would be able to work with him again. For now, she'd been assigned the role of task force coordinator working alongside Special Agent McBride.

McBride, resplendent in sunglasses, stood next to her, silent as they gazed upon the corpse of John Razinski, Gregor's father. Rose had read his file on the way over, all single page of it. Razinski senior had existed beyond the parameters of real life. He'd never paid a cent of tax in his seventy-two years on earth, had no medical insurance or voting record. The only official record they had for him was as the owner of a fixed trailer on the outskirts of Hardwick.

Not that his body had been discovered there. Unlike the rest of Razinski's family who had been slaughtered where they lay the previous night, Razinski senior and his eight-year-old granddaughter had been taken from their residence to the railroad line which split the backwater town in two. All evidence suggested that it was by the tracks that the pair of them were executed. Two bullets for each. One to the heart, one to the brain.

Rose stared at Razinski senior dispassionately, her mind pondering the cliché of the apple rarely falling from the tree. She'd already convicted Razinski senior, imagining an upbringing of abuse for his monstrous son. Hopefully the granddaughter had escaped the worst of it for her brief time on earth.

Both bodies had been left in plain sight next to disused railroad tracks.

'It's obviously a signal. They wanted the bodies discovered,' said McBride, breaking the silence. The agent had a lilt of an accent to his speaking voice that Rose couldn't yet place. 'They're reminding us of their power.'

'Hardly needed following what happened at the compound.'

Rose turned away from the bodies. 'Maybe it's not us they're signaling to.'

'It sure as shit isn't the Razinskis. They've wiped out the whole clan in one fell swoop. Three generations.'

They were at an impasse. Over forty dead agents, and now the Razinski family, with no indicator of who was responsible save for a vague link to an organization that possibly didn't exist. Rose's hand reached for the burner phone in her pocket, her memory returning to last night with Lynch. She recalled his hesitancy with a secret smile and wondered again why she'd let him leave. 'We need to start looking at the Gunn family. It all started with them. I also need the Rota at the compound for the last six months including all prisoners and interrogations. Could you access that information, McBride?'

'You'll have it within the hour.' McBride stared at her through the protection of his shades before leaving her where she stood.

Rose left Razinski senior to the ERTU and walked towards the tracks. Despite their reason for being there, an air of calm hung over the place. The tracks ran through a narrow valley. She bent down and ran her fingers across the cold hard metal, imaging the trains that had passed through this very spot over the years supported by the lumps of metal under her flesh, the twin ribbons of steel which stretched for thousands of miles across the country.

Rose understood the lure of the railroad. Like the open road, it was romanticized. At one time, the railroad would have been the main source of income and employment for the small town of Hardwick. It would have supported hundreds of similar communities nationwide and there was something melancholy about viewing this empty and defunct stretch of line still trailing the countryside, a living memorial to the glory of the past.

She pushed herself up, feeling a slight pull in her calf muscles and thought again about Lynch. She wanted to call him but couldn't use a burner phone in view of everyone. She stopped and gazed out at the surrounding hillside, wondering if whoever was responsible was watching them, savoring their handiwork, before returning to the extended trailer van they were using as a mobile incident room.

McBride had already compiled a file for her. 'These are the logs for the compound for the last six months,' he said. 'Some of it is blanked out for clearance issues but we can always go to Miller if we need to.'

Rose nodded. 'Do you have anything else for me?'

'We've been looking into CCTV coverage for this area. Nothing within a two-mile radius of this spot and nothing in the homes of the rest of the Razinski family. The best Intel we've uncovered so far has come from a neighbor of Lyndsey McIntosh, a distant cousin of Razinski, who spotted two dark vans on the night of the attack. We're tracing plates of similar vehicles who have entered the town in the forty-eight hours preceding the attack up until present. However,' McBride flicked his laptop around and pointed to the screen showing a map of the area punctuated by a number of yellow pin marks. 'As you can see it's possible to enter and exit both the town and the area where Razinski senior and his grand-daughter lived without detection. This whole place needs a security kick.'

Rose sighed. Security cameras were unlikely to be of great concern to the town's chiefs. She'd seen too many places like this over the years, a forgotten America riddled with unemployment and poverty. 'Let's keep going. Coordinate with the team investigating the Gunn murders and report to me tomorrow morning. I've got a little light reading to do,' she said, waving the file he'd given her and leaving the van.

SHE'D DECIDED to use a hotel for the night as it was a three-hour drive home and she would have to be back at the site in the morning. It was dusk by the time she reached the lobby. The significance of the case and her role within it was starting to become apparent. To lead such a case was an honor and potentially career changing though not neces-sarily in a positive way. Rose collected the key from the receptionist, a beaming woman smothered in make-up, and made her way to the room.

The isolation of another non-descript hotel room was nothing new. After showering she lay on her bed in her robe, taking comfort from the familiarity of the box room and the patterns and order of living on the go.

The file made for dense reading and it took some time to make sense of the various reports. All personnel were from the Bureau. The only people to have visited the compound in the last six months still unaccounted for were Balfour and Lynch. If the Railroad existed, it was conceivable they had a number of insiders within the Bureau and that one of them had either been present at the compound, or had access to the daily routine there. With Balfour missing, he had to be considered as the potential link

Her eyes blurring, Rose shut the file and called room service. Her eating had been so piecemeal since the Gunn murders it was a wonder she had any energy at all. She ordered burger and fries from the less than inspired menu, before calling her sister on her cell phone.

Abigail Rose was her only sibling. She was currently at law school at the University of Texas in Austin, following the same route Rose had taken, albeit with different aspirations. Technically she was Sandra's half sister. They had different fathers, neither of whom were on the scene.

'Sis,' said Abigail, causing Rose's face to break into a smile for the first time that day. Abigail's voice was a melodic soprano. 'I was going to call you later, actually,' she said, in her sing-along fashion.

'Oh really?'

'Really. Guess who's secured an internship with Judge Felicity Harris?'

'Your roommate? Rachel isn't it?'

'How was I so fortunate to get such a witty sister?'

'Congrats, Abi, that really is wonderful news. You deserve it.'

'I know,' said Abigail, oblivious to her lack of modesty. 'I was thinking of going to see Mom this weekend to share news, if you're free?'

Rose noticed the change in her sister's cadence, the elongation towards the end of the sentence, the deepening of her tone. 'Not this weekend, Abi. I'm on one hell of a case at the moment.'

'When aren't you?'

Rose sucked in her breath, ignoring the coldness in the rhetorical question. 'It's such great news though, Abi. There'll be no stopping you now.'

Her sister didn't respond. She pictured her gripping the phone, internally debating whether to start an argument or not. 'When was the last time you saw her, Sandra?'

Rose sighed. 'Abi, now's not the time. Let's not spoil this good news with a fight.'

'I'm not fighting, Sandra, I just wish you'd speak to me.'

Rose inhaled again, the walls of the room appearing to encroach on her space. Her mother lived in a care home in Austin, near to where Abi studied. She'd been diagnosed with dementia five years previous and it had been a few months since Sandra had last visited. Although the guilt ate away at her like a parasite, she couldn't bring herself to visit on a more regular basis. The last time she'd been there her Mother hadn't recognized her. It had happened before but on this visit there'd been a blankness to her Mother's eyes she'd never encountered before. It was like looking at a different person, as if history had been rewritten and all her childhood memories of her mother had been deleted from it.

'I'm not exaggerating about the case, Abi. It's a big one. I couldn't get away...'

'Even if you wanted to,' said Abigail, interrupting.

'I'm going now, Abigail. It really is great news about your internship. Talk soon.' She hung up before her sister had time to continue the argument.

Room service arrived and she ate on the veranda. The burger was better than anticipated, thick and well seasoned. She pictured Abigail back in her shared apartment, full of rage and resentment. She was right to want more from her and Rose was thankful her mother still had Abi to look after her. She was failing both as a daughter and a sister but the thought of seeing her mother now filled her with a dread she was unprepared to face.

After mopping the remaining ketchup from her plate with her last cold French fry, she returned to McBride's file of the compound staff. It was like reading a litany of death. So many good people, so many families ruined forever. She read the names of Balfour's guards, the ones who'd effectively saved her and Lynch's life by guiding them to the gas masks. She discovered the names of the other fallen bodies, the agents who'd surrounded Razinski's prison, the guard from the outer perimeter, the woman she'd chatted to as she waited to speak to Lynch for the first time. All gone, extinguished from the world in less than a few minutes and she would have been one of their number had blind luck not intervened.

She read page after page, noting the names of those who'd been as fortunate as her by either having left the rotation or by being off shift.

A knock on the door jolted her as she was reading an entry with potential. She hadn't called room service again so edged her way back into the room and retrieved her firearm. Standing to the edge of the door she called out. 'Who is it?'

She relaxed on hearing the reply though her pulse was still in overdrive.

'Rose, let me in. It's Lynch.'

16

Lynch had followed Rose back to the hotel. He'd waited in the van for the last two hours giving her time to eat and unwind, parking beneath the low-hanging trees to the rear of the parking lot where he could access the coming and goings through the entrance of the hotel.

It had been thirty seconds since he'd knocked on her door. She'd answered but had yet to open up. It was possible she was calling it in and that within minutes a back up team would be present. It was a risk he'd decided to take.

'Rose, come on. I feel like an idiot out here.'

The door opened, Lynch presented with the scene of a vacant room.

'You're not going to hit me with an iron bar are you,' he said, entering, his hands in the air in mock surrender.

Rose closed the door behind him and he dropped his hands. She was wearing blue jeans, and a plain t-shirt. Her red hair was wet and fell onto her top creating a number of small damp patches. 'You alone?' she asked.

'Who would I be with?' Lynch moved towards to mini bar. 'Do you mind?' he said, taking a bottle of beer.

'Be my guest. I take it you've been following me?'

'I saw you by the railroad today. Razinski's father?'

Rose nodded.

'The daughter?'

'Eight-year-old girl. One to the chest, one to the head,' said Rose, pointing to the places on her own body.

Lynch swallowed hard. Daniel had been seven when they'd taken him. 'They don't fucking discriminate, do they?'

Rose took a bottle of beer from the mini bar and moved to the veranda. 'You left in a hurry this morning.'

Lynch didn't hear any accusation in the words. 'Apologies.'

'Not asking for apologies.'

'I thought your colleagues would be turning up and I wasn't in the mood for answering any questions.'

'Or explanations.'

'I need another one of these,' said Lynch, returning to the mini bar in the hotel room. Apart from Rose's suitcase, there was no sign that anyone occupied the room. The bed sheets were laid fresh, nothing in the room out of place. Perfect for a quick getaway. He retrieved the last two bottles of beer and returned to the veranda.

Rose took the second bottle and drank heavily. 'What aren't you telling me, Lynch?'

Lynch drank before answering. 'I think I've been very open with you.'

'What I don't understand is this increase in activity. If the Railroad exist then they've managed to avoid detection for years. Now, all of sudden, they're responsible for all these deaths. Hardly the action of a secret organization.'

Lynch had considered this and had no explanation beyond Razinski. 'They came for Razinski. He must have known something.'

'And his family?'

'I imagine initially it was a warning to him. They killed his family to keep him quiet, and took his father and daughter as security.'

'Why kill them once Razinski was dead?'

Lynch frowned, unsure if Rose was testing him somehow with her supposed naivety. 'These are not rational people. They believe they can do whatever they want. They would have killed partly out of fun, partly as a warning to other members of their organization. Would you cross them now?'

Rose's hand reached for her pale cheek. 'You speak of them as this entity. Surely Razinski was one of them before this?'

'Exactly. My research suggests they act exactly like this. A clandestine cell network as Razinski suggested at the compound. Razinski was one of them until he became weak and had to be expelled.'

'Every organization needs a leader. There has to be a hierarchy of sorts.' Rose reached for her iPad. 'One of your older reports highlighted someone called the Controller,' she said, reading from the glaring light.

Lynch laughed, thinking about Razinski's dying word: Mallard. 'I'm still not sure if someone was having a joke with me on that one. You've read Thomas the Tank Engine?'

'Daily,' said Rose, deadpan.

'That big guy. They call him the Sir Topham Hatt over here. In the UK they call him the Fat Controller.'

'Not very PC.'

'British sense of humor I guess. Anyway, that's where the name comes from.'

'But you had some leads on this Controller. He's potentially the head of the organization?'

'I was getting close, before...'

'Your son?'

Lynch nodded, taking a final swig of the warm beer. 'I was in Fort Worth meeting an informant who didn't show, who I never heard from again. The informant had given me good information prior to that. Either he'd been taking me for a ride all along, or they'd used him to get to me. And that I'm afraid, is the closest I ever got to this Controller.'

Rose gazed out towards the night sky, now decorated with specks of glowing silver. 'And your subsequent investigation?'

'Subsequent to leaving the Bureau?'

Rose nodded.

'The name appears. He's as much of a mystery as the organization itself. You question people about him and you see them change before your eyes. It's like talking to the devout about their God.'

'Some God.'

'A mythical deity who holds sway over the masses, who watches from a bastion of authority as terrible things happen? Yes, some God.'

'You're convinced he exists?'

'He exists alright, in one form another.'

Rose drank the last of her beer. 'I'm all out.'

Lynch would have liked nothing more at that moment than to call room service for another round of drinks but held his tongue.

'Did you ask Razinski about the Controller?' asked Rose.

Lynch remembered the look of fear on Razinski's face as

he'd mentioned the Controller. The way a man seconds from dying was scared of someone he would never see again. He couldn't be sure if Rose had overheard his final words. 'He may have been mentioned.'

'You don't give much away, do you, Lynch?'

'I've learnt the hard way.'

'You know you can trust me?'

'I've heard that too many times as well.'

'I heard you sneaking off that morning. I could have stopped you.'

'You could have tried,' said Lynch, trying to sound light.

'I could have called this in when you knocked on the door.'

'Have you?'

'You'll have to find out,' said Rose, absently pulling at a loose strand of hair from the front of her eyes.

Lynch stood up. 'I should get going.'

'You need to tell me what Razinski said to you, Lynch. We can help each other.'

Lynch hesitated. He wanted to share the information and felt he could trust Rose. It wasn't that stopping him. 'If the incident at the compound has told us anything it's that they have people on the inside.'

Rose stood and edged towards him. 'That's very likely but withholding information is not going to help anyone.'

'It will help me.'

'Will you take something from me before you leave?' asked Rose, holding her ground.

'Show me.'

Lynch followed her into the room where she opened up her suitcase and withdrew a small silver box.

Lynch opened the box revealing a metal covered capsule. 'What is it?'

'It's a tracking device.'

Lynch made a flinching motion. 'Delightful.'

Rose laughed. 'It activates when you twist the top. It may prove to be useful. I will be the only one who has access it to it.'

Lynch pocketed the device, undecided as to whether he would discard it as soon as he was outside.

'Okay then,' said Rose.

Lynch stood less than a foot away from her, close enough to reach. He felt like a teenager on a first date. 'I have your number,' he said.

'And I yours. Goodnight, Samuel.'

'Goodnight.'

17

Lynch held the tracking device in his hand and considered throwing it onto the street. Everything about Sandra Rose so far suggested she could be trusted. If she'd wanted him in custody he would have been there by now. She'd told him the device was not activated and he believed her. He placed it inside his wallet and drove away.

The sky had darkened but the intense heat of the day had yet to fade. He drove with his window down, savoring the cool breeze and the outdoor smells of the countryside. An excitement permeated his body. A feeling he hadn't felt for a long time. It reminded him of the times inside the Bureau before things turned bad.

Wary of being followed, he checked his mirrors on a regular basis as he made his way to his next destination. He needed to speak to a former colleague, Bryce Gibbs who resided a few hours away, north of Dallas. Lynch had called ahead and Gibbs agreed to meet that evening, even though Lynch wouldn't reach his place until after midnight.

Gibbs had originally worked with him on the Railroad

investigation but had been pulled off the case six months into the operation. Gibbs left the Bureau four months after Lynch. Lynch wanted to confirm his suspicions about Balfour and to find out any information the former agent had about Mallard.

Lynch reached the city apartment at eleven forty-five pm. Gibbs was waiting for him outside, a newly lit cigarette hanging from his mouth.

'This is some welcome,' said Lynch, shaking hands with his former colleague.

Gibbs was diminutive in height but not stature. He was almost as wide as he was tall, his chest rigid with muscle. 'I'm a bit worried about the company you're keeping at the moment, Sam,' he said.

'You've heard?'

'Whispers. Something about a compound explosion. This to do with the Railroad?' Gibbs offered him a cigarette which he declined.

'The less you know the better.'

'Amen to that. So what can I help you with?'

'It's best if you don't share this with anyone, Bryce.'

Gibbs lifted his cigarette in front of him, the smoke drifting in the night air before evaporating. 'I'm not sure if I'd want to risk it.'

'I have a possible lead on the Controller. Tentative at best.'

Gibbs nodded, not giving much away. 'Go on.'

'You remember Wilberforce Mallard?'

Gibbs smiled. 'The billionaire playboy, turned recluse? I remember his absurd name. Wasn't it Wilberforce Mallard the fifth?'

'The sixth.'

Gibbs chuckled. 'Somehow that's worse. I remember some of the work we conducted on him. It was a bit vague, as much of our work was. Heir to some rail fortune. I remember he was impossible to track, his funds spread very wide and very well protected.'

'You recall anything else?' said Lynch, fearing he was wasting his time.

'No criminal record. I do remember it being strange, the lack of information we had on him. I can only recall one image we had on our database. Which, considering the money he had was a bit unusual. There was a talk that he was a front, that he didn't really exist but that was from unverified sources. There was nothing to suggest a link to anything untoward. The reason we looked into him in the first place was his family's link to the railways in the past.'

Lynch nodded, disappointed but not surprised by the information. 'Thanks, Bryce. That tallies with what I remember.'

'If I think of anything else I'll let you know. On that number you called on?'

'Yes, thanks again.'

'No worries. Look, it's none of my business but you look a bit drained. You should get some rest.'

'You're probably right. I'll find somewhere for the night.'

Gibbs grimaced. 'I'd invite you to stay, but I have a family now, you know?'

'Of course, Bryce. Apologies, I shouldn't have called this late. Thanks again.'

Gibbs went to say something but held his tongue. Lynch imagined he wanted to say something about Daniel but couldn't find the words. 'Look after yourself, Sam.'

'You too.'

LYNCH HEADED BACK towards Hardwick wanting to be near Rose in case there were any more developments. Fifty minutes into the journey he began to take notice of the dark blue sedan in his rear view mirror. He'd noticed other vehicles during this time but the blue sedan had remained in a constant holding pattern three to five hundred yards behind him. The driver could simply be going at the same pace as Lynch but during the period Lynch had constantly changed speed and lanes as he'd been trained to do in the past. He'd passed other cars on the highway, and had been passed in return, but the blue sedan had stayed at a constant safe distance behind.

Lynch sped up, keen to see if the sedan would follow. He was four miles from the next exit – a service stop where he intended to refuel and buy provisions. It took three minutes for the sedan to appear in his rear-view mirror. Lynch was in the outside lane, the sedan in the middle.

He was being followed. He reached for his wallet and considered throwing the tracking device away though that made little sense now that he was being tailed. He slowed down into the inner lane and smiled as the sedan did the same.

They must have realized he'd discovered them by now.

LYNCH PULLED over into the gas station and filled the van. He kept his eyes on the pump, relying on his peripheral vision to discover if the sedan had followed him.

With no sign of the sedan, he locked up the van and made the short walk across the forecourt, his skin clammy with the night heat. A cold blast greeted him as he entered the shop as asinine music pumped through the shop speakers. He bought provisions for the following day including a six-pack of beer, three of which he would drink once he'd stopped for the night.

He left his goods in the shopping basket and used the restroom before paying. His movements were methodical, well measured. His ears and eyes alert to every customer who entered the shop. After relieving himself he examined the tracking device Rose gave him. He'd seen them before, though they were more advanced than the ones he'd used in his time. From what he knew of them they were indeed activated by twisting the capsule. That was not to say this particular device had not been tampered with.

He held it over the toilet bowl as a small bug, trapped in a spider's web by the windowsill, struggled to escape. In the end, he pocketed the device deciding there was a small comfort in Rose knowing his whereabouts. He made slow movements back to the shopping area, checking first the clerk who sat slumped behind the cashier desk, eyes full of apathy, and next an elderly couple, resplendent in shorts, khaki t-shirts and sun-visors, buying provisions of their own. He retrieved his shopping basket and moved towards the clerk, never once letting his attention waver as the teenager silently packed his groceries into a bag and muttered the price.

Outside, the heat hit him in a wave reminding him of disembarking from an airplane into a hot summer's day. His eyes flitted to each car in the gas station and further afield down the side streets. There was no sign of the blue sedan but he kept vigilant. He placed his grocery bag on the side seat and checked his gun. The area was well lit but he couldn't stay the night there. He wanted to make another few hours into his journey. So, checking once again in his rear-view mirror, he pulled out of the gas station and back onto the highway.

Five minutes later, the blue sedan reappeared. Lynch was impressed. Although they seemed happy to give away their position on the highway, they'd managed to track him to the gas station and back without him noticing. It made him think it was the Feds. But why would they follow him? It would have been simpler for Rose to bring him in; they could have questioned him and avoided such theatrics. That left the more worrying thought that it was the real Railroad following him this time, not the pair of amateurs who'd tried to scare him at the storage lock-up.

For the next thirty minutes, he followed the same routine: accelerating and slowing, the blue sedan never once driving past. Tension riddled his body. He had a headache and was dehydrated from the two beers he'd had at Rose's hotel. One way or another, he'd have to lose the car behind him. The next turn off was five miles away.

He slowed down to fifty and planned his move. According to his Sat-Nav the turn led to a small town. There were a number of secondary roads he could navigate through to his destination. The sedan was less than two hundred yards away now, three cars behind him. Lynch tried to relax his body. He loosened his shoulders, breathing as he took a light grip on the steering wheel. As the turn off approached he began accelerating, slow at first so as not to arouse suspicion then full on as he yanked the car off the highway without indicating and sped down into the darkness of the small town road.

Dismissing the threat of oncoming traffic, he took a hard

right at the first junction catching a glimpse of the sedan in his rear view mirror as he made the turn into the thankfully desolate road and sped up the hill. He was at over ninety by the time the road flattened out. According to the Sat-Nav, the back road had seven miles of uninterrupted driving left. The tension returned, his arms locked into position as he gripped the steering wheel, his eyes darting from side to side in search of a turn off where he could hide the car.

The Sat-Nav displayed a turn to the right a mile away. On the map, the glowing screen of his cell phone, the turn was a truncated line less than a centimeter long, possibly an entrance to some farm property. He rounded the corner, the sedan still not within his viewing area. He glanced alternately from the road to the Sat-Nav. The machine counted down the next turn in one hundred yard intervals until Lynch saw it, the possible opening he'd been searching for. He kept the speed up until he was fifty yards away. Lifting his foot off the accelerator, he eased the brakes switching his headlights to full beam. He squinted, assessing the potential of the turn off. Now yards away, he pressed heavier on the brakes and swung the car into the turning.

He was in luck. The driveway was indeed a link to some farm property and to the left was an opening, a dirt track about as wide as his vehicle. Lynch wasted no time turning into the side road. Ignoring the sound of branches scratching the exterior of his van, he expertly steered the vehicle into the narrow area where it was safely encased by a covering of trees and shrubs.

He switched off the engine and lights and opened his door, squeezing himself through the tight gap. The door wedged against the bark of one of the acacia trees. He hadn't anticipated the complete darkness. He switched on his flashlight in time to see some form of wildlife sprinting into the undergrowth. With his gun in one hand, the flashlight in the other, he edged back down the dirt track in time to see the lights of a car approaching him at speed. He killed the light, the car streaming past, oblivious to his presence. It moved too quickly for Lynch to recognize it but he was confident it was the blue sedan.

He paused for breath noticing the tension ease from his body, his shoulders falling, his arms and legs looser as he let out a heavy breath. It wasn't over yet. Whoever was following him would soon realize they'd been duped and would turn back checking for entrances such as this. He returned to the van and retrieved a rifle and ammunition from one of the holdall bags. Locking up, he moved back to the main road and crossed over, slipping behind a hedge on the other side and cursing as his foot slipped into a small puddle of water. He loaded the rifle and pitched it towards the road and waited.

LYNCH IGNORED the dampness seeping into his shoes. He'd been in similar positions many times before and was prepared to stay here until it was light. In the last forty minutes, he'd counted thirty-two vehicles, eighteen heading west and fourteen heading east. In the darkness it was difficult to ascertain the color or make of the vehicles, but he was sure the blue sedan had yet to pass him.

Lynch was alone in the alien world of nocturnal sounds. He sensed the hive of activity behind him, scurrying creatures, and insects chirping into the night sky. He took a strange comfort in the fact that he was an intruder in their midst, enjoying their companionship as he waited.

It was another twenty minutes before he saw them. They drove past him first of all, slower than the other vehicles. Ten minutes later they returned on the other side of the road and stopped by the turning.

They parked fifty meters away from Lynch's vantage point, close enough for him to fire off a shot if necessary. They sat for some time with the engine running, two people in the front, the passenger with a lit cigarette in his mouth. It was as if they knew he was in the hedge and were waiting for him to make his presence known. Lynch kept low, the rifle hidden behind the bushes but still pointed in the direction of the car.

Five minutes later, the passenger left the car. Lynch fixed his arms into position, the rifle locked and ready to go. The driver opened his door and joined his companion at the back of the car. They exchanged words, neither of them withdrawing a firearm, and made their way across to the small side road where Lynch's van was parked.

Lynch eased himself out of the ditch and scrambled across a thin covering of grassland on his hands and knees, his eyes fixed on the shadowy figures across the road. A truck made its way up the hill and Lynch flattened himself as the two men froze. As the lorry drove passed, Lynch used the opportunity. Springing onto his feet he dashed across the road. He jumped onto the small landing of soft grass and rolled behind an acacia branch.

It was tough going in the darkness. He used the light of his phone to guide him, concerned the flashlight displayed too much illumination. He'd always had a good sense of direction in these circumstances and moved from covering to covering until he was close to the side entrance where his followers had moved. They were heading down the dirt track towards the van.

If he'd known for sure that they were the Railroad he'd have had no hesitation in taking them out. The figures were visible enough for him to make a clean hit without it resulting in a fatality but he couldn't take such a risk yet. It was possible the two men were Agents and that Sandra Rose had lied to him.

He peeled away from his hiding spot and tiptoed along the path until he was yards from the men. Lynch tensed before making his move, sprinting towards the men with as little noise as possible, knowing hesitation could be fatal. He lifted his rifle as he ran and crashed it down onto the skull of the shadowy figure to his left.

The butt of the rifle made a satisfactory impact, the man's legs giving way in an instant as he crumbled to a heap on the ground. The second man was quick to react but not as quick as Lynch. As he moved to reach something from his inside jacket, Lynch leapt forwards and aimed a short, sharp jab into the man's throat. His collapse to the ground was less dramatic than his colleague's but was significant enough for Lynch to take control. As the man bent to his knees, unable to breathe, Lynch brought the butt of his rifle up again and smashed it, with less force this time, into the back of the second man's head.

The man let out dry gasps as he fell face-forward into the ground. He was still conscious as Lynch jumped onto his back, his right knee pinning the man down as he cuffed him. Confident he was secure, Lynch turned his attention to his unconscious colleague. Cuffing him first, he rolled him onto his side pleased to hear the shallow breathing coming from the man's chest. He secured a number of firearms from both men before standing back as the second man found voice.

'They told me you're a hard man, Lynch,' said the man.

Lynch didn't respond. In situations like this it was often most prudent to listen.

'You know who we are,' continued the man. 'Why haven't you finished us off?"

Lynch wasn't sure if it was an act but the man sounded genuinely perplexed by the situation. Lynch sensed something else in the man's voice. He was clearly afraid but Lynch wasn't sure he was afraid of him. Lynch hauled both men up into the back of the van, securing their legs and hands with flex cuffs before shutting the back doors. The largest of the pair was still unconscious and Lynch put him in the recovery position. His pulse was strong but there was a thick abrasion to the back of his head.

'Who sent you?' said Lynch, to the second man who sat slumped over in the back of the van his hand behind his back.

The man's face contorted into a grin, his eyes remaining cold.

'I warn you now, boy,' he said, his voice a thick Texan drawl, 'that you'll be getting no information from me.'

'Well see about that,' said Lynch, withdrawing his gun.

The man smiled again and broke into a strangled laugh.

'That's the best you've got? Just do it, boy, I'd welcome the oblivion.'

Lynch didn't want to waste time. It was getting light and they risked being discovered. He needed information and there was only one language the man understood. Lynch shuffled across the back of the van, his gun in his left hand.

He winced at the smell coming from the man's fallen comrade.

'What's your name?' said Lynch.

The man snarled before clicking his throat and spitting in Lynch's face. Lynch wiped the spit away and aimed his right elbow onto the side of the man's head. The impact was significant. Spittle drooling from the man's mouth as his head lolled onto his chest. Lynch grabbed his hair and pulled his head backwards. The man blinked, his eyes dotted with bloodlines, a thick bruise already spreading from his eye.

'That wasn't nice,' said Lynch.

The man shook his head a number of times, more spittle flying from his mouth. Lynch stood back and was about to continue the interrogation when he noticed something on the man's forearm.

Lynch retrieved his hunting knife as the man shifted in his confinement. He didn't fight his binds but for the first time since encountering him Lynch sensed fear. Lynch moved back. He checked the sleeping man before getting closer to his friend. Sweat poured off the prisoner's forehead, soaking his now closed eye before snaking down onto his chest. 'Do you think that bothers me?' he said, as Lynch moved the knife nearer.

'You wouldn't be pushing back if it didn't,' said Lynch, pressing the knife into the fabric of the man's shirt, ripping it downwards until his chest was revealed. Lynch repeated the maneuver on both sleeves of the shirt until the garment fell away completely. Lynch waited, and the prisoner slowly lifted the lid of his good eye. When he saw what Lynch had done, he breathed out a sigh of relief.

'Now you know,' said the man.

Lynch nodded. He'd seen the fake marks before but these were real. They matched Razinski's.

On the man's chest were five identical tattoos: railroad lines, each with ten sleeper tracks crudely carved into the victim's skin. Each tattoo was raised, like Razinski's they more scar tissue than tattoos. On the man's left arm were four more tracks, each longer than the ones on his chest.

'What are those for?' said Lynch.

The man looked down, something akin to pride coming over him.

'Those are the real deal,' he said, 'from the Big Man himself.'

'The Big Man?'

The man shook his head in regret.

'You mean the Controller?' said Lynch.

'Listen, aren't I supposed to have a lawyer?'

It was Lynch's turn to laugh.

'I think we've passed that point. Why were you following me?'

The man shook his head.

Lynch was no expert in this form of interrogation. In his time with the FBI he'd occasionally crossed lines when he'd felt it necessary, usually with a modicum of regret. The same rules didn't apply now. He wanted to find his son and nothing would stop him. He pushed the knife towards the man's neck, his tendons standing to attention as if somehow he could protect himself from the weapon.

'You're going to tell me everything I need to know.'

The man leant forward pushing the taut flesh of his neck into the blade. Through gritted teeth he said, 'I'm not telling you shit,' as a line of blood trickled down his skin.

Lynch didn't want to lose face but if the prisoner pushed

forward anymore it was possible he could do some lasting damage. He withdrew the knife and crashed his elbow onto the same spot on the man's left eye.

The man's head snapped viciously to the right, a spurge of blood filtering across the back of the van as someone knocked on the door.

18

Lynch didn't hesitate. He reached for the still conscious man and punched him square in the mouth to stop him speaking.

The back of the van was mirrored glass, darkened so the interior couldn't be viewed from outside. He withdrew a gag and tied it firmly across the man's mouth before withdrawing his firearm. He was in a compromised position but at that moment had no other course of action. It didn't matter who was on the other side of the door. One way or another it would cause problems. He cursed himself for his lack of professionalism. He'd thought the location was secure but, in retrospect, he should have driven away, should have kept moving; should have checked if he was being followed.

'Who is it?' he shouted, pretending to have just woken from sleep.

'Sorry to bother you,' came the voice. 'It looks like you've got yourself into some trouble. I thought I might be of assistance.'

'No, you're fine,' said Lynch, 'just resting up for the evening. Thanks for your concern.'

Lynch waited, hoping the do-gooder had taken the hint. Seconds later there was a second knock on the door. Lynch cursed and retreated to the front seats of the van.

'I said go away,' he shouted, mustering as much authority into his voice as possible.

The do-gooder didn't respond. It was then that Lynch understood. The person outside of the van was no simple passer-by. He crouched into the footwall on the passenger side seat. He tried to glimpse at the rear-view mirror but it was still dark outside and he could see little more than shapes and shadows. He sucked in a deep breath. Exhaling, he opened the door as quietly as he could and slid out onto the ground.

'I wouldn't move if I were you, Mr Lynch,' said the man holding a gun, mere meters away. 'These babies don't tend to miss in such close confines.'

Lynch was face down in the mud. He couldn't see the assailant but he recognized the voice.

'Balfour.'

'Whoa, buddy,' said Balfour, 'you got me. I still need you to release your gun and then we can talk.'

Thoughts rushed Lynch as he lay in the mud considering his next course of action.

'Throw the gun over here, Lynch, and you can get on your feet and we can have a little chat.'

Lynch threw the firearm over and pushed himself up onto his knees before standing. Balfour moved towards him, picking up the gun.

'Samuel Lynch,' said Balfour, shaking his head. 'Well, I'll be. Still trying to do my job for me, I see.'

Lynch was relieved Balfour had dropped his gun. 'Have you been following me?' he asked.

Balfour leant forward and helped him to his feet.

'Indirectly, yes. I've been tailing the two men you have in the back of your van at present. I presume they're secure?'

Balfour was acting like the compound had never happened, that he was the only agent unaccounted for.

Lynch nodded, playing along.

'And would you like to tell me what the hell is going on?'

'Me?' said Lynch. 'The last time I saw you, you were unconscious at the compound. How's the nose by the way.'

Balfour nodded, his hand involuntarily reaching for his face. 'I remember. At least, I remember being knocked unconscious and left to die.'

'That's not exactly what happened, Balfour.'

'Not exactly?' Balfour gave him his practiced smile, the side of his face swollen from where he'd been knocked out at the compound.

'We came back for you.'

'So Agent Rose claims.'

'You've spoken to Rose?' Was that why he was here now? Had Rose given him details of the tracking device?

'I haven't spoken to anybody. I've been tracking those two men in the back of the van. I managed to follow them from the compound and now I find you here.'

'Come on, Balfour, I'm supposed to believe that? Why didn't you call it in? How did you know what Rose said?'

'I have access to the Bureau's database. Unfortunately, I can't trust anyone there. Anyway, I can't discuss that with you anymore. You've technically committed a felony.'

'Technically bullshit,' said Lynch. 'Those two were following me and I've just turned the tables. You know what they are.'

'I know what they are and I know what they're capable of,' said Balfour, 'but that still doesn't give you the right to take the law into your own hands. And I'm not just talking about here.'

Lynch had lost all patience. Balfour had always been sanctimonious from the very day he'd stepped into Lynch's office all those years ago, and Lynch was sure he was loving this moment of power. Not that Lynch bought a single word he was saying.

'You wouldn't even be here if it wasn't for me. It was my investigation into the Railroad. This is effectively my case you're working on.'

Balfour laughed. 'That's history, Lynch. Christ, it's ancient history. Things have moved on a great deal since then. And you, as I'm sure you recall, are no longer an FBI agent. That's why I'm going to have to bring you in.'

Lynch folded his arms. 'This must be some sort of wet dream for you, Balfour. Are you going to cuff me as well?'

Balfour still had two hands on the shotgun. 'Now, let me think. Shall I cuff the man who was last seen at an FBI compound where a high security prisoner was murdered along with forty plus colleagues of mine? Would you consider yourself a flight risk, Lynch?'

Balfour's hand moved slowly to his belt where he withdrew a pair of handcuffs.

'You know the drill,' he said, throwing them towards Lynch.

Lynch considered his moves. He had a second gun in a holster behind his back. But Balfour was trained for such maneuvers and he was sure the man wouldn't hesitate to take him down. He had all the justification necessary. Reluctantly, Lynch cuffed his left hand and placed it behind his back before falling to his knees. Balfour moved towards him, ramming his foot into the small of Lynch's back.

.'Sorry about this, Lynch,' said Balfour, dragging Lynch's right arm back and cuffing his wrists together. 'Let's get you back to base and we can clear this up. If it's any consolation you can ride up in the front with me.'

BALFOUR PLACED him in the passenger seat before checking on the two men in the back. The unconscious man was still out on the floor of the van. Lynch watched the proceedings as best as he could through the rear-view mirror. The second prisoner moved his head towards Balfour as he released the gag in his mouth, narrowly missing contact with the agent's head.

'Now, now, sir,' said Balfour. 'It seems you've got yourself into a bit of a situation.'

'Fuck you,' came the simple reply.

'I see you checked out the tattoos on the man,' said Balfour, returning to the driver's seat. 'You think they're genuine?'

'I know they're genuine,' said Lynch.

Balfour reversed the van back down the lane. Outside the sun was rising, the light blue sky tempered with pale red and orange.

'This shouldn't take long,' said Balfour. 'We'll get you back. Get your side of the story then we can begin interrogating these two.'

Lynch didn't buy the friend act. Balfour had hated him for the brief time they'd been colleagues and he imagined his feelings for him hadn't changed in the interim period. Railroad member or not, Balfour was the complete Machiavellian character. He'd known it from the first time he'd met him. He'd played the friendship card then but Lynch had seen it for what it was. After Lynch left the Bureau, he watched from afar with a growing disdain as Balfour rose through the ranks. Nothing had pointed to him being a member of the Railroad, but every fiber of Lynch's being was convinced he was lying now.

'Where are you taking us?' asked Lynch, forty minutes into the journey.

'I told you, a secure office. I don't want to say too much in front of those two.'

If Balfour was on the level, it was likely this was the end of the road for him. Unless Rose could sway things in his favor, he was likely to do time for holding the men in the van whatever their backgrounds and motives for following him.

'How did you manage to trap them?' said Balfour, under his breath.

He sounded impressed but Lynch wasn't so easily flattered.

'Have you actually tried to stop them, or do you just let them do what they want?' he replied, noticing the impatience in Balfour' face.

'Who are we speaking about here?' said Balfour, playing dumb.

'The same people who slaughtered all your colleagues at the compound.'

Balfour feigned distaste. 'You're talking about the Railway? I'll come clean with you, Lynch. As you guessed at the compound, we did continue your work but at present that organization is not officially recognized. You can't stop something that doesn't exist, Lynch.'

'You've seen for yourself that they exist, Balfour.'

Balfour's reply was inaudible.

'How is the rest of your investigation going?' asked Lynch. He wanted Balfour to continue talking, to catch him in a lie or to divert his attention.

'You're a civilian now, Lynch, and it shows. I'm not going to share any information with you so drop it.'

'It was my investigation all along.'

'Was, Lynch. And that was a long time ago.'

Balfour was acting distracted, his answers short and impatient.

'At least the Bureau acknowledges them now,' he said, analyzing Balfour's facial movements as he contemplated the statement.

'Acknowledges them?' Balfour replied, a slight twitch in his left eye.

'The Railroad.'

Balfour shook his head, emitting a mirthless laugh. 'Why do we always label these things? These pointless names. The Railroad? Jesus, it sounds like some children's television show.'

The anger in the small cabin of the van was palpable. 'It sounds like you're defending them,' said Lynch, Balfour's face reddening.

'I'm not defending them. I'm suggesting we treat the situation with some respect.'

'Treat them with respect?' asked Lynch. He was playing a dangerous game with Balfour but given his current situation he had nothing left to lose.

'Maybe we should, Lynch. You ever notice the similarities? The behavioral traits? Let's call them the Railroad, for simplicity sake. What did your research uncover? A secret organization with a structured hierarchy. Sound familiar?'

'What the hell are you talking about, Balfour? You're missing out the part where they abducted hundreds of people a year, the majority of which were children.'

'Fuck, what do you think we do?'

'You think the FBI disappears children from Railroad lines?'

'Don't be a dick, Lynch. The FBI, the CIA, whatever fucking agency. We kill innocent people all the time. I've killed people as an agent, so have you.'

'Yes, people on the wrong side of the law.'

'Our laws, yes. Let's say for argument sake that the Railroad have a different set of laws, their own moral rules.'

Lynch sighed. Balfour was revealing his true self but that only made matters worse. 'For one, you're confusing morality and legality. Jesus, Balfour, when did they get to you?'

Balfour smiled, his eyes blank. 'You don't get it do you, Lynch?' He turned his face to Lynch, his eyes small and dark. 'They never got to me. I've always been one of them.'

Lynch closed his eyes before looking away from Balfour's dark gaze. He'd suspected as much but it still came as a crushing surprise to hear the words from Balfour's mouth. He focused on the road. It was light now, and he could see the faces of the drivers in the oncoming lane flashing before him, oblivious to his situation. Balfour had locked the door so he wouldn't be able to jump out of the moving vehicle even if he could somehow maneuver his tied hands into position.

How deep did the infiltration go? If Balfour could evade detection then it was conceivable the whole Bureau was affected. 'You were the leak then? You were responsible for those deaths at the compound?'

Balfour had relaxed. The unburdening of his position had clearly buoyed his spirits. 'We couldn't risk Razinski talking. He was a good soldier, but still. He had to make the sacrifice.'

'And his family?'

'Precautions.'

A wave of nausea came over Lynch. He thought about the three beers in the back of the van, wishing he had access to them. 'Precautions? Can you hear yourself, Balfour? Those people were mutilated.'

Lynch understood he would probably do better speaking to himself but Balfour's reply still shocked him.

'No one is denying a certain amount of pleasure was taken. Our members have certain...tastes.' Balfour elongated the word 'tastes' relishing Lynch's discomfort.

'What the hell *are* you people?'

'It's a good question, Lynch. More apt than you can imagine.' Balfour took a sharp turn to the right down a hidden entrance. Breathing hard with the exertion, he mouthed, 'remember, Lynch, we're not so different to you. We may even be the same.'

19

After parking, Balfour dragged Lynch from the van. They were outside an abandoned building, possibly an old factory, in a secluded area surrounded by a copse of trees. Balfour led him into the metallic structure. The heat inside was cloying, tempered with the smells of slaughtered animals and excrement. Balfour pushed him through a set of doors into a second room, Lynch trying his best not to struggle at what he saw.

Lynch had seen torture rooms before. Some had a sickening clinical feel, all neat lines and pristine surfaces like an operating theatre. Others were like this.

Although his pulse must have been in the high nineties, Lynch didn't struggle. Balfour had a weapon and he was cuffed; he would have to wait for an opportunity.

'Sit,' said Balfour, pointing to one of six metallic chairs screwed into the linoleum-covered floor.

As Lynch crouched down onto the seat, Balfour tied his cuffed hands to the back of the chair.

'Never hurts to take precautions,' said Balfour, echoing

his earlier words. 'Here,' he said, spraying a jet of water into Lynch's face.

Lynch hid his desperation as precious drops of water dripped into his mouth.

'I hope you don't mind waiting, Samuel. Back shortly.'

Balfour skipped out of the building, leaving Lynch in the stifling heat. Sunlight pierced the gaps in the metal walls, Lynch turning his eyes away from the row of rusted tools nailed onto one of the walls.

Despite everything he'd known of the man before, Balfour coming out as one of the Railroad was a shock. It would have taken an extraordinary amount of planning and patience to hide such an allegiance from the Bureau, and as far as Lynch could recall Balfour had been an FBI agent for close to fifteen years following a period in the US marines.

There had been no official handover. Following Daniel's disappearance, Lynch's role at the FBI was gradually side lined; his superiors reaching the conclusion that he was obsessed with the Railroad. One day it was his project, the next his files were handed to Balfour and his access rescinded. Balfour never once spoke to him about the matter and now he fully understood why.

'You've met Mr Ojeda here before,' said Balfour, leading the second of the two attackers into the room. The man was still handcuffed, a gag stuffed into his mouth preventing him speaking. Balfour led him to the chair next to Lynch and cuffed him in identical fashion. Not once did the man struggle.

Lynch tried his best to hide his confusion as Balfour wiped a loose strand of hair away from the man, a manic smile carved into his face. 'Mr Ojeda has been a bit of a bad boy. You didn't follow instructions properly did you, Marcus?'

said Balfour, in a child-like voice. He stood in front of Ojeda shaking his head, the smile fading, and slapped the man across the side of his face with the back of his hand.

'What the hell is going on, Balfour?' said Lynch.

The manic smile returned. 'A number of lessons, Samuel. Be a good boy and stay patient. All will be revealed.'

Balfour left the room, returning five minutes later with the second assailant. The larger man had returned from his enforced slumber. He staggered across the room, his arms cuffed behind him, Balfour guiding him like a blind man. Still smiling, he cuffed the man to the chair on Lynch's left.

'Your Good Thief, Lynch. Care to forgive him?' said Balfour, clearly pleased with his religious analogy.

'Enough of the games, Balfour. Tell me what's going on.'

Balfour crouched down opposite him. 'It's like this, Samuel. Mr Morgan here has also been a bad boy. Haven't you, Brendon?'

The big man struggled against his binds before giving in and slumping back into his chair.

'What are they supposed to have done?'

'Why the concern, Samuel? I thought you'd like these two brought to justice?'

Although he cared little about the fates of the two men who'd followed him, Lynch had no appetite to see the men killed in front of him. 'There's no justice to this, Balfour, as you well know.'

'I don't know what he sees in you, Lynch, I truly don't.'

'Stop talking in fucking riddles, Balfour.'

'I've said too much. Let me put it this way. We see justice in slightly different terms, Samuel. Take Mr Ojeda, here. He has a penchant for, how can I say this delicately, young flesh. Don't you, Marcus? Not to my tastes, but we don't discriminate. If anything we facilitate, but with such privilege comes great responsibility. Doesn't it, Marcus?' said Balfour, repeating his question with a snarl.

'Mr Ojeda and Mr Morgan here had one simple job. They were to follow you undetected. Seemingly, they messed this simple task up resulting in this unholy mess.'

'Why were they sent to follow me, Balfour? Who is the person who sees something in me?'

'All part of the plan, Samuel. Though this,' Balfour threw his hands out towards the wall decorated with tools. 'Well, this is a little extra. A little early education. For you at least. For Mr Ojeda and Mr Morgan, the lesson has taken too long to learn.'

Lynch struggled against his cuffs, much to Balfour's amusement. 'You're going to kill them for a simple mistake.'

Balfour snorted. 'Oh, I'm going to do a bit more than that.'

LYNCH TRIED his best to tune out what was happening. He closed his eyes and thought of happier times. He accessed the precious memories of Daniel he'd worked so hard to store. He pictured Daniel in the back yard throwing a ball around, times on the beach, Daniel playing with Sally in the sea. He concentrated on the sights and sounds, even recollecting the smell of the fresh cut grass, the salt of the water, while next to him Mr Ojeda and Mr Morgan thrashed in their seats as Balfour made one cut after another on their bodies.

'You see, Samuel, my tastes are a little more sophisticated than Mr Ojeda's,' said Balfour, his words floating towards him invading his memories.

'I won't even tell you what Mr Morgan is into. Takes all

sorts, I guess. Acceptance, Samuel, that's what it's about. Even you could be accepted. You and I have similar tastes, after all.'

The last statement ripped Lynch from his reverie. He blinked his eyes open, dismayed by the redness on Balfour's torso. He turned first to Ojeda then Morgan, lowering his eyes when he realized they were both still alive. 'Nothing about you and me is similar, Balfour.'

Balfour took an elongated knife from the wall and held it to Ojeda's arm. The man was shaking, his eyes closed. 'What if I told you Mr Ojeda and Mr Morgan were responsible for little Daniel's disappearance?' said Balfour, moving the knife swiftly up the back of Ojeda's arm removing a layer of skin like a potato peeler. 'What then, Samuel? What if I told you they had taken him, what they had done to him? Would you be so forgiving then?'

Pain rushed through Lynch's chest. He tried to hold onto the positive memories of his son, the vacations, the simple days of lounging around reading books, playing bizarre games with toys scattered across the floor, but all he could think of now was the period following Daniel's disappearance. As Balfour suggested, he had little compassion for Daniel's abductors and if the two unfortunate souls either side of him were to blame then he had imagined punishments far worse.

What did it matter now? Even if it was them it wouldn't bring Daniel back, wouldn't eradicate the years lived without him, the torture he'd suffered along with Sally of not knowing. And it was apparent he would be the next act in Balfour's sick little game. He didn't want to surrender but couldn't see a way out save for some last minute rescue from parties unknown. The kind of rescue that only occurred on television.

'Did they take him?' he asked, mustering all his remaining strength.

Balfour stopped working. Lynch tried not to look at the skinless forearm of Ojeda, as his former colleague waved his knife in the air as he contemplated the question. 'These two?' he said, incredulous. 'No, these are not our prime operatives. If they were, they wouldn't be sitting next to you now.'

'I saw the tattoos, they're part of your organization.'

Balfour shook his head. 'All this time and you still know so little. Fuck it,' he said, and with ferocious effort jabbed his knife into Ojeda's throat. 'He'd had enough,' he continued, as Ojeda made his last few desperate movements of life.

Balfour took off his blood-soaked shirt and turned his back on Lynch. 'This is what you should have been looking for,' he said, revealing a back decorated in blue and green tinged scars. Hundreds of tracks lined Balfour' back. It was like looking at a distorted railroad map, something a child would draw. Balfour swiveled back to him, his eyes closed as he savored the scene he'd created.

'What's the difference?' said Lynch.

'The difference lies in who made the incisions.'

'The Controller,' said Lynch, thinking back to what Balfour had said – *I don't know what he sees in you.*

'I've said too much, now if you don't mind I need to return to my work.' Balfour darted towards him, stopping at the last second before digging his knife into Morgan's forearm.

Lynch fought back the nausea as Balfour treated Morgan to a repeat performance. He closed his eyes once more and searched for the positive memories. His mind wanted to dwell on what Balfour had told him. It questioned how Balfour had survived in the FBI with such marks on him. How had no one ever seen them? How had he survived medicals without it showing on his file? It suggested a level of collusion that was truly terrifying. The thought taunted Lynch, made him feel his whole life had been a waste. Fear and anger surged through him as he thrashed in his chair, summoning every last amount of strength as he pulled at the cuffs, the hard metal slicing his skin and sending shockwaves of pain through his body as he continued pushing, trying for the impossible.

'It's over now,' came a voice.

Lynch struggled for a few more seconds before stopping and opening his eyes.

Balfour stood over him. In his peripheral vision, Lynch saw the subhuman form of Morgan who seemed to be completely without skin. 'It's over,' repeated Balfour, his voice somehow soothing.

Lynch stared straight ahead as Balfour walked over to a bag and bent down to retrieve something from within. Lynch studied the crisscross scars on the man's back, now coated with a film of red, as if there was still time to glean something important from the patterns.

Lynch took in a deep breath, trying to ignore the smell of blood, vomit, piss and excrement filling the room. He began to shake, hated himself for doing so, as Balfour edged towards him, a syringe in his hand.

'It will all be over soon,' said Balfour, cooing like a mother placating a child as he stuck the needle into Lynch's neck.

The needle was painless. Lynch closed his eyes and pictured Daniel as a baby, lying on his back, tiny arms and legs dancing in the air.

The last thing he felt was the warmth of his tears as they ran down his face into his open mouth.

20

Rose slept fitfully, having regretted allowing Lynch to leave the second he'd shut the door. There'd been an awkward moment when she'd thought he was about to kiss her. In the end their farewell was tentative and despite her regret she concluded it had been for the best.

The situation was far from perfect and if Miller or Roberts found out she was still in contact with Lynch it could mean her job. But there was no way to bring Lynch in without force and she would rather have him on her side at the moment.

It was five am and she'd been awake for an hour. She considered calling Abigail. Their last conversation had been strained and being on bad terms with her sister always put her on edge. But Abigail would need time and a call now would only serve to escalate the tension between them. Deciding to give it another day, she poured some coffee and went through her notes.

Balfour was her main focus. She glanced through the agent's records. Nothing in his reports from the time he'd joined the FBI fifteen years ago after an illustrious career in the Marines hinted at any link with an outside organization. It was unthinkable that he could have duped so many people for so long.

She ploughed through the details of every case he'd worked on at the Bureau searching for an embryo of a clue, a link with the Railroad, but if something was there it wasn't obvious. The first mention of the Railroad came six years ago when Balfour took over from Lynch. Prior to that, Balfour had headed a task force over in Dallas looking into a drug ring running over three states.

From what Rose could ascertain, the move from Dallas to San Antonio had been something of a downgrade, a sidestep at best. In Dallas, Balfour headed a huge spiraling team covering the three states whereas Lynch's investigation into the Railroad organization was little more than a one-man job. It could be considered as the first red signal. Why would Balfour move from such an important position to something so unrecognized? The obvious explanation was that he was a member of the Railroad and had infiltrated the FBI to protect his organization, but the very thought seemed absurd.

Rose searched deep into the files uncovering those responsible for Balfour's transfer. She jotted down the names; SAC Kendall and ASAC Stevenson from the Dallas branch and, closer to home, the names of Miller and Roberts.

She thought back to the grilling she'd taken from the last two names twenty-four hours ago, now concerned that the two senior officers were trying to cover their tracks. Miller had appointed Balfour and, in effect, had sacked Lynch.

None of it made sense. Lynch had received little or no support for his research into the Railroad so why bring in such a big hitter to head up the defunct investigation? Were Miller and Roberts somehow involved?

It would be a difficult angle to investigate and an almost impossible one to prove. She had to start at a lower level to find out who was in contact with Balfour and where the connections with the Railroad began.

She started reading his files from the time he'd taken over from Lynch. Balfour's investigation into the Railroad was half-hearted at best. He'd been assigned to numerous other cases during the last six years and most of his focus had been away from the Railroad as if he was just playing lip service to the investigation. She was about to put the file down when she spotted a name she recognized. Special Agent Romano Collins. The man had been assigned to Balfour's team three years ago and she recognized his name only because it was on her to-do list.

She uploaded the case notes on her laptop and saw his name; number five on the list. She clicked through to his file and read back her own notes. Romano Collins had been assigned to the FBI compound where Razinski was taken. Only he'd been off work on the day of the attack, his position taken by Agent Maurice Sanchez who'd been fatally shot during the raid. Collins was still off sick. She called McBride and told him her findings.

McBride sounded groggy at the other end of the line. 'Can't this wait till morning?' he said.

'It is morning,' said Rose. 'How soon can you get to my hotel?'

McBride groaned and Rose suppressed a laugh.

'Could you give me at least an hour?' he said. 'It would be nice to see a hint of daylight before I have to start working.'

'Forty-five minutes,' said Rose, hanging up.

She ordered breakfast and a large pot of coffee from room-service before showering and changing; she read through her notes again as she ate, rushing at her food and slurping her coffee as if the offerings would be taken away from her at any second. She could feel the oncoming indigestion sitting low in her chest.

SHE MET McBride in the parking lot. He looked worse than he'd sounded on the phone, nursing a coffee and wearing dark sunglasses despite the grey of the morning sky.

'You better have one for me,' said Rose, as McBride lowered his window.

'Here you go, Boss.' McBride's voice was gruff, close to inaudible.

Rose drank the coffee and tried not to think about how much caffeine she'd consumed in the past twenty-four hours.

'We're going to pay Collins a visit.'

'Have you tried calling him?'

'It's a surprise visit, between you and me,' she said.

McBride nodded.

'I'm not too late on that?' she asked.

'Believe it or not I've had more important things to do in the last forty-five minutes then call headquarters,' said McBride. 'As far as I'm concerned I'm working for you so I'll follow your orders. Even if that does mean waking up at five am.'

'Quit moaning, McBride. You've got the coordinates?'

'Yep.'

'Okay, I'm taking my car. Follow me.'

Despite his protestations, Rose was far from convinced about McBride's loyalty. Miller and Roberts had appointed him and chances were high that he was reporting back to them.

The city streets were relatively empty at that time of day and they made quick progress to Collins' apartment block on the eastern outskirts of San Antonio.

Rose parked on a side street and waited outside for McBride to find a spot. 'Take off those stupid things,' she said, pointing to his shades.

'It's a fashion statement,' said McBride.

'Yes, a bad one. Now take them off.'

McBride sighed and did as instructed.

Romano Collins lived on the fifth floor of a beaten down apartment building. The doors to the front of the building were secure so they couldn't access the entrance until an elderly couple dressed in identical tracksuits left five minutes later.

They took the elevator to the fifth floor, McBride unable to stand still in the moving room. 'You're not claustrophobic are you, McBride?'

McBride frowned and looked away.

Rose held her tongue and allowed the other agent to leave the elevator first.

Collins' apartment was two doors down from the elevator. Music blared from the interior despite the early hour. McBride stood to the side as Rose knocked on the door.

The music stopped but the door didn't open. 'Who is it?' came the voice from within.

'Agent Collins, this is Agent Sandra Rose and my colleague Agent McBride,' said Rose, holding her badge up to the peephole. She kept her hand steady as Collins remained silent. 'Can we come in?'

Rose counted in her head as she waited for Collins to respond. She'd reached seven when the locks turned.

Collins was in his robe. Rose immediately began looking for threats. She couldn't tell if the agent was armed. She shifted her gaze behind the man but the door was only half open so her vision was impaired.

'Apologies for the get up. I've been signed off sick for a few weeks now,' said Collins, clutching his robe. Collins did look ill. His eyes were bloodshot and drawn, his face grey and peppered with spikes of stubble. Rose inched closer and smelt alcohol. He'd either started drinking very early or carried the smell from the previous night.

'Can we come in?' asked Rose.

'What's this about?'

'The compound,' said Rose, studying Collins' face for a reaction and noticing a widening of the eyes, and a slight flare of the nostrils.

'Look, the place is a mess. Could you give me ten? I'll get changed and we can go for a coffee.'

'This won't take long, Agent Collins,' said Rose, standing firm.

'Fuck,' said Collins, turning and heading back into his apartment.

Rose kept close as Collins led them through a short corridor into a living area where he slumped down on a leather armchair. He hadn't been lying about the mess. Every inch of space was covered with fast food containers and empty bottles of alcohol. Rose made an initial estimate of forty bottles of lager and six bottles of whisky.

'When was the party?' said McBride, opening a window in the kitchenette area.

'I don't have to defend myself to you.'

'You think this is going to help?' said McBride, holding up an empty whisky bottle.

'What's it got to with you, pal?'

McBride shook his head and placed the bottle back down. 'Bit convenient, eh?'

'What's that?' said Collins.

'You being off sick when the attack happened.'

'Come on, man. Why do you think I'm drinking? I should have been there.'

'You feel bad to be alive?' said Rose.

'Christ, are you going to sit down. No, I don't feel bad to be alive. I feel bad for all the people who died there.'

Rose moved a mound of clothes off the armchair opposite Collins.

'Something like that makes you think, and not in a good way,' said Collins

'What was the issue?' said McBride, pacing the room and lifting various bottles as if he could find some answers from the hollow receptacles.

'Heart palpitations. I'm sure you've already checked that out.'

'How long?'

'I'm due for a check up next week.'

'You mention your excessive drinking to the doc?' asked Rose.

'This is not a normal thing,' said Collins, sounding indignant.

'You didn't get through all this last night though it would certainly explain the palpitations,' said Rose. 'I haven't got access to your medical records but I trust this is something you will share at your next appointment.'

'What the hell is this?' said Collins, getting to his feet.

'Sit down, Agent Collins, don't get yourself over-excited, we're just tying up loose ends.'

Collins glared over at McBride who'd stopped pacing. 'Fine,' he said, holding his hands up and falling back onto the seat. 'What do you want to know?'

Rose had studied the apartment when Collins had been distracted. She was trying to ascertain if the agent had a firearm nearby. It was possible he had one on his person beneath his robe and she didn't want to risk anything yet. It could be down to the alcohol but Collins' behavior was off. He was being defensive and she didn't buy his story.

'I have to ask you this, Agent Collins,' she began, waiting a beat before continuing. 'Did anyone ask you to take time off work sick?'

Collins didn't hesitate in his response. 'What the hell are you suggesting?'

'I'm not suggesting anything. Put yourself in my position, Agent Collins. I'm sure you'd be asking the same question. We're trying to find the people responsible for multiple murders of federal employees. This is not something that's going to disappear easily. I need to ask these questions. I need to find these answers.'

'Look, I was signed off a week before. Everything is above board. Just check with medical.'

Rose nodded at the repetition of Collins' argument. 'Have you heard of the Railroad?' said Rose, changing tact in an attempt to disorientate Collins.

Collins answered quickly. 'I'd heard of their possible existence. Found it a bit hard to believe if I'm being honest.'

'Found?' said McBride.

'Found, find. I never understood how a criminal organization could go undetected for so long to the point that we weren't even know if they even existed. That suggested to me they didn't exist.'

'But did they approach you?' said Rose.

'Oh come on,' said Collins.

'If we search this place, are we going to find anything?' said McBride.

Collins shifted on his seat. 'Such as?'

'Drugs, money?' said Rose, noticing the perspiration on Collins' forehead, the slight tremble in his hand.

'Just alcohol,' said Collins, rattled.

Rose didn't like grilling a colleague. She didn't know Collins personally but he was one of them and it grated having to push him like this. Chances were he was suffering from the events at the compound. She'd seen survivor guilt enough times during her career. Colleagues turning to drink or drugs following a major incident they'd survived where others had perished. Yet, if she didn't push Collins then she may never find those responsible.

She took in a deep breath. 'Will you take off your robe for me, Agent Collins?'

Even the unreadable McBride was shocked by the request, his forehead furrowing at Rose's request.

Collins looked to McBride for support. 'What the hell is this?' he pleaded.

'It's a simple enough request. Show us you're not one of them and we'll leave you alone to indulge whatever this is.'

'Fuck you. You think I'm one of them, those fucking monsters,' said Collins, getting to his feet.

Rose lowered her hand, ready to reach her for her firearm if necessary as Collins continued his rant. 'Here,' he said, undoing his robe and throwing it onto the armchair. 'Satisfied,' he continued, spinning on the spot, completely naked, his pale skin free from any marks save for the occasional mole and tuft of hair.

'That's enough,' said McBride. 'Put your clothes on, Agent Collins. Rose, a word.'

Rose joined McBride in the kitchenette, McBride's wide bulk taking up the majority of the space. 'What the hell was that?' he said.

'Now we know. We don't have time to mess about with delicacies.'

'Shit,' screamed McBride, reaching across her and shoving her down.

As Rose fell to the floor, her initial thought was that McBride had turned on her. But as she landed, she made out the shape of Collins in the living area. The man was still naked and held an FBI issued Glock 22 in his right hand. It dangled by his waist, perversely close to his genitalia. McBride's gun was pointed at the man.

Rose wasted no time. 'What the hell is going on, Collins?' she said.

'Drop the gun, man,' said McBride.

'I had no option,' said Collins, swinging the gun in front of him, his limp penis swaying with the motion.

'Whatever has happened we can sort this. I'm going to stand up now, Agent Collins,' said Rose, getting to her feet. 'Tell us what happened.'

'You don't understand.'

'Try me,' said Rose.

Collins closed his eyes, a high-pitched sound escaping his lips. Rose tensed, waiting for Collins to turn his gun on them.

Collins stopped wailing, his eyes darting open as if he'd been spooked by a sound. 'They said they would take Becky and Lisa.'

'That's your wife and little girl?'

'Ex-wife. They said they would take them. Do you know what that means? Because I do.'

'I understand, Collins. You had to protect your family.'

'No, no, no, no, no,' said Collins, shaking his head with rapid force. 'They showed me what "taking them," meant. They wouldn't kill them, this was something so much worse.'

'I understand. No one is going to blame you. Just drop the gun and we can talk.'

'I don't care what the fucking Bureau think. Why would I care about that? What are they going to do, put me in jail and throw away the key? Send me to death row? Big fucking whoop. I couldn't care less about that. My only concern is them.'

'The Railroad?' said Rose, trying her best to keep her tone calm.

'As soon as you leave here they'll take me. And they'll take Becky and Lisa for the sake of it. There's only one way I can stop this happening.'

'No, Collins, we can help you,' said Rose.

'Put the gun down, Collins,' said McBride.

'Sorry. You're going to have to put me down otherwise I will shoot you and I don't want to have that on me as well.'

Rose tried to change the momentum of the conversation. 'Romano, what about Balfour and Lynch? How are they involved?'

Collins spat on the floor. 'How do you think I'm in this situation?'

'Balfour? Lynch?

'Yes, fucking Balfour.'

'How long have you known?' asked Rose.

'What fucking difference does that make? He's always

been one of them. He's an original. Higher rank than Razinski.'

'An original?'

'I don't know. From birth or something. Razinski was recruited.'

'And Lynch?'

Collins smiled. 'They've got some big plans for Mr Lynch. I'd try to get to him before it's too late.'

'Fuck,' shouted McBride, as the naked figure of Collins lifted his gun and aimed it at them.

He did it slow enough that they were under no immediate threat. Protocol suggested that they aim for the chest and Rose did so. She wouldn't forgive herself if McBride died because she'd tried to keep Collins alive.

Collins took four bullets - two from each of them - to the chest and was dead before he hit the floor.

21

'What a complete mess,' said McBride. They were outside - McBride smoking, sunglasses on - waiting for the incident team to arrive.

Rose agreed. She put herself in Collins' position. Would she have done anything different if they'd threatened Abigail? Would she have helped the Railroad to protect her sister? The injustice of it was too huge for her at that moment.

'What do you think about this talk of originals? Some freaky shit right there,' said McBride.

Rose agreed. The further they looked into the Railroad organization the murkier the facts became. Collins suggested that Balfour was somehow born into the organization as if it were some kind of organized crime family, whereas Razinski had been recruited. It would explain the lengths to which they'd taken their revenge on Razinski's family once he'd been captured. The set up made them sound all the more impenetrable.

'And what he said about Lynch?' continued McBride, when she didn't answer.

Rose had been thinking about little else. She needed to warn him. She would have to call him at some point soon whatever the risk. 'We need to find him,' she said, thinking about the tracking device she'd given him.

'Listen, Rose, it's none of my business but do you know where Lynch is?'

Rose looked at McBride. It was the first time he'd broached the subject since they'd worked together. He sounded genuine but he was too close to Miller and Roberts to be trusted.

'Come on, McBride. Do you think I would hold something like that back?'

'In normal circumstances, no, but if you know where he is then now would be the time to bring him in. There are too many people involved. They won't be able to get to him.'

'You weren't at the compound. I would tell you where he is if I knew. Now can we drop it?

'Ok. So, who replaced Collins at the compound?'

'Agent Maurice Sanchez. He was found dead at the scene.'

'What do we think Collins gave them?' McBride paced the street, taking an angry drag of his cigarette before throwing it down and grinding it with the heel of his shoe.

'Collins was the head of security. He would know of any weaknesses at the compound. You couple that with Balfour then they were set.'

'Christ, imagine it coming to that. What do you think he meant by "taking them"?'

'I don't want to think about it,' said Rose, as sirens approached.

Rose was perturbed but not surprised to see Miller and

his side-kick, Roberts, exit the first car on scene. Miller stayed by the car as Roberts walked towards them, her face so full of rage it was laughable. She stopped two feet from Rose, her mouth tight-lipped, a gnarled vein snaking across the left side of her forehead bulging against her skin. 'Words fail me,' said the woman, her lips barely parting.

If only, thought Rose. 'Collins was working for the Railroad under duress,' said Rose, knowing how insufficient her words sounded.

'Death by cop,' added McBride.

'Death by fucking cop? Why was he not disarmed first?'

Rose leant towards Roberts, not willing to be pushed any further. 'With all due respect, Ma'am, he was an FBI agent on sick leave. We had no reason to ask for his firearm.'

'Surely subsequent evidence suggests otherwise,' said Roberts, with a little less authority.

'Yes, well hindsight is a wonderful thing. Maybe if Agent Balfour had not been assigned to the Railroad investigation we wouldn't be in this situation in the first place,' said Rose, noticing a slight twinge in Roberts' right eye as she took a step backwards.

'That's neither here nor there,' said Roberts. 'What were the specifics of Collins' involvement with the Railroad?'

'He claimed he was being blackmailed. They threatened to take his ex-wife and child if he didn't comply.'

In the sunlight, Roberts looked her years. The light was no friend, highlighting the deep creases in her face and the bags beneath her eyes. 'I need you two to return to head office and leave this to someone else. You will need to do an immediate debrief and then I want your focus on finding those responsible for the compound. Check Collins' bank account. I'm sure there would have been some financial inducement. There always is. And where are we on the location of Mr Lynch?'

'Still no sign,' said Rose.

'Find him,' said Roberts. She was about to head back to the car when they recounted Collins' revelation about Balfour, Roberts' face turning a shade of white. 'Get back to the office,' she said, turning away without another word.

Rose watched her return to the car and briefly exchange words with Miller. Of the two Miller seemed the most approachable, though this was possibly due to their good cop, bad cop, routine. 'Guess we better get back,' said Rose.

McBride nodded, and without a word placed his sunglasses on like some lone maverick.

'Dick,' said Rose, smiling.

THE DEBRIEF WAS ARDUOUS, Rose enduring questions she saw coming from miles away. Eventually, they were released, the OPR, the FBI's internal investigation, satisfied with their answers to Collin's death and his revelations about Balfour.

Still, Rose was surprised by the speed they were allowed back on the case. She presumed the importance of the events at the compound meant she and McBride were allowed back on the case sooner than usual.

However, McBride was less impressed. 'Whole day wasted,' he said, as they sat in the canteen rehydrating with glasses of iced water and fruit juices.

'You feel they were just going through the motions?' said Rose, recounting the robotic line of questioning.

'To tell you the truth, Rose, I'm finding it hard to trust anyone at the moment. I keep internally questioning everyone. From Miller downwards.'

Rose understood the paranoia. In many ways she was more suspicious. After Dylan's betrayal and today's events she felt unable to trust anyone, even the colleague sitting in front of her. 'So what's your story, McBride?'

'My story?'

'Why are you so damn quiet for one?'

'I'd like to think of myself as being thoughtful,' said McBride, deadpan.

'You're a thinker, hey?'

'Deep,' said McBride, the slightest of curves forming on his lips.

The atmosphere of distrust had given Rose an idea. 'You remember when we asked Collins if he would show us his chest?'

'Remember? I don't think I'll forget his swinging dong.'

Rose couldn't help but laugh, the gallows humor was a coping mechanism she was more than used to. 'How would you react if I'd asked you to take your top off?'

'You want to see me naked, Agent?'

'You wish. Seriously though, would you be bothered?'

McBride considered. 'Perhaps not, but then I'm not in cahoots with anyone.'

'So if we asked people here to prove they were not with the Railroad, you think we'd have a problem.'

McBride took a long drink of apple juice. 'You want to see everyone here naked?'

'Only as a means to aid our investigation.'

'Yeah, right.'

A STACK of boxes was waiting for them in the incident room. Agent Callahan was hanging two giant posters on the office walls. On closer inspection they were maps of railway lines. One nationwide, one for the state of Texas. Each map was decorated by hundreds of different colored pins.

'Meticulously recovered from the home of Samuel Lynch,' said Callahan. 'The files are from his place as well.'

'Thanks, Sean,' said McBride.

Callahan nodded and left the office.

Rose moved towards the maps. 'Missing people?' she said, gazing at the pins.

'Christ, he was obsessed,' said McBride.

They spent the next few hours alternating between research on Lynch and on Balfour.

Balfour was an only child and his parents had died within six months of each other when he'd been serving in the Marines. Rose contacted a couple of his former colleagues from Dallas but none of the agents were talkative over the phone. His former superior, ASAC Rostron had only positive things to say about him and all but one of his current team had been eliminated at the compound.

Rose thought further about the tattoos she'd seen on Razinski. Collins had been clean, but it didn't mean Balfour or others in the department were. She broached the subject with McBride again who looked less than impressed.

Rose checked her watch. Four pm. 'You think Miller and Roberts are in?'

'I guess so. You really sure you want to do this?'

Rose puffed out her cheeks. 'No. But you better come too.'

Rose couldn't remember seeing the building more alive. All leave had been cancelled as the investigations into the compound attack continued. So far, the attack and the secret of the compound itself had been contained from the press but opinion pieces regarding the explosion appeared daily.

Everything from a terrorist attack to an alien invasion had been suggested and it was possible Miller's hand would be forced at some point to reveal the truth.

Rose noticed a stiffening of backs, and an intensity of work, as they walked past the packed office of agents sitting at their desktops.

'They fear you,' said McBride, as if reading her thoughts.

'Fear me?'

'You're head of the investigation. You're in with Roberts and Miller. You were at the compound and survived. Fear, respect, hate. All goes hand in hand.'

'You could have missed out the hate bit,' said Rose, as they reached the exterior of Miller's office. 'Special Agent Sandra Rose to see Agent In Command, Miller,' said Rose, to Miller's PA

'You don't have an appointment,' said the PA, without looking at her diary.

'Correct,' said McBride. 'Please tell him Agent McBride is here as well.'

The PA glared at McBride as if he'd cursed in front of her. Rose watched fascinated as McBride held the woman's gaze for what felt like over a minute before she finally relented and got to her feet. She returned a minute later and told them to go through.

Miller ignored them as they entered, his attention focused on the oversized screen in front of him. He left them standing for a few minutes before taking off his glasses and glancing up at them. 'Rose, McBride. I didn't know we had a debrief booked in,' he said.

'Sorry, sir, this couldn't wait.'

Miller nodded to himself. 'You better take a seat, then. Nasty business with Agent Collins. Exemplary record.'

Not anymore, thought Rose. 'He was placed in a very difficult situation, sir. In part, that's why I wanted to speak to you.' Rose watched Miller's reaction closely. She was searching for any inkling of signaling between Miller and McBride, but the SAC kept his eyes focused on her throughout.

'What are you asking me, Rose?'

'Sir. When we were questioning Collins, we, I, asked to see his torso. I wanted to see if he had any of the Railroad tattoos we'd seen on Razinski.'

Miller frowned. 'And did he?'

'No, but he didn't like being questioned about it.'

Miller pushed his lower lip out. 'Can't blame him for that. A form of accusation I suppose.'

Rose thought back to Collins' outrage, his disrobing, and the gun dangling from his side. 'It was a question that had to be asked. The thing is, sir, I think we need to ask a few more people the same question.'

Miller linked his hands together and swayed back on his chair. 'I see. Who exactly do you want to check, Agent Rose?'

Rose glanced sideways at McBride. 'Everyone.'

22

'Everyone?' said Miller, laughing.

Rose remained stone-faced. 'It's the only way.'

Miller leant towards her, his hands now clasped together in front of him. 'You want to conduct some sort of strip search for the whole of this building? You want to ask seasoned service men and women to prove they are not part of some - and this is at least one of the major sticking points, Rose - form of as yet unacknowledged organization.'

'An organization that is responsible for the deaths of at least forty-two of our agents, sir,' said McBride, to Rose's relief.

Miller turned to McBride, his gaze venomous as if McBride had somehow betrayed him. 'You can't be serious. It would never wash. Anyway, do you think anyone under cover would be stupid enough to leave distinguishing marks on their body?'

Rose had thought about this. 'It's a ritual, sir. It's a badge of honor. My best guess is they wait until they are enshrined within the organization before taking on their marks.'

'What about medicals? We have procedures to avoid this sort of thing.'

'Not really, sir. I worked out that if I had such a tattoo on my back then the last time someone checked would have been ten years ago, and that wouldn't be in an official capacity.'

'When would you want to do it?'

'Now, sir.'

Miller tilted his head and stared at Rose, wide eyed.

'That's why I came to you now, sir. You need to order a lock down,' said Rose, regretting her choice of words.

'Need?' said Miller, his face reddening.

'Sorry, sir. I didn't mean anything...'

Miller raised his hand. 'Enough. How to you plan to run this?'

'Sir, I hope I'm not speaking out of line...'

'The time has long passed for that, Agent,' said Miller.

Rose noticed a hint of a smile from McBride next to her. 'Ok. We need to recall Special Agent Roberts. Then the four of us need to...'

'Strip naked?' said Miller, wide eyed.

'Yes. Roberts and I can deal with the women, and McBride and yourself with the men. I would suggest everything is recorded, sir.'

'Not content with humiliating your colleagues, you want them captured on video too?'

Rose started to speak but Miller raised his hand again. Rose had a sudden urge to reach over and snap the patronizing appendage at the wrist but stood her ground.

'This is a logistical nightmare,' said Miller, summoning his PA. 'Lynda, get me the head of security now.'

. . .

AN HOUR later the FBI field office in San Antonio was in lock-down. Roberts had returned and was prowling Miller's office. She'd failed to make eye contact with Rose since receiving the news about the checks.

'It starts with us, I guess,' said Miller.

Along with Roberts and Miller, McBride and Jenkins, the head of security, accompanied Rose. Miller began unbut-toning his shirt. 'Jenkins, you've permission to withdraw your firearm,' he said, sighing.

Miller was clear and McBride went next. 'My turn,' said Rose, unbuttoning her blouse.

'You're okay doing this here?' said Miller.

'Of course I am, sir,' said Rose, noticing Roberts frowning. Miller and McBride turned their backs as she undressed, Jenkins looking pained as he checked her for marks.

'You're really going to make me go through this,' said Roberts, once Rose was given the all clear.

'Just get it done, Janice,' said Miller.

Roberts undressed, her eyes focused on Rose who lowered her gaze. She was cleared and McBride withdrew his gun as they checked Jenkins.

'That was fun,' said Miller. 'Okay, McBride and I will lead the male checks. Janice, you work with Rose. Jenkins, we will need to go through the security team first as we will need your team to supervise. I want no second guesses. Everyone is guilty until proven otherwise.'

The checks went quicker than Rose had anticipated but not everyone accepted the situation with grace. Humor was in short supply and by midnight, when the last of the agents and support staff had been checked, it was extinguished.

. . .

'WHAT A GIGANTIC WASTE OF TIME,' said Roberts. It was past midnight and they were back in Miller's office.

Rose didn't consider it a waste of time but wasn't about to contradict her. They'd all but eliminated everyone in the building from being connected to the Railroad. It wasn't conclusive but it made her feel a lot easier about her work colleagues.

'What next?' said Miller.

'I want to speak to Balfour's former colleagues back in Dallas,' said Rose.

'You going to strip search them too?' asked Roberts.

Rose stared at the woman who returned her gaze, her fury evident. Roberts was used to getting her own way and she resented Rose's involvement in the case. Everything about the woman was contained. Her lips were squeezed tight together, wrinkles blossoming on her face. 'If what Collins says is true about Balfour then it's possible he has recruited other members from within.'

It was Miller's turn to get agitated. 'You think you're going to march into another FBI department and start questioning officers? You need to start getting real, Agent Rose. I can just about accept today's little adventure but you're getting ahead of yourself. Our focus now is finding Samuel Lynch and Balfour. Lynch is the catalyst in this whole thing. No one had even heard of the Railroad until his little obsession. Chances are he will know where Balfour is.'

Rose turned to McBride, outraged but unsurprised by the Miller's comments. Lynch's investigation had been a genuine one. If he'd been listened to earlier then everything could have been avoided, and the suggestion that Lynch knew Balfour's location was insulting. She was about to voice her objection when McBride made a slight shake of his head.

'That is all,' said Miller.

Rose left with McBride, heat surging through her body.

'They need a scapegoat,' said McBride, once they were in the bowels of the building where their cars were parked.

'You think they're going to blame Lynch for what happened at the compound? I was with him, McBride. This is bullshit.'

'Then we need to find him. Get some rest, Rose. We can reconvene tomorrow. Put today behind us and start again.'

Rose watched McBride drive off, wondering again if the agent could be trusted. She opened the car and retrieved the burner phone from the glove compartment. 'Right, Lynch, where the hell are you?' she said, calling the number from memory. She tried three times, but there was no answer.

23

The ringing in Lynch's ears was incessant and piercing, and was accompanied by a distant chiming noise. It felt like he was suffering the mother of all hangovers. He was back at his apartment viewing the three gigantic agents through his web cam. But how did he know one of them was called Lennox?

A scratching noise roused him. He blinked his eyes open into darkness. Something was trying to eat his hand. He reached down and swatted the vermin away. 'Fuck sake,' he said, patting himself down as the creature ran into the shadows. Somehow he was alive and unbound.

Whatever Balfour injected him with was still in his system. He felt nauseous getting to his feet, struggling with his balance in the darkness, the poison polluting his bloodstream. He stumbled towards a crack of light in the distance. He took small steps, fearing he would trip over one of the men Balfour had slaughtered and would not be able to get back up. The air was thick with the smell of cleaning products and he feared he was trapped. He upped his pace towards the light, his steps reckless, and tripped, stumbling head first into a wooden barrier.

The impact knocked him backwards and he fell to the floor clasping his head. He waited until the pain subsided. His eyes had adjusted to the darkness and he saw more cracks of light through the wooden panels. Getting to his feet again, a terrible heaviness in his limbs, he reached for the handle. Fearing this was all an elaborate joke, he turned the handle shocked by the glare of sunlight. He fell through the opening, a warm breeze caressing his skin, and vomited onto the stones of the driveway.

Darting pains shook through his head as if someone was hammering nails into his skull. He wanted to curl into a ball, let the poison finish its work one way or the other, but the sunlight was too much of a shock to his senses. He pushed himself up and realizing the van was still in the driveway made his way across to it.

He was in too much pain to be surprised by the sight of his keys in the ignition. He opened the back door and searched for liquids settling on the four pack of beer he'd purchased another lifetime ago. He clicked one of the cans open and downed the hot liquid in two gulps, seconds later throwing it up. Sweat covered him as he opened the second can, this time taking small sips. The beer was warm and tasteless but at that second it was the greatest thing ever. He sat in the back of the van and allowed the liquid to settle.

Balfour had let him live and he had no idea why. His head was still full of sharp pains and his thoughts were incoherent. He searched through the van once more for something more substantial than warm beer, and was rewarded with the discovery of a giant bag of chips. It wasn't ideal for someone dehydrated, but he ate with a greedy relish supplementing each mouthful with a swig of beer from the third can.

Gradually things started to clear. 'Shit,' he said, his voice hoarse, as he concluded he'd been set up to look responsible for the deaths of the two Railroad employees. He took some final sips before making his way back to the barn. He pulled open both sides of the door, light flooding the interior.

He'd expected to see the two bodies of the Railroad guys but the area was vacant. It had been scrubbed clean, every sign of the torture and murder of the two men erased in clinical fashion. Lynch rubbed his eyes, his limbs loosening. What the hell was going on? Balfour could have killed him but he'd let him live for no apparent reason. He'd cleaned up the area where he could have fitted Lynch up for the murders. Who would believe his version of events at this stage? Lynch had always spoken out against the Railroad. They'd taken his son so why would anyone believe he'd not slaughtered the two men covered in the tell tale railroad track tattoos?

It didn't make sense but Lynch wasn't going to wait there to find out what Balfour had in store for him. As he retreated to the van he remembered the chiming noise that had woken him from his drug-induced sleep. He reached inside his pocket and retrieved the burner phone he'd purchased with Sandra Rose. The phone was still charged and a bleeping icon displayed the missed call. He clicked on the symbol. An unknown number. They'd both selected to withhold their outgoing number in case they became separated from their phones so chances were high this was from Rose.

Now was not the right time to call her back. Although she was the closest thing he had to someone he could trust, he didn't know if she'd been calling under duress. If it was important, she would call again.

After checking beneath the van, he climbed into the driver's seat and, closing his eyes, started the engine. To his relief, it spluttered into life. Balfour still had plans for him and he wouldn't disappoint. He pulled down the dirt track until he reached the desolate main road. Balfour had driven for an hour after picking him up, so he presumed he was somewhere north of the town of Oakley where he'd confronted the two Railroad employees. He took a right, pulling down the visor as he drove towards the sun.

It was ten minutes until he saw the first sign of life, a silver Prius travelling in the opposite direction, its driver a lone female. He smiled, surprised at the emotion rushing through him at the sight of another human being. He lifted the burner phone, feeling its weight in his hand. It would be good to see Rose again, to even hear her voice. Their last encounter had been strained, their goodbye awkward. He checked his wallet with his right hand as his left hand held the steering wheel steady. The tracking device was still intact and for one desperate moment he considered activating it.

The sight of a roadside diner banished his melancholy. Lynch pulled over to the metallic-paneled shack, the sign reading 'Kim's Diner.' His van one of only two in the parking lot. He checked himself in the rear view mirror, sighing at the bedraggled figure within. Balfour had left him with his money so he left the van and made his way across the hot concrete to the diner.

He reached the door in time to see a waitress opening up. 'You're early, hon,' she said. 'Come on in.'

A blast of cool air hit him as he entered the diner. He took a seat in the second booth with good vantage points of the exit and the panorama of the narrow dining area. He thought again about the tracking device. Had Balfour placed a similar device on him? They'd known where to find him ever since that first day at his apartment when Lennox and his goons had turned up. But how to avoid detection? He would have to dump the van and all his possessions within. He would need to find a new set of clothes and burn the ones he was wearing. He would even have to dispose the phone and the tracking device Rose had given him. Only then could he be sure he wasn't being followed.

'Coffee, hon'?' said the waitress, tearing him from his thoughts.

'That would literally be heaven,' he said.

The dark black liquid singed his throat but he didn't care. He ordered pancakes with eggs and bacon and demolished the stack within minutes. The waitress kept bringing coffee and he kept drinking it. The poison was leaving his body, his strength returning. He'd somehow escaped death and the avoidance was making him stronger.

'Where you heading, hon? asked the waitress, topping his cup again without question.

'I'm going to see my son,' said Lynch.

The diner was filling with morning customers, catching breakfast or coffee before a long day at work. Lynch thanked the waitress and tipped her heavily before returning to the van. Opening the back doors, he did his best to rearrange the area where the two men had been held captive. A bloodstain marked one area and Lynch covered it up with a picnic blanket. He took a map of Texas from his backpack and laid it out on the floor, marking where he was and where he was heading. He overlay the map with a second map, this one of the railroad lines in the area. He'd studied so many railroad maps in the last few years, both state and nationwide. He could picture each and every one of the hundreds of lines by memory. The swirling tracks told a story. They danced across the folded pages of the map, each distinct from the other. At times Lynch had considered the millions of people who had travelled the railroad lines of America over the decades, the millions of lives, the billions of different journeys. At any given minute, somewhere in the country people were travelling by train, from small commuter journeys to epic sweeps of the country. And somewhere a group of people were watching these tracks. Biding their time, waiting for the chance to strike.

His phone pulsed, the vibrations spinning it across the corrugated metal of the van's floor as if it were alive. Lynch grabbed the buzzing device. An unknown number. Sandra Rose?

He clicked *answer*, his heartbeat increasing. 'Yes,' he said, not willing to state his name just yet.

A male voice, warm and deep responded on the other end of the line. Lynch couldn't be sure but he felt that he'd heard it before, a sound at once familiar but not.

'Ah, Samuel Lynch. We speak at last,' it said.

24

Lynch stepped outside the van, surprised to see his hand was shaking. 'Who is this?' he demanded.

'I think you know, Samuel. You've been waiting half a life-time to speak to me.'

Lynch's blood drummed through his ears. He was taken by the soothing quality, the rich baritone of the man's voice. Even through the shitty phone Lynch felt its deep texture. Each word resonated with him as if they'd been selected personally for him. 'Tell me who you are and what you want or I'm hanging up.'

'Don't be like that, Samuel. Are you not curious as to how I found your number?'

Lynch blinked, a tiredness washing over him. He'd already considered the question and concluded that Balfour had taken the number when he'd been unconscious. But a second alternative occurred to him now. Rose was the only person to have his number. Could she somehow be part of this?

'Surprise me,' he said.

'Where would the fun be it in that, Samuel?'

Lynch jumped out of the van and scanned his surroundings. Was he being watched? 'Balfour has put you up to this.'

'Very good, Samuel. Mr Balfour sends his regards.'

'And you are?'

'Please, Samuel. For someone of your aptitude, this sounds a little naïve. Look in your heart, you know to whom you're speaking.'

Could this really be him, the man he'd been searching for the last six years, since even before the day Daniel disappeared? Was this the head of the Railroad, the Controller?

'What should I call you?'

'No need for names, Samuel.'

'Mr No Name, then.' Lynch considered calling him Mallard, to gauge his reaction, but for the moment it felt like a piece of potential knowledge best kept to himself.

'Very good, Samuel.' The man paused, unhurried. 'Samuel, it's wonderful to finally talk to you. It's been too long.'

Lynch was surprised to be so relaxed when every inch of him wanted the man on the other end of the line dead. 'Why didn't Balfour kill me?'

'Samuel, if we wanted you dead you would be dead. If we wanted you dead now, we'd kill you now. We can see you. Pacing the parking lot like a lost sheep. A little lost sheep.'

Lynch froze. He scanned the area again, looking at the rooftop of the diner and further into the surrounding hills. It could be a bluff, a parlor trick of a guess, but something in the Controller's voice suggested otherwise. 'So why not kill me?'

The Controller laughed, the sound rich and melodic. 'Samuel, why would we eliminate you?'

'Because when I find you, I will end you?'

'Well, exactly. Who would destroy someone with such admirable qualities, such lofty aspirations? You've gone through so much, Samuel. There's been so much trauma in your life. You've endured things that would have destroyed all but the strongest, and yet here you are - still pursuing what many, if not all, would describe as a lost cause. You are, to use the current vernacular, a walking legend, Samuel.'

Tiredness seeped through him again. The Controller's words were evenly paced, musical in their delivery. They had a rhythm as if they were practiced, as if he was an actor recounting lines with perfect delivery.

'What do you want?'

'You may not believe it at the moment, Samuel, but we are very much alike. We are both singularly focused. I can help you, Samuel. I can obtain the redemption you seek, Samuel. Samuel, trust me and I can be your salvation.'

Lynch blinked his eyes rapidly, a combination of the heat and the odd delivery of the Controller's voice getting to him. His words reminded him of the words used by Balfour, that bizarre suggestion that they were alike. 'Is Daniel still alive?' he asked.

'Good, Samuel. You're beginning to understand. We need to meet, Samuel. I wish to see greatness face to face. Could you do that for me, Samuel?'

The cell phone weighed down his hand, the talk of Daniel ridding him of his strength. 'Where and when?' he said, trying to muster authority in his words.

'Good, Samuel. We'll send you the details. Try to forget what Mr Razinski told you and please don't inform Sandra Rose of your plans. We know where she is, Samuel. And your ex-wife, Sally. We know where everyone is, Samuel.' He paused again, and Lynch felt the absence of the man's voice.

'Samuel, goodbye for now. It was wonderful to make your acquaintance and I am literally counting down the hours until we meet.'

The Controller's voice was replaced by a beep and a dialing tone. Lynch collapsed to the ground, stricken, as sunlight attacked him from all sides. The Controller's departure had left him bereft and he couldn't understand why. He presumed it was the mention of Daniel, the resurgence of hope the Controller had given him that his son was still alive.

The asphalt ground was hot. Sweat drenched him, yet he was unable to move as the Controller's words replayed through his head. 'We know where everyone is,' he'd said, and Lynch felt the man's eyes lurking on him from some unseen vantage point and wondered if he viewed him with pity or disgust.

He crawled to the relative safety of the van, the Controller's words echoing through his head like an earworm. Normal protocol would be to share information about the conversation. In all his years of tracking the Railroad, it was the first significant communication he'd had with its would-be leader. He moved the burner phone from hand to hand, recounting Rose's number less he forget it. The Controller had told him not to call her, or anyone else. The threat was implicit, the same type of threat told to the family of kidnap victims. *They told us not to contact you*, he'd been told on countless occasions, and his advice had always been the same. Getting the authorities involved was always the correct decision. So why was he loath to take such advice now?

He started the engine and pulled away for no other

reason than it was an action and he needed to do something, even if it was to drive aimlessly.

The Texan scenery proved too little a distraction. As he drove, Lynch kept sneaking glances at his phone. He wasn't sure if he was waiting for a call from the Controller, or if his subconscious was telling him to call Rose. He was playing a waiting game and it wasn't a position he was comfortable being in.

Deciding the Railroad and the Controller wouldn't dictate him to, he stopped at a branch of Buc-ee's, a Texan service station, he ordered some food and purchased a second phone. Waiting for his food order to arrive, he contemplated his options. He needed to check on Sally and that would be his next move.

With the windows up, the van acted like a greenhouse but Lynch kept them shut as he ate his salami sub. The heat made him woozy, the sweat drenching his shirt as he savored the sauces and oils as if he was eating for the first time. He wondered if any of the poison Balfour injected him with still lingered in his blood stream. His thinking wasn't clear, it was tinged with doubt and insecurity as if he was suffering from an excessive hangover.

Opening a bottle of water, he gave in and wound down the windows. The air outside was warmer than in and he was forced to turn on the engine and start the air conditioning. He wanted rest but needed to keep going. He finished the water and tapped the dashboard. He was avoiding his next call. It was always difficult to speak to Sally but he hadn't spoken to her since he'd made her drop everything and leave her home. Although it had been for her safety, he doubted she was going to be so forgiving. He was almost relieved when Rob answered instead.

'Rob, it's Sam. Is Sally there?'

Rob sighed and Lynch wondered why he always seemed to answer Sally's phone for her. 'Samuel, I really must protest. You call us out of nowhere and instruct us to leave our home for no apparent reason and then we hear nothing from you. What's going on?'

Lynch laughed. He knew he shouldn't but he'd never heard Rob stick up for himself before. He could almost feel him shaking on the other end of the phone. 'Just put Sally on please, Rob.'

'No, Samuel, I won't. I realize you're in a difficult place and can empathize. Of course I can. I know what Sally has gone through and I know it's the same for you...'

'Let me stop you there, Rob.'

'No,' said Rob, with a touch more vehemence. 'You need help, Samuel. You need to see someone about this obsession.'

Lynch gripped the phone. He had nothing against Rob. The man was in an impossible situation, but he couldn't let his last comment slide. 'Obsession? Fucking obsession? If you ever call my son an obsession again, regret will not begin to describe the emotion you will be feeling. Do I make myself clear to you, Rob?'

'I can see you're upset.'

'Can you now? Well fucking done. I'm more than upset, Rob. I am at breaking point. For the love of God, put Sally on the line.'

Rob's voice fell to a whisper, his earlier bravado evaporated. Lynch regretted his outburst. It was the result of everything that had happened over the last few days but that wasn't an excuse. 'She's not here.'

Lynch clenched his hands. 'Rob,' he said, with a slowness

reminiscent of his conversation with the Controller. 'Where the hell are you?'

There was no immediate answer, only Rob's labored breathing. Lynch was about to ask again when his ex-wife's partner spoke. 'We are back at our house. We tried to contact you but you didn't respond.'

'Fuck,' shouted Lynch. 'Listen to me now, Rob. Whatever your misgivings about me put them to one side and do this for Sally. You need to call her and get her back to the house as soon as possible. Go inside and lock the doors and windows. Turn off all the lights and try to find a safe place to hide. I will be there in two hours.'

25

Lynch sped down the road, glad to have a destination once again despite the circumstances. He'd been tough on Rob but to his credit the man held his ground. Hopefully, he'd taken his advice. If the Controller could locate *him* in the middle of nowhere, could destroy the most secure of FBI compounds, then it wasn't going to take much to attack Sally and Rob at their home.

Although he was racing towards them, Lynch thought it was a fait accompli. If the Railroad wanted them dead they would be dead at some point and nothing he did would make a difference. He considered calling Rose again but her involvement would only cause more confusion, and she was the only one of the Bureau he could remotely trust.

He reached Sally's house in ninety minutes. She lived in a picturesque estate off the main road in Katy. Lynch parked up at the first opportunity and made a slow approach to Sally's road. The houses were all individually designed with the shared characteristics of red tiled roofs, and white walls. Most houses had their shutters closed due to the heat and, as he walked along the deserted streets, the chirping song of the cicadas his only company, the place had the feel of a ghost town.

He stopped two hundred meters from the house and surveyed the area for signs of life. He called Sally but she didn't answer so he continued his movement towards the house. The weight of his gun was a comforting feeling as he edged closer. He remembered Rose's description of the Gunn house and the desecration heaped upon it by Razinski. Images of Sally and Rob ran through his mind, gruesome collages of their dismembered bodies that he tried to blink away, his eyes watering in the heat.

Reaching the drive, he checked their SUV. He kept his gun holstered as he moved to the back of the house, hoisting his body up and over the locked wooden door. Members of the Railroad could be waiting in ambush but that there was nothing he could do either way. The Controller had told him they could have taken him out at any time and he believed him. His only choice now was to play along and wait for a chance to present itself.

He landed hard, his right knee jarring on the concrete. He edged along the fence, and stopped as he caught a reflection off the windows of a small yard office. The reflection was of a nervous looking man standing leg locked, a gun held in shaking arms pointing to the space Lynch was about to enter.

'Rob. It's Samuel. Put the gun down now,' said Lynch. He wouldn't have been surprised if Rob let off a shot through sheer panic.

'It's my house,' said Rob, his voice as shaky as the hands holding the gun.

'No one is disputing that, Rob. Put the gun down and we can talk. Where is Sally?'

'How do I know if I can trust you?'

'Don't be so fucking stupid, Rob. I appreciate you're protecting Sally but why the hell would I come here to hurt you? I was the one who warned you. I told you to leave in the first place.' With a sigh, Lynch took out his own gun. 'Put the gun down, Rob, this is how accidents happen.'

Lynch watched the indecision on the face of his ex-wife's lover. The stubborn bastard was yet to drop his weapon and Lynch feared he would shoot if he walked into the yard, either by reflex or some warped sense of protection.

A third voice came from the shadows. 'Drop the weapon, Rob,' it said.

Sally.

Rob turned and looked towards the back of the house. He lowered the gun to his side.

'We can trust him, Rob. He was Daniel's father,' said Sally, speaking to Rob as if he was in shock.

'Rob, I'm going to walk over but I need you to drop the gun completely. Do you understand?'

'Do as he says, darling,' said Sally.

Rob dropped the gun like a child being forced to drop their favorite toy. Sally rushed forwards and wrapped her arms around him. Lynch, fighting a stab of jealousy, moved into the yard. Before he had a chance to speak Sally was onto him.

'This is the end, Sam. What the hell have you done?' Tears streamed down her face as she stared at him, her eyes wild and accusatory, enlarged veins pushing at the skin of her neck.

'Has something happened?' said Lynch, surprised by the onslaught.

Sally and Rob clung to each other as if fighting gravity.

'There,' she said, nodding towards the patio table. 'Someone dropped them off, said they were for you but that we should take a look.'

Lynch edged towards the table and the A4 manila envelope. He stared at the innocuous looking object, his pulse racing as he contemplated what evils lurked within. For the second time in recent memory, he gazed at his shaking hands as if they were betraying him as he lifted the envelope and reached within for its contents.

He shielded his body from the lovers as he began to cry. His chest convulsed as he flicked through image after image of Daniel. In each picture he was wearing the same clothes, the same confused look on his face as if he was pleading to the camera. Lynch pictured his son calling for his parents as some stranger took the photographs and he fell to his knees, an inconsolable despair overcoming him.

He didn't know how long he stayed that way for. The vagaries of time disappeared as a rekindled grief took over his senses. He could have been there for hours before Sally placed her hand on his shoulder and whispered soft words to him. With Rob's help, Lynch found himself lifted to his feet and then onto a chair. He sipped at some iced water and gazed at Sally and Rob, the looks of incrimination all but eradicated.

'That was what he was wearing the day he went missing,' said Sally, her eyes red-raw.

Lynch drank some more water, trying to process what had happened. He rubbed his eyes, trying his best to switch off his emotions. 'Who gave you these?' he asked.

'They were delivered through the letterbox,' said Sally.

'You didn't see the person who delivered them?'

'No. Jesus, what's going on, Sam? I feel like we're back to

where we were. I'll never forget Daniel, you know that, but this? I'm just not sure that I can, Sam.'

She clung to Rob, who failed to make eye contact with him but said, 'tell us what is happening, Samuel. You owe Sally that much at least.'

He told them as much as he felt able from Lennox appearing at his house, to the call from the Controller, omitting anything he considered would frighten either of them more.

'Why now?' said Sally.

It was a good question. Had the catalyst been Razinski or had the Controller been planning this from the beginning? 'I'm not sure.'

Sally's eyes welled up as she leant towards him. 'I need to know, Sam, and don't bullshit me. Do you think Daniel is alive?'

Lynch choked down his tears as he remembered what Razinski had told him.

You wouldn't recognize your son now. The boy you know is gone.

He didn't want to give her false hope but it was too late for that. The pictures of Daniel had brought everything back for her, the grief she'd battled through, the guilt and anguish. She'd never fully recovered from Daniel's disappearance but she'd at least come to terms with it. He went to speak but stopped until he regained his composure.

He exchanged a look with his ex-wife, the first real glance they'd shared since his arrival at their house. Taking a deep breath, he said, 'yes, I believe he is.'

26

The bullpen was an unwelcoming place the following day, a cold silence accompanying Rose's walk to the incident room.

McBride didn't look up as she entered the room. 'Boss,' he said.

Rose sighed. Her night had been restless. She'd tried Lynch four more times but his phone had gone straight to voicemail without ringing. It was likely he felt the phone was compromised and had jettisoned it. She now had no way of locating him unless he switched on the tracker device.

He was missing and it was her fault. Pouring coffee, she marveled at the detail of the two maps covering nearly every inch of wall space in the room. Each pin represented a missing person and Lynch had prepared a file for them all.

'Rose,' said McBride, holding his phone in the air. 'We've had some Intel recovered from the attack at the compound. Some closed circuit video we thought destroyed. It's being sent over now.'

Five minutes later, the files arrived on McBride's computer. The attack at the compound felt like a lifetime ago.

So much had happened since. Rose was surprised by the
clarity of the images. Three assailants, each wearing gas
masks, appeared at the third checkpoint deep within the
compound, executing the waiting guards with military precision. Rose recalled the sight of the guards as she'd exited the
compound with Lynch. She continued watching, transfixed
as two of the masked assailants removed canisters and
launched them into the main area of the compound. The
three men waited for two minutes before making their way
into the mist, automatic guns held out in front of them as the
picture hazed over.

McBride played the video at double speed. The image
appeared frozen apart from the swirling smoke clouding the
room, until fifteen minutes later when the three men
returned. Rose lowered her eyes remembering the damage
the men had caused.

'You were still inside at this point?' asked McBride.

'Yes,' said Rose.

Six minutes later, Rose appeared on the screen followed
by Lynch.

'You gave him a weapon?'

'Working with him was my only chance at that point.'

The recording finished and McBride started it from the
beginning. 'No sign of Balfour.'

Rose wanted to keep an open mind but with Collins' testimony, she had to believe Balfour was the insider.

'Do you think they let you escape?' said McBride, uncomfortable with the silence.

It had crossed Rose's mind. 'To what end?'

'And why did they let Razinski live? It's one hell of an
oversight considering how precise they were everywhere
else.'

'Razinski was as good as dead. He was in and out of consciousness, covered in wounds. He wasn't going to survive more than minutes.'

McBride nodded but looked unconvinced. She didn't begrudge him his suspicions. She couldn't believe they'd staged it so Lynch could speak to Razinski before leaving, but it was conceivable they'd allowed her and Lynch to survive.

'Maybe they wanted survivors to report what had happened?' said McBride.

Rose had once tracked a serial killer who'd always left a witness. It was a form of power. It recorded the destruction, and left the observer always looking over their shoulder waiting for the killer to return. She agreed with McBride's assertion. An oversight from such seasoned operatives seemed unlikely.

Rose's phone rang, the noise startling her out of remembrance. It was Abigail. 'I need to get this. Speak to the tech team and go through every second of this footage. There must be something missing,' she said, leaving the incident room.

'Abi,' she said, finding a vacant interview room where she could speak to her sister alone.

There was no response and Rose's initial reaction was one of panic, the events of the last few days putting her on edge. She took a deep breath. 'Abi,' she repeated, 'you there?'

The sound of gentle sobbing filtered through the phone. Her sister went to speak, her voice high and breaking.

'Take a breath, honey,' said Rose.

'It's Mom,' came the faraway voice.

Time stopped as Rose waited for Abigail to elaborate.

'She's had a stroke. A big one by all accounts.'

'Where are you?' said Rose, fighting her emotions.

'We're at the hospital. Can you come?' said Abigail.

The question was hurtful though she didn't blame her sister for her asking it. She hadn't been the best daughter or sister of late, so why would Abigail presume anything had changed?

'I'm leaving now,' she said.

ROSE DROVE to Austin in a vacuum. She'd told McBride she would return as soon as she was able but didn't offer an explanation. Every guilty feeling she'd ever had concerning her mother replayed in her mind as she drove. The time when she was eight and she'd scribbled her name onto her bedroom wall in pencil, the times she'd said "I hate you" during teenage arguments, when she'd stayed out all night following a high school party, the look of relief, anger, and betrayal on her mother's face forever etched into her mind. However, most of the guilt was reserved for the last few years where Rose had separated from her family, her mother in particular. It didn't matter that it was fear keeping her away. She'd acted selfishly, and that could never be undone. Her mother had suffered a stroke, could be dying, and the last time she'd had a chance to see her she'd made her excuses and avoided the journey.

Abigail was in the main reception area of the hospital. They embraced without words. Rose clung hard onto her sister, Abigail's wiry frame holding her with the same intensity. Eventually they let go of each other, both smiling as they wiped away tears.

'Let's go see Mom,' said Abigail. There were no words of recrimination and for that Rose was thankful.

They caught the elevator to the fourth floor and Rose

followed behind her younger sister, like a child following her parent, to the ward where her mother was resting. Abigail stopped by the entrance. 'She's not in a good way, Sandra,' she said. 'Much worse than normal.'

Abigail was trying to protect her but nothing she could say would stop her going through those doors. 'Come on,' she said. 'Show me.'

Rose caught the tremor in her sister's hand as she led her through to her mother's room. 'Mom, Sandra is here,' said Abigail.

Rose stood at the edge of the bed staring at the skeletal frame beneath the bedclothes. The figure bore no resemblance to her mother. She'd last seen her two months ago, and although she hadn't recognized Rose she'd at least been in relative good health.

'She's been losing a lot of weight recently,' said Abigail, noting Rose's confusion.

Rose approached the bed and placed her hands on the twig-like structure of her mother's arm. Her skin was yellow, laced with patches of white as if her skin had been peeled away. A thick plastic tube protruded from her mouth and Rose fought the urge to pull it free, the foreign object having an unnatural hold on her mother. 'Mom,' she said, as if asking a question.

The body didn't move, and Rose glanced towards Abigail as if her sister held all the answers. 'She hasn't been responsive since they brought her in.'

'Who found her?' asked Rose, taking her hands from the paper-thin skin of her mother's arm.

'One of the nurses. We're not sure how long she was out before they found her.'

The nursing home hadn't called her and although she

understood why – Abigail dealt with everything concerning her mother's care –it still bothered her she hadn't been notified. 'When will she come out of this?' she demanded.

'They're not sure. We need to discuss some things, Sandra.'

'Such as?' said Rose, hearing the defensiveness in the tone.

Abigail lowered her eyes. 'Such as whether or not we let them resuscitate if this happens again.'

'YOU WANT TO GET AWAY,' said Abigail.

They'd moved to one of the hospital's coffee shops. The haunted faces of patients and their loved ones surrounded Rose as she sipped a tasteless black coffee, her sister staring at a full cup of mint tea. Abigail's initial magnanimous mood had all but vanished, her tone now accusatory.

'What does that mean?' said Rose.

'Ever since you've arrived, you've wanted to leave. Typical Sandra behavior, can never stay for the difficult stuff.'

'Now's not the time, Abi. We're both upset.'

Her sister sat stone-faced, glaring at her. 'Go then.'

'I don't want to go.'

'It's fine. I can deal with it. There's nothing you can do and I'm sure there is an important case you must be working on.'

'What does that mean?' asked Rose.

'You always have an important case to work on. That's why you never visit Mom in the first place.'

ROSE WINCED as she took another sip of coffee. She hadn't

thought about the case once since she'd arrived at the hospital but much of what Abigail said was correct. She was failing as a daughter and now it was too late.

'That's not why I don't visit, Abi.'

'No?'

Her sister's tone hadn't softened. It was the wrong time to have the conversation but Abigail clearly wouldn't be moved. 'I realize it's wrong, Abi, but I can't stand to see Mom that way. It's as if it isn't her.' Rose was her own fiercest critic and she acknowledged the selfishness in her words.

'So, you just want to abandon her. Give up on her?'

'Of course not, Abi, but it used to destroy me seeing her like that. She didn't even know my name.'

Rose saw the redness in her sister's eyes but didn't go to comfort her. It would be the wrong move at the moment.

'Don't you think I feel that way sometimes, Sandra? Jesus, you're unbelievable. What gives you the right to even say that? She's your Mother. You wouldn't be who you are if it wasn't for her and that's how you repay her? She brought us up practically on her own after my dad passed. How can you even say that?'

Rose rubbed her face, wished herself anywhere but there. There was a silence to the coffee shop as everyone listened to their argument. The customers of the coffee shop stared at them, glad to escape their own issues for a time.

'I can only say how I feel. It's unfair, but I knew you were looking after her and I thought my monetary contribution was enough.'

Rose regretted the words as soon as they'd left her mouth.

'You can shove your money, Sandra. If you can't bring yourself to see her then you can forget about helping her in

any way. Graham and I will see to her medical costs. You get
back to the real love of your life.'

Rose lowered her head. Abi was right so she accepted the
abuse. 'I'm going to say goodbye to her,' she said.

There was such rage in Abigail's eyes. It was heart-
breaking to see her sister look at her that way and Rose
wondered if they would ever get past this.

'I'll see you later,' said Rose, to silence.

Time stood still as Rose left the coffee shop. The eyes of
her fellow customers followed her as she made self-conscious
steps away from her sister. Back in the corridor of the main
building she let out a deep breath, a coldness sweeping
over her.

Her Mother hadn't moved. She lay at the same awkward
angle, the alien tube still protruding from her. Rose stared
hard at the bag of bones and tried to reconcile the vision with
the memories she had of the vibrant woman who'd raised
her; the woman who'd been a confidante and teacher, a
friend, and at times a necessary disciplinarian. She searched
for a glance of the Mother who'd taught her more about life
than anyone she'd ever met, or ever would, but her eyes
failed her.

'Are you in there, Mom?' she said, again touching her
fleshless arm.

The woman in the bedclothes didn't move.

Rose kissed her on the forehead and left.

Rose blinked at the midday sunshine. She hadn't checked on Abigail before leaving, deciding it was best to give her sister space. Opening her car, Rose checked her voicemail doing her best to push the guilt she felt about her mother deep inside her.

Surprised that there were no new messages, she called McBride.

'Boss?' said McBride, with what Rose presumed was irony.

'Any development on the CCTV images?'

'Nothing yet. Tech team are hopeful we may have one more surviving recording but they haven't contacted me yet.'

'I should be back in two hours. You'll be at the office?'

'Yes. Everything OK, Rose?'

'Yes, thank you. I'm making my way back now.'

Rose tried to focus on the case but was assailed by images of her mother. Should she return to the hospital? Part of her wanted to, knew she would regret it if her mother was to pass in the next few hours. But what could she do? What was the use of sitting, staring at her dying mother? If she'd been able to communicate, Rose was sure her mother would tell her to get back out there. Solve the riddle of who destroyed the FBI compound, who was responsible for the deaths of so many colleagues, so many innocent people. If her mother could speak, that was what her mother would tell her to do and she would honor that with everything within her. It was the least and, at that moment, the only thing she could do for her.

The air conditioning whirred in the car as she made slow progress along I-35 back to San Antonio. She tried Lynch's burner phone as she drove, frustrated as it went straight to the automated voicemail message. Lynch was difficult to analyze. It appeared that he'd been poorly treated and misrepresented by the Bureau. Although Balfour likely had a large part to play in this, it still troubled her that his situation had been handled so unfairly. What did it say about the organization when a person of Lynch's experience could be sidelined so easily?

And then there was the disappearance of his son. Understandably this had impacted his life, and he carried that grief with him on a daily basis. She'd glimpsed an occasional remoteness in his eyes, as if he wasn't present. She imagined he blamed himself for his son's disappearance, and knew for sure he wouldn't stop trying to find him until the possibility was destroyed one way or another.

One thing was still clear. Even after everything they'd endured together, from the night at the compound, to the night they'd spent together, she was still no closer to really knowing the man. Maybe that was why she felt a spark of anticipation at seeing him again, why she hadn't shared any details of their communication with anyone at the Bureau.

After parking underground, she was about to leave the

car when the burner phone rang. 'Yes,' she answered a little too eagerly.

'It's Lynch. Rose, I need your help.' His voice was distant, an octave lower than she'd become accustomed to.

'What is it?' she said, checking no one was listening in her near vicinity.

Lynch told her about the photos of Daniel delivered to his ex-wife, seemingly taken on the day of his son's disappearance.

'Jesus, Samuel, I'm sorry to hear that. I don't know what to say.'

'You don't need to say anything. Can you get someone to watch over Sally and Rob?'

Lynch gave her the address as multiple possibilities played through Rose's mind. 'I'll send someone over. I'll need to see the pictures, Samuel,' said Rose, dropping her voice to a whisper.

'I can't come in, Rose. Not now.'

Rose paused. She was going against protocol but the photos were a development. 'I'll probably have to call in a favor from the local sheriff's department. Are you going to be happy with that?'

'As long as they're well-trained and not green. You need to stress the danger. I'll debrief them as long as they don't try to take me in.'

'We need to meet. Can you come to my apartment this evening?'

It was Lynch's turn to hesitate.

'You can trust me, Samuel.'

'Okay. Text me the address. I'll bring the photos with me. Tell the local cops that.' 'I'll let you know when they're on their way.'

Rose hung up assessing what Lynch had told her. Why would they send him pictures of Daniel now? Lynch's ex-wife lived in Dimmit County, not that far from where the Gunn family were executed. She called Captain Iain Haig with her issued cell phone.

'Special Agent Sandra Rose. I thought you'd forgot about us,' came the slow drawl voice of the County Captain.

'Iain. Good to hear your voice. You may have heard we've had some minor issues since we last met.'

'So I understand. How may I help you, Agent Rose?'

'It's a tough one and I'm going to need you not to divulge the details to anyone.'

'Shoot,' said Haig, without a moment's hesitation.

Rose relayed as much information as she could about the events following Razinski's arrest. She told of the ambush at the compound, omitting Balfour's involvement, through to the photos arriving at Lynch's ex-wife's residence.

'Those poor folks. I'll take personal responsibility, Agent Rose, you have my word on that.'

At that precise moment, Captain Haig's word meant a great deal to her. He'd seen first hand what the Railroad could do, had suffered the loss of a fellow officer at the hands of Razinski. 'Thank you, Iain. Please call me if there are any developments.'

'You want me to bring Samuel Lynch in when we arrive?'

'No. He's coming to see me and I'd rather have him on our side. Please let him keep the pictures.'

'Yes, Ma'am,' said Haig, hanging up.

She left the call and took the elevator to her floor. As at the hospital, she felt everyone's eyes on her. Feelings were still high after the strip searches. She was pleased when she saw McBride leave the incident room and walk over to her.

'Bad news,' he said, as soon as she was within earshot.

'That's heartening.'

'The extra footage was damaged. All we've got is what you've seen.'

'Wonderful. Any more bad news?'

McBride's eyebrows fluttered up and down. 'Yes. We've run facial recognition tests. Obviously, the fact they're wearing balaclavas didn't help. OTD were hoping to get a match through the eyes but there was nothing except for some vague body shape measurements.'

It was disappointing but she hadn't expected anything different. 'What's the latest on Collins?'

'We've been trawling internet history, his bank and credit card details, normal stuff but nothing unusual yet. Miller has suspended his team, what's left of it. We've been questioning them all day but everything points to him working alone. The threats on his family would have been enough to secure that.'

Rose looked around her and wondered how many of her colleagues could so easily be intimidated. After what had happened at the compound, she imagined the number would be higher than before. Again, she considered what she would do if someone came for Abigail. Despite the fact that they weren't speaking, she would do everything in her power to protect her, even if that meant losing her own life. But would she be so weak as to capitulate like Collins? He'd been put in an impossible situation, had blamed himself for the death of everyone at the compound. Rose had sympathy for his situation even though she believed she would do things differently if it ever happened to her.

She decided not to tell McBride about the photos Lynch had received. She wanted to see Lynch first before involving her colleague. It was far from ideal, especially as Haig was involved, but McBride would be obliged to tell Roberts and Miller and Rose wasn't ready for that yet.

She spent the rest of afternoon watching interviews of Collins' colleagues. Most were cooperative, if a little put out at the imposition. Collins had an exemplary record. He'd gone off sick as soon as the Railroad had blackmailed him. He'd had three sick days in eight years so it was accepted without question that he could take some time off if needed. There had been no reason to suspect him, so no one had.

She slammed her laptop shut. It was becoming apparent that the only person who could lead them to the Railroad was Lynch. It was enough of an excuse to leave the office early. She debriefed McBride before leaving and heading down into the underground parking lot.

An hour later she was back at her apartment block. She sat in her car, the air conditioning on full and stared at her two cell phones. There was no message or missed call on either. No news from Abigail or Lynch. Accepting no news was an absence of bad news, she left the car, her skin instantly prickling with the heat of the late afternoon. She walked across the parking lot to the building's entrance, relieved as she entered the cold air-conditioned interior. A concierge service was beyond her meager government salary, the foyer area deserted.

All her nervous energy left he as she entered her apartment and collapsed on the sofa. She was too tired to move but didn't want to nap in case it stopped her sleeping that night. She opened her eyes wide and forced herself onto her feet.

Only then did she see the brown envelope by the door.

Sally was still ghost white as Lynch paced the living room of the house he'd once called home.

The photos lay on the dining table. Daniel aged seven. Six years ago. The day he'd been taken. Lynch wanted to look at them again, to study the images for a clue, but couldn't bring himself to do so. Once he'd recovered from the initial shock of seeing the photos, he'd placed them in a plastic container so Rose's forensic team could test them later.

He moved to the window, staring out at the vacant road waiting for Rose's to arrive. Each time he thought about the photos a curious mix of nausea and breathlessness came over him. The confusion in his son's eyes would forever haunt him, but much worse was the hint of accusation, the pleading look he gave the camera; the suggestion that his mother and father should come for him and stop this unfunny game.

Lynch closed his eyes as if doing so could blink away the memory of the photos and his failure to protect his son. But, when he opened them again, nothing had changed.

Two patrol cars arrived five minutes later. Thankfully the

sirens were switched off and if any of Sally's neighbors noticed their arrival they did so from behind the shutters and closed windows.

'Wait here,' said Lynch.

Rose had done well. A tall muscular man walked up the drive towards him with confident steps. 'Samuel Lynch?' said the man, with a thick Texan accent.

For a moment Lynch thought he was going to be arrested but the man stopped meters away from him and waited for a reply.

'I'm Lynch'

'Captain Iain Haig. I believe we have a mutual colleague, Special Agent Sandra Rose.'

'Thank you for coming,' said Lynch.

'Don't thank me. Thank Rose. I believe your ex-wife is in the house,' he continued.

Lynch nodded.

'Anyone else?'

Lynch hesitated. 'Her boyfriend,' he said, searching for a hint of derision from the police captain.

He got none. 'Take me to them,' said Haig, clicking his fingers at the two patrol teams who moved towards the front of the house.

Lynch led him through to the living area and introduced him to Sally and Rob.

'Ma'am,' said Haig. 'Can you tell me exactly what happened?'

Sally stared at him as if he was a non-entity and Rob surprised Lynch by getting to his feet. 'The photos were delivered this morning,' he said.

Lynch pointed to the plastic sheet on the dining table.

'This is your son?' said Haig.

'It appears these were taken on or near the day of his abduction,' said Lynch, nodding. 'He was wearing that when they took him.'

Haig lifted the plastic covering. 'This was six years ago?'

Lynch nodded. 'I'm going to take them to Agent Rose. We're in agreement on that?'

'So I believe,' said Haig. 'I guess you have no reason not to take them to her'.

He stared at Lynch searching for a sign of weakness. Satisfied, he handed the pile of photos to him. 'We can take over now. They'll be safe with us. The sooner you get those to Agent Rose, the better.'

Lynch tried to say his goodbyes but Sally was not responding to anyone other than Rob.

'You look after her now,' said Lynch.

Rob shrugged. The man was going up in his estimation all the time. He thanked Haig and walked to the van. Plugging his cell phone into the dashboard charger, he pulled away trying not to think of all the times he'd seen Daniel playing in the street sometimes with his friends, sometimes alone.

As he headed into the city he kept glancing at his phone, desperate to hear from either Rose or the hypnotic voice of the Controller. Everything was coming to a head. The Controller had promised to call him and Lynch had promised to himself he would end the man's life.

What twisted game was the Controller playing? Ever since that day Lennox and his two goons had arrived at his front door Lynch had become embroiled in something beyond his control. Was it all meant to happen? Was the execution at the Gunn house part of the Controller's master plan? Was it a way to get Lynch out into the open and a means to destroy the FBI compound? Or was the attack at the compound simply a result of Razinski's arrest, a power play, a form of retribution by the Railroad for taking one of their own?

Whatever the reason, Lynch felt manipulated. He was being orchestrated in a game not of his choice. Somehow, he had to redress the balance and, if the Controller presented that opportunity, he had to be prepared to capitalize on it.

The traffic was at a standstill. He flicked at the van's radio, searching for something worth listening to, a mindless tune to take his mind off the photos of Daniel, but was only presented with country classics and soulless music. He'd only slept fitfully over the last few days and it was beginning to take its toll but part of him feared sleeping; the nightmares waiting him would be all too real.

He thought about Sally and the profound effect the photos would have on her. He'd envied her once, the way she'd eventually come to terms with Daniel's disappearance, but now he shuddered to think what she was going through. She would blame herself, would consider her acceptance a betrayal of her son. She'd decided long ago that Daniel had passed away and now she would be forced to face she may have given up too soon.

Maybe this was all a game by the Railroad, a way to prolong the torture of the parents they'd stolen from. Both the Controller and Razinski had told him his son was alive. Lynch ground his teeth as he remembered Razinski's dying words, the suggestion that he wouldn't want to see his son again.

He couldn't have been more wrong.

The sky had darkened by the time he'd reached Rose's

address. Lynch's paranoia made him drive around the block five times before parking up, searching for potential threats.

Across the road from Rose's apartment building an Irish bar with blacked out windows was doing a roaring trade, revelers filing in and out of the entrance, some staggering, others being carried by their comrades in arms. Lynch was tempted to join their numbers - an evening of oblivion was just what he needed - but he'd made a promise to Rose.

He took the photos from the passenger seat and wrapped Daniel's sweater around them. His firearm securely in his holster, he made the slow walk to the building's entrance. The faint smell of bleach and cleaning products greeted him as he entered the main foyer of the apartment block. There was no one there to greet him so he made his way uninterrupted to the elevator and pressed Five. Like the foyer, Rose's floor was deserted. The whole building had an eerie feel to it. There was a lack of sound and Lynch wondered if all the apartments were somehow deserted. He reached Rose's door and knocked on it, standing to the side out of instinct.

'Who is it?' said Rose, her voice dull and lifeless.

Lynch stepped out so he could be viewed through the peephole.

'It's Lynch.'

Rose opened the door and stood aside, ashen faced, staring at him as if he was an apparition.

Lynch went for his gun but Rose shook her head. 'Come in,' she said.

He followed taking anxious looks around the sparsely decorated apartment searching for signs of an intruder. But Rose slumped down on the sofa, pointing to the dining table and a single glass of single malt whisky.

'I don't touch the hard stuff,' said Lynch, trying to lighten the mood. Something was off with Rose and he didn't know how to handle it.

'There's something you need to see,' said Rose. 'Sit down.'

'What is it Rose? You're freaking me out.'

'Just sit. Please.'

Lynch did as instructed.

'I got home an hour ago and this came through the door,' she said, handing him a brown manila envelope.

Lynch took the offering from her shaking hands.

'More photos?' he said, his head spinning.

'I'm afraid so,' said Rose. 'But they're not from the day of the abduction.'

29

Lynch's first thought was not to look. During his time with the FBI, and subsequently, he'd seen things he'd never be able to erase. Grotesque images forever burned into his memory that would come to mind at inopportune moments, visions worse than the most hideous of nightmares.

What was seen could not be unseen. Lynch kidded himself that if he left the envelope where it was, he could go about his life without ever knowing the true horror of its contents.

'Do you want me to tell you what's inside?' said Rose. The color had returned to her cheeks as if she realized she was in the supportive role now.

Lynch shook his head, unable to speak.

'Can I get you some water? A beer perhaps?'

With trembling hands Lynch took the proffered bottle from Rose, downing the contents in three large gulps.

'Show me,' he said.

Rose handed him the envelope gingerly. Lynch took a deep breath and pulled the photos from the envelope. Daniel glared back at him, and for the first time Lynch understood what Razinski had told him.

You wouldn't recognize your son now.

The boy in the picture had changed. Maybe it was only something a father could spot. Cosmetically he looked little different. His hair had been cut short and his features were intact. If the newspaper he was holding was anything to go by the picture had been taken a year to the date of his abduction when he was aged eight. A year had gone by and little had changed.

Unless you studied the boy's eyes.

Daniel's eyes reflected the change in him. They were completely vacant as if Lynch was viewing a photo of a waxwork. The second photo was an complete replica of the first. Daniel was sitting, in poor lighting, holding that day's newspaper, glaring aimlessly into the camera lens.

'That's him?' asked Rose softly, placing a hand on Lynch's shoulder.

Lynch continued through the short stack of five photos, each similar to the last, searching for a hint of life in his son's eyes.

'It's him,' he said, gripping the last of the photos tightly as if doing so could evaporate it from existence.

'Let me take those,' said Rose. She took the four loose photos and placed them in the envelope and waited for him to let go of the fifth.

Lynch was transfixed by the image of his son. His mind played tricks on him, listing the awful things that could have occurred during his son's missing twelve months. He tried to be hopeful but his mind reminded him of the atrocities he'd seen over the years: the abuse and suffering which occurred on a daily basis in America's shadow-land.

'Let go now,' said Rose, her voice floating towards him as though part of the air.

Her hand rested on his shoulder, releasing the pincer like grip he had on the photo.

She moved away from him, placing the photos back on the table and he felt her absence. His shirt was damp against his skin and as he wiped his face he realized streams of tears had fallen from his eyes. He shuddered as Rose sat down again, her hand on his, and despite his grief and desperation he accepted the kisses she offered and held her hand as she stood and led him to the bedroom.

LYNCH WOKE LATER WITH A SCREAM. Blinking, he tried to hold onto the images that haunted his nightmare but they'd already faded from memory. His heart hammered against his chest, the rhythm wild and uncomfortable.

Rose placed her hand on his, his whole body covered in a thin film of sweat. 'You were dreaming,' she said. 'Try to get some more sleep.'

Lynch remembered to exhale. He lay back down but sleep wasn't coming. 'When did you receive the photos?' he asked.

'About an hour before you arrived. I must have either walked over them as I entered the apartment or they were slipped under the door when I was here without me noticing. I think the former is more likely.'

Lynch clenched his teeth. 'I don't understand why they'd send them to me now after all these years. They must have known I was coming to see you. What is this game?'

'I'm going to have to report this. And the photos sent to Sally's house.'

'Of course. You can take them in as soon as possible. I

doubt they'd be as foolish as to leave a trace on anything but, who knows, we might get lucky.'

Rose absently stroked his arm. Lying here with her was the most comfortable he'd been with another woman since splitting with Sally.

'It would make sense if you came in as well; explain your side of the situation.'

'There's a few things I haven't told you,' he said, telling her about the two Railroad operatives and Balfour's torture session.

Rose sat up in bed. 'You're sure Balfour killed them?'

'He did more than kill them but you'll struggle to find any evidence.'

He didn't tell her about his conversations the Controller. If he told her now she'd be compelled to bring him in for questioning and he couldn't afford that yet.

'I'll give you the coordinates of the place he killed them but give me twenty-four more hours,' he said. 'There must be at least one mole in your department and I can't risk it coming in yet.'

'There's plenty of moles, I've seen them all,' said Rose with a laugh.

'You've lost me there, Agent,' said Lynch, cheered by her smile

Rose explained the search she'd conducted on the whole of the FBI headquarters.

'So you've seen the whole building naked?' he said.

'Women only.'

'That's something I suppose,' said Lynch. 'I bet you're Miss Popular now?'

'You better believe it.'

'Obviously, just because there are no Railroad tattoos doesn't mean everyone's clean.'

'No, of course not. I wanted to go to Dallas and speak to Balfour's former colleagues but the SAC, Miller has stopped me so far.'

'He probably thinks you're going to strip search everyone.'

'You jest but that's exactly what he said to me,' said Rose. 'But with these photos I think I have justification.'

Lynch got out of bed, noting it was only four am.

'You should try and get some more sleep,' said Rose.

Lynch smiled at her. It sounded like a great idea but he was too wired. He showered, turning the heat up to its highest temperature, the piercing jets painful to endure. He washed the dirt of the day from his skin. Rose was right. He should go in but if he did the Controller might not call again. He was sure the next set of photos would arrive soon. By then, he wanted to be face to face with the head of the group who'd kidnapped his son.

Rose had brewed some coffee by the time he'd changed; the black liquid heavenly as he sat and drank.

'Twenty four hours?' said Rose, repeating his earlier request. 'This time tomorrow morning, if you've got no further then you'll need to come in with me.'

Lynch nodded, handing her the plastic file with the photos of Daniel. He picked up his son's sweater wondering if the boy in the second set of photos would have outgrown it. 'Until then,' he said, hesitating as he'd done that morning at the trailer. This time Rose relieved his embarrassment by leaning over and kissing his cheek.

He left her apartment with a sense of optimism despite the latest developments. Maybe it had been the night he'd shared with Rose or the sense that things were coming to a head, but he felt perversely lifted as he walked out into the early morning sun, the sound of birdsong lifting his spirits further.

Inside the van, he placed Daniel's sweater into the bag on the passenger side seat and was starting the engine when his phone rang. Had they been watching all night? He didn't care; he just wanted it to be over with.

'Yes,' he said, already knowing who was on the other line.

30

'Good morning, Samuel,' said the cool, soothing voice of the Controller.

Lynch's first thought was to signal Rose but the Controller advised him against it.

'Let's not do anything rash now that we are so close,' said the man.

Somehow they had eyes on him. If he'd been followed all this time then it had been exemplary surveillance work. That, or Lynch's judgment was getting worse with age.

'You must have seen the photos by now,' continued the Controller, with that odd cadence, the words a rich baritone slowly spoken with strange intervals. Again, Lynch found himself drawn into the man's speech patterns. It was staged but Lynch couldn't help but be affected.

'Is he still alive?' asked Lynch, cursing himself for the slight tremor in his voice.

'You have my word,' said the Controller.

Unlike Razinski he didn't add anything about his son's

current state. 'What is it you want from me? Why after all these years are you sending photos of my son?'

The Controller spoke as if he hadn't heard the question; the sign of a true politician.

'I want to meet you, Mr Lynch. You are an extraordinary person. You proved that all those years ago when Daniel disappeared and you've been proving it ever since. Only you, out of everyone, never lost faith. Even your wife...'

'Don't bring Sally into this,' said Lynch, interrupting the Controller's monologue.

'Apologies, Samuel, that was crass. But you get my point. The authorities and your colleagues; how did they treat you, Samuel? At best they viewed you with pity but most viewed you with scorn. And do you know why, Samuel? Because they feared what was happening to you could happen to them, and they blamed you for not taking the easy option; for not accepting that your son had disappeared for good. But you've shown them, Samuel, you've proven all those doubters wrong and now you'll get your reward.'

'As long as my reward is seeing Daniel then I'm happy with that,' said Lynch.

'Oh, it goes much beyond that,' said the Controller. 'You are a rarity, Samuel, and I'd like to get to know you better. We can do great things together, you and I.'

Lynch grimaced. Did the Controller really mean what he was saying or was it another part of the game, a ploy to undermine him. Could he truly believe Lynch would have anything to do with him after everything he knew, after the years he'd stolen from him by taking his son?

He'd heard the refrain from the Controller's underlings. Razinski and Balfour had tried to suggest he was like them; that he could be one of their number. Lynch couldn't believe they'd truly meant it. But if there was a chance of seeing Daniel again then he was willing to play along. 'Okay.'

'Wonderful,' said the Controller. 'I'm pleased you're starting to come round to my way of thinking. I have so much to show you, Samuel; a world you never knew existed, something you can't even comprehend yet. But I meant what I said. You can be part of this world, Samuel. You're not like the others. You're more like me than you'll ever know. Come, let's meet and I can show you everything.'

'Just say when and where,' said Lynch.

'That's all been settled naturally, Samuel. Now, it's going to sound hackneyed after all the silly nicknames your friends have come up with for my colleagues and me but I think we should meet on a train. How does that sound?'

'Sounds fine to me.'

'Wonderful. Your train leaves tomorrow at seven am from San Antonio. Naturally, we've upgraded you. You'll have your own cabin. I can hardly wait until we finally meet, Samuel. But, Samuel, I do have to warn you and, remember, I can see you even now sitting in that little van of yours. You must come alone. And you mustn't tell the fragrant Agent Rose about this conversation because if you do, Samuel, we will never meet. And you will never see Daniel alive again. Until tomorrow.'

With that, the Controller hung up.

31

Rose watched Lynch leave from her apartment window. He walked like a man with a giant weight on his shoulders, and the cache of photographs on her dining table explained why. To some, what happened last night would be viewed as a lapse in her professional judgment. Lynch was a civilian, and potentially a suspect, but it was too late for regret.

Lynch was understandably upset and she'd comforted him. There had been no manipulation on either side, and in the morning there had been a sense of ease as they lay together. Something she hadn't experienced in years.

It made what she'd done when he'd been sleeping feel like a betrayal.

She called Abigail before showering. There was no news on their mother. Abigail spoke in short sentences like a sulky teenager and Rose said goodbye before she lost her temper.

She spent a long time in the shower until the fatigue of the last few days disappeared and she felt a faint sense of optimism.

An hour later she met McBride for breakfast at a pancake

house a block from her apartment building. The chairs in their booth were covered in a thin lining of green faux-leather decorated with patches of discoloring and grease. McBride was dressed in his standard get-up of black suit, tie, and shades. His hair was slicked back, some of the strands held together in clumps revealing patches of scalp. It was not the best look for him but she made no comment. The approaching conversation would not be an easy one.

McBride ordered a stack of pancakes with bacon and syrup. 'In this heat it's fine to carb up,' said McBride.

Rose ordered the same. 'I saw Lynch last night,' she said.

McBride leant back into the plush seating. 'That came out of nowhere.'

'He called me. Someone dropped these at his ex-wife's house.'

McBride picked up the folder of photographs. 'This is his son?' he said, dispassionately.

'It would appear they were taken on the day of his disappearance.'

McBride shook his head. 'Jesus. And he brought these to you.'

'Lynch called me to say they'd been delivered. I've set up a team at his ex's house. County Captain Iain Haig's team.'

'And you didn't think to bring Lynch in?'

'I don't consider him a suspect.'

McBride laughed. 'No? You going to explain that to Miller?'

'No. You going to tell?'

The pancakes arrived and they began eating, McBride still sitting back in his chair. 'There is more,' said Rose, placing the second set of photos onto the table.

McBride stopped eating and leant forward to the plastic covered photos. 'This is Daniel?'

'A year later. Lynch verified it was him.'

'Christ, look at his eyes. Fucking monsters,' said McBride, under his breath.

'These were delivered under my door, an hour before Lynch arrived.'

McBride ate a forkful of pancakes before speaking. 'You think he could have placed them there?'

'Why would he do that?'

'Come on, Rose. You know as well as I that there is no rhyme or reason with some people. You also know that most abuse occurs from family members.'

Rose knew that at least eighty per cent of the time a child's abuser was known to them but was in no mood to concede to McBride. 'What, you think he abducted his own son and is playing some weird game with us?'

'Stranger things, Rose, stranger things,' said McBride, gulping at his coffee as if it was medicinal.

Rose thought about the two nights she'd spent with Lynch, and the sense of loss and desperation she'd seen in him when he'd viewed the second set of photos. She'd met some of the world's great deceivers in her time, but if McBride was correct about Lynch she would happily give in her FBI badge.

'You didn't see him,' she said, sounding like every deceived victim she'd ever encountered.

McBride lifted his hands palm up. 'Where is he now?'

'He has a lead he is pursuing.'

'The plot thickens. An ex-FBI agent running his own vigilante campaign? I don't suppose he deigned to share this information with you?'

The waitress arrived and Rose accepted the refill of her coffee. She was withholding information from McBride, something she'd never done with a partner. It wasn't that she didn't trust him, more that withholding at this moment felt like the right move. 'We need to speak to Balfour's former colleagues,' she said, deflecting the question.

'Didn't Miller advise against that?'

'What is it with you and Miller, McBride?'

'What the hell does that mean?'

'First you pick me up from my hideout, then drop me at Miller's office. Next thing, we're working together.'

'You're paranoid, Rose.' McBride pushed out his lower lip, pretending to sulk, and Rose did her best not to laugh.

'I'd never worked directly for Miller in my life until that day. I've been working with Callahan for the last five years. We were assigned to collect you, told nothing, and then I was assigned to work with you. I'm not his rat if that's what you think.'

Rose pretended to pout. 'I wouldn't say rat exactly,' she said, with a hint of lightness.

'Look, if you want to go see Balfour's former colleagues let's do it. We can go now and tell Miller afterwards. As far as I'm concerned, you're in charge. However, I would appreciate it if we can be open from now on about everything.'

'Deal,' said Rose, nodding. 'I put a tracker on him.'

'Lynch?'

Rose nodded. I gave him one before but he didn't activate it so I placed one in his phone last night.

McBride hesitated. 'Shall I ask how?'

'No.'

'So you know where he is?'

Rose held up her phone displaying the app that was tracking Lynch.

THEY SET OFF AFTER BREAKFAST. Dallas was at least five hours away. They were driving for twenty minutes before McBride brought up the subject of Lynch again. 'So where is he now?'

Rose had already checked but she glanced at the app on her phone anyway. 'Still in San Antonio.'

McBride nodded

'We should have done this sooner,' said Rose, as McBride pulled onto I-35.

'What, you and I on a road trip? Yes, it's been a long time coming. We should stop and get some beers.'

'Balfour's colleagues. Why do you think Miller stopped us questioning them?'

'You know what inter-department politics is like.'

'Even so, Balfour is potentially responsible for the murder of over forty Bureau staff. Who cares if some noses are pushed out of joint.'

'I imagine it's hard for the suits to admit that one of their own could be responsible.'

Rose agreed. Why blame the Bureau when they had an outsider they could tie everything to? A light manipulation of the facts could easily put Lynch in the frame. A former FBI agent let go from his position following the disappearance of his son, someone with the skill, experience, and motivation to carry out such an attack. What better candidate to wreak havoc on his former employers? Rose had seen people lost in the system before. The power of national security could go a long way. Lynch understood this, and he must have a lot of faith in her to have trusted her with the photos.

She glanced again at the flashing red signal on her phone. She'd convinced herself she'd planted the chip on Lynch out of protection for the man, but her motives were clouded.

She zoomed in on the map and wondered if it was purely a coincidence that he was less than a mile from San Antonio Train station.

32

Lynch spent the night at a hotel near the station in San Antonio. Before leaving, he packed a small holdall to take with
him, leaving the rest of his belongings in the van. He held
Daniel's sweater before packing it, inhaling deeply as he
banished thoughts of the two sets of photos.

Pulling the cell phone from the charger he considered
calling Rose. He wanted to tell her where he was going but
the Controller had warned against it. He hated being in such
a compromising position, but the Controller and the Railroad
had been one step ahead of him all this time. The delivery of
the photographs had only cemented his thinking. If he told
Rose now, he risked never meeting the Controller and
blowing his chance of seeing Daniel alive again.

He left the vehicle and headed towards the station on foot,
the instant change in temperature causing him to break out in
sweat. The rational side of him began to niggle as he walked
through the entrance of the station that was little more than a
holding room. As an agent, he would never have counseled

someone to do what he was about to. It was potential suicide. Whatever the threat, he would have always insisted on the authorities being involved. He recalled a banker whose daughter had been held for ransom. Lynch had advised the man not to negotiate without the agency's involvement but the banker had panicked. A day later he dropped over three million dollars at a secure site, only for the body of his daughter to be discovered a week later in the Bayou River.

So why was he going alone now? Ever since the day he'd disappeared, Daniel had been his obsession. Prior to that, the Railroad had been his obsession; both obsessions had led him to this moment. Between them, they had cost him his son, his wife, his career, and a good amount of his sanity. It made no sense to stop now.

He'd spent the last day and evening researching Wilberforce Mallard the sixth, on the off chance that the man he'd been speaking to went by that name. His research revealed nothing he didn't already know. The information was suspiciously thin and he wished now that he'd confronted the Controller with the name when he'd spoken to him.

The station was a disappointment. As a child he'd loved such places. Railway stations, airports, even the dowdy bus depot of his hometown had been like doorways, portals to other worlds beyond his understanding. Such romanticism had faded over the years, and run down station had lost its appeal.

'I have a ticket to collect,' said Lynch, to the cashier at the collection section.

'Name?' said the rotund woman, sitting behind a glass partition as if she was on display.

'Lynch.'

The woman's eyes ran up and down his body, her face devoid of warmth, as if she knew something he didn't. 'ID?'

Lynch sighed and placed a credit card through the small opening.

The woman took the card, flared her nostrils, and punched something into her system. 'First class return to St Louis?'

'I guess so,' said Lynch, pleased the ticket wasn't one-way.

His response elicited a frown from the woman who paused before printing the tickets. 'Enjoy your trip, sir,' she said, handing the tickets and his card back, without a trace of a smile.

'Thank you ever so much,' said Lynch, breaking into an exaggerated smile ignored by the cashier. 'I don't suppose you can tell me who purchased these tickets on my behalf?'

The cashier stared at him as if he was insane. Lynch walked away without discussing the matter further.

With forty-five minutes to kill before boarding, Lynch found a coffee shop and ordered a black coffee and a breakfast croissant. He checked through his belongings, using a spare socket to charge the burner phone that was now his only communication to the outside world. Again he considered his options. Experience told him the Railroad was capable of anything, and that being in public on a train wouldn't keep him safe. He knew that the correct move would be to get Rose involved, but once more he dismissed that sensible option. However much he wished it wasn't true, he had to concede that the Controller and the Railroad were in charge, and always had been.

He washed down the dry food with the last of the coffee and made his way to the platform. The Texan Eagle looked little different from any other Amtrak train Lynch had encountered, its carriages a mixture of dirty metal and blue paint. The Controller had treated him to his own compartment and a smiling stewardess, the antithesis to the cashier, checked his ticket and guided him to his cabin, which was air-conditioned with a large seat that opened out as a bed. Lynch checked the itinerary on his phone and was dismayed to see that the journey to St Louis lasted thirty hours.

The train pulled away, the carriage swaying side to side as it picked up speed. The rhythm soothed Lynch and he closed his eyes, waking three hours later as the train pulled into Austin.

Bored, Lynch left his cabin and wandered through the train, taking a seat in the viewing area halfway down the train, checking the exit points on both sides of the carriage as he went. He was the lone occupant in the carriage and the paranoid side to him suggested this was part of the Controller's plan. As the train eased away from the platform, he moved taking a seat at the far end of the carriage so he could better view any potential threats.

Seconds later, the carriage door opened. Lynch was poised, ready to reach for his gun, only to relax as the smiling stewardess walked passed him. Lynch sat back in the chair and tried hard not to fall asleep as the train made its slow, rhythmic way, along the tracks.

Lynch was glad to see other passengers join his carriage over the next few stops. He assessed every one. The two businessmen who'd already started on their gin and tonics, the lone college student with her grimy rucksack, a married couple dressed in designer clothes, unsmiling as they listened to whatever played through their earphones, and a lone man in denim jeans and black t-shirt.

The lone man caught Lynch's attention. The man hadn't

seen him, busying away at his laptop four seats down. Of all his fellow travellers, he appeared the most likely to be the Controller though Lynch doubted he would be so obvious.

JUST AFTER THREE PM, the train pulled into Dallas. Lynch kept glancing at his fellow passengers. It didn't help that he didn't know who he was looking for. The man in the black t-shirt appeared oblivious to his attentions, his eyes never once leaving the glowing screen of his laptop.

Lynch got to his feet and left the carriage. The smiling stewardess stood by the train door waiting to greet the next batch of passengers.

'May I stretch my legs?' he asked her.

'Yes, sir, of course. We'll only be here for twenty minutes so please don't go too far,' she said, the kind smile never once fading from her lips.

Lynch jumped down, landing hard on the concrete platform. A number of passengers were boarding the train though none were entering the cabins. Lynch scanned the surrounding area. The platform overlooked a parking lot and he studied the vehicles within but could see nothing amiss.

'Ready to re-board?' said the stewardess, once the last of the passengers had boarded the train and the doors had been slammed shut by the stationmaster.

'Thank you,' said Lynch. The woman stood aside, the light smell of her perfume drifting towards him as he made his way back to his cabin.

Lynch checked his cell phone but there had been no messages. He made notes as he waited for some form of contact, recounting each day and event that had unfolded since Special Agent Lennox had rudely awakened him. Was there something he'd overlooked which could unravel the mystery of why he was sitting here alone on a train with no real idea of his destination, or who he was likely to meet once there?

The stewardess knocked on his door. She beamed a smile turning her head to him as if they were conspirators together in some unknown secret.

'May I get you anything?' she asked, in her southern drawl.

Lynch surveyed the drinks on offer, his eyes alighting on a row of beers in the fridge compartment, all the more enticing for their coldness.

'Diet soda,' he said.

'Glass and ice?'

'No, thank you. And just leave the can, I'll open it,' said Lynch, an old paranoia creeping in.

'Of course, sir,' said the hostess, leaning in a little too close as she placed the drink and a complimentary snack in front of him.

'Let me know if you need anything else,' she said, lowering her eyes.

Lynch sipped at the diet soda as the train rushed by identikit scenery, flat featureless land tinged with green and yellow. He was becoming more and more paranoid that the Controller had duped him. Maybe he'd wanted him out of the way? Maybe it was just another of the Controller's power plays?

He returned to the viewing carriage, his fellow travellers oblivious to his scrutiny, and continued walking towards the rear of the train. In standard class, the atmosphere changed. The carriages were nearly at capacity, filled with groups of travellers, families and lone travellers grouped together. The air-conditioning was struggling to cope with the number of bodies and Lynch was coated with a film of sweat as he made his way further down the train. The walls of the standard carriages felt narrower, the ceilings lower, their claustrophobic nature a stark contrast to the viewing carriage back along the train.

As he approached the end of the train, Lynch noticed it was slowing. He checked out of both sides but couldn't see anything untoward outside. The last stop they'd made was at Marshall. Texarkana, the next scheduled stop still an hour away. As the train eased to a stop, he walked back first to his cabin and then the panoramic viewing carriage. He caught the eye of black t-shirt man just before two Texas Rangers boarded the train.

33

The Rangers entered two carriages further up the train. Lynch took a seat and checked his phone. He lowered himself down so he wouldn't be easily visible when the Rangers entered his carriage.

Less than a minute later, the connecting door opened. Lynch caught a glimpse of the Rangers through the gaps in the seats. The light tan uniform, the thick black utility belts containing amongst other items their state-issued firearms. The carriage was hushed and one of the pair cut the silence. 'All non-US citizens are to move to the back of the train. Bring your passport and necessary visas.'

Something was amiss. Lynch sensed it in the way the Ranger spoke, as if he'd been reading from a script. Were they here for him? The female backpacker got to her feet and nervously made her way towards the officers. 'Through there, Ma'am,' said the second Ranger, pointing towards the next carriage.

Lynch took out his burner phone and typed in Rose's number. The backpacker returned a few minutes later, a smile on her face, just as a second train pulled onto the parallel track next to them. The train caught everyone's attention and when Lynch looked out of his window he understood why. He'd never seen anything like it. The train was only three carriages long. Each carriage was a perfect image of glass and chrome. The black-mirrored exterior curved upwards from the base of the train. It was impossible to see any joins in the exterior of the machine. Even the engine compartment was sleek chrome. Lynch searched for an engine number but the shiny coat was blemish free.

Alarmed, Lynch typed a message to Rose. He had to share the information about Mallard before it was too late. He sent her a hurried message before snapping open the phone and removing the battery and Sim card which he palmed as the Rangers walked down the carriage.

There were too many people to do anything. If they were coming for him then he would have to leave. He reached into his wallet and took out the tracking device. Without hesitation he activated it. Using the metal casing, he ripped a hole in the lining of his jeans where he placed the device.

Seconds later, the taller of the two Rangers stopped by his seat. 'Mr Lynch,' he said. 'Please come with us.'

Lynch picked up his holdall and got to his feet. The smaller Ranger took the bag from him and instructed him to place his hands behind his back. Lynch could have made a move, but the other Ranger had his gun out and Lynch couldn't risk a shoot out in such a closed environment. 'Who the hell are you?' he said, as the Ranger snapped a pair of metal cuffs on his wrists.

LYNCH KEPT HIS HEAD HIGH, making eye contact with as many

people in the carriage who would match his gaze. The two men who'd apprehended him were either not Rangers or were insiders, corrupted like Balfour. They cuffed him without warning or stating his Miranda rights. They didn't even ask him who he was, the slimmer of the two men having verified him with a photo on his phone.

He struggled to keep his feet as they bundled him out of the train onto the desert gravel between the tracks. He dropped the Sim card, and grunted as he missed the last step, his knees struggling to hold his balance. From the windows, he saw the shocked faces of the passengers pressed up against the window like prisoners. He saw the distaste in some of the faces, the presumption that he'd done something wrong. It would make no difference protesting and could lead to a mass slaughter, so he kept his silence as he was led up the steps of the second train.

Classical music greeted him as he entered the train's interior. The sound quality was concert perfect and was a fine complement to the interior of the carriage. Lynch had been on-board a few private jets in his time, but none of them could match the opulence of his current surroundings. Everything was decorated to the highest spec, leather armchairs, polished wooden trimmings, a deep patterned carpet.

'Sit,' said the overweight Ranger.

Lynch did as instructed, collapsing onto the plush leather of one of the sofas his cuffs digging into the material behind his back. 'Can you take these off?' he asked, to silence.

He glanced out of the window, surprised to see the train was moving, the only sound he could hear the classical music piped through the speakers.

Although his ego was bruised from being captured,

Lynch considered recent developments as positive. The situation was desperate but he was a step closer. The Controller must have arranged his capture. That suggested he would get to see his foe for the first time, and meant he was closer to seeing Daniel again.

As the thin Ranger kept a close eye on him, his obese partner searched through the contents of his bag. Lynch's skin went clammy as the man took out Daniel's sweater, looking at it with distaste before placing it back in the bag. 'Clear,' said the man.

'You going to tell me where we're going?' said Lynch.

'You'd be better served holding your tongue,' said the thin Ranger.

'Just making chit chat,' said Lynch. He'd been watching the two men ever since being dumped in the carriage, searching for patterns, potential weaknesses in their movements. He'd yet to see one. They kept their distance, one of them maintaining eye contact at all times. He played with the cuffs on his wrist but they were secure. Houdini himself would have struggled to break such binds. He'd yet to be stripped-search which was a blessing. His major hope now was that Rose's tracking device was still working. It seemed to be an oversight on the part of the Controller but in Lynch's experience such minor things were often the undoing of such people.

The two Rangers stood to attention as a side door, one Lynch hadn't been aware of, slid open. Lynch had been hoping to see the Controller but was neither surprised nor disappointed to see the man who walked through the opening.

'Samuel, how are you?'

'Balfour. How about loosening these cuffs?'

Balfour grinned and sat on the leather armchair opposite him. 'Like the pad?'

'Yeah, it's lovely. Yours or the Organ Grinder's?'

Balfour's left eye twitched, a split second gesture suggesting the comment had bruised him. The former agent linked his fingers together. 'You realize you no longer exist? You have disappeared and will never reappear.'

'Why don't you kill me then, Balfour?'

'Believe me, I would love to. Fortunately for you, you have a choice.'

'What choice?'

'There will be time for that, Lynch. I'm not one hundred per cent sure you will enjoy the options but who knows, you may surprise me.'

'I don't know what you're talking about, Balfour, but believe me when I say that when I have the choice of killing you or not, I will be taking the former.'

Balfour's face changed. It was more than a look of annoyance. It shifted shape, his eyes narrowing, his mouth constricting. He stood up and moved towards Lynch, thrusting his hands onto his throat so Lynch's head was pushed back. 'Listen, you sad little man. If I'd had my way you'd have been eliminated long ago. If you think there'll ever be a time where you have the chance to do anything to me, you're sorely mistaken.'

Lynch wrinkled his nose, trying not to smell the garlic on the man's breath. He allowed Balfour's fingers to push into his windpipe without fear. Balfour had shown his weakness by the attack, had confirmed to Lynch that he was not the one in control.

Balfour withdrew his hand, his face snapping back to a

polished façade of civility. 'Enjoy the rest of the journey,' he said, disappearing through the hidden door.

The two fake Rangers kept guard on him as the train progressed. 'Are you one of them or just the hired help?' asked Lynch, to be met with silence again.

Lynch glanced outside the panoramic windows that framed the exterior in perfect clarity. The glass took up most of the side of the train. If he concentrated, the view was so unobstructed that Lynch felt as if he was floating through the desert scenery. The hidden door slid open once more tearing him from the illusion. A statuesque woman entered the carriage carrying a tray of drinks, her clothes wrapped so tightly against her body that they acted as a second skin, leaving little to the imagination. Lynch noticed the hypnotic effect she had on the two Rangers as she moved towards him. 'Mr Lynch, I hope you're enjoying the journey,' said the woman, breathy as if she was doing her best Marilyn Monroe impression.

'I'm having a great time,' said Lynch.

The woman smiled. Lynch tried to guess how old she was but couldn't work it out. Her skin was flawless. As she beamed her perfect smile, there was no sign of any creases. Only her eyes gave her away. They looked straight through him, her pupils dilated. Lynch presumed she was one of Balfour's prisoners, permanently drugged, forever compliant. 'Please take a drink,' said the woman, unscrewing a bottle of mineral water.

He didn't want to disappoint the woman but he didn't want anything she was offering. 'Sorry, not thirsty.'

The woman smiled but held her ground as if not fully understanding what he was saying. 'Please,' she said, her face still formed into a perfect smile. Her beauty was hard to look at, harder still considering why she was there. Lynch turned his mind back to the hundreds of cases he'd studied in the past, the children young and old who'd disappeared near the railroad lines. Was she one of them? Was Daniel suffering a similar fate somewhere aboard this train? The last thought shook any compassion from him. 'No,' he shouted.

The woman moved aside as the obese Ranger barged past her. 'There is an easy way to take the drink. And there is a much harder way. Now drink up.'

The woman tipped the bottle towards his lips. Lynch let the liquid fall into his mouth before turning and spitting it into the face of the obese Ranger. The man groaned and from behind him, Lynch felt the heavy blow of something hard on the back of his head. The impact caused his eyes to blur and the last thing he saw before slipping out of consciousness was the grinning face of the obese Ranger - contorted in his blurred vision to something monstrous -smiling before aiming his fist towards him at alarming speed.

34

Rose was back at headquarters in San Antonio when her phone beeped. It was the burner phone she used to communicate with Lynch and she'd forgotten to put it on silent. It vibrated in her pants pocket, the chiming sound echoing in the emptiness of the incident room.

Yesterday's visit to Dallas had been a burn out and McBride had been sulking with her ever since. No one wanted to discuss Balfour with them. Rose's theory that Balfour's former colleagues were more likely to talk to them face to face had been misjudged. The incident at the compound was not the secret that she'd imagined, and neither was Balfour's disappearance. No one would talk to them in case they incriminated themselves. McBride had pointed out that it was something they could have discovered without the inconvenience of travelling halfway across the state but had said very little to her since.

The small screen displayed two messages and she recognized the number as Lynch's burner phone, the one she'd planted with a tracker chip. She'd been following his progress on her tracking app since that morning, soon discovering that he was either on, or closely tracking the seven am train from San Antonio to Chicago.

She clicked on the message icon on the burner phone. If she was surprised by the first message, she was stunned by the second. Checking her smartphone, she confirmed that Lynch's estimated location matched the location on his tracking device. The first message had given her little other information other than he'd taken a train to St Louis. The tracker showed he was still in East Texas between Marshall and Texarkana.

The second message was rushed. It read:

They are going to take me. Razinski said to me, Mallard

EVEN FOR LYNCH that took some beating. Being taken by the Railroad on a train. The tracking device was stationary and she feared he'd destroyed the phone and her only way of tracking him. She called the phone, unsurprised that it went straight to voicemail. If someone had come for him, then Lynch would have jettisoned it. She ran her hand through her hair, as a thousand thoughts rushed her, when her tracking device beeped again. Lynch's second tracking device, the one she'd given him at the hotel, had just been activated. The beeping signal matched the other tracking device.

McBride was sitting at a table in the office, his back to her. Rose placed the burner phone on the table next to McBride's sunglasses and called his name.

'Have I just woken in the nineties?' asked McBride, staring at the chunky cell phone.

'It keeps me in contact with Lynch,' said Rose, sitting down next to him.

'I see.'

'Take a look at the messages.'

'Look, if you've got something going on with this guy just leave me out of it.'

'Just look at them, McBride.'

McBride feigned a look of hurt surprise before picking up the phone. Puffing out his cheeks, he said, 'We know he caught a train.'

'Look at the second message'

McBride was unfazed by the next message. 'How would they 'take him' if he was on the train? Doesn't that trip take a number of hours?'

'The train is due in Texarkana in forty minutes. It's not supposed to stop at his current location.'

'You think they're taking him from the train?'

Rose didn't know anything at that moment, her mind was working overtime trying to work out what the hell was going on. 'You come across anyone called Mallard?' she asked.

McBride shook his head.

Mallard could be FBI or be protected somehow by someone within the Bureau. They needed to access Lynch's files.

'What did that message mean?' asked McBride.

Rose came clean. 'Lynch spoke to Razinski before we left the compound. Razinski said something to him which he refused to share.'

'Mallard?'

'I guess so.'

McBride rubbed the bridge of his nose. 'So Lynch has been conducting a one man search for this Mallard all this time.'

'He must have been in danger to have shared that by text.'

'He must have been desperate to have listened to a degenerate like Razinski.'

'Lynch isn't stupid, McBride. He wouldn't have believed him without good reason.'

'He may not be stupid but he's deluded, or at least blinkered. He would believe anything if he thought it would bring back his son.'

Rose's pulse quickened. She felt compelled to defend Lynch even though McBride's words were fair. 'Remember that Lynch was the first to investigate the Railroad when no one even believed in their existence. Maybe if we'd listened to him then we wouldn't be in this situation now.'

McBride shook his head, wincing as he drank his coffee. 'What's next?'

'We obviously need to find out who Mallard is and we need someone to meet that train,' she said, trying to find the timetable online. 'It gets into St Louis tomorrow morning.'

'That gives us a bit more time, I guess. I'll call the St Louis field office now.'

'I need to be there,' said Rose.

'Not another road trip, Rose. Yesterday killed me.'

'I'll fly there.'

McBride contemplated his coffee before replying. He sat awkwardly as if his neck was stiff. 'You're going to need to tell Miller and Roberts about the current situation. You might be able to use one of the helicopters.'

'I guess they'd find that out soon enough anyway.'

'Maybe so, but I don't want to be the one telling them.'

'My hero.'

McBride grinned but didn't respond.

IN THE EARLY HOURS, Rose took off in a Bell 407 helicopter from the rooftop of the San Antonio field office. Miller had reluctantly agreed with the caveat that Lynch had to be taken in for questioning once the train arrived.

After checking with the rail authorities, Rose discovered that his train had remained stationary for less than half an hour, yet both tracking devices showed that Lynch hadn't moved in the hours since he'd sent his text; the devices had either failed or been destroyed, but Rose still checked her app every few minutes.

She'd left McBride at headquarters, searching Lynch's files for a mention of Mallard. She used the journey to update her case notes, strategically omitting certain aspects of Lynch's personal investigation. It was only days since the attack at the compound, but it felt like a lifetime ago. Her memory of the incident was tempered by the video footage she'd viewed and the subsequent development, in particular the photos of Lynch's son.

Since joining the Bureau, the thought of having children had hardly occurred to her. She'd had a couple of semi-serious relationships in that time but hadn't met anyone she'd consider sharing a life with. To many, her sister in particular, this was an admission of failure, but Rose was content with her life. Dating an FBI agent was a novelty for most men; a novelty that soon wore off once they understood the full extent of her work and her tunnel-vision approach to it. Rose had never settled for second best in her work, and certainly wouldn't do so in a partner, but she didn't need to have had a child to understand what Lynch was going through. She had a niece and nephew via Abigail, whom she loved as unconditionally as any parent.

'Yes, but you can hand them back,' Abigail would say to her, not meaning to be cruel.

She'd seen Lynch's determination a number of times during cases. Parents were always the last to give in, to accept the inevitable. She'd dealt with enough missing children cases, had seen first hand the devastation of not knowing, of forever wondering what had happened to a loved one.

A team were waiting for her at the St Louis field office. They rushed her to the back of a car, her companion an impossibly young blonde woman who introduced herself as Agent Madeline Gray. 'We have a team ready at the train station,' said the woman, as the car meandered through the St Louis traffic.

They reached the station with five minutes to spare. A small SWAT team surrounded the platform where Lynch was due to arrive. 'Slight overkill,' said Rose.

Gray shrugged her shoulders. 'Orders from your SAC.'

'Figures.'

As the train pulled into the platform, the SWAT team made their way onto the platform. 'That's one way to put the frighteners on the passengers,' said Rose, as she followed.

The train stopped, and SWAT team members boarded the train. Rose followed Gray onto the first carriage, and informed all the passengers to stay in their seats. She made her way down the corridors through business class, to the cramped carriages of standard, all the time expecting to see Lynch.

'He'd reserved a private cabin,' said Gray, joining her. She was accompanied by one of the train's crew, a tall woman in a smart grey dress.

Rose showed the woman a picture of Lynch. 'Did this man board the train?' she asked.

'Yes, Mr Lynch. He was the one who was...'

'Who was what?' said Rose, to the agitated crew member.

'Who was taken,' said the woman, lowering her voice as if it was a secret.

Rose blinked at the woman, speechless, as one of the SWAT team approached her.

'Ma'am, I think you should talk to this gentleman,' he said, pointing to a passenger sitting in the viewing compartment. The man was wearing denim jeans and a black t-shirt, his face decorated with a goatee beard. 'Says he saw Lynch,' said the SWAT member, standing aside to allow her to sit.

'You saw this man?' said Rose, showing the man a picture of Lynch after introducing herself.

'Yes, he was sitting down there,' said the man, pointing to the far end of the carriage.

'When did he get on?'

'He was already on the train when I got on at Austin.'

'So where is he now?'

'They took him.'

'Who took him, sir?'

'I thought you'd know. The Rangers took him when we stopped.'

The black t-shirt man's name was Preston Bullard, a tech consultant visiting one of his clients in St Louis. Rose instructed the SWAT team to evacuate the carriage so she was alone with the man.

'Why did you take the train? Wouldn't it have been easier to fly?' she asked the goatee-bearded man who was inexplicably relaxed considering recent events.

'I like trains,' said Bullard. 'I have my own bed and I spend a big part of the journey working and I can bill hours for that.'

Rose stared at him.

The man smiled. 'You got me. I'm scared to fly.'

'So, tell me again, what happened when the train stopped?'

'As I said, the Rangers came on board the train. They asked for all foreign citizens to make their way down to the canteen carriage. I'd seen it happen before so it wasn't a shock to me.'

'Did anyone from this carriage leave?'

'Yeah, there was some girl. She looked like a backpacker.'

'So this girl left the carriage and then came back?'

'Yep. She must have had all her documentation up to date,' said Bullard, who appeared to be enjoying the interrogation.

'And this man? The man you said the Rangers took.'

'Well, I wasn't paying much attention but I did notice he must have left the carriage at some point as his seat was empty for some time.'

Rose nodded, not answering, prompting the man to speak further.

'To be honest, I just got on with my work. But I noticed about five minutes after the train stopped that the man returned to his seat over there.'

'Did he look shaken in anyway?'

'Honestly, I didn't pay him that much attention. But he looked fine to me.'

'Which seat did he sit at?'

'That far one by the door,' said Bullard, pointing.

'So, tell me what happened when the Rangers returned to your carriage.'

'There were two of them. One was quite heavy set. I noticed they were both carrying guns. That always spooks me. Initially, they walked up to the seat three tables down.' Bullard pointed to the other end of the train. 'They stopped there and conferred. I had my earphones on. I turned down the volume to try and hear but they were whispering. It was as if they expected someone to be in those seats.'

'And then what happened?'

'The younger guy, who was much slimmer, spotted your man in the seat and pointed to him.'

'And did 'my man' do anything?'

'It all got a bit dramatic if I'm to be honest. The two Rangers ran down the carriage and they arrested the guy.'

'And did he put up a fight?'

'Not that I was aware of. Before I knew it they'd hand-cuffed him and were leading him out.'

'Did you see where they took him?'

'No, I stayed in my seat. I'm sure if you asked some of the others in the carriage they'd tell you. They were glued to the window like children at the zoo but I'd lost interest. I imagine they put him on the second train.'

Rose stopped. She stared at the man who'd somehow forgotten to mention this new piece of evidence.

'Second train?' she asked.

'Yes, I presume that's where the Rangers had come from. After we stopped, this second train pulled up. It was quite intriguing actually.'

'Intriguing?' asked Rose, shaking her head, incredulous that the man had forgotten to mention the arrival of this second train.

'Yes. Do you guys have your own private trains?'

'What?' said Rose.

'Well, I've never seen anything like it before and I take the train all the time. The carriages were a different shape and size to your normal run of the mill Amtrak services.'

'In what way?'

The man played with a wedding ring on his left hand, moving it up and down on his finger.

'Well, it was sort of futuristic, if you know what I mean?'

'No, I don't,' said Rose.

'The carriages were like pieces of art. They didn't have

any edges. They were beautifully crafted; chrome, with large blacked out windows.'

'Did you notice any insignia on them?'

The man slipped his wedding ring back on.

'No, as I said, I didn't pay much attention but if you ask some of the others, I'm sure they'd be able to tell you something.'

THE STEWARDESS and the other passengers on the train verified the story. Rose detained Bullard until his background had been fully checked. Next she spoke to the train's engineer, Will Koeman. Koeman verified the story about the Rangers and the mystery train. 'I got the call from the NOC twenty minutes before we stopped,' he said.

'NOC?'

'National Operation Centre.'

'Anything unusual in that?'

Koeman pursed his lips. 'It happens. Not for some time though. With the commuter trains it's not such an issue. If I was hauling freight it would be a different matter. It would take an age to get the thing up and running again.'

'This other train. You ever see anything like that?'

'It was a new one on me. One thing struck me as odd was the lack of an engine number. Maybe it was hidden beneath all that shiny chrome. The NOC will have all the details.'

Rose thanked the engineer before making some calls concerning this mysterious second train. She was surprised to discover that it was possible to use private trains on the railroad system, though her initial set of calls to the NOC had yet to resolve what this particular train was and who, or what organization, it belonged to.

She left the details of that to Gray and called McBride. She told him about the Rangers and Lynch, and shook her head as he began laughing.

'What's so funny, McBride?'

'It just gets better and better. So we're now on the lookout for some sort of ghost train,' he said.

'It's not a ghost train. Apparently these private vehicles exist. It's a different world, I tell you. How is the research going on Mallard?'

'I may have something positive for you there. Although it sounds as far fetched as this ghost train of yours.'

'Just tell me, McBride.'

'There's not that much in Lynch's notes, but there is mention of some hot-shot socialite who goes by the name Wilberforce Mallard. Wilberforce Mallard the Sixth, believe it or not; ex-trust fund baby, now in his fifties. Extremely wealthy, and I mean extremely. Trouble is he stays out of the public eye. He's fifty-two but the last official picture of him on record is of him as a thirty-one year old.'

'So, what does the guy do? Doesn't he work?'

'These sorts of people don't have to work. I'm doing more research but the guy has fingers in everything. Thousands of investments spread throughout every imaginable industry. I started trying to make contact but it's proving nigh on impossible. I'm being passed from department to department, lawyer to lawyer.'

'So, we don't even have a location for him?'

'Not yet, Rose, but I'll get one. The more obvious concern is the link between him and Razinski. I find it impossible to believe that Razinski knew Mallard. I think we may have to face facts that Razinski sent Lynch on a fool's errand.'

'Maybe but he's the only link we have now so we have to

follow it up. Let me know when you've got an address for him. Or, ideally, a meeting arranged.'

'Will do, Boss.'

McBride went silent and Rose closed her eyes waiting for him to vocalize his thoughts.

'So, what are we going to tell Miller about Lynch?' he said, eventually.

'Leave that with me,' said Rose, wondering how she would explain Lynch's abduction

'Don't forget to mention the ghost train,' said McBride.

'Fuck off, McBride,' said Rose hanging up.

THE TRAIN ENGINEER gave her a pinpoint location for the area where the train had stopped. From St Louis, she was taken by helicopter to a stretch of land between Marshall and Texarkana. The area was humid, the only sound the gentle hum of insects and the distant drone of the cars on the interstate.

Rose twisted her neck, severe fatigue having set in following the helicopter rides. Although it was unlikely she would discover anything worthwhile here, it felt important to attend. A distant part of her hoped she would find Lynch's burner phone, or a further note from him. She stood by the tracks, picturing the two trains, trying to make sense of the fantastical description of McBride's so-called ghost rain.

Rose was joined by Captain Westcott from the local Rangers department. He stood in the background, continually rubbing the back of his head as if he had a skin infection. Westcott oscillated between embarrassment and acute rage that someone had impersonated officers from his department. Rose felt for the man, but the last thing she needed was another head of department to worry about.

'What is the normal procedure? The train driver knows when you're due to stop?' she asked him.

'Yes, Ma'am. We liaise with the National Operations Centre, the NOC, in Fort Worth. They notify the engineer to stop the train at a specific location. We have to liaise with the NOC for safety reasons. We only do it every few months.'

'We've checked with the NOC and no call was made.'

'Apparently not, Ma'am.'

'Could anyone from your department get straight through to the driver?'

Westcott lowered his eyes. 'Nope.'

'Okay, when your men enter the train what is the procedure?'

'The train guards will sometimes ask for ID but rarely. Why would they try to stop two armed Rangers?'

'Fair point.'

'Do you think anyone from your side could have tipped the assailants off?' asked Rose.

'Now listen here, Missy.'

'Save it,' said Rose, holding up her hand. 'You won't be the only force to have suffered the effects of an insider, if we understand each other.'

Westcott grunted. 'We have a few bad apples, but I refuse to believe any of them would be prepared to stoop this low.'

There was the doubt in the Ranger's eyes, as if he was appreciating the full extent of the day's events for the first time. Rose showed him images of the Railroad tattoos on her phone. 'You need to check your whole team, including civilians, for this. With immediate effect.'

'And if we find anything?'

'Treat with extreme caution and let me know.'

36

It was close to midnight by the time Rose reached her hotel room in Marshall. The transient nature of her job didn't usually bother her but the constant change of scenery had been getting her down of late. The interior of the various hotel rooms she found herself in over the years had blurred into one. As she switched on the television set and poured herself a miniscule shot of gin from the mini-bar, she realized she could be anywhere in the country.

The search for an informer within the Rangers had so far proved unsuccessful. Captain Westcott was proving to be a far from willing partner, which had prompted her to start an investigation into the man himself.

Rose didn't expect much. Whatever organization they were dealing with was clearly at least two steps ahead of them. They wouldn't be so unprofessional as to leave one of their own in danger.

Somehow, they'd managed to kidnap Lynch in broad daylight.

McBride's ghost train was beginning to appear to be just

that. So far, all enquiries had turned up blank. The NOC had no record of the second train and claimed it would be impossible for such a train to go undetected. Yet Rose had over a hundred passengers who swore they'd seen this second train, including the engineer on the Texas Eagle.

Rose collapsed on the armchair and tried to focus on the banalities being played out on the television screen. The task proved impossible. Every few minutes her attention would turn to her iPad and the installed app tracking Lynch's whereabouts. She remembered the adage that a watched phone never rang but still her heart skipped a beat every time she glanced at the screen. The two tracking devices were inactive red dots on the screen, the last known coordinates at the location where Lynch was taken. The device Lynch activated had worked for four minutes and twenty-eight seconds. Long enough for Lynch to have been taken from the train and for the device to have been destroyed. It was the obvious explanation but not the only one. It was possible to mask GPS signals and for Lynch to still have either device on his person. Rose would be notified if either device was reactivated but still couldn't look away from the screen.

With a sigh Rose pushed herself up and walked to the mini bar. She glanced through the contents, satisfied there was enough alcohol within to send her to oblivion. She picked up a second small bottle of gin, the glass cold on her skin, and weighed it in her hands. She rarely gave in to such instincts but was so overwhelmed with exhaustion that it felt like a logical move. She was about to unscrew the top when the sound of her mobile phone rescued her.

Abigail's name flashed on the screen like a danger warning. Guilt gnawed at Rose as she considered not answering. Not because she didn't want to speak to her sister, but because she feared what she had to say. She answered on the fifth ring. 'Hi Abi,' she said, trying to hide the mounting emotion in her voice.

Her sister didn't answer.

'Abi?' said Rose, forcing her phone against her ear, a sense of desperation in her voice.

'Abi,' she repeated, a panic she wasn't used to spreading through her body, her normal rational mind destroyed by the silence on the other side of the line.

From nowhere, a blast of sound reached her followed by the sound of her sister crying.

'Oh, Abi, you scared me,' said Rose, vaguely aware that she too was crying. 'What's happened?'

Rose allowed her sister time. She listened to her crying, desperate to comfort her younger sibling but not knowing how. Eventually she cried herself out and between sobs said, 'It's Mom. They're considering turning off her life support machine.'

Phone in hand, Rose collapsed back on the armchair once more. She felt as if she'd been punched in the gut. The news was not surprising - she'd been expecting the call ever since she'd left Abigail at the hospital - but part of her thought this day would never come. Her subconscious hope had been that life at the hospital could continue without her, that if she didn't worry too much than the worst couldn't happen, that her mother would never die.

'Sandra? You still there?'

'Sorry, Abi. I...'

'You don't need to say anything.'

'What exactly did they say?'

'She's not coming back, Rose,' said Abi, with a certainty that alarmed Rose.

'Is there no one else we can speak to. A second opinion.'

'It's time, Sandra. They're going to run some more tests over the next few days but I can tell it's just a formality. She's not responding to anything, and with her condition...'

Rose didn't want to argue. Abigail was the one who'd looked after her mother over the last few years and she respected her judgment. They spent the next hour reminiscing, sharing tales. The trips they'd made as young girls to the coast, the scent of their mother's only perfume as she'd held them close. Rose recounted the one and only time her mother had got drunk in their presence. Rose had been nineteen at the time and they'd been celebrating their mother's birthday. Sad laughter came from both of them as they recalled her swearing at the waiter at a local restaurant who she'd believed had given her the wrong drink.

'What was it she called him again?' said Rose.

'A bucking fastard.'

Rose's laughter turned once again to tears as the enormity of losing her mother rushed her once more. 'When are they going to do it?' she said.

'It's our decision. We need to sign the consent forms. I'll let you know, Sandra,' said Abigail.

'I'm sorry you're going through this alone, Abi. I'm sorry I haven't been a better sister...Or daughter.'

'Don't be ridiculous, Sandra. You know I love you.'

Rose struggled to speak. 'I love you too, Abi,' she said eventually, her voice choked with tears.

UNABLE TO SLEEP, Rose spent the rest of the evening searching for details on Mallard. McBride had sent over Lynch's notes. As McBride suggested, Mallard was something of an enigma. She was unable to find any further photos of the man save the one from twenty years ago. He'd been a handsome man then, a strong jawline and an effortless style that was an obvious by-product of his extreme wealth. The picture had been taken with a high-powered lens, Mallard leaving an apartment block in New York seemingly unaware someone was photographing him. Then nothing.

There was no credit for the photograph and Rose wondered why and how it had been taken. McBride's report was piecemeal. Wilberforce Mallard The Sixth was the sole heir of the Mallard fortune and appeared to have no immediate or extended family. She scrolled through pages and pages of company names where it was believed Mallard had some sort of interest. It was impossible to know for sure without trying to audit him. Such a procedure would take an age, and it was unlikely they would be given permission to audit the man. All they had to go on was Lynch's frantic text, and the dying word of Razinski.

Rose was about to give in for the night when she spotted a name she remembered. One of Mallard's companies had a controlling interest in Hanning Industries. The name sounded familiar. Rose searched through her notes confirming that Edward Gunn, Razinski's first victim, had been working for the company at the time of his death.

She called McBride.

'You do know what time it is, don't you?' said McBride.

'You were asleep, I suppose?'

'That's not the point.'

'We should go tomorrow,' said Rose, ignoring McBride who sounded like he'd failed to resist the temptation of his own mini-bar.

'You've seen the list of companies Mallard has an interest in?'

'Yes, but this is the first one which links Mallard and Gunn, and thus Razinski.'

'Thus?'

'Fuck off, McBride. I'll see you back in San Antonio first thing.'

37

Lynch's uneasy sleep was punctuated with images and senses rather than dreams. He was descending the world surrounding him insubstantial, colored in fiery shades, to the extent it was almost liquid.

It was a relief to wake to find he was still sitting on a leather sofa. He blinked open his heavy eyes and realized he was no longer on a train. He was in a large open space, the curved walls and ceiling of which were painted white and interspersed with numerous spotlights lighting the area to an unnatural degree. The interior gave the place a dated futuristic feel. It reminded Lynch of sci-fi movies he'd watched in the eighties, the clean white surfaces suggesting a purity and hospital-like cleanliness, the effect of which was destroyed by the five armed guards dotting around the room dressed head to toe in black.

Lynch tried to move, remembering the drink he'd refused on the train that had probably been fed into his system. It was only then that he realized he was no longer handcuffed; he tried to stand up, only for his legs to betray him. Whatever poison they'd forced into him was still travelling through his bloodstream. His limbs were heavy and ineffectual as if he was drunk or severely hung-over. His head pounded and he reached for the tenderness on his skull where the fake Ranger had struck him. Falling back down on the sofa, he studied the armed guards searching for the obese Ranger but the guards were all new to him, each lean and poised for movement.

Ghost-like, the woman from the train appeared next to him. 'Rest, Mr Lynch,' she cooed.

Lynch had little option but to take her advice allowing the softness of the leather to envelop him, the material adjusting to the shape and movement of his body as if it was made just for him. 'Where am I?' he said, surprised by his rasping voice.

'Here, drink this,' said the woman, as picture-perfect as the last time he'd seen her.

Before him was an antique china tea set, steam billowing through the spout of a pot painted with elaborate swirls depicting the ancient east. 'You must think I'm stupid,' he said.

'Please accept my sincere apologies for what transpired on the train. The guard who struck you has been dealt with.'

Lynch wondered what the full extent of 'dealt with' meant. 'I don't care about that coward's sucker punch. I was thinking more of the poison you forced down my throat.'

'A mere sedative,' said the woman, with a sympathetic look. 'There is nothing but hot sweet tea in this pot. May I?' she said, filling his cup.

A sweet aroma filled the room. Lynch failed to place the smell, something reminiscent of wild flowers and cinnamon. The woman filled a second cup and, savoring the aroma, drank the liquid. 'If we'd wanted to drug you we could have done it at any time. Please, Mr Lynch, for me.'

The cadence of the woman's speech reminded him of the telephone conversations he'd had with the man he believed to be the Controller. She spoke as if every word was considered, the delivery slow and deliberate. He wasn't convinced by the display of her taking the tea but her words made sense. Why drug him again when they could have upped his dose at any time?

He picked up the cup noticing hints of other smells from the hot liquid, cinnamon and the faintest scent of ginger. If he'd been alone with the woman he would have thrown the tea in her face and followed the action by bringing the china cup hard down on her head, but the armed guards were watching. The other option would be to take the woman captive but he imagined her life was expendable. Instead, he continued drinking surprised at how dehydrated he'd become and studied the area biding his time to strike.

'Where are we?' he asked the woman, who'd sat down next to him.

'Somewhere special,' she said, her face painted with a fixed smile.

'Do you have a name?'

'You can call me Clarissa.'

'Clarissa. Are you one of them, or are you a prisoner too?'

Lynch studied Clarissa's face as she failed to answer. Behind her mask of beauty, he noticed the fear in her eyes. Her pupils were still diluted which suggested she was drugged, though her speech and demeanor were normal. She remained focused on him, not once glancing at the guards dotted around the circular room. 'All will become clear,' she said eventually, as if the response had just been fed to her in an earpiece.

Lynch reminded himself that these were the people who'd taken his son, who were responsible for the thousands of people who'd vanished by the tracks and for the mass slaughter at the compound. Could Clarissa really be one of them? Would the removal of her clothes reveal hidden track tattoos like the others? 'Did you know Razinski?' he said, trying to surprise her into revealing something.

'All will become clear,' she said, repeating her new mantra.

'What about Mallard?'

Clarissa rose from her seat with a silent grace. 'Please, drink your tea. Someone will be with you shortly,' she said, gliding across the circular room and exiting through a set of sliding doors integrated into the curved walls.

At no time did any of the guards change focus as she made her exit. Lynch was impressed by their professionalism. He wanted to check that the tracker device was still inside the hem of his jeans but it was impossible without drawing attention from the men. He hoped that somewhere Sandra Rose was reading his signal and tracking his location. It was possible he'd inadvertently infiltrated the lair of the phantom organization but he wasn't about to take that as granted. The Railroad had avoided detection for so long that it was highly unlikely they would let their guard down so easily.

He drank more tea and waited. He thought about Sally and Rob, about Rose and Daniel. After all these years of trying to find Daniel he was on the threshold. So why did he feel deflated?

He was distracted from his thoughts by the opening of the sliding doors through which a procession of people entered.

The first was a heavily-muscled man with long blond hair. He was wearing a wife beater and every inch of the visible skin on his arms and neck was decorated with the crude marks of the Railroad organization. Lynch estimated there were hundreds of tracks on the man's arms and shuddered to think what he'd done to gain them. Two nondescript men followed, if they had tattoos they were covered by the tailored shirts and light-colored summer jackets they wore. Next was an overweight woman in her late fifties, her crumpled face decorated with layers of makeup that only served to make her look older. The last to enter the room was Balfour. Lynch saw the triumph on the man's face and promised he would one day rid the man of the look.

'Lynch, good to see you again,' said Balfour, with no hint of irony. 'May I?' he added, taking a seat next to him.

Lynch noticed a change of attention in the guards as Balfour sat. They were more on edge than they'd been when Clarissa had sat next to him. Did they think it more likely that Lynch would attack the former agent? Or did they consider Balfour more valuable than the glamorous waitress?

'What's with all the theatrics, and the freak show?' asked Lynch.

'You're in the presence of greatness,' said Balfour.

Lynch glanced at Balfour's four companions who milled around the circular room with a restlessness he shared. 'Jesus, you are deluded. So this is all your work?'

BALFOUR SIGHED as if Lynch had somehow insulted him. 'This is the inner sanctum. The people in this room dictate your future, and that of your son's.'

Lynch lent towards Balfour at the mention of Daniel,

each of the guards lifting their automatic rifles in his direction. 'When this is done, Balfour, I will take your life and that's a promise.'

Balfour smirked. 'If I had my way, Lynch, we would have eliminated you long ago but others have a higher opinion of you than I do.'

'So am I ever going to meet this organ grinder or do I have to spend my life speaking to his monkeys?' said Lynch, repeating the phrase that had antagonized Balfour before.

'You have a chance, Lynch. Personally, I hope you blow it but you have a chance,' said Balfour, through clenched teeth. He rose to his feet before Lynch had time to respond and began pacing the room like the others.

An air of anticipation filled the area. Lynch sensed it from the guards and the five people Balfour had described as belonging to the inner sanctum. The anticipation was tinged with a nervousness that reminded Lynch of a class of unruly kids waiting for a head teacher.

A shaft of light darted down from the glass ceiling, illuminating a patch of the circular floor and for a brief second the room lost its sense of mystery. It became just a room, subject to the elements and the physical world. It was no longer imposing, and the people within it lost their menace

As if in response to the intrusion of the lights, the doors slid open and everyone except for Lynch fell to attention. Clarissa shimmied into the room, gliding across the floor as if floating on air.

Behind her, a huge smile etched onto his face, was someone Lynch thought he would never see.

38

If McBride was hung over then he was doing a good job of hiding it. The sunglasses helped. Though woefully out of place in the grey light of the early morning, they made him unreadable. He smiled at Rose as she clambered into the passenger seat of his Bureau issued car. He was clean-shaven and she didn't lean close enough to check if the feint waft of aftershave masked the smell of alcohol.

'Good night?' asked McBride, before she had time to speak.

Rose had slept fitfully, her thoughts alternating between her mother, sister, and Lynch. 'I've slept better,' she said.

'Me too. I've been trying to find out more about Mallard but haven't got any further. After your call I did some more research on Hanning Industries. From what I can ascertain, Mallard's portfolio includes a fifty-five per cent controlling interest in the company which would be a significant chunk of change for most people, but nothing for someone of Mallard's ilk.'

'Does his name appear on any of the documentation?'

'No, he's not a member of the board and doesn't person-ally appear as a shareholder, but when you dig further you see the links. Companies owning companies, with Mallard somewhere at the heart. All perfectly legal but designed to keep Mallard himself at arm's length.'

'I presume this is all managed for him?' asked Rose.

'He must have a small army working for him. I can't imagine he gets involved in the day-to-day stuff. Why the hell would he? I'd be surprised if he's worked a day in his life. I can't even imagine that kind of wealth.'

'Some things money can't buy, McBride.'

'It's what it can buy that scares me.'

Hanning Industries was situated on private land twenty miles outside of Houston. The complex was built over two hundred acres and the gated entrance reminded Rose of the FBI compound where she'd fled with Lynch. McBride had secured a meeting with the company's CEO, Lyle Niven, for that morning. Rose checked her iPad hoping for a flicker of activity on Lynch's tracking app, as a heavyset man in a blue uniform, who'd gleefully shared with them his previous experience as a cop, checked their credentials.

'You're free to go through, Agents,' he said, returning to the car ten minutes later. 'Park in sector one, space seventy-two.'

'Thank you ever so much,' said McBride, with such heavy irony that Rose was forced to smile.

The parking space was right outside a vast sprawling building painted a perfect white. Panoramic folding doors shifted apart as they made their way through the early morning sunshine into the building's foyer where a pencil-thin man with a covering of sandy-colored hair greeted them.

'Special Agent McBride and Special Agent Rose. My

name is James Rawlings. I am Mr Niven's personal assistant. Please follow me.'

The interior of the building had a surprisingly industrial feel in comparison to the pristine façade of the outside. 'Our research and development site,' said Rawlings, as if needing to explain.

'What do you research and develop?' asked McBride, as Rawlings led them through a labyrinth of corridors.

'We are effectively a construction company but we work in many arenas. In this department, we could be testing the durability of the smallest nuts and bolts to examining the integrity of immense structures such as bridges.'

'And railroads?' said Rose.

'We have worked on numerous railroad projects,' said Rawlings, not losing step or turning back to make eye contact.

The corridors were wide and high ceilinged. Despite the whirring air conditioning, Rose felt particles of dust in the air that she brushed from her hair and skin.

After what felt like an extended time, long enough to have walked the perimeter of the building at least once, Rawlings stopped outside a service elevator.

'Mr Niven is waiting upstairs,' said Rawlings.

The elevator took them to a glass cube-shaped room looking down on a sprawling factory where most of the work was being conducted by robotic machinery.

'Quite something, isn't it? I'm Lyle Niven,' said a smiling man, surveying the scene below him. Niven was in his late seventies, a neat shock of white hair matched by the trimmed beard on his face. He walked over to shake hands first with Rose, then McBride.

'Special Agent Sandra Rose and Special Agent McBride,' said Rose.

'A pleasure,' said Niven, the smile not once leaving his face. 'May I get you something to drink? You've had a fair journey.'

'Coffee would be wonderful,' said Rose.

Niven was a genial host. He poured them both coffee from an antique silver pot and asked them about their journey. 'So I imagine it's time we got to the point?' he said, after they'd had the first sip of coffee.

'Yes thank you for your time,' said Rose. 'We're here to discuss one of your former employees, Edward Gunn.'

Niven frowned. 'This is not the first time I've had the privilege of speaking to someone from your organization regarding Mr Gunn. I thought we'd put that unfortunate business behind us by now, but obviously not.'

Behind Niven's front of geniality, Rose sensed the steely personality that would have propelled Niven to such a lofty position. She wondered how long the politeness would last. 'There have been some new developments.'

'We only buried that poor family last week,' said Niven. 'What possible developments could there have been? Furthermore I was under the impression that you had caught the man responsible?'

'I'm afraid we're unable to confirm or deny that,' said Rose. 'We need to ask you some questions about the setup of your organization.'

Niven frowned, affecting a quizzical look. There was a hint of amusement to the gesture. 'You realize we're a publicly owned company,' said Niven. 'Any information you wish to know could be found quite easily. I imagine you already have all the information you need.'

'You are aware of the company shareholder structure,' said McBride.

'No, sir, I am the mere Chief Executive of Hanning Industries. How the hell would I know something as insignificant as the share structure of my own company?' replied Niven, all sense of civility fading.

So this was the point of no return. Niven was no longer humoring them. McBride's question had been purposely obtuse and it had the desired effect. 'Excuse my colleague,' said Rose. 'We do have something more specific to ask you.'

'Then please do,' said Niven, the redness in his cheeks a stark contrast to the whiteness of his beard.

'Could you tell me who has the controlling interest in Hanning industries?' asked McBride.

'Jesus Christ, why don't you just get to the point?' said Niven, who had clearly taken a dislike to McBride. 'We both know Barker Price Inc. has a fifty-five per cent share of the company. A cursory glance through our records would have shown you as much. Now tell me what this is really about?'

'We are trying to find out more details about Barker Price Industries,' said Rose.

'Specifically?'

'Can you tell me what dealings you have with their board members?' asked Rose.

'What dealings? We deal with them all the goddamn time. My assistant can give you the details of all our meetings. I am afraid it won't make for very interesting reading.'

'Who would you usually correspond with?'

'Their lawyers mainly, Agent Rose,' said Niven.

'Have you ever come across someone by the name of Wilberforce Mallard,' asked McBride.

Niven didn't hesitate. 'No, but it is one hell of an interesting name.'

'That it is,' said Rose. We believe Mallard has a controlling interest in Barker Price Inc.'

'There would be records of that,' said Niven. 'He either does or he doesn't.'

'Now you know as well as I do that is not necessarily the case,' said McBride

Niven attention was being drawn elsewhere, to the robotic factory beneath their feet. 'I have to be honest with you both, I'm not sure that I really care. Can you tell me what this has to do with me and Edward Gunn for that matter?'

'Would your company ever have worked on a special project for Barker Price?' asked Rose.

'No. The type of projects we work on are huge in scale. I would know about any projects we would have worked on for them.'

'Could it be possible that Mr Gunn worked on a freelance basis for this corporation?'

'I'm not sure what you're getting at here, Agent Rose. Gunn was a full-time employee of Hanning industries. Even if he'd wanted to, he would never had the time to work freelance.'

'Do you have a list of all the projects Mr Gunn was working on before he left Hanning industries?' said Rose.

Niven laughed 'Mr Gunn's belongings were taken away by your colleagues. All his laptops and files. Don't you people ever talk to each other?'

'So if we did a thorough search of this building we wouldn't find anything belonging to Mr Gunn?' asked McBride, ignoring Niven's scorn.

'If you think you're going to threaten me, Agent McBride,

then you clearly do not understand me very well. I think this concludes our meeting,' said Niven.

'Thank you for your time,' said Rose, shaking hands with Niven who gave her the faintest of nods.

'He was hiding something,' said McBride, once they were back at the car.

'Probably on first name terms with Miller and Roberts.'

'Which reminds me, they want a report. Or at least a sighting of your ghost train.'

'You really are in a foul mood today, McBride, do you know that?'

McBride shrugged, put on his shades, and started the car.

Gunn's personal belongings had been taken to a holding depot back at head quarters. Rose didn't want to face Miller and Roberts anytime soon so she accompanied McBride to the basement storage area.

A disheveled-looking civilian by the name of Hussein was on storage duty and he wasn't taking kindly to the fact. He was busy drinking coffee and reading a magazine. He scowled when Rose asked him for everything he had on the Gunn case and initially didn't even look up.

'By everything what do you mean exactly. We have a room full of stuff. As it is part of an open case, we still have everything we recovered from the house that day,' he said, flicking over a page of his reading material.

Rose shook as she remembered that day. The decapitated bodies arranged in a circle, the terrible stillness of the room, and the ludicrous smile on Razinski's lips.

'We need everything you have from Gunn's work. His laptop and all his paperwork,' said McBride.

'It would have been easier if you'd just said so,' said Hussein, dragging himself from his seat and magazine.

He returned twenty minutes later carrying a box of hard-ware belonging to all members of the Gunn family. "Thought I'd process them now to save me having to go back,' said Hussein, with a smirk.

'These have been analyzed?'

'Of course. Written report is in the file and if you have access you can view on the system.'

McBride took the pile of laptops, e-readers, and tablets from Hussein. 'It's great to see someone who loves his job,' he said.

They both retreated to the offices, Rose stopping to pour some coffee for the long day ahead. When she returned to the incident room her heart sank. McBride was sitting at his desk, one of Gunn's laptops in front of him. Hovering behind him, a look of thunder on her face, was the ASAC, Janice Roberts.

'Special Agent Rose, good of you to make an appearance,' she said. 'I think it's time we had a talk.'

39

It was like a magic trick. No one in the room moved. The guards, the inner sanctum, the glamorous assistant, even Balfour, all stood frozen in awe at the sight of the man standing ten meters in front of Lynch.

His face tilted to one side, eyes wide, his lips formed into a curious smile, everyone in the room held their breath as he began to speak. 'Mr Samuel Lynch. At last. This truly is a pleasure.'

The sound of the man's voice sent reverberations through Lynch's skull. It belonged to the man he'd spoken to on the phone, the man who was always one step ahead of him.

The Controller.

'Mallard,' said Lynch, full of disdain.

'Very good, Mr Lynch.'

Wilberforce Mallard. Lynch had only seen the one photo of the man, taken twenty years ago, but it was definitely him. He'd aged well, his body shape lean and muscular. His face had only a hint of ageing, and his eyes shone with uncanny brightness. 'We could have done this a long time ago, Mallard.'

'Now where would the fun have been in that?' said the Controller, his voice the same soothing baritone Lynch had heard on the phone. 'May I?' he continued, indicating the sofa next to Lynch.

'Be my guest,' said Lynch, mimicking the man's tone.

'Thank you.'

Mallard moved towards him and the room rushed back into focus. For the brief time they'd been talking it had been as if it was only the two of them. The periphery of the room, the sycophants drooling at the sight of their master vanished, and Lynch had existed as if in a bubble. Mallard's movement ignited the room. The guards tensed, raising their guns and pointing them at Lynch.

'I imagine you have some questions for me,' said Mallard, taking a seat less than three meters away from him. Despite everything - the atrocities the man had committed, the fact he'd taken Daniel - being in the man's presence was having a strange comforting effect on him.

'Where's my son?' said Lynch, trying to shake the hold Mallard had over him.

'We will get to that.'

Lynch lent towards Mallard causing one of the guards to rush over and push him back.

'Now, now, Travis, let's be polite to Mr Lynch. He is under a bit of duress. Why doesn't everyone take a break. Travis, you and Roy over there can stay,' said Mallard, gesturing to one of the guards. 'Everyone else, please excuse us for the time being.'

Everyone in the room did as they were asked. Only Balfour lingered receiving a smirk from Lynch in return.

'Please, Mr Balfour,' said Mallard, prompting Balfour to nod and retreat without a word.

'Can I get you anything else to drink?' Mallard asked him.

'Where's my son?'

Mallard nodded. 'You've come such a long way, you deserve some answers, I understand that.'

'Why don't you provide them then?'

'We have all the time in the world,' said Mallard, holding his arms wide as if he could control time itself.

'I'm curious, you're the one responsible for all these disappearances from the railroad lines?'

Mallard turned the palm over his right hand over, shrugging as if being modest.

'You're the Controller?'

Mallard shook his head, once again with false modesty. 'That term was not of my choosing. Why do you think we do that, give silly names for things we don't understand?'

'I understand you very well,' said Lynch. 'You have delusions of grandeur like the rest of them, but you're no different.' Lynch pointed to his head. 'You're off, Mallard. Something up there is wrong. I don't know if you were born that way, or if Daddy didn't love you, but something has messed you up.'

'Maybe. Or perhaps that's the only explanation you can come up with.'

'Tell me then, Mallard. Why do you take these people, these children? How can you justify it?'

Mallard lent closer and the two guards tensed. 'Why should I justify it?'

'Why should you justify it? You're destroying lives. Not only the ones you take, but the ones you leave behind.'

'Is that why you carry that pathetic keepsake with you at all times?'

The drugging had made him sluggish, but Lynch was sure he could reach Mallard before the guards executed him. He took some satisfaction in the fact. If he landed the perfect hit, if he could drive the man's nose into his brain, then it would almost be worth it. Mallard wanted him to react but he did nothing but smile.

'Very good, Mr Lynch,' said Mallard, clapping his hands. 'You realize we could have taken you out anytime we wanted. That's partly what makes us so special. We could have come for you and you could have done nothing about it. Like now in many ways. But I saw something different in you, Samuel. I saw a glimpse of myself.'

'You are out of your fucking mind.'

'Think about it. How many people have you met like you over the years? I mean truly like you? I'm sure you have some stellar colleagues at that old organization of yours, Miss Rose for one, but there's no one really like you. You get things done, Mr Lynch. You are not afraid to use force, to kill if necessary.'

'The difference is I have the backup of the law.'

'The law,' said Mallard, with disdain. 'The law was created by men like us to give us license to control others. I don't adhere to any legal guidelines and your connection to the law is tenuous at best. Think about the two men you held captive before Mr Balfour intervened. What would you have done to them if he hadn't stopped you?'

'I would have found the truth,' said Lynch.

'And would have used whatever force you deemed necessary. Let's not pretend you would have stayed within the law's remit. So how do you justify your actions?'

Lynch thought about the fury driving him that night. Mallard was correct in suggesting he would have killed the two men for information on Daniel. There was no point arguing that his circumstances were different. It was what Mallard expected. Instead he said, 'so what about you? What makes you think you're so special?'

Mallard sat back and clasped his hands. 'It's a good question and most people would be unable to accept my answer. I've hoped for some time that you would under-stand. The rest of them, my esteemed guests you met earlier, thought it was a mistake. They don't believe you are like us.'

'Like us?' said Lynch, content to let Mallard speak.

'I imagine you've dealt with some low-level criminals before. Drug dealers, drug abusers for that matter. Picture some crack head whore off the street. How do you feel when you encounter someone like that? I imagine you think you are from a different species, that you have evolved to some-thing different from her.'

'I don't tend to think in those terms.'

'Maybe not but subconsciously I guarantee you are think-ing, "I am not like her." How many times have you felt like that? I imagine you feel that way about me, about us, that our so called criminality makes us a different species.'

'What are you trying to tell me, Mallard? That you've evolved?' Lynch had encountered such delusions before. There was power in taking another's life, or being in control of another person, and such power bred this type of deluded thinking.

'That's a very simplistic way of looking at it but if you look deep within yourself you would have to accept that you consider yourself better than other people. It's the human condition. Everyone thinks they are special. And some of us are.'

'Why? Because you take innocents and destroy them? Any fucker with a gun can do that.' Lynch was losing patience. He was desperate to hear something about Daniel, and although he understood he needed to humor Mallard there was only so much he could take.

'Now that's not quite true, is it Mr Lynch? Out of everyone, you should appreciate the scope of our operation. You were the first one to really speak of our existence. When all those around you doubted you, you started to link all the disappearances. No "fucker with a gun" could do that, and then Mr Lynch, you are only scratching at the surface.'

'What is it you want, Mallard?'

Mallard moved his face so it was only inches away. It took all of Lynch's strength not to turn away, such was the intensity of the man's gaze. He couldn't remember ever meeting someone with such poise, such absolute confidence. 'I think that's enough for the time being. You have a lot to consider.'

'You abducted my son, you fucking monster,' said Lynch, through gritted teeth, prompting the attention of the two guards.

Mallard got to his feet, and smiling said, 'and this is something you are going to have to move past.'

40

McBride was not invited upstairs to meet Roberts and Miller. Roberts led Rose through the office like an errant child. They took the elevator to the top floor in silence. Rose feared she was about to be taken from the case. She understood the reasons why but wasn't about to easily surrender this late in the day.

'Special Agent Rose, do come in.' Miller stood by the entrance of his office door as if he'd been eavesdropping.

'Sir.'

Miller gestured her over to a set of sofas. 'Please sit,' he said.

Rose sat, Roberts and Miller sitting either side of her. It was an obvious intimidating tactic but Rose refused to be flustered.

'You've had a few interesting days since we last spoke to you,' said Miller.

'Sir.'

'Would you care to tell us what the hell is going on?' said Roberts, taking the bad cop role.

Rose updated them, telling them what they already knew.

'And your recent visit to Hanning Industries?' said Miller.

'News spreads fast. We've just left that building.'

'I know. We just had a very irate Mr Nevin on the phone,' said Roberts, unable to hide the agitation in her voice.

'Some new evidence has come to light,' said Rose, furious at having to justify her investigation.

'The case into the Gunn massacre has been passed on to another team as you well know,' said Roberts.

Rose stared at Roberts wondering what her angle was. She reminded herself that these two people were responsible for hiring Balfour and sacking Lynch. 'We believe there was a potential link between Hanning Industries, Mr Gunn, and the disappearance of former Special Agent Lynch.'

'Which is?' said Miller, with his practiced politician smile.

Rose explained about Wilberforce Mallard. How Lynch had been pursuing the man and Mallard's financial interests in Hanning industries.

'Rather speculative, wouldn't you say, agent Rose?' said Miller.

'It's a starting point,' said Rose.

'What about this Mallard character? Have we managed to speak to him?'

'We're in the process of locating him,' said Rose, sounding more defensive than she wished.

Miller blew out his cheeks as if he had something stuck between his teeth. 'This is a big case, Agent Rose. I'm coming to the opinion that it might be a step too far for you at this stage.'

'With all due respect, sir, that's utter bullshit.'

If she shocked the two senior Agents, they hid it well. 'Obviously I wasn't given the time to investigate the Gunn massacre myself. I have been working tirelessly ever since that day in the compound. Everything that has happened has been out of my control. This is an organization which managed to infiltrate an FBI compound, one of the safest sites in the world.'

Roberts lifted her palm to stop her speaking, Rose having to fight the desire to take the woman's hand and snap it at the wrist. 'What I still can't understand is how Mr Lynch was allowed to escape custody.'

'He was never under arrest,' said Rose, dismissively.

'Don't you think it would have been wise to have brought him in for a more thorough interrogation?' said Roberts, refusing to be diverted from her theme.

'You have spoken to the man since your time at the compound?' said Miller.

'Yes, sir.'

'And did you not think it would be a good idea to bring him in?'

Rose didn't answer.

'The thing is, Agent Rose, it is apparent to us that Samuel Lynch has been waging an investigation of his own. We know for a fact he continued investigating the so-called Railroad long after his dismissal from the Bureau. As he's not around we cannot hold him culpable if you get my meaning.'

Rose understood very well. There was a game of pass the buck going on and she was the last link. She was about to defend herself, to tell them that she needed seventy-two hours to find the man, when there was a knock on the door.

McBride didn't wait for an answer. He breezed through the door apologizing to Miller and Roberts. 'There's been a development on the ghost train situation,' he said.

Although pleased at the interruption, Rose sighed at the ghost train comment.

'Do tell,' said Miller.

'It appears it may not have been a figment of everyone's imagination after all. We've managed to locate it,' said McBride.

'YOU'RE A LIFESAVER, MCBRIDE,' said Rose, once they were in the car-park.

'It's my mission to serve. I thought you might be having a hard time.'

'They need someone to pin this on when it all goes south. And that someone is me.'

'I figured,' said McBride, opening the car door.

'So where is this train?'

McBride twisted his mouth. 'Yes, well I may have exaggerated that aspect. We haven't found the train exactly. We've found someone who can confirm it exists.'

'We've interviewed over a hundred people who confirm it exists,' said Rose.

'Yes, but this is official confirmation.'

McBride started the car and pulled out of the underground parking lot into the midday sunshine. He was already wearing his sunglasses, and Rose took hers from her inside jacket. McBride explained that he'd spoken to an operative who worked at AMTRAK. The man had confirmed that a train listed as Z/YTY243 had been granted access to run on a line close to where Lynch's train had been stopped. It had only just come to light that the signal boxes had been hacked and that the train had managed to move onto the line parallel with Lynch's train.

'Were there any other trains due on that line?' asked Rose.

'Not for another two hours.'

'So where did the train go after that?'

'That is the question. The hacking of the system went further than the signal boxes. There is no trace of where it went next.'

'A train can't just disappear.'

'It can, apparently,' said McBride. There are a number of private railroad lines that are able to gain access to the main network. My contact believes the train could have slipped onto one of these networks without detection, such was the extent of the hacking.'

'Great, so where are we heading now?'

'OTD are looking at the hacking. It's going to prove impossible to search for the missing train as the area is too wide. I found something else though. I was going through Gunn's files and I saw a missing entry. I thought we could discuss that with the lead investigator.'

THE AGENT in charge of the Gunn case was Special Agent Laura Jenkins who, like Rose, worked out of one of the Bureau's satellite offices in Laredo. Jenkins was twenty years Rose's senior. She'd seen the woman before but they'd never worked together. McBride had agreed to meet the woman at a coffee shop in downtown San Antonio. Jenkins was waiting for them when they arrived. She was drinking coffee but didn't offer either of them anything.

'So what's this about?' said Jenkins, getting straight to the point. She had a faint hint of the east coast to her accent.

McBride went through the laborious process of explaining the recent developments in the Mallard case.

'Never heard of Wilberforce Mallard,' said Jenkins. 'We looked into the structure of Hanning Industries but didn't delve so far as to look at its shareholders.' There was a hint of defensiveness to Jenkins' actions that Rose understood. 'Our investigation focused on Gunn's colleagues and interactions. Everything pointed to him being a straight-down-the-line kind of guy, he appeared to be a family man, no sign of extra-marital affairs from either party, children were doing well at school.'

'No trouble with work colleagues?' asked McBride.

Jenkins took a sip of her coffee maintaining eye contact with them.

'If there was any disharmony no one was talking, his boss Nevin loved the guy. He was one of his hardest workers and he was compensated as such. He was on a mid-six-figure salary.'

'You know we're going through his files at present?' said Rose.

'I'd heard,' said Jenkins. 'What is it you're expecting to find?'

'Not expecting to find anything. We'd like to find a sign that Gunn was somehow working for the holding company.'

'Something to link him with Mallard?' said Jenkins.

'It's a long shot I agree,' said Rose. 'But right now we have nothing else to go on.' Jenkins nodded as she took a second sip of her coffee and leaned back in her chair, her body language easing. 'You could look at his past work history. He's been at Hanning Industries for twelve years, but he worked on a number of freelance roles prior to that.'

'Anything that sparked your interest?' asked McBride.

Jenkins frowned. 'He did some work in Mexico helping an architectural firm with the design of a vast industrial complex. You might want to see who put the money into that, but from my investigation, which I assure you was thorough, I found nothing that was suspicious. Obviously if there had been anything that linked Gunn to Razinski we'd have found it by now. My conclusion is the same. The attack was random, at least in the sense of Razinski's choice of victims. He could have been stalking them for months but he left no viable trace and everything suggests that Gunn had no inkling of Razinski's existence.'

IT WAS one dead end after another. Although Jenkins had started the conversation defensively, she'd mellowed by the end and Rose had no reason to question her findings.

'What do you think about this Mexican compound idea?' asked McBride, once they were back in the car.

The logical part of Rose thought they were diving further and further away from reality and researching some freelance project Gunn had worked on twelve years ago felt like a step too far. 'I'll go through his laptop again tonight. See if there are any plans for this place, see if there is any connection to Mallard.'

McBride nodded, but she noticed the defeated look in his eyes. It was being left unsaid but he was probably thinking along the same lines as her: the chance of finding Lynch now was close to zero. At some point they would have to accept that he'd been taken, that he'd become another of the Railroad's victims.

LATER THAT EVENING Rose was surprised to find that her sister was not at the hospital. Rose had made the journey unannounced, hoping the drive would clear her head. She was struck by the same feeling as always when she entered through the hospital doors, the antiseptic claustrophobia, the desire to run from the remembrance of her own mortality. She was relieved to see one of the coffee shops was still open. She purchased a coffee and took a seat nursing the drink like a drunk on their last beer. She was killing time, delaying the inevitable. It was hard to admit, but she feared facing her mother alone.

A young man in his early twenties sat at the table next to her smiling with a giddy enthusiasm. Rose clocked the wedding ring on his finger and presumed he was an expectant father. Why else would anyone be smiling in such a place? She checked through the messages on her phone, her mind darting from the close to lifeless body of her mother somewhere else in the hospital, to thoughts of Samuel Lynch. She knew what the Railroad were capable of and tried not to dwell on the atrocities Lynch could be enduring at that precise moment. Twice she went to call Abigail but each time she hesitated. She had to see her mother alone, needed to say the things she should have said so many years ago.

'So it all comes down to this,' thought Rose, as she eased her way through the doors of her mother's room. She gazed at the frail figure prone on the bed, at the alien tubes and pipes keeping her alive, and struggled to equate it to her mother. When the dementia had first set in, Rose had spent more time with her mother than she had in the previous ten years. She'd wanted to capture the woman she'd known, as she was before the terrible disease had its way with her, but it had proved to be a mistake: life went on. It made no sense to sit around waiting for further symptoms. Slowly her mother started getting on with life and so did Rose, wrapping herself up with work and trying to forget the gradual decline that was happening to her parent. It had been her mother's doing. They'd been sitting on the sofa together watching some nondescript television show when she'd said, 'this can't go on forever.'

'What do you mean?' said Rose.

'You can't stop time, darling. Sitting here watching me won't stop it happening, all it does is remind us of the inevitable.'

Rose had felt hurt then and now regretted the emotion with a terrible force. Only she could be so selfish as to consider her own feelings at such a time. She tried to place herself in her mother's position but it had proved impossible; how could you conceive of losing one's mind? It truly was a fate worse than death.

Yet, she now regretted the time she'd stayed away. She stood at the end of her bed, only just realizing she was crying. Her mother wasn't going to recover and life would never - could never - go back to the way it was before. Rose placed her hand on her mother's face and remembered everything the woman had done for her, the things she'd achieved raising two young girls single handed while holding down a day job, securing their education and future: the support she'd given Rose when she first decided to join the police force and latterly the Bureau, her sense of humor and empathy, her courage and selflessness. As Rose held the skeletal figure of her mother in her hands, she thought that if she amounted to becoming half the woman her mother was she would have led an extraordinary life.

41

He could have mistaken the cell they locked him in for a hotel room. Lynch had the comfort of a double bed, a desk and chair, and en suite bathroom. A small fridge humming at a gentle frequency was filled with various food and drink, though nothing alcoholic. Only the asylum-cleanliness, the pristine whiteness coating every inch of the room, the lack of windows and the locked door suggested he was anywhere other than a three-star hotel somewhere in the middle of nowhere.

He collapsed onto the bed, surprised and begrudgingly exalted to find Daniel's sweater waiting there for him. He clasped the material towards him, inhaling deeply, ignoring the other interloping smells, until he caught the remembrance of Daniel deep within the material. It was close to being unbearable, knowing that he might be only meters away from him at that very moment. After all these years, he was the closest he'd ever been to seeing his son again though he was sure Daniel's sweater hadn't been left for him as a means of compassion but as another tool to keep him down.

Lynch lay back thinking about Mallard's words. It was a tactic, another way of undermining him, but the words had served their purpose. He was now dwelling on the similarities between himself and Mallard. He didn't do what Mallard did. He wasn't a hunter, killing and abusing for the pleasure of it. But he had killed in his time, had gone beyond simple legal procedure to bring someone to justice. It may not make him as bad as Mallard but it highlighted a similarity. Mallard accused him of thinking he was better than others and it wasn't easy to argue against that. It was not something he did consciously but he'd acted that way before. He liked to think it was a necessary part of his job – when he was at the Bureau, and latterly in his role to find his son – but he didn't always take other people into consideration if they got in his way.

'Fuck,' he screamed into the void of the room. He was falling for Mallard's games. It was a simple interrogator's technique. Leaving the suspect alone with their thoughts and insecurities. Lynch paced the room and tried to focus on something positive. He thought about the years he'd spent with Sally and Daniel before his son was taken, focusing on all the wonderful times they'd shared together. His mind drifted to their vacation to Yellowstone Park when Daniel was only four - Daniel's amazement at the wildlife, the secret smiles he'd shared with Sally at their son's enjoyment. But however hard he tried, his mind kept returning to the darker times. The days and nights he was absent, the guilt he felt at missing weekends with his son because of some case he deemed important, and eventually his obsession with the Railroad that had led to his disappearance. If he hadn't become embroiled in that, had listened to the advice being freely offered at the time, then maybe he could be home now with his wife and son.

He screamed again and ran as hard as he could at the door. No doubt those fuckers were watching, savoring his desperation. The drugs still coursed through his body and it became apparent to him that this was all a ruse, another move from the Railroad play book; that Daniel wasn't alive, and he'd rushed into a position of jeopardy without a second thought.

He needed to start acting like a professional again.

But first he needed to sleep.

The lights darkened in the room as his head fell on the pillow, confirming his suspicion that he was being watched. He clung onto Daniel's sweater as exhaustion propelled him into an uneasy, dreamless sleep.

He woke an indeterminable time later, the lights in the room responding to his movements. It was the sort of feature, motion sensors perhaps, he would have expected at an exclusive hotel. He scanned the room but couldn't find any hidden cameras, yet he pictured the glamorous waitress, Clarissa, watching him from behind a bank of television screens.

He stretched and moved to the table, where a continental breakfast of cereals, bread, cheese and ham slices was laid out for him. He peered into the metallic jug, buoyed by the sight of the steaming hot coffee. He felt refreshed as if his internal organs had worked through the poison. He was more alert and his appetite had returned. He was at their mercy - - the food and drink could contain any sort of drug, or lethal poison – but he began anyway, pouring a large cup of the black coffee before starting on the bread and meats. Mallard wasn't finished with him yet and that gave him hope.

He was convinced an opportunity would arise and he needed to be ready.

TIME PASSED but in a way Lynch had never experienced. The lights in the room remained on until he lay down for sleep and he had no means of telling what time of day it was or even how to measure the passing of time. The effect on him came as a surprise. Although he was fed and he busied himself exercising and reading the trash novels left in the room, he soon became fatigued. He tried to measure time by the periods he was awake and asleep but it was impossible to measure either. Even the meals, which were given to him via a trap door, didn't help. He would wake from a sleep to be given a large meat dish, would receive breakfast moments before planning to go to sleep. He'd counted ten meals since he'd been placed in the room so estimated he was somewhere in his fourth day. Occasionally he would panic, worried that he would be stuck in such perpetual solitude. How long could he last like this? Solitary confinement was still used in penitentiary systems, both civil and military. He'd sent suspects into solitary in the past and their situations had been much harder than his. He had a solid bed, regular food, light and warmth. In comparison to the solitary confinement cells he'd used working for the Bureau this was pure luxury.

It reminded him how different time was on the outside. In confinement, time crawled but for the jailor time passed by at normal speed. It was a harsh lesson being on the other side of the equation.

It was six meals later before he really began to feel his

isolation. During the last few sleeps he'd started to appreciate the silence of the room. No sound leaked in from outside and he pictured himself in some form of soundproof container in the middle of the desert. He began to miss company of any kind. He would have given anything at the moment to hear another human being. It didn't matter the content, he just needed to hear another person's voice.

One sleep and three meals later he got his wish.

Lynch had finished his meal, a lamb stew with a particularly heavy sauce, when a voice filtered through the trap door.

'Mr Lynch, please can you place your hands in the dispensing area. You need to be cuffed before you move.'

It was the voice of the glamorous waitress, Clarissa. She sounded animated and Lynch wondered what it took to remain in such good humor, what reserves of strength she had to continue behaving that way. Her voice was a blessed sound. It emphasized the silence he'd endured. Lynch placed his hands into the trap, the feel of the cold steel on his wrists a pleasant sensation. Once cuffed, he staggered back into his cell where the door slid open like a scene from a science fiction movie.

Clarissa stood in the opening. Time hadn't changed her appearance. She was identical to the last time he saw her, from the clothes she was wearing to the parting of her perfectly coiffured hair.

'Mr Lynch,' she said, bowing slightly, her voice smooth like honey.

Lynch fought an overwhelming urge to move towards the woman. Such was his need for human contact, he would have happily let her embrace him. Instead, he smiled to himself imagining this was how Stockholm syndrome began. He looked back at Daniel's sweater on the bed. 'Where are we going?' he asked, refusing to play the victim. The woman may or may not be working under duress, but either way she was one of his captors and had to be treated as such.

'Please, follow me,' she cooed, turning on her heels and walking away.

Lynch followed, two guards appearing from the shadows to accompany him. He memorized the route as he was led through various darkened corridors, up and down staircases until they reached a wooden door approximately eight meters in height.

'May I?' said the waitress, placing a pair of sunglasses over his eyes as she opened the imposing doors. Beams of bright sunshine filled the corridor as he stepped through the threshold savoring the caress of the warm air on his skin. He was standing in a flat, desert-like area. Yellow-brown ground stretched in all directions, the landscape desolate save for a small building to his right and the outline of another building in the distance. The panoramic view was all the more special after his time in confinement. Lynch savored every second as the waitress led him across the desert, at the same time trying to ascertain his location and possible escape routes.

They'd been walking for five minutes when the building in the distance started to take shape. It was the remnants of an old church. What Lynch had thought was a chimneystack was in fact a crumbling steeple. 'Are we going to mass?' he said, turning to the guard on his left who ignored him.

The waitress stopped five hundred yards later, the church still some way in the distance. 'Please,' she said, pointing to the building.

'You want me to go alone?' said Lynch.

'Please.'

Lynch began walking at first surprised, then concerned, that the guards were not following. His hands were still cuffed behind his back and the movement was laborious. As the church approached, it became hard not to think he was walking to his death. He braced himself, as if he would be able to feel the sniper bullet enter his skull.

The sound of the gun failed to materialize, and yards from the church entrance Lynch had the absurd impulse to start running. The church was little more than a shell. Light escaped through holes in the roof and the dust-strewn bricks of the exterior appeared precarious at best.

Lynch looked behind him to see the waitress and the two guards standing in the middle of the land staring at him. Behind them he saw the outline of the building where he'd been captive.

The door of the church creaked open and Lynch recognized the guard from the train. It was the same man who'd sucker punched him. The guard smirked as if reminiscing. 'This way,' he said, pointing his gun towards the interior of the church.

'One day we'll face each other when I'm not wearing these,' said Lynch. 'We'll see who's smirking then.'

'I look forward to that,' said Sucker Punch, clenching the automatic rifle tighter.

Lynch walked through a set of wooden doors into the church proper. The interior was little better than the exterior. Scaffolding climbed the walls of the church as if holding it in place. The room was vacant. No pews for worshipping, only an altar at one end of the space, interspersed with candles but devoid of the Christ figure.

Sitting on the altar, his back to him was Mallard.

'Quite a show,' said Lynch, pacing the stone ground that would have been the aisle. 'I appreciate the effort you've put into this.'

Mallard lifted his arms and turned to face him. 'You can leave us,' he said to the guard.

42

Three days after visiting her mother in hospital, Rose was in a Mexican restaurant on the outskirts of San Antonio with McBride. Their investigations into the Gunn and Mallard connection had proved futile. The Mexican compound Gunn had been working on was a government facility. Nothing in the files or their various follow-ups linked Gunn to Mallard in any way and they had reached a dead end. Miller and Roberts were close to taking them off the case.

Rose had involved directly in a cover up before. Now she was being woven into a lie. The official line for the bombing at the FBI compound pinned the blame to a splinter cell of a terrorist group. Such rationalizations were easy for the press and public to swallow and they took away a great deal of pressure from the Bureau. As both Miller and Roberts had pointed out to her, they had no proof either way.

Rose hadn't argued; it would have been like talking to herself. She'd barely slept in the last three nights, her time spent on conversations with Abigail, research on the case, and thoughts of Lynch. She accessed Lynch's tracking app on what felt like a minute-by-minute basis, desperate for any indication he was still alive. She understood even more clearly now how Lynch had spent all those years searching for his son, how he'd never given up.

Some cases she'd walked away from, but this would forever haunt her.

'Do you need to wear those sunglasses?' she said to McBride, who'd taken to sporting the eyewear at every inappropriate occasion, no doubt as a playful means of antagonizing her.

'The lights are bright in here,' said her colleague, filling his taco shell past brimming point. Half the contents fell back on his plate but he shoveled the food into his mouth without a thought.

Rose's iPad was laid flat on the table. McBride shook his head as she glanced at it, the screen loaded to Lynch's tracking app.

'You know that thing is either broken or destroyed?' said McBride, refilling the falling contents of his taco shell. 'Are you going to look at it every day for the rest of your life?' he continued, his mouth full of food.

'Don't they teach you table manners where you come from?' said Rose, for once irked by her partner's behavior.

McBride was right, but how could she ever let it go? She feared the day she stopped looking at the tracking app would be the day it was activated. They sat in sullen silence, Rose contemplating the journeys she'd made ever since that day at Gunn's house. What would her own tracking device tell her? What miles would it record? What pointless misdirection would it taunt her with? The thought gave her an idea.

An athletic-looking waiter dressed in a tight black shirt brought over their bill.

'Your turn,' said McBride.

'Ever the gentleman,' said Rose, taking out a credit card from her purse as the idea blossomed. She paid the bill and with a large intake of breath shared her plan with McBride.

PERVERSELY, McBride took off his sunglasses once they were outside in the dazzling sunshine. Rose gave him a pitying look but didn't rise to the bait. 'So what do you think?' she said, as they got back into the car.

'It strikes me as the workings of a desperate obsessive,' said McBride.

'You mean an investigator who is being thorough?' said Rose.

'I suppose it depends on which way you look at it. You know this means we'll have to visit the depths of the building again. I just hope to god Hussein isn't working, I'm not sure I could face his upbeat attitude so early in the day.'

An hour later they discovered that Hussein was on duty. Once again he was reading and continued until he'd finished his current magazine article before giving them his attention. 'Yes?' he said, staring at McBride and Rose as if they'd never met.

'We called ahead,' said Rose. 'We want to examine Edward Gunn's car.'

Hussein stared at Rose as if she wasn't there, as if he could see right through her to the back of the building. And then, as if from nowhere, he produced a set of keys.

'Lower garage seven,' he said, handing the car keys to Rose. 'There were three family cars, have fun.'

'What is that guy's problem?' said McBride, who'd placed his sunglasses back on despite the darkened corridors.

'Can you even see with those on?'

'I don't talk about what you're wearing so please don't comment on my style,' said McBride, with his now familiar mischievous smirk.

'You know one day I'm going to take those glasses and snap them, don't you?'

'One of many pairs, Rose.'

The number of cars in lower garage seven surprised Rose. The vehicles were all from crime scenes or taken from suspects. The value of the vehicles must have reached the millions. Automatic lights on the walls and ceilings sprang into life, sending a shaft of light onto two bright red Lamborghinis.

'Are these the new company vehicles?' said McBride, placing his sunglasses inside his jacket. The rest of the vehicles were a mixed bag, from battered up coupés to luxurious German cars used for chauffeuring.

'Here we are,' said Rose, reaching the Gunn's cars.

'Two drivers, three cars,' said McBride.

The thought had already occurred to Rose. The Lexus saloon was company issued from Hanning Industries but the other two cars, a sleek Mercedes sports car and fully featured British Land Rover were privately owned.

'Maybe they like off-roading?' said McBride, opening the door of the Land Rover. 'Nice,' he said, as the interior light shone on the white leather. 'So where do you want to begin?'

'The Land Rover,' said Rose.

It was speculative at best but Rose couldn't shift the idea that Gunn and Mallard were linked. McBride switched on the ignition and the interior electronics came to life. Rose played with some buttons until she found what she was looking for: Gunn's Sat-Nav system. 'Here goes,' she said, trawling through the various layouts of the system until she found the correct button: *Saved Destinations*.

'Please, sit,' said Mallard, nodding to the marbled covering of the altar steps.

'I can't with these on,' said Lynch, turning to display his handcuffs.

'How remiss. Travis, take off Mr Lynch's handcuffs, will you?'

Sucker Punch appeared from the shadows. He grabbed Lynch and pulled him tight. 'One wrong move and it's all over for you,' he whispered into Lynch's ear, flecks of spittle coating Lynch's skin.

At another time Lynch would have considered disarming the man and sending a wave of bullets into him and Mallard, but he was still weak from his captivity. Instead, he offered the guard a grin intended to infuriate him and sat next to Mallard.

Mallard nodded to Sucker Punch, seemingly unconcerned that Lynch was now free of cuffs. He was wearing the same clothes as last time, head to toe in black. Lynch tried to determine how long ago that occasion had been but time was becoming an illusion. 'How long do you intend playing these games, Mallard?' he said.

'I don't play games, Mr Lynch. I told you the last time we met that I saw something in you long ago. I thought some time alone would give you cause to consider my suggestion.'

The sensible move would be to play along with Mallard's assertions, to say the words Mallard wanted him hear. Lynch held Mallard's gaze and understood that wasn't an option. Mallard would see through him. 'I considered your suggestion and I don't buy it,' he said.

Mallard smiled like a salesman facing an objection. 'That would be a grave pity, Mr Lynch. As I said, we could do wonderful things together.'

'Do you really need me, Mallard? You seem to be doing OK for yourself as it is. You've got your guards, they're terrified of you but they're yours and no doubt loyal. You've got your wealth, and your connections with the law agencies. What the hell do you want with me?' Lynch's pulse was racing but Mallard remained calm.

'People like you and me are rare, Mr Lynch. So very rare. I scour the earth for like-minded souls and can literally count on the fingers on my hands the number of people I've met who are like me.'

'Your inner sanctum?' said Lynch, with a laugh.

'Yes, and one or two you've yet to meet.'

'You're including Balfour on this list?' said Lynch, dismissively.

'Let's not drag personal conflicts into this, Mr Lynch. You and Mr Balfour are much more alike than you could ever imagine.'

'That's where your argument falls down, Mallard. I'm nothing like that prick.'

Mallard leant closer. 'You really don't know yourself, Mr Lynch, do you? Or if you do, you choose not to fully accept what you are.'

The calming baritone of the Controller's voice soothed Lynch. He shook himself, fighting the feeling. 'I'm nothing like Balfour.'

'You have different tastes, certainly,' said Mallard, with a knowing smile. 'Yet fundamentally you are alike. Both of you would stop at nothing to get what you want. You have a very flexible approach to morality when it comes between you and your goal.'

Mallard had alluded to this before and alone in his cell Lynch had dwelt on his previous actions, the lives he'd taken or forsaken in his desire to find Daniel. He'd sacrificed his marriage and all existing relationships. In the last few weeks so many people had died, in part because of him. From that point of view, Mallard was correct. He did have a flexible approach to morality at certain times, but then who didn't? Morality was a fluid concept. Lynch had witnessed parents protect murdering children, countless colleagues and friends who'd cheated on partners and kept silent. Lynch had made a choice. He'd placed Daniel above everything else. He wasn't the first parent to do this and wouldn't be the last. It didn't make him like Mallard or any of them.

He was signing his death warrant but he couldn't play along with the charade anymore. 'You're wrong,' he said, standing.

Mallard nodded. 'I'm disappointed to hear that, Mr Lynch.' He clicked his fingers and Sucker Punch appeared once more, cuffing Lynch before he had time to react. 'Perhaps it's time we reunited you with your son.'

Rage overcame Lynch at the mention of Daniel. Sucker

Punch was still behind him so he threw his head back, a sharp aggressive motion making solid contact with Sucker Punch's nose. Lynch ignored the mumbled complaints of the guard and ran straight towards Mallard who was holding his ground, a curious smile on his face. With his hands cuffed behind him Lynch was off balance. He ran head first at his captor like a bull chasing a red rag. Mallard was ready for him and sidestepped with ease. Lynch managed to remain upright and swiveled around to face Mallard.

'Even you are not going to win this particular fight, Mr Lynch.'

Lynch shook his head, a line of spittle flying from his mouth. 'He's still alive?' he said, determined not to display his rising emotion.

'We're both men of our word. Now, I suggest you compose yourself before Mr Travis here takes revenge for his unfortunate injury.'

Lynch smirked at the fallen guard who held his broken nose as if it would fall off. 'I'm ready.'

'Then follow me. Get up, Travis.'

Mallard walked across the altar of the church followed by Lynch, the sound of their footsteps echoing on the marble floors. Travis moved in behind Lynch, his breathing ragged, the smell of blood and fear pouring from his body. Mallard bent down and lifted a trap door and disappeared below. Lynch peered over the opening, surprised to see an ornate wooden staircase leading down.

'Steady now, we wouldn't want you falling,' said Sucker Punch, as Lynch took his first step.

Thirteen steps down, expensive artwork hung on the walls of a well-lit room, the modernity reminding Lynch of the circular room where he'd first met Mallard.

'Our gateway,' said Mallard, pointing towards a second set of doors.

Lynch followed his captor. The adrenaline in his system was unwelcome, a result of fear and unease rather than excitement. Mallard pulled open the doors and Lynch was surprised to see the interior of an elevator similar to any he would expect to see in an upmarket office building.

'Very few people get to see what you are about to, Mr Lynch. At least, not from this side.'

Lynch fought his apprehension, his determination coming from the promise of seeing Daniel again. He was unable to tell if the descent was an illusion. He couldn't sense any movement as the doors shut and they stood in silence. Mallard was lost in thought, a serene look on his face as he swayed on the spot.

Minutes later, the elevator stopped with a gentle bump. The doors opened and Mallard ushered him into hell itself.

44

McBride was owed a favor by one of the OTD team, William Hawken, who agreed to analyze the data downloaded from the three Gunn vehicles. 'Shouldn't take me more than thirty minutes,' said Hawken, who was dressed more like a vagrant than a member of the FBI. His overgrown salt and pepper beard draped down onto the chest hairs beneath his floral patterned short-sleeved shirt.

As Rose waited in the canteen area with McBride, she felt the eyes of the other agents boring into her. She had become a celebrity in the Bureau for all the wrong reasons. Many of her colleagues still blamed her for the events at the compound. The building was full of misinformation and Rose was experienced enough to realize there always had to be a scapegoat.

'What exactly is it you're hoping for?' asked McBride, who either wasn't suffering the same insecurity or was hiding it better than her. He was tucking into a burger, sauce dripping from the bun onto the side of his chin. He chewed on his last mouthful before shrugging his shoulders as he waited for her to respond.

'I don't believe in coincidence,' she said.

'Yeah but there are coincidences and coincidences,' said McBride, wiping his face with a napkin. 'Mallard's business interests are vast. If you looked hard enough you could probably link him with practically everyone.'

'Something's not right here. You know it as well as I do. The Gunn family wasn't killed by accident. It wasn't a random murder, it was planned. Razinski may have taken things too far, but he was meant to be there that day.'

'Maybe so,' said McBride, finishing another mouthful of burger. 'But the link to Mallard is so slim it's almost non-existent.'

'Have Miller and Roberts got to you as well?' said Rose, sounding sharper than intended.

'I will pretend I didn't hear that. Listen you know I'm on your side it's just that...'

'What?' said Rose, interrupting. 'You want me to give this up and be known as the agent who was responsible for the multiple deaths at the compound? You want me to give up on Lynch as well? He was one of us, remember. If we had listened to him to begin with this could all have been prevented,' she said, realizing after she'd spoken that she was repeating an earlier argument.

'I'm not saying we give up on it, more refocus. Continue our work on Balfour, see what we can find there.'

A distant part of her accepted he was right. If she'd been viewing the case from the outside she would have given the same advice. She was working on little more than a hunch, and hunches were something she couldn't abide. Real police work was completed by hard work and diligence, by analyzing facts and evidence. Hunches were for a bygone era, for rogue detectives, for fiction and television. She would wait to see what the tech team came back with and plan from there. If a new approach was what was needed then so be it.

'You not going to eat?' said McBride, eyeing her half-eaten burger.

'Jesus, you sound more and more like my mother,' she said, regretting her words as soon as they'd left her mouth. 'I'm getting coffee. Do you want anything?'

McBride took a bite of her burger and put his thumb up.

HAWKEN WAS at the table by the time she returned with the coffees. He smiled as she walked over and took one of the cups from her. 'Good news or bad news?' he said.

'Anything,' said Rose, drinking from the second cup of coffee before McBride had a chance to take it from her.

'Well, the bad news is that the majority of journeys in all three cars were pretty routine. Gunn's work vehicle recorded daily trips to and from work. Mrs Gunn's vehicle had a similar predictable pattern. I've printed out a list of all destinations and corresponding routes. I'll leave the proper investigating work to you, maybe what you're looking for is in there.'

'Thanks,' said Rose. 'You mentioned something about good news?'

'Yes,' said Hawken, taking another drink of coffee, some of the liquid clinging to his beard. 'Good news is perhaps a stretch too far. Interesting might be a better choice. The Land Rover appears to be used for one particular recurring journey, long trip too, very long trip. Five hundred odd miles away from Gunn's home into the wilds of West Texas, Davis

Mountain country. What was interesting, what caught my eye, was the way the journey stopped.'

'Stopped?' said McBride.

'Yes it's really quite interesting between 490.2 and 490.9 miles into the journey, and this was always depending on minor deviation to the route, the signal just stops.'

'So that is where he stopped the car?' said Rose.

Hawken lifted his finger. 'No, that is exactly the point. The signal stopped but the car was still going, our diagnostics tell us the car continues for another twenty to twenty-five minutes on each of the trips with no GPS signal showing. On the return journey the same thing happens. The car runs twenty to twenty-five minutes with no signal whatsoever and then at the some point it springs to life.'

Rose took the file from Hawken and studied the coordinates shown on the map.

'So he just turned off the GPS whenever he reached this point?' she asked.

'No,' said Hawken, the smile on his face broadening until the side of his eyes were full of deep wrinkled lines. 'That is the interesting thing. It wasn't done manually, it was automatic. If I didn't know better, I would have said the car went underground at this point. This would be the most logical explanation for his GPS failing.'

'Is there any other reason his GPS would stop working?' asked Rose.

'The only other thing I can think of is a malfunction with the car's GPS, but this isn't the case as it works fine; or that someone was jamming the signal.'

'How can you do that?'

'It's not that difficult. It's illegal, but quite easy to do. We use such technology in certain locations if you get my drift?'

'In this instance?' asked McBride

'No, no, no,' said Hawken. 'I'm just saying. Could be a military organization, could be some private land, could be a rogue civilian, could be coincidence.' Hawken got to his feet. 'I'll leave that up to the professionals,' he said, making a bizarre circular gesture with his hand like a commoner signaling to royalty.

'Thanks, Will, I owe you one,' said McBride.

'My pleasure,' said Hawken. 'Let me know what you find once you get there,' he said.

McBride glanced Rose, his face downcast presumably at the thought of a five hundred mile journey.

Rose matched Hawken's smile. 'We will do,' she said.

'YOU DIDN'T THINK we were going to sit on this did you?' said Rose, the following morning at five am. She was doing her best to cheer up the somber looking McBride.

'I guess not,' said McBride, who sat in the passenger seat, dark glasses on, nursing a coffee, staring at the window like a teenager on vacation with his parents.

After meeting with Hawken, they'd studied the area where Gunn's GPS signal failed. She didn't know what to expect when she got there. The main issue, as Hawken had pointed out via email, was that Gunn could have gone in any direction once his signal had gone blank. In twenty to twenty-five minutes, he could have travelled another twenty to forty miles or even more depending on his speed. Which left them with a huge circumference tracking area. Rose oscillated between optimism that she was on the right track, and fear that her investigation was spiraling out of control. Sometimes letting go was the hardest decision and, from an outsider's position, it could look like she was clutching at imaginary straws.

They headed out of San Antonio on the I-10. The road was desolate, the scenery seemingly unchanging. Even after all these years Rose had yet to overcome her sense of wonder at the vastness of the state. Isolated houses dotted the never-ending landscape, the occasional built up area flashing by on the edges of the interstate. It was beyond her understanding how people lived in such solitude. Although happy in her own company, and at times welcoming such isolation, there was something unfathomable about being so far from civilization. She pictured the inhabitants of the lone houses and wondered if they were staring back at her as she drove, and if they felt comfort in the occasional passing stranger.

They stopped for an early lunch in Del Rio, near the air force base.

'How are we on securing a meeting with Mallard?' asked Rose, cracking a taco shell.

'I'm not even sure if Mallard exists,' said McBride, turning towards her and catching her faraway gaze. 'I'm just passed from one lawyer to the next and the fact that I'm a government agent doesn't appear to give me any leeway.'

'Can we not send it higher up the food chain?' said Rose.

'Miller and Roberts, you mean?' said McBride, with an ironic laugh. 'They washed their hands of this case some time ago. They're not going to get involved, contacting some reclusive billionaire with the vague connections we have.'

'Well... keep trying. I do appreciate you sticking by me on this.'

The left corner of McBride's mouth curled into a smile. 'Anything for my partner.'

'So we're partners?' said Rose, matching his smile.

'It looks that way,' said McBride, reaching into his jacket pocket for his shades.

'Don't you dare.'

McBride's hand hovered by the seam of his inside pocket before he placed it on his forehead and gave her a mock salute. 'I wouldn't dream of it, boss.'

FOUR HOURS later they were approaching Otisville, the area where Gunn's GPS had failed. 'It should be any second now,' said McBride, looking at the map on his phone.

They'd left the highway and were on a minor road, barren land surrounding them on every side. Rose's sense of isolation had intensified over the last thirty minutes, the broken tarmac of the road and their car the only sign of modernity in their entire field of vision. 'Now,' said McBride, hitting the dashboard with undue force as his GPS signal disappeared. Rose continued driving for fifty more yards before pulling over.

'Jesus this is convenient,' said McBride.

Rose had stopped at a crossroads, the road continuing straight ahead and forking to the left and right. 'You ever feel like you're in a game, Agent Rose?' said McBride, gazing in all directions.

'Continually,' said Rose.

They were ten miles south of Otisville. Rose's research had revealed that the Rock Island Railroad, a now defunct network running from St Louis, had once passed close to the area.

They left the car, Rose checking her phone for the dead signal. Heat rose from the road. Above her, she heard the faint buzz of the electrical wire that stretched across the sky, held together by wooden pylons. It was desolate but still contained signs of life.

'Never thought I'd have to use one of these again,' said McBride, unfolding a map of the local area.

Rose squinted at the small area McBride pointed to on the map. 'If we go east, we'll reach civilization sooner,' he said.

'We don't want civilization,' said Rose, pointing south. 'Gunn drove a further twenty-five minutes without GPS coverage.'

'True, but he could have gone any direction. He could have moved inland, meandered through these small country lanes.'

Rose rubbed the sweat from her brow, droplets of the salty liquid stinging her eyes. She could tell McBride thought it was a lost cause. It would be easy to drive away from this and return to normality but the loss of GPS signal was an anomaly that had to be investigated. 'Come on, we've come this far. Might as well see it out.'

McBride grimaced, and placed his shades on. 'You're the boss,' he said.

They took the road west, McBride glued to his iPad. Twenty minutes in and the road had deteriorated further in quality. The road markings vanished, and the various potholes were testing the viability of the car's suspension.

'You realize we're totally screwed if we break down now. This is the sort of thing you read about, though it's usually clueless tourists rather than seasoned FBI agents.'

'Relax, McBride, we're a maximum twenty-five miles from an area with reception. Probably much less. As long as we've got our legs we'll be ok.'

They passed a smallholding, a wooden shack with

boarded up windows. In the distance, behind the building, Rose saw the outline of ancient railroad tracks, the sleepers covered by weeds and dirt. The remnants of the steel tracks made her feel she'd made the right choice by continuing west.

The road ran parallel to the tracks for the next five miles before diverting and stretching into the distance. If McBride had seen the tracks, he chose not to comment. 'That's twenty-three miles now and still no signal,' he said. 'Suggests we made the correct choice, though why the hell he came out here I don't know. He could have been meeting someone, I guess. Good place for an exchange.'

The thought had occurred to Rose though she was convinced that something was occurring here beyond illicit meetings.

'We're back,' said McBride, flashing his iPad at Rose. Twenty-three point six miles since the GPS went out.

Rose stopped the car. Although there was no crossroads this time, the area looked identical to before. 'He must have taken one of the turnings,' she said.

'Yeah, maybe. That's if this was the correct road. There's too many possibilities. We're never going to discover where he travelled.'

'We could do a flyover, check for locations.'

McBride sighed but didn't answer.

Rose was about to turn back when both their phones rang at the same time. They checked, both had received voice message from headquarters.

'Special Agent Rose, McBride, joint message for you.' It was the voice of Hawken, McBride's tech consultant.

Rose switched on the speakerphone.

'I was intrigued by the little conundrum you find yourself

in so took it upon myself to do a little bit more research. I entered all the addresses the three Gunn vehicles had visited in the last six months. One recurring address I had seemingly overlooked. I thought you might be interested as it is a flagged address. Mrs Gunn visited the same address eighteen times in a three-month period. The house belongs to a Captain Iain Haig. I believe you are acquainted with the man, Agent Rose?'

Rose hung up, her heart racing.

'That's the same Captain Haig who was at the Gunn scene?' asked McBride.

Rose nodded. 'And the same Captain Haig who's been protecting Lynch's ex-wife.'

45

Lynch didn't believe in haunted spaces. A former colleague once told him about a house she'd come close to purchasing. In the end her reason for not doing so was based on the house having a 'bad feeling'. She asked him if he understood what she meant and he'd nodded politely, not having a clue what she meant.

He hadn't understood how a building could have a bad feeling until the second he'd walked out of the elevator doors.

The area had much in common with the Bureau compound where they'd taken Razinski. It had the same open feel, a vast area with the atmospherics of an underground bunker. There the similarities ended. At first glance, the space appeared devoid of personnel yet Lynch could hear the hive of activity somewhere in the distance.

'What do you think?' asked Mallard, with an obvious pride.

Lynch would have shrugged his shoulders if his hands hadn't been cuffed behind him. 'It's a warehouse of some sort.'

'Very good, Mr Lynch. What you see in front of you is a but a fraction of the space.'

'Great, where's my son?'

Mallard laughed. 'Where are my manners? Of course, but it would be remiss of me not to show you around first, no?'

Lynch followed Mallard, eyes alert to his surroundings. Numerous cameras pointed towards him and as he turned a corner he saw the first of the guards. Each wore the same black uniform and carried identical firearms. Lynch wondered if they were private hire or if each was a member of the Railroad. 'So this is a kind of club house for your society?' he asked.

Mallard had stopped next to another set of doors, thick steel monstrosities that stretched from floor to ceiling.

'Club house?' said Mallard, his attention elsewhere.

'For your society. We call you the Railroad.'

The alertness returned to Mallard's eyes. 'I'm aware of what you call us,' he replied, smiling.

'Where are your tattoos?' continued Lynch, trying to provoke a reaction from the man.

'We call them honor marks,' said Mallard.

'Honor marks? You're fucking kidding me?'

'Why would I do that, Mr Lynch? I'm deadly serious.'

'Tell me about the marks, then.'

'First, let me ask what you think they are.'

'I've seen similar many times before. The penitentiary system is full of sick fucks inking their skin to mark their conquests. Murders, rapes, I imagine your tracks are little different.'

'That's where you're wrong,' said Mallard, slipping his mask of perfection and revealing the ugly truth.

'Enlighten me.'

Mallard gazed at the new set of doors as if they held some great conundrum. 'You appreciate I am aware of your questioning techniques?'

'Sure, you're in charge here, Mallard. You tell me what you want.' Lynch was intrigued by what lay behind the doors but wasn't about to let on to Mallard. With neither man speaking, he could hear the hum of activity from behind the steel barriers.

Mallard turned him. Once again, Lynch was struck by the intensity in the man's gaze; it took all his strength to maintain eye contact. He felt Mallard assess him and waited for the verdict. 'It would be easier if I demonstrated it to you,' said Mallard, as the steel doors began opening.

A wave of heat swarmed towards Lynch as he followed Mallard through the opening. Two further guards greeted Mallard by lowering their heads. They ignored Lynch as he moved into the secondary compound, trying his best to make sense of what he was seeing.

At first glance it reminded Lynch of the visions of Area 51 he'd seen in films and television – ship containers piled on high stretching into the distance. On closer inspection, he noticed a semblance of order. The large containers were arranged in order. Each was painted black, illuminated only by the occasional spotlight shining down on them like an artificial sun.

Mallard watched him with a mounting glee, waiting for him to reach his conclusion.

'They're rooms,' said Lynch.

'Good,' said Mallard, prompting him to elaborate.

'Prisons.'

'You've got it,' said Mallard, with a joyous rise to his voice.

'Have you seen this?' he continued, pointing to the gravel beneath their feet.

Lynch had noticed the parallel metal tracks on the ground stretching towards the makeshift prisons.

'Too much?' said Mallard.

Lynch was stunned as a miniature steam train approached them, the kind he'd seen in theme parks as a child. The train pulled a single carriage containing two rows of pristine leather armchairs. It was the juxtaposition of seeing the children's novelty train in such a forbidding area that threw him. He couldn't help but wonder if Daniel had ridden the train; if he now resided in one of the metallic containers in the distance.

'Shall we?' said Mallard, hauling Lynch onto the train carriage.

Lynch swallowed, his mouth dry and wordless as the train pulled away.

'You see we recruit our members, Mr Lynch. Yes, we are elitist. As I mentioned, there are only a select few who can understand what we are about.'

'What are you about, you sick fuck?'

The train stopped outside one of the containers. The number forty-nine was painted outside in a dull green. 'Come,' said Mallard, dragging him from the carriage. Lynch shuddered as he moved towards the container, Mallard running his fingers over the painted numbering. He slid a metal shutter across and peered inside as Lynch searched for an escape route.

'Look,' said Mallard, his face flushed.

Was it Daniel? Lynch wasn't sure he could look into the container.

'It's not your son, if that's your concern,' said Mallard, as Lynch stood his ground.

Lynch didn't move, nausea rising within him as his mind considered what lay behind the shutter.

'If you want to understand us, Mr Lynch, this is your chance.'

Lynch fought the urge to attack the man. They were alone but he was sure somewhere in the shadows a gun was pointed at him. He had to do it for Daniel. He moved towards the shutter, Mallard grinning as Lynch placed his head into the opening. His eyes were still closed as he felt the weight of Mallard's hand on his back.

He opened his eyes and was rewarded with a laugh from Mallard. 'That, in part,' said Mallard, 'is how you receive an honor mark.'

46

'Shall I call it in?' asked McBride.

'No. I don't want anything to alert Haig. Call Hawken and tell him to keep the information to himself.'

Rose was loath to leave the area, especially considering the amount of the time it had taken to reach there. She tried to process Hawken's information as she drove to Dimmit County, drowning out the noise of McBride talking to the OTD agent in the background. How was Haig linked to all this? She remembered his professionalism at the Gunn house, how he'd kept his troops in order despite Razinski having killed one of his men.

It couldn't be a coincidence. If Mrs Gunn had been travelling to Haig's house on a regular basis then Haig should have declared it. They needed to speak to him when they had the chance, before someone else got to him.

'Hawken hasn't told anyone,' said McBride. 'Happy to keep it to himself for now.'

'Can he be trusted?'

McBride frowned as if insulted by the question. 'So what was this Captain Haig like?'

Rose recapped the incident.

'So Haig called it in to us?'

'Yes. Razinski demanded the Bureau were called in and Haig obliged even though one of his men were down. I did a bit of research on him on the way to the scene. Ex-military. Appeared to be well respected by his team.'

'You think he knew Razinski?'

'Until now, no.'

IT WAS after midnight by the time they reached Dimmit County. They stayed the night in a hotel on the outskirts of the city before taking a two-hour journey to Haig's department in the morning. They parked up a hundred yards from the station. Haig arrived an hour later, alone, carrying a tray of coffees.

'That's the kind of boss I need,' said McBride.

'Be careful what you wish for.'

They waited ten minutes before moving in. They were greeted by a Deputy who barely looked old enough to put on the uniform, despite the tiredness emanating from his eyes. Rose didn't remember the man being at the Gunn house. 'How can I help you?' said the youngster, in a thick Texan drawl.

Rose showed the deputy her badge. 'Special Agents Rose and McBride. We're here to see Captain Haig.'

This got the officer's attention. He flushed red, his body rigid as if he was trying to stand to attention. 'Yes Ma'am, please wait here,' he said.

Rose shifted her body to the left, checking the weight of

her firearm inside her jacket. She sensed McBride was on edge as well. Too much had happened in the last week for them not to be on high alert. If Haig was somehow connected to the Railroad then they needed to be prepared for the worst.

'Special Agent Rose, a lovely surprise.' Captain Ian Haig stood in the doorway. He was wearing a short-sleeved shirt, his marine tattoos displayed proudly on his muscular arms.

Rose's eyes darted to the gun at Haig's side. 'Captain Haig. This is my colleague, Special Agent McBride. Apologies for not calling in advance.' Rose hoped her tone was neutral, professional yet approachable, though she feared she sounded too formal.

'No problem. Please come through. Can I get you anything? Some coffee perhaps?' Haig smiled at them as he held the door open.

'Coffee would be great,' said Rose.

'See to that, Mitch,' said Haig.

Rose recognized some of the faces in the bullpen from the Gunn house and received a nod of recognition from the heavyset Deputy she knew only as Check-Shirt, who'd attacked Razinski at the scene. She hadn't blamed him then and certainly didn't now. She returned the gesture as Haig led them through to his office.

A flicker of hesitation came over Haig as he sat behind his desk. 'How can I help you?' he said, holding Rose's gaze.

Rose didn't immediately respond. She stared back at Haig. Part of her wanted him to come clean. He'd acted so professionally at the scene that she still found it difficult to believe he had anything to do with Razinski and the Railroad. 'You knew Edward Gunn,' she said, after a time. Her eyes never left his, studying his response like a poker player.

Haig's left eye twitched but he didn't speak.

'And Laney Gunn as well,' added McBride.

Haig shrugged, a false smile on his face. 'You make me feel like I need an attorney,' he said, with a lightness betrayed by the sweat on his brow.

'Are you going to tell us or are we going to tell you?' said Rose.

Haig's eyes glazed over as he went through some internal struggle. He was either deciding to come clean or was about to spin some elaborate tale.

Rose waited. Haig was an experienced interrogator and would know all the tricks but she wanted him to speak first.

'Okay, what do you think you know?' he said, eventually.

Rose exchanged looks with McBride. 'We know you visited Mrs Gunn on more than one occasion prior to her murder,' she said.

'And the murder of her whole family,' added McBride. 'You live alone, Haig?'

Haig nodded.

'Widower?'

Haig nodded again as if unable to speak.

Anger spread over McBride's face. 'What was it then? An affair, or was it love?' he said, with a sneer.

'I made a mistake,' said Haig.

'A mistake?' said McBride, incredulous.

'I met Laney outside of work. We went out for a few coffees and then started seeing each other. She was married, yes, but it was a loveless marriage.'

'You're going to need to give us some more to go on here, Iain,' said Rose. 'How long were you seeing her for?'

'About fourteen months. It wasn't really serious. I saw her once or twice a month at most.'

'You do this a lot then?' said McBride. 'Little extra service from the local law enforcement.'

Haig bristled. 'What's it to do with you, son?'

'Come on, Iain. Think straight. You have an affair with a woman who ends up murdered along with her family, and one of your officers for that matter, and you don't volunteer any information about it. It's the end of your career for one, you must realize that,' said Rose.

Haig stared at her. 'Of course.'

'But it can be much worse, Iain,' said Rose, growing impatient.

'What do you want me to say?'

'You can start by telling us why the hell you didn't react or say anything at the Gunn house.'

'What was I going to say? That I was screwing the woman with no fucking head?'

'Yes, that's exactly what you should have said,' said McBride, standing. The anger was not an act. He leant over Haig's desk, inches from his face. 'Forty-one people, forty-one of my colleagues, died because of your inaction.'

Haig matched his gaze. 'I didn't know Razinski. This had nothing to do with me.'

Rose shook her head, dismayed to hear such pitiful words from a man she'd once respected. 'I really struggle with that, Iain. It doesn't matter if you knew Razinski or not. Whether it's relevant or not, your affair with Laney Gunn is a possible motive for Razinski's actions. You know as well as I do that this information could have proved vital to the investigation. Your inaction could have led to those deaths and you're going to have a lifetime to consider that. Now do your conscience a favor and tell me what you know about the Gunn family.'

The enormity of Haig's situation was beginning to dawn

on him. His hands were shaking and he failed to make eye contact with either of them. 'Laney was a high school teacher,' he said, with a failing voice.

'And Mr Gunn?'

It was a split second hesitation but Rose caught it. 'He was something big in construction. A consultant architect on large projects.'

'Worth a lot of money?' asked McBride.

'Fuck off, McBride. I wasn't after their money.'

Rose paused, considering the speed of Haig's response, the supposed injustice in his voice. A picture started formulating in her mind. 'Did you investigate him?' she asked.

'What do you mean?'

'What I mean Captain Haig is, did you use government time and money to look into the background of Edward Gunn and the work he did for Hanning Industries?'

Haig didn't respond and it was all the answer she needed. She pulled out her firearm, McBride at first surprised, doing the same. 'What did you find out?' she said.

'What the hell is this, you can't draw your gun on me.'

'You're under arrest, didn't we say?' said Rose, nodding to McBride to cuff the man.

She kept her gun pointed squarely at Haig's chest as McBride moved behind Haig. At this stage she didn't think Haig was one of the Railroad but she wasn't willing to take that chance. McBride managed to cuff him, pulling his arms behind his back before pushing him into his seat.

'I repeat, what did you find out?'

'Fuck you, I want my attorney.'

'Fuck me? You're responsible for the death of forty-one federal agents. You're a potential terrorist. It will be a long time before you see any legal representation. Now, help yourself and tell me what you know.'

On cue, McBride slammed the man's head onto his desk the side of his face catching the corner of his plastic computer keyboard.

'This is literally your last chance for a semi-happy ending.'

'Ok,' said Haig. 'Let me sit up.'

McBride dragged him back again. 'Speak,' he breathed into Haig's ear.

'Okay. I thought there was something off about the guy. He didn't treat Laney very well. Nothing physical but he didn't treat her right.'

'We'll need a bit more than that,' said McBride, pacing the room.

'Mental abuse, she was his personal slave. Then Laney started telling me he would disappear for days on end with no word of warning. He wouldn't call or answer his phone. When he reappeared he wouldn't discuss where he'd been.'

McBride stopped pacing and sat down next to Haig.

'So you started looking into him?' said Rose.

'Can't you take these off, this is humiliating. I don't want the guys to see me like this?'

'Answer me, Iain.'

Haig clenched his teeth, his face full of concentration as if he was trying to break the cuffs around his wrists. 'Yes, I started looking into him. Wouldn't you?'

'What did you find?'

'Not as much as I'd have liked. Everything I found out about his work at Hanning was legit. Obviously my range of investigation was hampered as it wasn't official. In fact, it was hard to find someone who had a bad word to say about him.

His public persona was completely different to his private life.'

'What aren't you telling me, Iain?'

Haig struggled in his seat. He was leant forward at an awkward angle, his chest pushed towards the desk. It looked painful and Rose had some sympathy for him. He'd walked into something beyond his control, his only real mistake was getting involved with the wrong people. However, it didn't excuse his subsequent actions and she was prepared to keep him where he was until he began to speak. 'We'll get to the bottom of this one way or another. Cooperate now and help yourself out. Do it for Laney, if not yourself,' she said.

'Do it for the men and women who died because of Razinski,' added McBride.

Haig remained silent his face grimacing with pain.

'This is your only chance, Iain,' said Rose.

Haig began shaking. 'There was one more thing. Ah, Jesus. Three days before the Razinski incident I followed Gunn. I'd had him under surveillance for a couple of weeks. I'd been waiting for him to make one of his forays so I could find out once and for all for Laney, and my own curiosity, where the hell he went when he disappeared. So I followed him. I got a hundred miles or so when I was hit.'

'Hit?'

'I thought it was an accident at the time but I'm not so sure now. I was pulling out of a crossroads at a little town called Ryegate, when a car pulled out from the left and ran into me. It was minor, but enough to stop me in my tracks. Gunn drove away before I had a chance to give chase and a few days later he was dead.'

'You have a plate for the car?'

Haig clenched his teeth again. 'I did. Full insurance

details and everything. Except when I got back and checked it was all fake.'

McBride could barely control his fury. 'Are you fucking kidding me, Haig? You're the Chief of Police here and you fell for that?'

'I was preoccupied.'

'Preoccupied?' screamed McBride, running his hand across Haig's desk and sending everything onto the floor.

The office door opened and Mitch stood on the threshold. The scene was too much for the young officer to comprehend and he stood mouth agape.

'It's OK, Mitch,' said Haig.

'Do you want me to call someone, sir? The Sherriff's not in today.'

'No it's fine. Get back to the desk.'

Mitch glanced at McBride and Rose before retreating in haste.

'Were you ever going to share this information, Iain?' said Rose.

'Don't you think I've suffered too? I had to standby as that animal took Laney hostage and did what he did to her and the children. I had to behave as if nothing had happened. I had to see the aftermath, Sandra. Had to pretend it was another homicide, albeit it a horrific one, when all along it was killing me inside.'

Rose shook her head. 'That's where you're wrong. If you'd come clean at the beginning you could have saved yourself. You could have saved all those people.'

'Jesus, don't you think I know that. I swore to myself that I would make amends.'

'And how's that working out for you?' said McBride.

Haig sat back on his chair, moaning as the cuffs dug into

him. 'I was waiting for the heat to die down but there's one thing I haven't told you.'

'Here we go,' said McBride.

'Speak,' said Rose.

'Yeah, about that. First, I want to make a deal.'

47

Lynch used his imagination to fill in the missing information. A female of indeterminable age lay on the prison floor, her figure skeletal-like. She stared towards him, her hollow eyes sunken deep into her skull. She was cast in darkness and Lynch was glad of the fact. He couldn't fully see the patterns on the walls, or what he imagined were the markings on the helpless girl. He turned away but Mallard pushed him back towards the opening. 'Look,' he heard the man say as he closed his eyes. 'This is how you get an honor mark,' said Mallard, whispering into Lynch's ear.

Lynch pulled back and vomited on the gravel floor. Mallard stood over him as he retched, hauling him to his feet when he'd finished. For the first time since meeting him, Mallard was angry. Was he somehow disappointed in Lynch's reaction?

'It takes a will of iron to live like this,' said Mallard, lost in an internal reverie. 'An acceptance of what you are, the limit of your capabilities.'

'It takes an utter lack of sanity,' said Lynch, wiping his chin on his shoulder.

'Do you remember the first person you killed, Mr Lynch?'

Lynch exhaled, his throat dry. He anticipated where the conversation was going, awaited another pathetic rationalization he didn't want to hear.

'I'm sure you do. I imagine it's a kind of release in your world. To jog your memory, his name was Ferdinand Rodriquez. You were aged twenty-three.'

Lynch lowered his eyes, remembering the gang member who'd drawn a weapon on him. He'd been little more than a boy, his eyes wide and confused.

'Your first official kill anyway,' said Mallard, lowering his voice. 'It was initially hard to accept, yes? The power you held. The guilt of taking another man's life despite the fact that he would have taken yours in a heartbeat. We never forget our first kill, Mr Lynch, do we?'

Mallard's words drifted towards him, out of sync as if they were being pumped through speakers rather than from his captor's lips. 'But that second kill? We remember, yes, but it doesn't resonate as much. Isn't that true, Mr Lynch. I've met many killers, thousands, and they all concede that point. Do you, Mr Lynch?'

Lynch struggled to stand still. The vomiting had weakened him and he felt drained and dizzy. He could have quite easily fallen asleep to Mallard's words.

'Kill three, kill four. Who cares?' said Mallard, with a relentless intensity. 'Each kill becomes easier until it no longer matters. The thrill never completely vanishes, does it Mr Lynch, but it fades.'

'What is it you want, Mallard?'

'I have so much to offer you, Mr Lynch. However, perhaps you need some time to think.'

Lynch wasn't sure if the train had been there all along but he found himself back in the carriage. He was disorientated, as if the blood pumping around his body was weighted with lead. He couldn't remember taking anything but he felt some form of poison in his veins.

The train chugged along the line, past countless versions of prison forty-nine, occasionally letting out a puff of steam. It was an absurd dream Lynch was desperate to wake from.

'Here we go,' said Mallard, as the train stopped before a container etched with the number One Hundred and Thirty-Seven.

Lynch stumbled as he was dragged from the carriage. Mallard uncuffed him but he was too tired to fight. A guard waited by the entrance, an open door welcoming him to a stone floored room with nothing for company save four blank walls.

'Enjoy your stay,' said Mallard, as the guard pushed Lynch into the room.

Lynch collapsed on the stone floor and turned back in time to see a grinning Mallard usher him into darkness.

'This is bullshit,' said McBride. 'Let's just take him in. We'll get the answers we need.'

McBride paced the room again like a caged animal as Rose tried to put the pieces together. Had Haig unwittingly come close to finding something he shouldn't? Had Gunn been eliminated because of Haig's proximity? If so, why did the rest of the family have to suffer? Maybe if the officer hadn't accidentally been patrolling the area at that specific time, Razinski would have eliminated Gunn and disappeared; though recalling her brief meetings with the man she doubted this was the case. Razinski would have eliminated the whole family even if he hadn't been holed up in the house, for the fun of it.

'What can you possibly have to bargain with?' she asked Haig.

'I know where Gunn was going on all those occasions. I imagine you want to know as well,' said Haig.

Rose stared at the man. 'We already know,' she said.

'If that's true, then we have nothing else to discuss,' said

Haig, calling her bluff.

'You've been there?'

'Not yet. I planned to go there and get some answers once this had all died down.'

'You know what's there?'

Haig smiled. It wasn't malicious, more resigned. 'If you've been there, you'll know all this. I'm not saying another word until I have something in writing.'

'What fucking world do you live in, Haig?' said McBride, moving behind the Captain and leaning down heavy on his shoulders.

Haig grunted. 'I have what you want, now give me what I want.'

'Which is?' said Rose.

'Immunity and relocation.'

McBride lent harder onto Haig's shoulders. 'Sure, we'll arrange a lovely new job for you while we're at it. Somewhere by the sea perhaps?'

'Listen, son, your bully-boy tactics aren't going to work with me. I've seen it all, experienced more than you can ever throw at me. Make this deal or I'm not going to talk.'

Rose recalled Haig's file, how he'd escaped from capture during combat. He'd suffered prolonged torture during the twelve days he'd been missing. 'How do you know where he was going?' she asked.

'I can't answer that without a deal.'

Rose slammed her fist on Haig's desk. 'Enough of this. If you want your deal, you tell me now how you know where he went. You tell me now, or any chance of a deal evaporates.'

Haig closed his eyes as McBride hovered behind him ready to strike. 'I placed a tracking device on his cars. His company car and that monstrosity of a people carrier he used.'

'The Land Rover?'

'Yes.'

'Bullshit,' said McBride.

'Come on, Iain, you know we have those vehicles in custody.'

'Of course I do. After I checked the insurance credentials of the guy who ran into me, I realized something was wrong. When Gunn got back home, I removed the device.'

Rose hesitated, concerned they were wasting time. Was Haig testing them, working out how much they knew?

'I'm not speaking any more. Get me the agreement and I'll talk. What have you got to lose? If I don't give you anything, I don't expect anything in return.'

'I'm sure you don't,' said McBride.

MCBRIDE LED Haig out into the silent bullpen, followed by Rose. The large deputy, Check-Shirt, who'd nodded to Rose earlier stood in protest. 'What the hell is going on, boss?' he said, blocking their path.

'It's okay, Chester. A simple misunderstanding. I'm going with these good people to clear a few things up.'

'Do you want me to call anyone?' said Chester, standing firm.

'No, everything is in hand. I'll be back shortly.'

Rose had allowed Haig the opportunity to call his lawyer who'd arranged to meet them back at headquarters. She'd followed this call by contacting Miller who set up proceedings to offer Haig a deal. They bundled the Captain into the back of the car. 'We need to search his place,' said Rose. 'You stay here and arrange a warrant. If he does have anything, I'd like us to find it before he signs any papers.'

McBride sneered. 'You're not really going to deal with this cretin, are you?'

'It's not my first choice but if he knows anything about Lynch's whereabouts then we have little option.'

'Do we really need a warrant?' said McBride, under his breath as Rose entered the car.

Rose pretended not to hear. 'Let me know when it's done,' she said, shutting the car door and diving off.

TWO HOURS LATER, Rose was back at headquarters. After a debrief with Miller, she sat in on the negotiations with Haig's lawyer. The man was out of his depth and when she showed the contract to Haig, he was unimpressed. 'It's a little vague,' he said.

'I will be back in exactly sixty minutes. If the document isn't signed the deal is off,' said Rose.

Leaving, she called McBride who'd managed to obtain a warrant from a local judge and had already started coordinating a search through Haig's home.

'We've secured a couple of laptops. I've sent them back for analyzing. Nothing looks out of place. If he does have anything I don't think he'd be stupid enough to leave it in the open.'

'I agree,' said Rose. 'Keep going though. I'll be speaking to him shortly. He knows something, McBride. I'm sure of it.'

'Let's hope he speaks,' said McBride, hanging up.

The contract was signed by the time she returned. Miller insisted on being part of the interrogation, as did the head of the legal department. Rose handed the documents to her counsel and began the interview, acknowledging the presence of Haig's lawyer for the tape.

'There's no preamble here, Mr Haig. You need to tell me everything you know about Edward Gunn.'

Haig nodded. He sat straight-backed on his chair, the worry having vanished from his face. 'I wasn't completely honest with you before,' he began.

'From what I can tell, Edward Gunn was a decent enough man. He didn't abuse Laney, physically or mentally. He was somewhat of an absent husband, hence my... relationship with Laney, but there didn't appear to be anything malicious about him.

'What I said about him disappearing for days on end was true though. Laney had mentioned it when we first met, but the days away were becoming more frequent. Laney told me each time he returned from being away it was like meeting with a different man. She described him as a ghost. She said he had dead, soulless, eyes, every time he returned. When she tried to approach him about it, he would clam up. In the end she came to me for help.'

'To the man she was cheating with?' said Rose.

'That's a rather naïve way of looking at things. Yes, we were lovers but she still loved her husband. I could respect that and promised to help.'

Rose wasn't convinced but played along. 'So what did you discover?'

'I started doing some surveillance work on him. Naturally, it had to be part-time. I followed him about, watched if he was up to anything unusual. This went on for a few weeks but nothing came from it. I trailed him to a couple of business meetings but nothing more interesting than that. He didn't go on any of his long haul jaunts and I couldn't spend all my time watching him, so I decided to put a tracker on his cars.'

Rose thought about Lynch's tracker device and realized she hadn't checked it in the last few hours. She nodded, waiting for Haig to tell her something of interest.

'Then one weekend he disappeared. Laney called me, told me he hadn't returned from work and had taken the Land Rover.'

Rose was confident what he would say next.

'I checked the tracking device and discovered his location. Otisville, West Texas.'

Miller glanced at Rose. 'The ghost town?'

Haig turned his focus to the senior agent, enthused by having a response. 'I'll say. I drove to the location but there was nothing there. Just endless roads, electrical pylons, the occasional lone dwelling.'

'We already know this,' said Rose.

'I thought as much,' said Haig. 'Obviously this anomaly piqued my interest. I guess you've checked that area and discovered there's no phone signal and that somehow GPS signals are jammed?'

'Yes.'

'I drove a few miles in all directions, looking for a sign of civilization. I found a few small farm holdings. Old cattle ranches mainly, long ago deserted by their owners. It would be impossible for one man alone to even start trying to find where Gunn had gone. I imagine it's proving impossible now.'

Rose didn't answer, nodding for Haig to continue.

'I decided I could follow him the next opportunity I had but two months went by and he hadn't made a move so...this is incriminating,' he said, turning to his lawyer for advice.

'I think we're beyond that now, Iain,' said Rose, interrupting.

'Yeah, I suppose so,' said Haig, gazing into the distance. 'I accessed his laptops one day when I was seeing Laney. One of my...someone I knew gave me a USB device and I managed to download the contents of two of Mr Gunn's laptops. I had the data analyzed but it was all work stuff, work for Hanning. Nothing incriminating, nothing suggesting why he was going to Otisville and beyond.

'Then, three days later I get a notification that the Land Rover is moving and I decide to follow, only for me to be ambushed with the car accident. Now I'm convinced something is wrong.'

'It took that incident for you to know something was wrong?' said Rose.

'It was confirmation.'

'So what did you do?'

'I ransacked his fucking house.'

Haig's lawyer rolled his eyes at his client's last statement.

'Laney was there. She gave me permission. She was worried about him,' said Haig, justifying his actions.

'Tell us what you found,' said Miller.

'I went through everything, every single thing in that house. I was there for sixteen hours minimum,' said Haig, warming to his role of storyteller.

'Didn't find anything. We put everything back in place before Gunn returned. Over the next couple of days I contemplated confronting Gunn but for all I knew it could be something innocuous. Some lover he'd taken to the wilderness. The car accident could have been simply an accident, the fake insurance documents fake insurance. And then Razinski killed them and it was too late.'

'I hope for everyone's sake that your tale doesn't end there,' said Rose.

'Obviously, I knew it wasn't a coincidence from the off. I spent all those days wondering what the hell it all meant. Then I found out what happened at the compound.' Haig gazed at the floor. 'All this shit about the Railroad. I started to think that Gunn was eliminated because of my interest in him, that somehow Gunn was working for them and that I was getting too close.'

'Why didn't they take you out instead if that was the case?'

'Well, exactly. My guess was that there was less heat this way.'

'A four person slaughter, and an armed attack at an FBI compound,' said Miller, with a snort.

'Look, I don't know. Maybe if my officer hadn't been on the scene, and if we hadn't cornered Razinski, the worst wouldn't have happened. Razinski would have killed Gunn and been done with it.'

'What else did you discover, Iain?' asked Rose.

Haig sighed, and turned to his lawyer who was trying to ignore him. 'It was after I saw those tracks engraved onto Razinski's arms that I remembered something from Gunn's house. I'd dismissed it before as there was no correlation. But after you told me about the Railroad organization I remembered a little booklet I'd seen. It was in his safe along with a few other books. It was an old book so I thought it might be valuable. It was a history of the railroads in the state.'

'Where is this book now?'

'I took it.'

'God damn, man. You tampered with evidence as well,' said Miller.

'You saw what happened to the Gunn family, what happened to your agents. If they could do that to the feds then what hope did I have if they came for me?'

'What did you find in the book, Iain?' said Rose.

Haig looked defiant. 'I told you. I know where they are.'

Rose wanted to believe him but struggled to see how an old book about railroads could reveal their location.

'For the love of God, tell us man,' said Miller.

'Gunn had highlighted a passage. A defunct freight line, last used in the early twentieth century. He'd underlined an entry. St Bernadette's Church. I ran a search for the place online but there were no results. If it ever existed, it's been erased from history. The town, the church, the railroad line. I've been to the County library, even went to the State library. I've gone through microfiche until it was coming out of my ass. The only proof that this place ever existed is in this little book. If you don't find them there then fuck it they don't exist. You can lock me up for good.'

'Believe me, we will,' said Miller.

'Where's the book?' asked Rose.

'In my safe. I presume you're already searching through my stuff?'

Rose nodded.

'In my office there is a loose floorboard beneath my desk where you'll find a floor safe. The combination is 52639.'

'Laney,' said Rose, glancing at the alphanumeric interface on her phone.

'Yes,' said Haig. 'Laney.'

49

Lynch's days alone in the faux hotel room hadn't prepared him for this. He wasn't quite in pitch darkness - at infrequent intervals light from the floodlights spilt through the corrugated iron of his prison - but it wasn't clear enough to see much beyond the outline of his hand in front of him. He feared this was it - he'd come so close to finding Daniel only for it all to end in a lonely prison cell – but tried to keep positive.

Mallard wasn't finished with him. The sensible move would be to surrender to Mallard's will and pretend he was one of them, that the whole experience had changed him. If he could gain Mallard's trust, he could escape. But would Mallard fall for this deception? Or had he already protested too much?

With the perpetual darkness he was unable to even guess the amount of time he'd spent in the prison. He fell in and out of consciousness, the distant memory of his dreams fading on waking. It felt like days since he was last supplied with food and water, and when the shutter of his prison door opened, light piercing his cell like a laser beam, it took all his strength not to beg for sustenance.

'To the far end,' came a voice from outside. 'Feed your hands backwards through the opening.'

Lynch shuffled across the floor to the back of the cell and placed his hands in a second trapdoor on the wall where his hands were cuffed behind him. He shielded his eyes as the prison door slid open and more light swamped the interior. He looked up in time to see a guard place a tray on the floor before the door was shut and he was returned to the darkness.

He tried not to rush the meager rations, ignorant as to when he'd next be fed. He'd been given dried bread with a non-descript form of meat, milk, and water.

He fantasized an escape route while trying not to dwell on thoughts of Daniel being stuck in such a place for all these years. He fiddled with the tracking device still in his jeans. If it had ever worked, it wouldn't do so underground but the small device was his last connection to the outside world.

In his darkest moments he reconsidered Mallard's words. Were they so different? Mallard had been correct in stating they were both killers and his homily about his first kill had struck a chord with Lynch. He could picture his first kill as clear as any day of his life; the clear blue sky, the hint of sulfur in the air, the gang member's lifeless body. The boy had meant to kill him but that hadn't made it any easier. He still dreamt of that moment despite all the other lives he'd taken since. Mallard was correct, it did become easier, but Lynch could still recall everyone he'd ever killed. He knew their names, the dates, and could replay each incident with unwavering accuracy. He doubted Mallard would be able to do the same.

Lynch rejected Mallard's argument about moral justification. His kills had come serving the law, or latterly in his quest to find Daniel. Whatever their similarities, Mallard couldn't really believe that Lynch would ever be one of them. Seeing the helpless woman in prison forty-nine was enough to clarify that. Mallard's constant assertion that they were alike must be part of a secondary ploy. Lynch imagined he was involved in some form of experiment, the goal of which was to turn him into one of the Railroad.

Lynch promised himself that would never happen, accepting his decision would ultimately mean he would lose his life.

50

Rose insisted that Haig accompany her back to his house. The threat of an attack was ever present as she made the journey, her eyes on constant look out for an ambush. Due to the risk of her communications being tapped, she didn't call McBride.

'It could happen to anyone,' said Haig, as she pulled off the interstate.

'You don't need to defend your actions to me, Iain. If you really believe that, then fine. But if we switched positions would you have sympathy for me? You had the chance to come clean about your relationship with Laney that day your officer was killed. Yes, it could have ended your career but you would have left with some respect intact. Now, you're little better than Razinski and the rest of them.'

'That's not fair.'

'Live with it,' said Rose, pulling outside the deposed Captain's house.

McBride was outside, shades on, smoking with two other

agents. 'What's he doing here?' said McBride, approaching her as she left the car.

'Thought I'd bring him along for the ride. Keep him where I can see him. What have you found?'

'We're trying to crack a floor safe at the moment, apart from that nothing.'

'I may be able to help you with that,' said Rose, replaying the information Haig supplied.

'It could be a trap. He could have rigged the safe.'

'The thought had crossed my mind. I thought we could get Mr Haig here to open the safe for us.'

'I like your thinking.'

Rose opened the back seat of her car and pulled Haig out, his body tense and heavy. 'We need you to do a bit of safe cracking,' she told him.

Haig blinked at the setting sun. 'I gave you the code.'

'Then it shouldn't be a problem.'

Haig glanced at McBride's unreadable face. 'You think I've put some form of trap on the safe? Why would I do that? We have a deal, don't we?'

'That's up to you. You help us find Samuel Lynch, lead us to the Railroad then yes. It starts with you opening the safe and it not going bang,' said McBride.

'This is absurd,' said Haig, stony-faced.

'Shall we go?'

The house resembled the aftermath of a college party. Furniture was overturned, books and files thrown to the floor. The agents had ripped apart all the electrical equipment, Haig's television lying in a hundred tiny pieces, the screen cracked. Despondent, Haig glared at the agents still going through his belongings but stopped short of complaining. The transformation in Haig's life would be hard for the man to accept. Hours ago, he was still a law enforcement agent and now his future was uncertain. At best, he would avoid jail time, his reputation forever destroyed. At worst, he would never see the light of freedom again. Rose pushed him forwards, her compassion for his situation limited.

'You found it then?' said Haig, walking into the bedroom where an agent was working on the floor safe.

'It's hardly the greatest hiding place,' said McBride, removing his shades. 'Jack, can we have the room.'

'Do your stuff,' said Rose, removing her gun from its holster.

'There's no need for that,' said Haig. 'These?' he said, rattling the cuffs.

She handed the keys to McBride, gun aimed squarely at Haig's chest. 'Don't give me a reason,' she said.

Haig shook his head, groaning as he bent down towards the safe and punched in the five numbers. 'There,' he said, pushing himself to his feet.

'Hands back behind your back,' said McBride.

Once Haig was re-cuffed, Rose retrieved the contents of the safe. Could it really be this simple? She scanned the piles of dollar bills and documents until she found what she was looking for. 'This it?' she asked, holding up the pamphlet.

Haig nodded and Rose instructed McBride to take him back to the car. The pamphlet was called the Railroad. Rose skimmed the content, stopping on the highlighted page Haig had mentioned. A fading black and white picture showed one set of parallel train tracks on a dust road, a wooden sign with the station's name, St Bernadette's, knocked into the ground. On the same page was a crudely pixelated picture of St Bernadette's church.

If Haig was correct and the railroad station and church

didn't show in the record books, then that meant one of two things. Either the Railroad had somehow eradicated all mentions of the area from the history books, or that the book she was holding was a fabrication.

McBride returned and she showed him the entries. 'The station looks temporary. I'm sure there were hundreds of these little stops on the railroad which were never officially recorded,' he said.

Rose agreed that was plausible. 'What about the church?'

McBride studied the picture of the derelict building. 'A brick building. I can't see how that goes unrecorded.' He snapped the book shut, brushing dust off the cover. 'Lionel Reeves. We only have this author's word that the building is actually a church.'

'Let me see,' she said, taking the book from him. The language inside was stilted, hesitant. The book pertained to be a history of the lesser-known railroad tracks and stations, but the first ten pages didn't suggest the author was an authority. Reeves had worked on the construction of these additional lines and his testimony rambled and was clouded in anecdotal remembrance rather than cold facts. As McBride suggested, the train stop may not have been official. If there were no records for St Bernadette's church, it might not be official either, brick building or not. She took pictures of each page on her phone and handed the book back to McBride.

'Let's get some proper researchers on this. Even if the names are incorrect, this place exists or existed in one form or another. If it was so important that Gunn was killed over it then Haig might be right. This might be where they're hiding.'

'Okay. Nothing much is going to be achieved today.'

'Continue searching the house. Take up the floorboards, and we can question Haig tomorrow.'

Outside, she called Miller and explained the finding.

'It matches what Haig told us?' said Miller.

'To a certain extent. Sir, considering the scope of the land surrounding Otisville, if we're going to find this place then I think we need to do a fly over.'

'Do you now?'

Rose didn't answer. Miller had been tough on her throughout the investigation but it would be pointless for him to stop her progressing at this point.

Eventually he relented. 'I'll arrange a helicopter for tomorrow. 'The ice is so thin that you could breathe on it and it would crack. Do you understand me Agent Rose?'

'Sir. Thank you,' said Rose, hanging up before the man had time to change his mind.

At home, Rose printed the photos she'd taken of the book and emailed copies to McBride. Glass of wine in hand, she read the book from beginning to end and started again. By the second read she hadn't mustered much love of the author though his tale was a fascinating one, describing his work on the gangs who'd laid the railroad in the early days of the rail network.

The great wealth amassed by the owners and operators of the railroad had not trickled down to the workers. The conditions Reeves worked under were horrendous, many of his compatriots dying only to replaced by new, eager workers. What caught Rose's attention most was the occasional foray into the branch lines, the tributaries off the main railroad. According to Reeves, this work was often secretive and Rose made a note to confirm the veracity of Reeves' claim with the Bureau's researchers.

Most of all she stared at the picture of the St Bernadette's railroad stop, and the collapsed steeple of the church and wondered if Lynch was somewhere nearby.

Pouring the dregs of her wine down the sink, she decided to shower before attempting sleep. The smell of the day's exertions slipped from her body as she scrubbed the dry sweat and dust from her skin. Tiredness seeped through her, a dull ache she was doing her best to ignore.

Haig was still in custody, the validity of the railroad book still in question. Rose didn't share the former Captain's unwavering belief that whoever was responsible was stationed in the region surrounding St Bernadette's, wherever that may be. Everything hinged on Gunn's relationship with Hanning Industries, and the fact that Gunn had gone to so much trouble to hide the book with its underlined passages. They would know more tomorrow, but if what he claimed was true - that St Bernadette's had been erased from history - then it might be one coincidence too many.

The phone rang as she was getting dried. She ran naked into the living room catching the phone on the last ring. 'Abigail,' she said, breathless.

'Rose,' said her sister, sounding distant.

'What is it, Abi?'

'It's Mom,' said her sister, crying. 'She's awake.'

Rose tensed, trying to comprehend what she was being told. 'Is she lucid?'

'She doesn't recognize me, doesn't recall having children. She's worse than before in many ways but she's alive.'

Beneath the grief and despair, was a harder edge to her sister's voice. It was a warning to Rose. That, as before, her mother's condition didn't matter, that she was alive was enough.

Rose refused to get into an argument. 'That's wonderful,' she said.

'When can you get here?' said Abigail, her words leading and cold.

The helicopter was booked for five hours time. It would take longer than that to reach Austin and back. At any other time she would have rushed to her mother's side, but there was nothing she could do for her mother in the hospital. Nothing had really changed. It was heart-breaking to admit it, she would probably never forgive herself, and Abigail would consider her attitude monstrous, but their mother was gone. She wanted to be there for Abigail, but she needed to find Lynch; needed to hunt down the monsters who'd caused so much misery to countless families.

'I'm sorry, Abigail, I can't come straight away,' she said.

'Save it. I knew you would do this.'

'Abi, I'll get there when I can. I need to do something first,' said Rose, talking to an empty line.

The music started every time Lynch fell asleep. Sometimes wild, jarring noise, discordant and electric. At other times, simple nursery rhymes repeated on loop for hours on the end. The same, mundane lyrics and basic chords rattled in Lynch's head. It was a well-known torture device, brutal in its simplicity. The mixture of repetition and sleep deprivation designed for full psychological impact on its captive.

Every time Lynch tried to sleep, they increased the volume or changed the tempo or tone of the music. Occasional snippets of time would pass where Lynch managed to block out the noise. He couldn't be sure if he'd slept or if his mind had gone into a fugue state. Desperate to keep his wits about him, he played memory games. He recalled everything that had happened since that day when Special Agent Lennox knocked on his door. His memory struggled, the words he used to recall lost within the continued strain of the noise filtering through the speakers. He began thinking only in images, picturing events as if watching a silent movie. Lennox and his two oversized henchmen, Sandra Rose and the compound, the ambush and all the subsequent events played on a continued reel, sound tracked by a toy piano and a high pitched rendition of 'Here we go round the mulberry bush'.

A vision of Gregor Razinski, trapped and dying in his glass prison, shimmered in front of him, the image so real that Lynch reached forward and touched the man's skin. Lynch muttered something to the dying man and reached out his hand.

With that, the music stopped.

The Razinski mirage faded as white noise rang in Lynch's ears and his eyes snapped shut.

If his head struck the concrete he didn't feel it.

WHEN THEY WOKE him some time later, Lynch wiped drool from his mouth as the guard rattled a baton against the metal of the prison door - the rhythm, the sound of a train roaring across the tracks.

'Turn around, against the wall,' said a voice. The guard sounded young, the voice thin and reedy.

Lynch complied, feeding his hands through the trap door. The snap of cold metal on his clammy skin was almost welcoming. Once Lynch was cuffed, the guard placed a tray of food on the cell floor. He failed to make eye contact and despite the hours of sleep deprivation Lynch was alert enough to see an opening.

'Samuel,' he said, to the man.

The guard pushed the tray into the center, the plastic scraping across the stone. The man was young, early twenties, the remnant of acne scarring visible in the gloom of the cell. 'I'm not supposed to speak to you,' he said.

'Just a name?' asked Lynch. Although he sensed weakness in the man, and a potential opportunity, Lynch's request was genuine. He was desperate for human interaction, the words spoken by the young guard the first he'd heard in an indeterminate time.

The man paused, the thin sound of nasal breathing filling the small room. 'Ethan,' he whispered, leaving the cell.

HOURS PASSED without the music returning. Lynch slept for as long as he was able, not knowing when he would next be attacked by the music.

Ethan.

The guard was soft-spoken, nervous. Could he really be one of the Railroad? The most obvious explanation was normally correct, and Lynch concluded that the man was there for his benefit, another mind game for him to contend with.

Time didn't exist in the cell. Lynch estimated five hours elapsed by the time the guard next knocked again on the door. 'Ethan,' he said, under his breath, as he shoved his hands behind him into the trapdoor.

'I shouldn't have told you that,' said Ethan, as he dropped another tray onto the floor for him.

'I won't tell if you won't.'

The guard smirked, meeting Lynch's eyes for the first time. Lynch was about to question him but it was too soon. 'Thanks,' he said.

OVER WHAT COULD HAVE BEEN days, Lynch searched for patterns in the guard's occasional appearances. The music never returned and Lynch felt as rested as at any time since his incarceration. Even the quality and quantity of food increased. The poison he'd ingested from the spiked water had vanished from his bloodstream and he'd begun to think straight once more, but he was yet to determine a pattern to Ethan's movements. The only constant was the initial procedure, of feeding his arms behind him into the cell opening so they could be cuffed. Lynch was formulating a plan to utilize this information when the guard knocked on the door once more.

'LONG TIME, NO SEE, ETHAN,' said Lynch, as the cold metal snapped down on his wrists. He stretched his hands, searching for space, for the flesh of Ethan's hands. Even if he could grab hold of the man they were separated by inches of thick metal. Somehow he would have to prevent the cuffs from locking, but it was too late this time.

Ethan placed another tray of food on the floor and retrieved the two buckets that constituted Lynch's bathroom.

'This a full-time job?' asked Lynch.

Ethan smirked, his scarred flesh crinkling into a spider web of fine white lines. 'It's not a job.'

'You're one of them?'

'You wouldn't understand.'

'Try me. You'd be surprised.'

Lynch's hands were still cuffed. He played with the metal, twisting his index finger until it found a small keyhole.

'All I can say is, you have it easy here,' said Ethan. He bent down so they were at eye level. Inches separated them but he was still out of reach.

'It doesn't feel easy.'

'There's much worse going on.'

'So you are one of them?' said Lynch, his voice harder than before.

'In a way.'

'How does it work?'

'We all have different tastes,' said Ethan, as if he was colluding with Lynch.

Lynch held the man's gaze searching for something he could capitalize on.

Ethan was warming to his subject. He sat cross-legged on the floor like they were best friends. 'I help out here and I get to fulfill my desires,' said Ethan, reminding Lynch of Balfour's words just before he'd skinned his colleague alive.

The guard was animated now, the sickness evident in his wide eyes.

'Which is?'

'You wouldn't want to know,' said Ethan, getting to his feet.

That was one thing they could agree on. The guard stopped by the door. 'I've been told to give you something.'

Lynch craned his neck. Ethan held something in his hand, something Lynch thought he'd never see again. Was that a smile on Ethan's lips? Lynch held himself, wanting to dart forward and snatch the object, but unable to move.

The door shut, and Lynch let out a soft cry as the guard dropped the patch of material, the remnants of Daniel's sweater, into the cell where it fell gently to the floor.

52

Guilt engulfed Rose as she made the journey to headquarters a few hours later. What sleep she managed had been restless, her tiredness greater now than before she went to sleep. Abigail's phone was switched off, and Rose feared this was the end, that there would be no forgiveness waiting for her especially if something happened to her mother.

McBride was already in the holding area at the top of the building waiting for her. Outside, the blades of the 407 blurred into one as Rose bent down and followed McBride into the back seat of the machine, pulling at the headphones that had the dual purpose of deadening the noise and keeping her and McBride in contact with the two pilots.

'You okay, Rose? You look a bit pale,' said McBride, as the helicopter began hovering above the FBI headquarters.

Rose had never been the greatest of flyers. Despite having flown recently in one of the machines, the thought that the only thing preventing her from falling to her death was the continued rotation of four blades of metal did little to comfort her. She frowned but didn't respond, thoughts of her mother keeping her preoccupied.

The pilots introduced themselves. 'I have the coordinates of where you want me to go. Towards Otisville, is that correct Ma'am?' said Rebora, the lead pilot.

'That is correct.'

'Not the greatest sightseeing but we'll get you there as soon as we can,' he said, through the static of the headphones.

The city soon disappeared, the ground beneath them thinning out until signs of civilization all but vanished. It was even easier to appreciate how vast the state was from above. The faded landscape stretched in all directions, pitted with the occasional dwelling and vehicle travelling on the roadways. The journey to Otisville was cut by almost a quarter and Rose wished they'd used the chopper the first time around.

'This is the location,' said Rebora, circling the spot where the signal in Gunn's car had disappeared.

Rose checked her phone.

There was no phone signal but the GPS was working.

'Can we circle out of here in cumulative circles?' said Rose.

'Yes, Ma'am,' said Rebora, moving the joystick and sending the helicopter into a turn.

McBride placed on his sunglasses and gazed out of the window. 'So we're looking for the ruins of a church which may or may not have existed,' he said.

Rose rolled her eyes. 'Something like that.'

The emptiness stretched on forever, punctuated by random buildings, abandoned barns, small homesteads, herds of cattle, and wild horses. Rose struggled to fathom the desolation, and was confused by the solitude she experienced viewing the barren land. She tracked the helicopter's progress on her IPad, as they covered over fifty square miles.

'Fucking needle in a haystack,' said McBride.

Reluctantly, Rose agreed. They wouldn't find anything this way. The researchers would have some feedback on the book soon; it couldn't be that easy to completely erase history.

She was about to instruct Rebora to return home when the pilot spoke up. 'Can't go any further,' he said.

'What's that?' said Rose.

'This area is showing as a restricted site. I'm not allowed to fly over it.'

'Military?' asked McBride, removing his shades.

'Not sure. All I know is that if I travel much further we will be in severe trouble, and more than likely danger.'

Rose checked the location the IPad. They were twenty miles inland from Otisville. She marked the place and questioned Rebora. 'You ever come across this sort of thing before?'

The pilot glanced at his partner. 'Now and again. As you suggested, probably military. Could even be Bureau for all I know but I can't take the risk of going any further. I imagine you would need some form of warrant. That would be a minimum though. I've heard of light aircraft disappearing in such places.'

'Very Twilight Zone,' said McBride.

'No, sir. Shot down.'

McBride shook his head, incredulous, glancing at Rose.

Was St Bernadette's beyond this invisible border? 'You sure you can't be persuaded, Agent Rebora?'

The pilot's silent colleague shook his head. 'No way, Ma'am,' said Rebora.

Rose cursed under her breath. 'Take us back then.'

She tried to take the positive from the situation; it was still early in the day. She could get permission from Miller, and be back here before noon.

Civilization began to creep into the landscape as they made their way back. McBride didn't speak, his attention still focused outside. Rose's thoughts oscillated between her mother and Lynch, guilt the overwhelming emotion. She still had a chance to rectify the situation with Abigail - all it would take would be another visit - but she couldn't say the same for Lynch. It was her fault he was missing, her pragmatic side taunting her that he would never be seen again.

She didn't thank Rebora or his colleague as she left the helicopter. She headed for the incident room, accompanied by McBride, where she began searching for the restricted area. She found it with little effort, a red mark on her screen approximately twenty square miles in area. There was no further information other than a brief description stating the area was restricted.

'There must be something more we can find out,' said McBride, hovering behind her shoulder.

Rose checked the clearance status on the area. 'We'll have to speak to Miller,' she said.

Miller stopped her before she had time to ask the question. He pushed his wire-rimmed spectacles up the bridge of his nose as he held his hand, palm out, in front of her. 'I know what you're going to ask, and it's classified,' he said, before either of them sat down.

'You know what's in this restricted site?'

'That's neither here nor there, Agent Rose. What I do know is we're not allowed anywhere near it.'

'There must be something we can do,' insisted Rose. 'With everything that is happening, we must be able to get clearance somehow. Who do we need to speak to?'

Miller didn't take kindly to the question. 'You're speaking to him,' he said, his voice dropping an octave as it rose in volume.

'Sir,' said McBride, about to protest when Miller stopped him by raising his index finger.

'This is getting quite embarrassing now. I've humored you Agent Rose, through your wild goose chases on the railroads, and your fly overs on the say of some work of fiction.'

'You've read my case notes then,' said Rose, beyond cares of insubordination.

'Yes, I've read your case notes, Agent Rose,' said Miller, reddening. 'How come we're only finding out now that Captain Haig was having an affair with Mrs Gunn? I'll tell you why, because you've taken your eye off the fucking ball.'

'We should have found out about Haig earlier. But with all due respect, sir, hours after arresting Razinski I was under gunfire attack at our compound and fleeing for my life. The natural course of my investigation has led to this very spot, to this dead area we can't enter.'

Miller's tongue darted, lizard-like, from his mouth. 'I can't help you. Bring me something more concrete than a poorly written book with some vague underlining and I'll see what I can do.'

'Sir, I...'

'That is all. Good day, Agent Rose, McBride,' said the SAC, pushing his glasses further up his nose and focusing on the mound of paperwork on his desk.

'WHAT NOW?' said McBride, back at the incident room a cup off coffee in his hand.

'If we can't fly over, we'll drive through,' said Rose.

McBride drank his coffee, silent.

'What?' said Rose, defensive.

'Even for you, that's a bad idea. You know the sort of shit goes on in those restricted areas. We know it's probably military or CIA. If they're going to the trouble of fucking with the GPS they're not going to welcome us turning up by car.'

'I don't think it's military or CIA.'

McBride smiled sardonically. 'Is that right.'

'Ok, let's say it is. That only raises further questions. If it's a government site, then why was Gunn visiting it?'

'It's a government site, Rose, that much is clear. Why else would we be forbidden from entering?'

'It could be private land. You know the sway some of these companies have nowadays. You've heard of Green Bank, in West Virginia?'

'The place with the telescope?'

'Yes. In parts of that you're not allowed phone or radio signals of any kind in case it interferes with the radio signals on the telescope.'

'Yeah, but you're allowed to fly over it. And it's registered, we know about it. All we know about this site is that it's restricted. It has to be government.'

Rose tired of the argument. She returned to her

computer, receiving an email about the Railroad. 'Here,' she said to McBride, pointing to the report on the screen.

The researchers had run checks on the images and text within the book but had failed to find any matches. They confirmed the existence of tributary railway lines disused for close to a century throughout the state, but so far no record could be found of St Bernadette's church, or a railway station of that name ever existing in West Texas.

'What does it mean?' said McBride, scrunching his eyes as he stared at the screen.

'It means we need to go back to the dead zone area.'

McBride rubbed the bridge of his nose. 'I may have another way,' he said.

53

All other tortures paled in significance. Released from his cuffs, Lynch crawled to the center of his cell and grabbed the piece of clothing, inhaling deeply as if the material was his only source of oxygen. He didn't know if he could smell Daniel anymore, the scent of his son fading with the passing of the years, but the sight of the sweater was enough to highlight his complete isolation. There would be no rescue. People disappeared all the time, the last six years of his life was testimony to that, so why should he be any different? He would spend the rest of whatever life he had left in the confines of his cell, the piece of Daniel's clothing a constant reminder of his folly.

Absently he fiddled with the tracker device he'd inserted in the hem of his jeans. The denim was soaked and clung to him - a sodden, filthy, second skin - but he could feel the outline of the tracker. If Rose knew his location she would have reached him by now. Head in his hands, Daniel's sweater against his nose, he started rocking. His eyes closed as he thought back to the time before Daniel went missing.

His old self was selfish and obsessive, focused only on work and not his family; yet he spent the next few minutes recalling the good times he'd banished from his memory: the boat trips the three of them made together; Daniel swimming in the sea at Galveston, the pair of them jumping into the waves; simple days lounging in their house; barbecues on the lawn; kissing Daniel goodnight after reading him a bedtime story. He regretted the negativity defining his last few years, wished he'd held more tightly to those precious memories, celebrating them rather than punishing himself by trying to forget.

The thoughts rekindled his strength. If these were to be his last days, and this cell his last resting place, then he would take what comfort he could from these positive memories.

Then the music returned.

EVERYONE HAD a breaking point and there was no accounting for how and when that point was reached. Lynch learned that early in his career. He'd seen the hardest of people crumble from innocuous events. He was still in the game but was slipping. *Here We Go Round the Mulberry Bush* was playing at half speed, the singer's voice a nightmarish distortion. Lynch clung to the remains of Daniel's sweater, rocking on the spot as tears streamed from his eyes, and concentrated on staying sane.

It was difficult thinking beyond the noise. In the rare moments he managed to tune out the repellent sounds of the distorted voice, he thought about Mallard and his insistence that they were alike. Again he wondered if that was some form of ruse, that it was all part of the man's grotesque game, his sense of fun. Lynch clung to the hope that Mallard still had plans for him beyond this basic, yet effective, means of torture.

IF HE SLEPT he didn't recall. One second the music was there, the next it had stopped. He unwrapped his limbs, still caught in a form of half-life. A tray of food was in the center of the cell. Gripping Daniel's sweater with one hand he ate without fear, the lukewarm water coating his dry mouth. Ethan, or one of the other guards, must have placed the tray in the cell when he'd slept. He was buoyed by the thought. If he could fool them into believing he was unconscious, then they could try the same thing again. Even if he managed to attack one of them, it was unlikely he would be able to get far, but it was a hope. An emotion he'd been drained of for so long.

Sometime later, Ethan's voice filtered through the cell's speakers. 'Arms, please, Mr Lynch.'

Absurd as it felt to confess it, there was a joy in hearing Ethan's voice. The onset of Stockholm syndrome it may well be, but the young man's reedy voice made him feel less alone. He fed his arms backwards through the trap gate, his fingers touching Ethan's thin arms before he snapped the cuffs on.

Ethan didn't respond. He pushed Lynch's cuffed arms back through the opening, before unlocking the cell door. 'You're wanted,' he said, hauling Lynch to his feet.

Lynch was unsteady. 'Can I have that?' he said, pointing to the remains of Daniel's sweater.

'Move to the wall, please,' said Ethan, watching him closely as he bent to retrieve the material. 'May I?' asked the young man, tying the material across his waist.

Lynch could have attacked him then. Cuffed or not, he had his head, knees, elbows, and a relentless will, but now wasn't the right moment. He didn't know what was waiting for him outside, and security would never be this lax again if he attacked Ethan without escaping.

Ethan guided him outside the cell, Lynch blinking at the light. 'Visitor?' said Lynch, with a false chuckle. 'How long have you been doing this, Ethan?' he asked, as the young man led him away.

'Since Mr Mallard discovered me,' said Ethan.

'Discovered you? What, does he send his scouts nationwide?'

'I guess so. He knows what's going on.'

Lynch kept talking to him, his eyes restless, analyzing and storing everything for later use. 'So, explain it to me. Was it some kind of job offer? Come work for me, and you can have your heart's desire?'

They stepped over a different set of railroad tracks, Lynch reminded of a ghost train he'd enjoyed as a child at the county fair.

'You wouldn't understand,' said Ethan, repeating the overused refrain.

'Why don't you try me? You call him Mr Mallard, is he known as the Controller as well?'

Ethan stopped by a corrugated steel door. 'Why don't you ask him yourself?' he said, activating the hydraulic system parting the doors. 'In you go.'

Lynch stepped through the opening into what resembled a replica of a boutique hotel lobby. The sound of running water filled the area as it fell from a marbled fountain into a pond stretching for over fifty meters.

'You like fish, Samuel?' Mallard sat on the edge of the pond, gazing at the hideous blue grey creatures swimming in the gigantic pond.

'Sea bass, lightly seared,' said Lynch.

'Very good, Samuel.'

Lynch looked at the fish. 'One could get the impression that you have a fetish for keeping prisoners.'

Mallard stood. 'I have to give it to you, Samuel, after everything you've been through you still manage to keep your smart mouth.'

'It's a gift.'

'That it is. Shall we?' Mallard moved across the room, his footsteps echoing on the floor.

Lynch didn't hesitate, not wanting to show any weakness. Mallard stopped by a bank of hundreds of small television screens. Lynch closed his eyes delaying the inevitable for as long as he was able.

'I've been watching you, Samuel.'

'No cable here?'

'It's fascinating. Everyone responds differently, that's what makes it so exciting.'

Lynch glanced at the screens trying his best not to focus on the helpless souls trapped behind the glass screens. 'I know everyone else is impressed with your little games, Mallard, but nothing is going to change my view. What are you over compensating for? Did your Mommy not love you?'

'Come, you're better than that Samuel.' Mallard pointed to the screens 'This is but a part of what we do.'

Lynch caught some unfortunate snapshots on the screens. Fellow captives. Some alone in their cells, some not. 'Why do you have this desire to show off? I don't care, Mallard, as simple as that.'

Mallard smiled enigmatically. How many people had he seduced with such a glance, with the drop of his voice? Evil always came in disguise. He played with some dials, and all the screens changed to form one giant picture: a single rail track trailing a desert landscape. 'My Great, Great, Granddaddy was a pioneer,' said Mallard, his voice warm and resonant.

'Is that so?'

'That is indeed so, Samuel. He was part of a consortium laying the first tracks on these lands.'

'Let me guess. It's his estate which pays for this?'

'I come from a fortunate bloodline, I confess. And yes, my Great, Great, Granddaddy made his fortune from the railroad but he was different to those other pioneers. Do you know how?'

'I'm sure I will find out shortly.'

'He was hands on, Samuel,' said Mallard, ignoring the jibe. 'He was an engineer. The railroad was his passion, it was in his blood.'

'But it wasn't his only passion.'

Mallard snapped his fingers. 'Exactly, Samuel. Great men. Great men don't settle for the mundane. They experience the extremes of life. You experience that in your work, others have to find it their own way.'

'By keeping people in little boxes.'

Mallard looked genuinely upset by the remark. 'It's much more than that, Samuel.'

'Explain it to me.'

Mallard glared at him and it took all of Lynch's will power not to cower. Mallard's authority was born out of his unfailing confidence. In all his years in law enforcement, Lynch had never encountered such unwavering belief. 'What we do here is incomparable. It is enlightening, it is evolutionary.'

'Torturing unfortunates is not evolutionary. You don't really believe that, do you, Mallard?'

'If you refuse to open your eyes then there is little I can do for you. We are gods, Lynch.'

Lynch began laughing, hysterical and uncontrolled, the trauma of his days in captivity finding voice, the sound distant and separate as if it wasn't coming from him. He fell to the floor, clenching his stomach, his laughter unstoppable.

Mallard smiled at his response. 'I see you're not ready.'

Lynch sat up. 'Tell me,' he said.

'Tell you what?'

'About Razinski, about my son, about all of this. Why you abduct innocent people near the railroad lines. Why you imprison some of them, what you do with the others.'

'Where else would we source them?' said Mallard, amused.

Lynch shuddered at the word source. 'Razinski?'

'Razinski was an oversight. He had a job which he took too far.'

'To kill Edward Gunn?'

'Yes.'

'Why Gunn?'

'Edward Gunn has been known to us for a number of years. He has been instrumental in some developments to our underground paradise. Unfortunately, his wife had started getting involved with the wrong people and we could no longer take the risk.'

'So you eliminated his whole family.'

The Controller shook his head. 'Sadly not. Mr Razinski was tasked with one elimination. Evidently, things got out of hand.'

'You could say that. How did Razinski know about me?'

'Mr Razinski was a smart man. He knew of you and your son. You've been a special project for us for some time now.'

Lynch controlled his anger at the mention of Daniel. 'So you eliminated him before he could talk?'

'We have Mr Balfour to thank for that.'

Fucking Balfour. 'And why am I still alive?'

'I told you. I had great things planned for you.'

'And now?'

'Now I increasingly think I've made a mistake. Which is a shame.'

'What the hell did you think was going to happen? I'm not a fucking monster.'

'I think that's the problem, Samuel. You think we're monsters when we're anything but. I think it's time we end our little chat,' said Mallard flicking a switch, the bank of television screens returning to the individual shots of the prisoners.

The hydraulic door opened and Ethan entered. 'Where's my son?' said Lynch, as he was led away.

'Don't worry, you'll be seeing him soon enough,' said Mallard, as Ethan dragged him through the door's threshold.

Lynch stopped struggling once outside. 'Did he make you like this, Ethan?'

'Mr Mallard? No. He helped me see my potential.'

Back in his cell, Lynch searched for the camera in the walls and roof of the prison but couldn't locate it in the gloom. He sat huddled in the corner, and retrieved Daniel's sweater from his waist. Beneath the sweater, he took out a paperclip.

He'd seen the clip when he'd been shown into Mallard's room. It was pushed flush against the wall of the fish lake and he had waited patiently for his moment. The hysterical laughter was only partly overacted. Mallard's talk of being god-like had triggered the extreme response in him, but as he'd fallen to his knees he'd palmed the paperclip.

He needed to keep his senses and sanity intact for just a bit longer. It was a waiting game and he would only have the one opportunity.

54

McBride called her two hours later and told her to meet him in the underground parking lot. He was waiting in his car, in the driver's seat, sunglasses on.

'Like to tell me where we're going?' said Rose.

McBride stared ahead. 'I could tell you but I'd have to...'

Rose shook her head. 'Don't, just don't.'

Rose had called Abigail numerous times since the meeting with Miller but her sister's phone remained switched off. In the end she'd resorted to calling the hospital. They confirmed her mother had woken from her coma but didn't offer much more information. She hadn't told McBride about her Mother and couldn't bring herself to do so now. She feared he would suggest she visit; her guilt was already at breaking point and she didn't need McBride's disapproval on top.

Thirty minutes later, McBride turned off the highway. He drove for another forty minutes pulling over at a secluded building surrounded by scrubland. 'Heads up, this guy can be a bit funny.'

'Funny?'

'You'll see.'

A wire mesh surrounded the one story brick building. Two dogs, Doberman cross breeds, greeted their approach with frenzied barks. As McBride pressed the intercom, one of the pair rammed its snout against the gate. It snarled, revealing a set of discolored teeth strong enough to rip through metal. Despite the midday heat, Rose shivered, her eyes moving from the snarling dog to the gigantic satellite dish on the side of the house.

A sharp noise came from the intercom. 'Who?'

'McBride.'

A lean man in army fatigues opened the door, a semi-automatic rifle strapped to his chest. 'Jesus, is this guy for real?' said Rose, under her breath.

'He has some security issues,' said McBride.

Both dogs cowered as the man approached and unlocked the gate. 'McBride,' said the man, offering his hand his gaze not leaving Rose.

'John. This is Special Agent Sandra Rose. Rose, this is John Bainbridge.'

'Pleasure, Ma'am,' said Bainbridge, offering his hand, his grip bone-dry and vice-like. 'Don't mind the ladies. They don't bite. Well, they do but only when I tell them.'

The dogs had transformed into docile pets and followed them to the house, stopping on the porch to stand guard. The interior of Bainbridge's house was minimal and sterile. Everything was chrome and glass. A computer server took up a quarter of the space, comparable in size with the equipment back at HQ. Bainbridge lent his gun against a wall and took out a set of spectacles from his fatigues.

'John is ex-military. Special ops. Tech specialist.'

The hum of electricity filled the room, Rose counting seven active computers.

'So you want to use my drone?' said Bainbridge.

'We need a flyover but it's a restrictive area,' said McBride.

'Military?'

'We're not sure,' said Rose.

'So I could get shot down?'

McBride shrugged his shoulders.

'It's some expensive equipment, McBride.'

McBride didn't reply and Rose wondered how the two men were connected.

'Fuck it. I can get this bird high. They won't detect her, and if they do we'll get the fuck out of Dodge.'

It took two hours for Bainbridge to set everything up. Rose spent the time calling her sister's answerphone, and checking her email. She was sitting outside, sheltered under the canopy of the porch, the two dogs curled by her feet, when Bainbridge told her they were ready to go. She followed him to the back of the house, surprised at the size of the drone. She caught McBride's eye when she noticed the insignia on the machine, receiving a short shake of the head from her colleague.

Bainbridge made some last-minute adjustments before standing back. 'Take some space and close your ears,' he said, as the drone roared into life. He used a tablet-sized controller, pitching the machine into the clouds. 'We can watch inside,' he said, as the drone disappeared out of sight.

It was a serious piece of kit. Three screens inside Bainbridge's house showed live footage from the cameras, the central screen displaying the banks of clouds the drone was dissecting. The machine would need some serious permits, which she doubted Bainbridge had, but such concerns were for a different time.

LESS THAN AN HOUR later the drone was flying high over Otisville. 'Here we go,' said Bainbridge, controlling the machine so it hovered over the periphery of the red zone. 'So what are we looking for exactly?'

Rose showed him the pictures she had of the church and the old Railroad line.

'Not much to go on. I can zoom down to ground level. Let's see what we can see.' There was a manic look to Bainbridge as the drone moved into the red zone. Rose didn't know, and for now didn't care, why the man had left special ops and had old military equipment in his possession. She needed to find Lynch and was willing to bend the rules to locate him.

The drone moved on, two of the cameras focused on the yellow dust of the ground beneath the clouds. The clarity was impressive. Although the drone was thousands of feet in the air, the camera picked out the environment in perfect clarity.

'There,' said McBride, pointing to the periphery of the screen.

Bainbridge maneuvered the drone revealing a chained fence stretching into the distance. The drone followed the path of the unending perimeter.

'What do you think it is?' said Rose.

'Could be used to contain cattle,' said Bainbridge. 'Or to mark territory. I've measured seven miles of it now. It's marking the perimeter of the red zone, though it begins two miles inside the coordinates you gave me.'

'Move in,' said McBride.

There were no cattle, no farm holdings, only an endless nothing.

'Are you getting a GPS signal?' asked McBride.

'Yes, of course. Why?'

'The GPS signal near the area has been disrupted somehow.'

Bainbridge frowned. 'Interesting. Whatever equipment they have down there wouldn't affect us. We're too high up.'

Rose caught a glimpse of a building on the screen. It flashed by, almost lost by the speed of the drone. 'I thought I saw something,' she said.

Bainbridge punched the screen, the drone changing direction.

'There,' said Rose.

The drone hovered, Bainbridge zooming in the camera. Beneath a covering of dust, and desert weeds, the screen displayed the outline of two train tracks.

'Can you follow that?' said Rose.

'I'll do my best.'

It didn't take long. The drone followed the disused tracks to a copse of trees. Rose checked her photo. Poking out of the thicket were the remains of a steeple.

St Bernadette's church.

'Fuck me, it exists,' said McBride.

'Can you mark the coordinates?' said Rose.

Bainbridge pressed a button on the tablet. 'Done. Now, can I get my bird the hell out of here?'

'Yes, of course. Thank you.'

When the drone returned, Bainbridge handed them video files containing still photos and the coordinates. 'You never got this from me,' he said, handing a USB stick to McBride.

'Thanks, John.'

'We're done?'

McBride nodded, and placed his sunglasses on.

'Done?' asked Rose, back in the car.

'He owed me.'

'Dare I ask why?'

'Best not. You want to go to Miller with this information?'

The question had been bugging her ever since the drone found the outline of the church. 'It's going to be difficult to explain how we got the footage.'

'Agreed.'

'Look, McBride, I'm sorry to ask this again but what is your deal with Miller? We never worked together before...'

'And you think I'm one of his minions?'

If McBride was hurt by the suggestion he didn't show it. 'Not minion exactly...'

'Listen, Rose. If you don't trust me by now, you'll never be able to. If I was reporting back to Miller then you'd be off this case already. I'm a company man, Rose, but I'm a loyal partner.' McBride took off his shades, and looked at her.

Rose couldn't help laughing. 'Ok, so you fancy a trip to this dead zone, partner?' she said.

McBride placed his shades back on. 'Just the two of us?'

'Just the two of us.'

55

Lynch practiced in the dark. On his front, pretending to sleep, he moved the metal clip from his wrist to his hand and back again. He'd practiced similar maneuvers before, successfully escaping from various forms of metal cuffs. It was an art he'd learned early in his career for such a situation as this, one almost made redundant by the ubiquitous flexi-cuffs favored nowadays. Fortunately, the same type of cuff was used on him each time the cell door was opened. A metal chain-linked cuff he believed he could pick.

When not practicing, he spent his time exercising. High explosive movements – push ups, sit ups, squats, conducted as fast as possible to get his heart pumping. Loosening the cuffs was a minor part of the operation; what he did once the cuffs were off was pivotal.

Although he didn't know when his next opportunity would arise, he decided not to make a move when Ethan knocked on the cell door later that day. The moment wasn't right. Lynch fed his arms back through the trapdoor as instructed. When Ethan was inside the cell and out of sight,

Lynch let the metal shard fall into his palm in one swift movement. He placed it inside the keyhole, testing that it would fit the lock before rolling it back up his sleeve.

'How was your meeting?' asked Ethan, sitting on the stone floor.

Lynch pulled his arms back and shuffled forward so he was opposite the young guard. 'Bizarre. What's with all the fish?'

'You tell me,' said Ethan, with a laugh.

On the outside, Ethan wouldn't have any problem integrating. He had an easy manner, was likable in a geeky sort of way. 'You ever wonder?' said Lynch.

'All the time,' said Ethan, not taking the bait.

'Seriously. You ever wonder what would happen when he has a change of heart.'

'The Controller?'

'I thought he was Mr Mallard to you.'

Ethan shrugged.

'Okay, what do you think will happen to you when the Controller has had enough of you?'

'That would be the end, I guess,' said Ethan, as if he'd not thought of it before.

'The end?'

'This is it, Mr Lynch. I understood that the day I entered here.'

'And that doesn't bother you?'

'What's that line? Better to have loved and lost than never to have loved at all?'

'Tennyson, Ethan, I'm impressed.'

The young man no longer looked so young. His expression changed, his face growing serious. 'The Controller gave it to me straight. He offered me paradise, with the proviso that it wouldn't last forever. Is it better to have paradise and lose it than never to have it all? No brainer for me.'

'This is your paradise.'

'No offence, but sitting here with you? No. But the other stuff?' Ethan's face changed again, a dreamy faraway look. 'It's better than I could have imagined.'

Lynch didn't want to imagine what could fill the young man with such pleasure. He glanced over at the remains of Daniel's sweater. 'You know where that came from?'

'No, and I don't want to know.'

Lynch continued, regardless of Ethan's objections. 'It belongs to my son. He was abducted by the Controller six years ago.'

Ethan sighed. 'I said I didn't want to know.'

'The Controller says he's here.'

Ethan stood up. 'I'm sorry, Mr Lynch. I don't know anything about that. There are a lot of people here. A lot,' he repeated, for emphasis.

'I don't know what you're up to, Ethan, but you could help me.'

'I'm sorry, man, I can't,' said Ethan, a hint of sadness in his eyes as he shut the cell door.

Ethan pressed his hands on his wrists as he unlocked the cuffs. Lynch couldn't tell if it was a sign of solidarity, but he knew what he would do the next time it happened.

56

Rose and McBride left for Otisville the following morning. Abigail's phone was switched off and Rose had phoned her mother's hospital three times in the last twenty-four hours, each time receiving the same non-committal response, that her mother was stable. The rest of her time she'd spent researching St Bernadette's church; it seemed Haig hadn't been lying. The place was written out of history. The only proof it ever existed was the flimsy paperback recovered at Haig's house, and the images they'd seen on the drone surveillance.

McBride had spent the day searching for the owners of the restricted land. The records were classified and together they decided that pushing Miller for help was a pointless exercise.

At best, it was an optimistic journey; at worst, foolhardy and unprofessional. McBride picked her up outside her building, surprising her with the amount of artillery he'd stored in his trunk.

'You planning on going to war?' she asked the agent.

'I'm planning on going into the unknown,' he replied, and six hours later that was exactly where they were.

The GPS signal started fading in and out as they reached the threshold near Otisville. From there, they navigated by paper map and compass, using the information uncovered by Bainbridge's drone. Thirty minutes in, the road was little more than a dirt track, the vehicle's suspension taking brutal punishment as McBride meandered through potholes and random outcrops. 'You think Gunn used to travel to this church?' said McBride.

'Don't you?' said Rose, no longer knowing what she believed. McBride had led her to Bainbridge and his drone, so she clung to her belief that he could be trusted. Aside from that, there was no one else but Lynch. Everything pointed to the church.

McBride pulled over. There was no shade and they ate their prepared lunch in the car, alone in the desert void. 'Where do you think we are?' he asked, holding up the map.

Rose pointed to the map. 'We should come to the fence in the next few miles.'

McBride drowned the remains of his water. 'Best get going then.'

They reached the fence thirty minutes later. It split the land in two, stretching in either direction as far as the eye could see. 'We could be forgiven for being suspicious at this point,' said Rose, as McBride drove northwest.

The vehicle curved inwards to the left as they eased along the dirt track. 'Pull over,' said Rose, after they'd been travelling for another twenty minutes.

A blast of heat hit her as she opened the door, a lining of sweat coating her skin in seconds. With the engine switched off, a peculiar silence descended over the area. Rose strained her ears to pick up any sounds, the chatter of insects, distant traffic, birds circling above, but heard nothing. She threw a stone at the fence to confirm it wasn't electric. It clattered against the wire, making a satisfactory clanging noise.

'We could cut through that easy enough,' said McBride.

Rose jumped at the sound of McBride's voice, as if it had no place in the silence of their shared wilderness. She used her binoculars to scan the space beyond the fence but all she saw was endless barren land. 'Let's keep driving. There must be an entrance at some point.'

She realized what had been bothering her as McBride started the engine and set off again. The place reminded her of the compound and her heart sank to think they might be trying to break into an area belonging to their own organization.

Minutes later, the sight of armed guards suggested she would soon have an answer.

McBride slowed the vehicle as Rose checked her weapon. She noted four guards, dressed in khaki fatigues, each holding machine guns. They were looking their way but were unconcerned by their presence as if expecting them.

McBride stopped a hundred yards from the entrance and together they left the vehicle. As they approached, the sound of their feet crunching on the stones beneath them, one of the guards moved towards the gate.

'Afternoon, Ma'am, Sir,' said the guard. He didn't smile but there was nothing threatening about his greeting. He had the professional, polished deference of an experienced military operative. 'What brings you here?'

Rose kept her focus on the three guards behind him as she withdrew her badge. 'Special Agent Rose, Special Agent McBride.'

The guard nodded but didn't glance down at her badge. 'How may I help you?'

'You can start by telling me what is beyond this gate.'

A hint of a smile formed on the guard's face, disappearing before it could fully form. 'Unless you have some paperwork to back up that request, then I'm afraid I can't help you.'

The guard held her gaze suggesting he wasn't to be moved. 'Military or civilian?' asked Rose.

'Again, Ma'am, I'm not in a position to answer that question.'

Rose glanced at McBride who was staring hard at the guard from behind his sunglasses. 'You going to stop us if we come through that gate?' said McBride.

'This is private land, sir. I would advise you not to tres-pass.' One of the other guards walked over and handed the first guard a piece of paper. 'Here,' said Guard One, pushing the piece of paper through chain-linked fence. 'A route out of here. You'll find it quicker than the one you took to get here.'

McBride smirked as he took the paper. 'You work for Mallard, don't you?'

'Sir, as I said...'

McBride held up his hand. 'I hear you.'

They retreated to the car, Rose shivering at the blast of cold air from the vehicle's air conditioning. 'What the hell is going on here, McBride?' she said.

'What did you expect? We knew it was gated and restricted.'

'That's helpful, partner.'

'Sorry, that guard got to me. They knew we were coming.'

Rose agreed. Did they know about the drone? Had they been watching them ever since they'd arrived in Otisville? The constant theme from that first day at the Gunn house

was the sense that those responsible were always in the know.
'Let's go,' she said.

'Where?'

'We'll drive the whole perimeter of this thing if we have to. I want to see that church.'

57

Ethan returned sooner than Lynch anticipated. Lynch fed his arms into the trapdoor without being asked, Ethan applying the same pressure on his wrist as before.

'What is it?' asked Lynch.

Even in the dim light of the cell, Lynch could see the color had left Ethan's face. 'He wants to see you.'

'Who, Mallard?'

'The Controller, yes.'

Had Ethan done something wrong? It was conceivable he shouldn't have been in dialogue with Lynch during the period of his incarceration. It would explain the fear in the young man's eyes, the quiver in his voice as he said, "The Controller.'" Maybe it was his training, but Lynch couldn't help but fear for Ethan. He reminded himself that Ethan was his captor, that each day he cuffed him before leaving food for him like an animal. Furthermore, he remembered the look of glee in the man's eyes when he'd described his experience here as paradise. Despite all this, Lynch couldn't shake the feeling that the man was here, at least in part, under duress. He didn't want anything to happen to Ethan because of him.

'You in trouble?' he asked, as Ethan led him from the cell.

'Nothing like that.'

Lynch felt the paperclip nestled into his grime sodden shirt. Had he missed his last opportunity to use it? Ethan led him back to the Controller, using a different route. Lynch mapped it in his head, noting the differing turns and changes of direction that led to the same destination of the peculiar aquarium.

'Good luck,' said Ethan, guiding him through the entrance.

The room was empty and Lynch moved towards the glass tank. Monsters and their pets, he thought, at the sight of multi-colored fish in their prison.

'Impressive, are they not?'

The Controller's voice echoed in the room, as loud and pronounced as a Shakespearian actor on stage.

Lynch turned to face the man, and did his best not to react to what he saw.

Mallard was stripped to his underwear. Every inch of skin below his collarbone was covered in tattoos. Lynch tried not to stare but he estimated hundreds if not thousands of tiny dark blue strikes on the man. Each miniscule horizontal dash a railroad sleeper, attached to separate parallel lines snaking across his body. Mallard's skin resembled a perverse railroad map, the hundreds of various lines intersecting and overlapping until it was hard to determine where one line began and the other ended. Lynch shuddered, remembering each horizontal dash represented the life of a human being.

'My life's work,' said Mallard, appalling Lynch by spinning on the spot.

'You think I care?' said Lynch.

'You care. You have an idea of what these lines represent. You understood long before anyone else, even if your grasp of their significance is minimal.'

For the first time since he'd met him, Mallard was truly animated. It was the first glimpse to this side of the man Lynch had witnessed. He was still controlled, still spoke in his resonant, hypnotic voice, but his words contained a sense of enthusiasm Lynch had not yet encountered. Was this the weakness he'd been searching for? 'I have nothing much better to do, Mallard. Why don't you humor me?'

'Do you know how hard it is to receive one of these?' he said, pointing to one of the marks on his arm.

Lynch moved closer, examined the raised skin on the man's flesh. He was a walking map of scar tissue. Lynch pictured the railway maps in his apartment, the missing people in the state of Texas who had disappeared by railroad lines, the thousands more nationwide. 'Whoever you're using could do with refinement work. Not the cleanest marks.'

Mallard smiled. Again, Lynch wondered how many people had been seduced by that simple gesture. 'That, as you know, is not the point. The theory, I believe, is that we receive a mark, a track, for everyone we kill?'

'Working theory I guess,' said Lynch. 'I always thought it a little old hat myself. Reminded me of those pathetic inmates with their tear-drop tattoos.'

Mallard sighed, unhappy with the comparison. 'Working theory. Very good. Samuel. Let me put that theory to rest. Let's take Mr Razinski as an example. He was a useful associate until the end. He earned a number of these marks. But what transpired at the Gunn house.' Mallard shook his head as if disgusted. 'That wouldn't have earned him anything.'

'Multiple homicide and decapitation not enough?'

'You jest but you have reached the correct conclusion. Anyone can kill. You, in particular, should understand that. No, to receive one of these you must do something a little more. It's obviously going to prove too hard to explain, so why don't I show you.'

Mallard placed his hand against the wall, pushing a button Lynch hadn't noticed. The wall moved apart revealing a glass partition. Lynch moved to the glass, entranced and appalled by what he saw beyond.

Even before it touched the cold surface, his face was coated in tears.

Alone in the cell, malnourished and blank-eyed, was Daniel.

58

Lynch banged on the glass but Daniel didn't look up. Razinski's words rang in his ears.

You wouldn't want to see him now.

His boy was skeletal thin - his rib cage visible, his arms and legs little more than skin-covered twigs – but that was the least of it. Lynch didn't want to look away, he'd waited so long for this moment, but it pained him to look at his son. Daniel had lost his sight. More correctly, his sight had been taken from him. So many traumatizing thoughts rushed through Lynch's mind that he became overwhelmed. What had they done to his boy? Daniel rocked from side to side and every fiber, every inch of Lynch ached at the sight.

The sound started somewhere deep within him, a place he'd never accessed before. It reverberated around his body as his face stayed glued to the glass panel. Lynch fought the dizziness as his roar reached its crescendo. He didn't think. His hands still cuffed behind him, he turned and rushed at Mallard his forehead striking the man's nose with one swift movement.

Mallard staggered but didn't fall backwards. Momentarily surprised by Lynch's attack, he stepped back and wiped the blood from his face. 'Good shot,' he said, laughing.

Lynch didn't stop. He moved towards the man, invading his space, trying to deliver blows with the only options left open to him - his head, knees, and feet – but Mallard side-stepped him with ease.

'We need to talk, Samuel. I understand that. But first you must calm down.' Mallard pressed a button, and the glass screen vanished.

'No,' screamed Lynch, as he sought a final glimpse of Daniel.

'Now, now, Samuel. He'll still be there when we've finished talking.'

Lynch fell to his knees. The world span in and out of view as conflicting desires rushed him: he wanted to die, to end the suffering that would never leave him; he wanted to free himself from the cuffs, and slaughter Mallard and his malignant friends where they stood; but ultimately he wanted to reach Daniel. He wanted to hold his son, kiss him, apologise, try to make him believe that it would be OK, that he could take him away from all this. The thought that the last of these would probably prove to be impossible only served to intensify his torment.

Time slipped by. Lynch found himself in a second room. Had he failed to notice he'd been carried away? He was sitting on a leather chair, coated in a film of plastic. His hands were still tied but the glamorous waitress arrived and offered him a sip of water that he accepted with a nod.

Seeing Daniel again should have been the greatest moment of his live. It was everything he'd strived for in the last six years. He should have prepared himself better. He thought back to Special Agent Lennox banging at his door, sparking the hope that Daniel was alive. It was only then that he'd truly begun to believe again. Before, although he'd not fully admitted it, the logical conclusion was that Daniel had died and that he was chasing his abductors. With the news that Daniel was alive – however dubious the source – he should have thought more about what that meant. Only now did he fully appreciate that he still thought of Daniel as the seven-year-old boy who'd gone missing. For his own sanity, he'd blanked out thoughts of what the last six years might have done to his son and a horrendous thought crossed his mind.

Daniel won't remember me.

The thought led to more tears. How had he never considered that before? Most, if not all, of Daniel's memories would be of his prison. He wouldn't remember a life outside and for the time being, Lynch couldn't comprehend the enormity of what that meant.

He had to regain his composure. There were greater concerns than his own mental well-being. He had to remain strong for Daniel. If it was to be the last thing he did, he would free him from his hell.

Lynch blinked, trying to banish the negativity. For the first time since being moved, he studied his surroundings and realized he was in a kill room. Every surface of the small room was covered in linoleum. Apart from the incident at the barn with Balfour, Lynch had been in such a room only once before. Had suffered twenty minutes of torture before being rescued by his SWAT team. He'd received counseling following that attack, and the memory occasionally woke him in a cold sweat.

His breathing became rapid, and he did his best to

manage it as he considered the meager chance of a similar rescue occurring now.

'Ah, Samuel,' said Mallard, entering the room behind him. The Controller placed a warm hand on the back of Lynch's neck before walking into view. The touch sent an involuntary shudder through Lynch's body, as if Mallard had tainted his skin with poison.

'I'm glad you're back with us. It was touch and go there. People can have such visceral responses to seeing their loved ones in distress.' Mallard was stripped down to his briefs. Lynch blinked, the patterns on Mallard's torso, arms and legs, merging into one distorted blob of color and scar tissue.

'That is all,' said Mallard, to the glamorous waitress, who disappeared as quietly as she'd emerged.

Mallard - the Controller – held his hand aloft, his eyes darting to the linoleum-covered room. 'So here we are, Samuel.'

Lynch wondered how many people had been tortured in this room, had eventually lost their lives. As if reading his thoughts, Mallard smiled and said, 'don't worry, Samuel, this is not for you. Prior to your relapse, we were discussing my markings.'

'You were,' said Lynch, surprised at the thin sound of his own voice.

Mallard ignored him. 'We were discussing how one receives such a mark. I think you understand now.' Mallard pointed to one of the tracks on his chest. Two vertical lines stretched from naval to sternum. The marks were thicker than the rest, the raised scar tissue protruding from his skin like a growth.

'Count the sleepers, Samuel.'

'Fuck you.'

Mallard sighed. 'This is my most important line. Reserved for my greatest conquests. There are eight sleepers, space for two more lines. Of course, I could have accepted one of those lines some time ago but I wanted to wait for you. I wanted to collect the set.'

From behind him, Balfour emerged through a plastic-coated door carrying a set of surgical instruments. 'Lynch,' he said.

Balfour bent before the Controller, holding a scalpel. He looked up at his master who nodded. Balfour placed the scalpel to Mallard's chest and sliced a line across his chest.

Mallard was almost orgasmic in his response. 'You see, Samuel, it's not enough to take a life. Not for us. You have to own it.' He shuddered with delight as Balfour placed a second cut across him. 'I'm not spiritual, but if I was I would describe it as owning another's soul.'

Lynch watched the scene with detachment. Despite the jeopardy, the risk to his and his son's life, he could see the absurdity in the situation. 'You are quite mad,' he said, forcing himself to laugh as Balfour placed ink on Mallard's open wounds.

Mallard was indignant. 'I was wrong about you, Samuel, and that is a shame. But I carry you here now. He pointed to the seeping wounds. 'You are forever mine. As is Daniel,' he said, pointing to the second of the two fresh lines on his chest.

Lynch looked from the makeshift tattoo to the imbecilic smile on Balfour still holding the scalpel, to Mallard lost in his perverse ecstasy, and much to the Controller's annoyance he repeated. 'Quite mad.'

59

Mallard called after him as he was led from the kill room but Lynch didn't look back. His mind was in overdrive. The measured, professional, part of him had managed to put all personal concerns aside. He was fully focused. The Controller had what he wanted. The two new tattoos signified, to his distorted mind, that he'd acquired Lynch and his son. Would he have any more use for them now? Lynch surmised that Mallard would take some joy in watching him suffer, and then would tire of him. His future would then be death, or prolonged torture in one of the cells. There would be time for remorse in the future. The present was a time for action.

The guard ushering him back to his cell was unknown to him. It was not the right time. The guard would be expected back, would be under surveillance. He had to wait. Ethan was the key. His captor had bonded with him and that made him vulnerable.

The guard pushed him into the cell. The place hadn't been cleaned and reeked of ammonia and excrement. Lynch heaved, as the guard instructed him to place his hands in the trap door and undid his cuffs.

This would not be the end of him. There would be an opportunity. Only one, but Lynch was ready to take it.

Over the coming hours, Lynch used every ounce of training, every hour of experience to prepare. Every time his thoughts turned to despair, dwelled on the vision of Daniel in one of his cells, he practiced the maneuver of dropping the paperclip from his sleeve to his palm. He kept active pacing the confines of his cell, doing occasional push-ups and sit-ups, wary of tiring himself out.

Twice he was instructed to place his hands behind him in the trap door. The first time an unknown guard emptied his buckets and made a rudimentary effort to spray the stone floor with disinfectant as if the place didn't smell enough already. The second time, the same guard placed a tray of food in the middle of the room. Both times, Lynch practiced the maneuver. He was ready, he just needed Ethan to show up.

He was asleep when the cell door knocked once more. His captors had refrained from piping in music and Lynch felt as close to being rested as was possible in this situation. 'Samuel, it's me,' said Ethan, through the peephole. 'You know the routine.'

Lynch took a deep breath, and pushed himself over to the trap door. He checked the metal was in place, and slipped his hands through the opening. Ethan grabbed his arms, and pulled them back. He put the cuffs on but to Lynch's surprise didn't lock them in place.

Lynch's breathing intensified as Ethan opened the cell door and locked it behind him. It couldn't have been an oversight.

'Bring your hands back in before anyone sees,' said Ethan.

Lynch did as instructed. He held his arms in front of him and the cuffs fell away. He was alone in the cell with Ethan, less than two meters apart. Whatever strengths the young man possessed, Lynch had the upper hand. He could attack now and end it before it began but curiosity kept him restrained.

The last time he'd seen Ethan, the guard had refused to look Lynch in the eyes as he led him to Mallard and to see his son again. 'You need to speak, Ethan.'

Ethan hesitated and Lynch was seconds from attacking him when he finally opened his mouth. 'I saw what they did to your son,' he said.

Lynch's experience told him not to trust the man. It could so easily be another one of Mallard's games. A false glimpse of solidarity. 'And?'

'I want out. I want to help you escape.'

'And how do you plan to do that?'

Ethan rubbed his face. 'There is a tunnel. Only a few people know about it. I've been here awhile now. My time is pretty much my own, with the exception of these duties. I can wonder around the facility without interruption. I've travelled through the tunnel. It goes on for miles. I thought it was never-ending but it's not.'

Lynch scratched his head. 'You can imagine it's quite hard for me to trust you, Ethan.'

'What other option do you have?'

Lynch closed his eyes and imagined attacking the man, taking his keys and weapons, and running amok through the area. He would find Mallard and kill him, would take delight in doing the same to Balfour before finding Daniel and leaving the place. But it could never be that easy. Ethan was right, he had little option but to trust him for the time being.

Lynch lowered his voice. He needed to know something 'What is it you do here, Ethan?'

Ethan shifted his legs and stared down at the floor like a dog caught doing something its shouldn't by its master. 'I can't say, Mr Lynch. I just need your word that once we're out we can go our separate ways and that you won't come for me.'

Ethan held his hand out and Lynch saw him for what he was: a scared boy, out of his depth. He grabbed his hand, considered pulling him close and smashing his nose, before letting him go. 'What time is it?'

'Ten pm.'

'Does this place run to normal timings?'

'To a certain extent. There is less guard presence at the moment. If we can get you out before morning it could be hours before they realize you're gone.'

'This tunnel. Is it man made?'

'I believe so, though it's not very well maintained.'

Ethan unlocked the cell, giving Lynch another chance to take him out. Instead, he followed the guard out of the room.

Ethan placed the cuffs loose on his wrists but didn't secure them. 'In case anyone asks,' he said.

Lynch stared at him, the balance of power fully shifted.

Ethan led him through a route he didn't know. Lynch tried not to focus on the rows and rows of prison cells, and the unfortunate souls within. He vowed to bring this place to its knees, but he had to be free to do so. 'We need to go somewhere first,' he told Ethan, freezing on the spot.

'What?' Ethan was incredulous, forcing the question under his breath. 'I don't know where they're keeping your son.'

Lynch flinched at the mention of Daniel. 'The computer room. I passed it with Mallard when I first entered this place.'

'The information you want won't be there. Not all the cells have cameras, and those that do don't have universal access.'

'You misunderstand my intentions, Ethan. Take me there now.'

Ethan closed his eyes, frozen to the spot. Lynch saw the indecision, and the realization that things had changed irrevocably between them. 'Fine,' said Ethan, through gritted teeth.

The journey was not a long one. Ethan weaved through the maze of prisons with the skills of a cat burglar, making Lynch wonder exactly how long the man had been part of the set up. Ethan pointed to the glass-paneled room. 'I'll need to access it with my card so they'll know I've been there.'

'What difference does that make if we're going to escape?'

Ethan frowned, considering the logic. 'This was a mistake,' he said, as a second guard rounded the corner and stood before them.

60

The second guard hesitated. Lynch didn't.

He flung his arms towards the man, his metal cuffs striking the guard's teeth, and followed the movement with a flurry of precision kicks and punches to his groin and throat. The guard fell to the floor as if dead, a thin wheezing noise escaping from his lips.

Lynch turned around to see Ethan pointing a gun towards him. Lynch nodded and, in a move he'd practiced thousands of times before, snatched the gun from him and smashed the butt of the pistol into Ethan's face.

Ethan collapsed, putting up less of a fight than the other guard, who was now trying to get to his feet. Lynch put that plan to rest with a kick square to the man's temple. The guard's eyes rolled into the back of his head and he hit the stone floor with a crack. Lynch checked his pulse before stripping him of his uniform and using cuffs to link the men together. He changed into the fallen guard's clothes, and ripped the shirt off Ethan's back to use as a makeshift gag for both men. Ethan looked at him, his eyes pleading.

'There's a lot of things you shouldn't have done, but pointing that gun at me was your biggest mistake.' Lynch cracked the gun to the back of Ethan's head and left the unlikely pair out cold as he moved towards the computer room.

Relieved that Ethan's pass card worked, Lynch entered the open area where the compound's IT equipment was stored. If he destroyed the small city of machinery in front of him it could lead to a disruption that would bring the compound to its knees and possibly aid Rose should she be tracking him. Now he just had to work out a way to do it.

His first try was brute force. Picking up a heavy office chair, he smashed it into the blinking lights of one of the servers and repeated the movement on every piece of technology he could see. Days of confinement had zapped his strength and soon the action was too much. Some of the lights still taunted him and he needed a better way.

He ran through the rest of the building, thankful for the lack of guards, and found what he'd been looking for. A storage unit, padlocked. From his shirt-sleeve, he retrieved the paperclip and broke through the flimsy lock. He presumed security was so lacking because of the situation. Everyone worked for the Controller, and no one in their right mind would turn against him.

'I'm not in my right mind,' he whispered to himself, taking two Koch submachine guns from the store. He stuffed his pockets with clips and was about to return to the IT equipment when he uncovered a steel protected case. Inside, nestled like eggs in a box were nine M68 military grenades. Not believing his luck, he carefully removed two of the green objects and walked carefully back to the computer room.

If this didn't do the job, nothing would. The church was

directly above them. He pulled the pins from both the grenades and threw them towards the machinery. As the explosion rang out, he pushed the magazines into the machine guns and moved into the shadows.

61

They'd stopped along the perimeter every five minutes, each time seeing nothing but blankness from within. It was now late evening, their way lit only by the car's headlights. 'You think Miller knows what's here?' asked Rose, returning' to the car after their tenth stop.

'Something spooked him.'

'You think a private citizen could own this place?'

'Mallard? Possible. Private land is private land and money talks. And he has all the money, or at least most of it.'

Rose considered the legal ramifications. Considering the security procedures they'd encountered so far, it would be days, probably weeks, before they'd get permission to enter the site; if they ever could.

McBride drank from a bottle of iced water. 'They knew we were coming. We haven't seen any cameras on the fences so they must be watching us from above.'

Rose considered the irony of another drone tracking their movement. 'We need to breach this fence,' she said.

'What we need to do and what we can do are two

different things. They'll definitely have eyes on us now. We've been warned off entering the site. We go through that fence we'd be executed, no question.'

Rose agreed but it didn't make the situation any less frustrating. There was no cover, no covert way they could breach the perimeter without being detected. If they were going to get through the fence they would have to reach the building within seconds and the location of the church was vague at best. The building was somewhere within the perimeter; it was there, they had photographic proof, but at that moment it all meant nothing.

'What's that saying? If you can't go through it, you go over it?' said Rose.

'That's not a saying,' said McBride.

'But a potential solution to our problem. The drone managed to fly over the site without being detected.'

'As far as we know. Even if that is true, it's different from flying a helicopter. And who would we get to fly it? It might sound farfetched but they may have air to ground missiles.'

'What, in a private residence?'

'Who knows what agreements they've made with the government. Anyway, we are only hypothesizing. It could be CIA.'

'Or military,' said Rose.

'Either, but neither would hesitate to shoot down an unknown craft. Not that we would get permission from Miller anyway.'

'So what? We just give up?'

McBride ground his teeth, the noise reverberating around the interior of the car. 'I don't know what to suggest, Rose,' he said, his voice rising. 'For what it's worth, I believe your assertions are right but this isn't the way to go about it. We need to get back to HQ and start working through the proper channels. We'll get permission sooner or later to investigate the place.'

'It will be too late by then,' said Rose.

'This is about Lynch?'

'Of course it fucking is. It's my fault he's disappeared.'

McBride looked away, as if gathering his thoughts. 'You're not going to like this, Rose, but did you ever think that he might be one of them?'

Rose was expecting the question but it still stung. 'I've considered it and dismissed it. You didn't see him at the compound. He went back to see Razinski under all that potential fire. He had the chance to take me out at any time and he's the one who led us to Mallard. His son was kidnapped for god's sake, why would he have anything to do with them?'

McBride held his hands up. 'Okay, Rose. Just sending it out there. Why do you think they've taken him?'

'Who knows why they do what they do?'

'It's getting late. Let's head back. We can find somewhere for the night and return tomorrow.'

Rose nodded, too agitated to speak.

McBride was about to set off, when in the distance a plume of smoke rose in the air followed by the sound of an explosion.

62

Within seconds, the area was flooded with guards. Dressed in the khaki uniform of the guard he'd attacked, no one took any notice of Lynch despite the MP5 machine gun strapped across his chest. They were too busy trying to put out the spreading fire, the chaos exacerbated by the smoke clouding everyone's vision.

Lynch stepped out of the computer area and headed back to the prison cells. Lynch used his spatial awareness abilities to track his course. Despite the best efforts of Mallard and Ethan, he'd created a mind-map of the immediate area. He found his way back to point zero – his cell – with no trouble. From there, he knew where he had to go. To the peculiar aquarium where he'd last seen the Controller. Where there was a window into Daniel's cell.

Lynch was under no illusions as he retraced his steps that either the Controller or Daniel would be there but he had to start somewhere. The pandemonium was spreading. People spilled out of the cells. They were surprised and avoided eye contact with each other. Lynch saw them for what they were:

captors not prisoners. He eased his finger onto the trigger of one of the rifles, and mustered all his strength not to use it.

He found the aquarium within minutes. Ethan had led him on a number of detours but the room was only meters from his cell. He didn't hesitate, bursting through the door with one of the guns held in front of him.

'Do I know you?'

The man in the room may not have recognized him but Lynch recognized the man. It was Sucker Punch from the train. Lynch saw the realization dawn, as the man's hand reached for his gun.

Lynch had spared Ethan's life, as well as the guard whose uniform he now wore, but Sucker Punch wouldn't be so lucky. He had no option. The guard wouldn't hesitate to put him down and the man's moment of hesitation was enough for Lynch to pull the trigger on the MP5.

The sound of the gun reverberated around the empty shell of the room, as bullet after bullet tore through Sucker Punch as if he was made of water. No remorse came over Lynch as he checked the man was dead and he recalled the Controller's claim that they were alike. But he was incorrect. Lynch felt no remorse, but he felt no pleasure either. The man would have killed him as soon as look at him. Lynch's only regret was that he wouldn't be able to question him about the Controller's location.

He tore the man's ID away, assuming he had greater access than the other guards, and moved to the concealed window. He punched in the four-digit code he'd seen Mallard enter, and held his breath as the wall partition opened.

He let out a breath, unsure if it was relief he felt as he viewed the empty space. 'Where are you?' he mouthed to himself, as the door behind him opened.

It was a risk but one worth taking. His usual response would have been to turn and shoot, but he needed someone alive.

Lynch fell to the floor, rolling over so he faced the door. The khaki uniform gave the guard away, Sucker Punch's accomplice. Lynch let off a line of bullets aimed at the man's legs.

The guard dropped, a dead weight crashing to the floor, and Lynch was on him within a second, dropping his knee onto the man's chest and securing his firearm. 'Remember me?' said Lynch, applying pressure to the man's right knee. Below the joint, the rest of his leg hung on by severed tendons and sinew the bone all but obliterated.

The guard struggled to breathe but was alert enough to cry out as Lynch increased the pressure on the wound. 'This will end two ways for you. I have to be honest, neither is great, but you reap what you sow. You tell me what I want to know and I give you the decision.'

Red-tinged spit dribbled from the man's mouth and Lynch was worried he would lose him before he got the answers. 'What decision?' said Sucker Punch's accomplice.

'Die immediately or later.'

'Some choice.'

'Where's my son?'

'Your son? I thought you'd want the Controller?'

'I'll get to him. Tell me where my son is?'

The accomplice smiled. 'We have a special place for him.'

The guard was trying to provoke him. Lynch could see he wanted to die. He smiled back, and placed his gun into the mess where the bottom of the man's leg used to be. The man tried to scream - his mouth gaped open as the veins on his neck and forehead protruded from his skin - but no sound left his throat. 'Tell me now, or your last moments on this earth will be full of agony even you can't imagine.' He held the gun in position for five more seconds. As he withdrew, the man's pain finally found voice.

When he'd stopped screaming, Lynch slapped his face. 'Where's my son?'

It took a minute for the guard's breathing to ease enough to allow him to speak. 'You promise you'll do it?' he said, his body shaking with each utterance.

Lynch nodded. 'But I won't ask you again?'

'He's in the cell next to you.'

Lynch closed his eyes. It made perfect sense yet the possibility had never crossed his mind. Of course they would have put him next to his son. Had they informed Daniel that he was in the next cell? Had they let him hear the suffering they'd heaped upon Lynch?

'You're a fucking monster,' said Lynch, getting to his feet.

'Do it,' shouted the man.

'Do what?'

'Kill me.'

Lynch held out his gun, aimed it square between the man's eyes. 'Now why would I do that?' he said, pulling the gun up and letting off a shot that missed the man's head by inches.

63

Rose and McBride watched the smoke rising in the darkening sky. 'It must be the church,' said Rose.

McBride laughed when she'd been expecting a sigh. 'That's quite an assumption, even for you.'

Rose had made many pivotal decisions in her career. The most recent at the Gunn house when she'd negotiated Razinski's release. Had that worked out for the best? She had no doubt that if Haig and his team had been allowed their way, Razinski wouldn't have escaped that place with his life and everything that followed could have been avoided. But that hadn't really been her decision. She'd followed protocol, would never let a prisoner come to harm because of the bloodlust of fellow officers, however heinous the crime.

This was different. If she breached the compound fence not only was she effectively trespassing, she was going against orders. However vague Miller's warnings, he'd been specific that she stay away from the site.

But some things were more important than protocol and orders. 'I'm going in. You coming with me?'

McBride was nonplussed. 'Better start making access then,' he said, retrieving wire cutters from the back of the vehicle.

Rose tried to remain calm as McBride snipped away at the metal but feared they were being watched. At that very moment armed patrols could be on their way.

'That should do it,' said McBride, cutting the last of a segment away from the fence. 'You sure you want to do this?'

'What's the worst that could happen?'

McBride sighed this time. 'I won't answer that.'

Rose drove, wanting to take responsibility for what was to come. She kept the lights off, using the fading plume of smoke as a guide. They hit a number of potholes, careered over hidden descents, neither commenting as their vehicle lurched from side to side and threatened to roll. Rose kept her eyes straight, focused on the undulating line, willing the church to come into view.

'I'll be damned,' said McBride, five minutes later.

In the distance, poking out of the land like a crop of young trees was the top of a building sunken into the ground. And five hundred yards in the distance, an anomaly in the vast nothingness of the land, stood the church.

Rose wasted no time. The smoke was still rising from the building, and she had the absurd thought that someone was being cremated within. She pushed the accelerator down, the vehicle sliding in the dust before springing forward.

'Rose, stop.' McBride slammed his hand onto the dashboard as Rose noticed the two figures emerging from the church, each carrying guns. She hit the brakes, and they both sank down in their seats before opening their doors as a line of bullets sprayed over their vehicle.

Rose rolled from the vehicle onto the rough ground, the

skin on the back of her hand ripping away as she snagged it on a rock. The bullets stirred the dust and she scrambled through the haze to the back of the car where she was pleased to see McBride.

She snapped open the trunk, and they withdrew additional firearms before dropping to the ground.

'There,' said McBride, pointing beneath the car.

Rose ducked down and saw the faint outline of two sets of legs less than fifty yards away. 'I'll take the right, you left. On three.'

She counted down. It was a tough shot. She loosened her arms, controlled her breathing and pulled the trigger six times, her shots ringing out in stereo with McBride's. The guards fell but they couldn't be sure what contact they'd made. 'Go,' she screamed, as they spun to either side of the car and ran at the two guards, sending a second round of bullets into the sky as a warning.

'FBI, stay down,' said McBride, as they reached the pair.

One of the men was unconscious, the other wasn't listening. He lay on the ground, his shin bone missing, yet he still had the strength to raise his gun and point it at McBride.

Rose didn't hesitate. She fired three times into the man's chest as she moved towards him and held the gun to the head atop his lifeless body. Her attention turned immediately to the other guard who was on his side, a puddle of blood soaking into the yellow earth.

She took the weapon from the man as McBride shouted questions at him.

'Fuck you,' said the guard, closing his eyes. He'd lost a lot of blood and Rose felt a weakening pulse in his neck.

They hunkered down, scanning the area, waiting for more guards to join their fallen comrades; but none emerged from the shadows of the church. Rose was about to move towards the safety of the building when she noticed something, a mark, a flash of blue, on the arm of the fallen guard next to McBride.

'Pull up his sleeve. Left arm,' she said.

McBride did as instructed, revealing the jagged line of a Railroad tattoo. 'Jesus Christ,' said McBride, as if only just coming to the realization that their foe was real and not imaginary.

'We have to call it in,' she whispered.

McBride nodded. 'All of a sudden I've got a signal,' he said, displaying the four bars on his phone. 'Miller?'

'You call Miller. I'm calling someone else.'

McBride understood. He called Miller and tried his best to explain the situation. From the way he held the phone away from his ear, she understood the call was not going well.

Rose took the opportunity to call Daisy Montero, an officer she'd befriended in the local Sherriff's department. She explained the situation as succinctly as possible.

'We can't go out there,' said Montero.

'There are two federal agents in lethal danger, Daisy. You have permission. Tell the Sheriff if you have to, but send some squad cars here now.'

'What about your team?'

'I don't know who I can trust, Daisy. The more people who know about what's going on here the better.'

'I understand,' said Daisy.

'I think that's my career,' said McBride, hanging up the same time as Rose.

'Miller should never have stopped us going here in the first place. I don't know what this place is but it shouldn't be benefiting from any legal protection. Tell me he's sending some back up in.'

'Reluctantly, yes. And you?'

'Local Sherriff's department. Just in case.'

'I like your thinking. I take it we're not going to sit here and wait?'

Rose tore an identification card from one of the guards. 'No.'

They moved towards the church, a second set of explosions ringing out into the night air.

64

Lynch had seen more people in the last five minutes than he'd seen in the last few weeks. They congregated near the explosion area, milling around one another, confused and worried. Lynch assessed them, trying to unravel what was bothering him about the way they moved across the space. Then it dawned on him: they were avoiding making eye contact. They moved in silence, eyes glued to the floor like shy teenagers at their first disco. Only they weren't being shy. They were being discreet, either ashamed or respecting each other's secrets.

They didn't look up as he moved through them, his ill-fitting uniform ripped and coated in blood. He wanted to know why they were there, what heinous crimes they'd committed, and what they'd had to sacrifice to be there; but there would be time for answers later.

He made his way back to his cell like an escaped zoo animal returning to the safety of captivity. The ease of his journey didn't surprise him, nor did the sight of the four prison guards waiting for him.

They'd barely opened their months by the time he'd let off his first round of fire. Eight rounds of bullets, two to each guard's chest. Even if they had Kevlar protection, at such close proximity the hits would, at a minimum, incapacitate them. Not that they were given the opportunity to retaliate. Lynch didn't stop moving. He fired four more times into the fallen bodies, before firing one bullet into the forehead of each guard.

They'd known he would return which meant he'd been watched all this time. He couldn't think of that now. There was a cell on either side of his old prison. He opened the peephole to the first and saw nothing but empty space. He moved to the next cell with limbs so heavy he thought they would hold him to the spot. He was reminded of childhood nightmares, dreams of being held in place by an invisible force when he'd been desperate to reach his parents' bedroom. But he was in control. He understood the fear making him hesitate and was strong enough to fight it.

He stumbled forward, his chest tight, and pulled the shutter open. With a deep breath, he gazed inside.

'Daniel,' he said, his voice lost in his throat.

Daniel sat on a single wooden chair gazing at the side wall that connected his cell to Lynch's.

'Daniel,' he repeated, fearing it wasn't only his sight that Daniel had lost.

The boy stirred and turned to face him. Lynch gasped at the sight of his son, so close to him, no barrier of glass in his way. 'Daniel, it's your Daddy,' he said, streams of tears coating his face. 'I'm coming to get you now.'

The bolt was a simple padlock, yet Lynch's hands shook and slipped as he tried the keys he'd found on one of the dead guards. He could have shot his way in but he didn't want to unsettle Daniel. Eventually he found the correct key, and the lock slipped apart. He had to stop as he began pulling the door open, his heart beating so fast he risked going into cardiac arrest. He took some deep breaths and eased the door open.

'Daniel,' he whispered. 'It's your Daddy.'

Daniel heard his voice and began to cower.

'Oh, Jesus,' said Lynch, putting his shaking hand towards his face. He edged forward. 'I'm here to help you, Daniel. I'm going to take you away. You can see Mommy again. Would you like that?'

Daniel was a teenage boy now but Lynch didn't feel strange speaking to him that way. He noticed a slight twitch in Daniel's face as he mentioned his Mommy. 'Mommy, yes? She is so desperate to see you again.'

Lynch leaned forward and placed his hand on the boy's shoulder. Daniel flinched but let him keep his hand there. It was too much for Lynch; he fell on his haunches and began to weep. What had they done to his son? As he grieved, he was overcome with such bitter anger that he thought he'd been changed for good. He wanted to go back to where the others were congregated and to execute each and every one where they stood. Readily, he would torture each one first, and would then find Mallard and spend the rest of his days putting the man through extremes of pain.

Then Daniel did something miraculous.

He placed his hand on Lynch's head and said, 'Daddy.'

Lynch stopped crying and stood up. Gently, he placed his hands to his son's face, something he never thought he'd do again. 'Daniel, we need to go. Do you understand?'

Daniel nodded and Lynch lifted him off his chair. Despite

the years, the boy weighed the same as when he was seven. 'Can you walk?'

'Yes.'

Lynch guided him to the edge of the cell. 'Wait here,' he said, securing the area outside the cell, the four slain guards heaped together in a river of blood.

He grabbed Daniel's hand and led him along the corridor, catching hold of him as an explosion sent them both crashing into the walls.

65

Candles lit the interior of the church. Tendrils of smoke drifted from the burning wax into the hollow shell of the building. Rose and McBride walked the perimeter of the church floor. There was no sign of the explosion they'd heard moments ago.

'Through here,' said Rose, pointing to a door at the rear of the raised level that had presumably once been the church's altar.

McBride kicked the door open, and Rose secured the area. The corridor was a modern addition to the derelict church. They followed the smooth white walls around two meandering corners until they reached another set of doors. 'An elevator?' said McBride.

Rose pushed her palms against the cool metal of the doors but was unable to force them apart. 'This can't be the only way in.'

As if in answer, the floor opened up.

'Jesus Christ,' said McBride, standing back just in time to

avoid being swallowed by the trap door blended into the carpeted floor.

Thick black smoke billowed through the opening, and they both fell to their knees on either side of the opening as two figures emerged each dressed in the same khaki uniform of the Railroad guards, both carrying weapons, both with gas masks strapped to their faces.

In the fog of the smoke, neither guard had seen them. They had their back to them and Rose faced considered firing, only the negative connotation of shooting someone in the back, and the faint possibility that they were innocent, preventing her.

McBride gave them a warning. 'FBI,' he shouted, as both guards swung their guns in his direction.

The movement roused Rose from her hesitancy. She fired at the two guards from her position on the ground and ran towards them as they fell.

McBride nodded and tore the gas mask off one of the guards. He handed it to Rose, but she shook her head and repeated the move on the other guard who was still alive. 'You want to live, tell me what is happening down there,' she said.

Rose began choking on the black smoke as McBride urged her to place the mask on. As the smoke clouded the guard's face, she heard him utter, 'it's the end.'

LYNCH COUNTED THREE DETONATIONS, the source infinitely more powerful than the hand grenades he'd set off in the computer area. The first must have been close as the residual blast had pushed him against the wall. He'd managed to grab Daniel, and shielded him as the wave sent him careering into the hard stone. He hadn't heard it, but he'd felt his bones crack. Daniel was unconscious in his arms, his pulse weak. Lynch held him tight with his left arm, and struggled to move the fingers of his right hand resting on the boy's head. 'We're going to have to move soon,' he whispered to Daniel. 'Soon,' he repeated, knowing his legs were no longer working.

THE END WAS A FINE DESCRIPTION. After descending the spiral staircase, Rose found herself in a version of hell. She was taken back to the compound, and the attack on Razinski and her colleagues. The cavernous space reminded her of that place, as did the sight before her.

Bodies littered the floor of the building, some dressed in guard uniforms, others in civvies. Most were victims of the black smoke curling around the beams of light that fell from the floodlights shaped high into the rock. Pockets of fire sprang up as they moved through the mass of bodies, into a second area where hundreds of shipping containers stretched into the distance. 'What is the place?' said Rose, her words swallowed by the breathing apparatus strapped onto her face.

McBride turned his head at the sound of sirens in the distance and pointed back the way they'd come.

Rose shook her head. 'We need to find Lynch,' she said.

McBride couldn't have heard her but he followed as she made her way towards the containers.

ACID-LIKE TEARS stung Lynch's eyes. He tried to blink them away, realizing he must have fallen asleep. He shuddered, his hand reaching for the bundle of bones in his arms. He let out a cry of relief as he felt the brittle beat of his son's heartbeat through his ribcage.

He refused to come so far only for it to end like this. He owed it to Daniel, owed Sally the opportunity to see her son once more. He took a deep breath and pushed himself off the floor, his weight landing on his right ankle.

The sound he made momentarily woke Daniel from his sleep. The boy's eyes flickered opened as Lynch tried to control the scream of anguish as his shattered ankle slipped, and cracked further.

'Looks like you 'ain't going nowhere.'

Lynch glanced up at a towering figure who was replacing a gas mask back onto his face. He thought back, trying to remember to match the sound of the man's voice. 'You're one of Mallard's harem,' said Lynch.

The man lifted his mask. 'I knew you would bring trouble with you.'

'You tell the Controller that? Or were you too scared?' said Lynch.

The man was impossible to read with his mask on. 'I wouldn't question him but I know what he would want me to do.' The man bent on his haunches. He removed his mask and coughed into Lynch's face. 'First I'm going to kill you. Then I'm going to take your son. I promise I'll look after him. I'll look after him forever, Lynch. You hear me? Forever?'

Lynch twisted his head, offering his ear to the man. Mustering his last ounce of strength, he dropped his right forearm onto the floor and picked up a shard of metal from the explosion. He gripped it tight, slivers of pain rushing through his broken hand, and he drove it as hard as he could into the man's throat.

The man's eyes widened. He tilted his head, his face a

question, the shard sticking out of his throat now coated in cascading blood.

'Forever,' said Lynch, as he pushed the man off him, the shard of metal plunging deeper into the man's neck as he landed.

'Forever,' he repeated, his eyes closing as he shielded Daniel as best as he could.

ROSE WIPED the soot from her burning eyes. The fires were breaking out everywhere now, and no one paid attention to either of them as they reached the first container. Rose pulled opened a slat in the side of the container and peered inside. At first, she couldn't see anything, the gloom inside almost impenetrable. She took off her gas mask and tried as best she could to clear her eyes. Blinking back stinging tears she made out the outline of a slumped figure in the corner. 'Stand clear,' she said, firing her revolver into the hinge of the lock holding the door in place.

Together, they pulled at the lock eventually forcing it free. 'What is this place?' she said, as she made her way across the floor of the cell, past buckets of human waste, to the child in the corner. She placed her hand on the figure, a girl no older than ten, and breathed a sigh of relief as the girl flinched.

'Here,' said McBride, placing his mask over the girl as three figures entered the cell and pointed their guns at them.

LYNCH SLIPPED in and out of consciousness, each time relieved to feel Daniel still in his arms. The smoke was clearing but the hope of being rescued was destroyed when another figure came into view, its face coated in shadow. 'I tried to help you,' it said.

Ethan still carried the wounds Lynch inflicted on him. His nose was flattened against the side of his cheek and his left arm dangled to his side.

'I had to find my son,' said Lynch, unapologetic.

'I tried to help you.'

'Why don't you help yourself by getting out of here while you can.'

'I'm afraid I can't do that. He wants to see you.'

'Mallard?'

'The Controller.'

Lynch laughed. 'The Controller.' He spat the words out of his mouth. 'He's not in control anymore, boy.'

Ethan looked at the dead guard to Lynch's side. He plucked the metal shard from the man's neck and lent forwards to Lynch, grabbing his broken right arm. 'You're coming with me.'

Lynch sucked in the pain, refusing to give it voice. 'You want me to go, you're going to have to drag me all the way there.'

'That can be arranged. But the Controller says you're to come alone.'

Lynch waved his useless hand at Ethan as he tried to pry Daniel from his arms. As Ethan got in close, Lynch struck his head hard against Ethan's broken nose but the boy kept fighting.

There was no way he was going to give Daniel up.

Ethan began to understand as much. He retreated and pulled out a gun. 'Let the boy go or I'll put a bullet in his head.'

As he said the words, his distorted face froze as a bullet

entered the back of his head. His body fell to the floor, revealing his assassin.

Agent Rose stood before him, her gun still held out in front of her. To her side, was her colleague, behind them three armed uniformed police officers.

Lynch had never seen a more wonderful sight in his life.

66

The knocking came in the middle of night. It took a few minutes for the sound to register, the incessant rhythmic thud of fists on wood the sound of a train rattling along the tracks.Lynch blinked his eyes open. The room was familiar yet alien to him. Behind him a machine pumped out the occasional electric noise, and his eyes followed the path of a tube snaking from a container high on his left to the vein in his arm. As he accustomed himself to his whereabouts, he was relieved to see the glass door of his room was ajar.

'You awake?'

The voice was soft, dream-like, and Sandra Rose glided into the room as if floating on air.

'What have they got me on?' said Lynch, his voice dry and hoarse.

'You've lost a lot of blood and fluids. A lot of everything.'

'This doesn't feel real. Am I dreaming?'

Rose laughed, the sound kind. 'No, I think your drugs are kicking in.'

Lynch's heart stopped as he remembered. 'Daniel?'

Rose smiled. 'He's here too.'

HE SLEPT SOME MORE, and when he awoke he tried to get out of bed.

'Samuel, wait,' said Rose.

Lynch was unable to move his arms and for a second he feared he was tied to the bed.

'Your arms are broken,' said Rose, placing a cold hand on his forehead.

Lynch glanced suspiciously at the white plaster covering his arms. 'I need to see Daniel.'

'Sleep some more. I promise I'll take you to see him in the morning.'

MORNING CAME and the effect of the drugs was beginning to wear off. Lynch's body felt more alive than he could ever remember, every inch of him in excruciating pain.

Rose understood the stricken look on his face and called for help. A nurse arrived and seconds later the pain eased. 'Daniel,' whispered Lynch, as he fell under once more

LATER THAT DAY, he was ready to see his son. The fug of the new drugs had worn off and although the pain was uncomfortable, he was willing to endure it for Daniel's sake.

Rose wheeled him through the hospital. Everyone they passed smiled at him as if he was an exhibit. 'Are you ready?' she asked.

'Thank you, Rose,' he said, as she wheeled him into the hospital room.

Daniel was awake, IV equipment pumping fluids into his veins, a mask over his eyes. 'I'll leave you to it,' said Rose.

Lynch nodded and glanced at Sally who was sitting in a chair next to her son, fighting back tears.

At first he was unable to speak. Every time he opened his mouth, he started to cry, and he wondered if he would ever be able to speak again. Sally nodded at him, willing him on.

'Daniel,' said Lynch. 'It's Daddy.'

The boy stirred. His eye mask lifted as he smiled, revealing the outlines of scarring where his eyes had been removed. 'Daddy,' he said.

Lynch hung his and began sobbing.

ROSE WATCHED FROM THE CORRIDOR, leaving Lynch to his joy and grief as he began crying and was consoled by his ex-wife.

It was three days since they'd found Lynch and his son at the underground prison. She'd spent nearly every waking moment at the place, and was due to return there shortly. Even now, they were still trying to make sense of what had happened. Over three hundred people had lost their lives in the last seventy-hours, the majority from suffocation. Many of them had died in their shipping container cells.

At headquarters, teams were working on the fallen prisoners. Matching them to the missing persons reports stretching back for years, sometimes decades.

Miller and Roberts had been suspended from their roles following the revelation they'd prevented Rose and McBride from visiting the compound, the ownership of which had now been linked to a holding company owned by the Mallard family. An agreement stretching back to the early twentieth century had given the Mallard family protective rights of the land. The press had already become involved, and the bureau and government were busy trying to answer legitimate questions as to why such a place existed.

The search for Mallard and Balfour continued. Neither man had been found at the compound. The explosions destroyed most of the infrastructure and, although some digital files were recovered, nothing of interest had yet been uncovered.

ABIGAIL MET her in the lobby of the hospital. She was dressed in black and stood frigid as Rose approached her. The sisters stared at each other as if about to attack.

Rose's mother had died during the siege at Mallard's compound. A single voicemail was waiting for Rose as she sat in the back of the ambulance rushing Lynch to the hospital.

'Well?' said Abigail.

Rose didn't say anything. What could she say? She hadn't been there for her mother's death, hadn't said goodbye, had allowed her younger sister to suffer that burden alone. She stepped forward and wrapped her arms around Abigail who stood frozen, her arms by her side.

'I'm sorry,' said Rose, squeezing harder.

They stood that way for what felt like minutes until Abigail's body finally softened. She lifted her arms and hugged her sister back, and Rose didn't want her to ever let go.

EPILOGUE

The Controller, still stripped to the waist, led the way through the narrow confines of the tunnel, the one designed by Edward Gunn, his feet either side of the disused railroad track twisting along the ground. Behind him, head bowed, followed the former FBI agent, Balfour.

All those years before, when he'd first taken Daniel Lynch, the Controller had suspected it would come to this or something like it. Lynch was a challenge of his own making. Lynch brought chaos, and an unwillingness to concede the Controller had never encountered. He'd been right and wrong about the man. They were more alike than Lynch would ever admit but not as much alike as the Controller had first envisaged.

He'd watched Ethan help Lynch escape, smiled as Lynch turned on the man and set off the first explosions. He could have intervened at any moment but the time had come to start again. It was he who had set off the second and third set of explosions much to the bemusement of Balfour who'd followed him around like a nervous puppy.

The whole operation had grown stale. They'd reached such a state of nirvana that they could get away with anything and where was the challenge in that? The Railroad legacy was over, he needed to start again. Not that he need start from scratch. The majority of his wealth was still undetectable, would remain so after the forthcoming FBI investigation.

A cold draught caressed his skin, signaling they were near the end of the tunnel. A car waited for them but he had one last operation to conduct before he began his new life.

Balfour stopped at the threshold of the tunnel's exit as the Controller removed the knife from his holdall. 'You deserve this, Mr Balfour. You've always been a tremendous servant.'

Balfour bowed.

'Where?' said the Controller.

Balfour pulled open his shirt revealing a chest decorated with intersecting railroad tracks, each carved onto his skin by the Controller's hand.

Balfour closed his eyes as the Controller made the incision.

'You deserve this,' repeated the Controller, lifting the knife and plunging it into Balfour's neck.

If Balfour was shocked, he didn't show it. He held the Controller's gaze as blood gurgled from his mouth and uttered something that sounded like, 'thank you,' before falling to the ground.

'You're welcome,' said the Controller, dropping the knife he'd used so many times before and heading out into the light to start again.

ACKNOWLEDGMENTS

I would like to thank the wonderful people of Texas for inspiring me to write this tale. In particular, big thanks to Beth Eardley, Warren Eardley, Regina Eardley, Walter Eardley, Laura Calhoun, John Calhoun, and the rest of the Eardley and Calhoun clans for always making me so welcome when I visit.

Thanks to Pat Jolly, Matt Wulff, Alexia Capsomidis, and Joe Brolly for early feedback on the novel and Matt Davies for the evocative cover.

Special mention and thanks to Ann Eardley for final read and editorial notes.

And as always, last thanks for Alison, Freya, and Hamish for sharing my Texas adventures with me

Printed in the USA
CPSIA information can be obtained
at www.ICGtesting.com
LVHW031620171123
764237LV00057B/1350

9 780995 774735